THE BEST OF ALL POSSIBLE WORLDS

'Carries deliberate echoes of Ray Bradbury . . . It's refined, meditative and life-affirming, and its exploration of gender politics and ethnology confirms Lord as the natural heiress to Octavia Butler and Ursula Le Guin'

FINANCIAL TIMES

'Karen Lord is perhaps aiming to take over the mantle of Ursula Le Guin as the myth-maker of sci-fi . . . [A] thoughtful and engaging novel [that] tells a story, indeed, but it is also a guide to getting along, a template for Utopia'

WALL STREET JOURNAL

'After her award-winning debut *Redemption in Indigo*, Karen Lord has returned with another stunning story . . . *The Best of All Possible Worlds* is a fascinating look at human relationships and cultural differences. Intelligent [and] well worth reading'

BRITISH SCIENCE FICTION ASSOCIATION

'Stayed with me for its sheer intelligence, the subtlety of its telling and the completeness of its imagination. Lord creates a sophisticated, believable and extremely poignant society with its own tragic history, yet is still powerfully considerate of the possibility that characters, structure, societies can change and transform. A thrilling and inspiring read'

BIDISHA

'Lord is a master at close observation . . . *The Best of All Possib[le Worlds . . .] e story'*

Also by
Karen Lord

Redemption in Indigo

KAREN LORD

Jo Fletcher
BOOKS

First published in Great Britain in 2013 by Jo Fletcher Books
This edition published in Great Britain in 2014 by

Jo Fletcher Books
an imprint of Quercus Editions Ltd.
55 Baker Street
7th Floor, South Block
London
W1U 8EW

ISBN 978 1 78087 168 4 (PB)
ISBN 978 1 78087 167 7 (EBOOK)

10 9 8 7 6 5 4 3 2 1

Typeset by Ellipsis Digital Limited, Glasgow
Printed and bound in Great Britain by
Clays Ltd, St Ives plc

For Dvorah, Gretchen and Ruthy.
You know why.

TABLE OF CONTENTS

BEFORE

He always set aside twelve days of his annual retreat to finish up reports and studies, and that left twelve more for everything else. In earlier times, he had foolishly tried retreats within comm-reach of his workplace, and that was not at all helpful. There would always be some crisis, something for which his help would be required. As his salary and sense increased, he took his retreats further and further away, until at last he found himself going off-planet to distant temples where the rule of silence and solitude could not be broken by convenient technologies.

This season, he had chosen Gharvi, a place with small wooden buildings scattered about a huge temple of stone, all set within the rain shadow of a mountain range. An endless ocean, both vista and inspiration, ran parallel to the mountains, and a beach between the two offered long walks to nowhere on either side. A place of two deserts, some said, for sea and land were bleak together – one boundless, one narrow, and both thirsty.

There was a place at home very like it, which had probably influenced his choice, but the sky was unique. The atmosphere was the cloudy blueish-lavender of a recently bioformed planet and the sun was scorching bright. It was so unlike the cool, strong blues and gentle sunlight of his home world that for the first few days he kept his head down and his door closed till night-fall.

On the twelfth day, he took his handheld, replete with work well completed, and put it in the box outside his hermitage door. He cooked and ate his evening lentils, slept soundly through the night and rose to prepare his morning porridge. There was a little water left over from the day before (he was ever frugal), but to have enough for washing he had to fetch the new day's supply from the box. The young acolytes of the temple always put suffi-cient water and food into each hermit's box before dawn. It was enough to stay clean, to fill the solar pot with porridge or pottage and to sip and slake the constant thirst that was the natural consequence of dry air and silence. The acolytes would also take away his handheld and safely transmit its contents to his work-place.

But his handheld was still there.

He paused, confused by this disconnect in the seamless order of the temple's routine. He stared at the untouched box. He looked up and frowned in puzzlement at the squat shape of the temple, vaguely visible through a haze of heat, blown sand and sea spray.

Then he shrugged and went on with his day, a little dustier, a little thirstier but convinced that an explanation would eventu-ally be made manifest.

The following morning, well before dawn, the sound of the box lid closing woke him from a sleep made restless by dreams of dryness. He waited a bit, then went to bring in the supplies and drink deeply of the water. His handheld was gone and a double ration of food sat in its place. He did not even peer into the darkness to catch sight of the tardy acolyte. Order had been restored.

'Dllenahkh, with your level of sensitivity and strength, you must go on retreat regularly.' So he had been told, long ago, by the guestmaster of his monastery. 'You are constantly looking to set things to rights, even within yourself. A retreat will teach you again and again that you are neither indispensable nor self-sufficient.'

Put bluntly, learn to stop meddling. Commitment is important, detachment equally so. He congratulated himself on his developing ability to keep curiosity in check and spent the next few days in undisturbed meditation and reflection.

One day, after a long morning meditation, he felt thirsty and decided to fetch more water from his supply box. He stepped out with his glass drinking bowl in hand and set it on the edge of the box while he tilted the half-lid and reached inside. His hands were steady as he poured water smoothly from the heavy narrow-necked jug. Moving slowly, he straightened and took a moment of blissful idleness, the jug left uncovered near his feet, to squint at the sun glare on the desert beach and the desert ocean, and to feel the coolness of the water creeping into his palms as he held the bowl and waited to drink. It was a child's game, to hold a bowl of water and mark the increase of thirst with masochistic pleasure, but he did it sometimes.

He brought the bowl to his mouth and had a perfect instant of pale-blue ocean, bright blue glass and clear water in his vision before he blinked, sipped and swallowed.

Many times after, when he tried to recall, his mind would stop at that vivid memory – the neatly nested colours, the soothing coolness of the glass – and not wish to go any further. It was not

3

long after that, not very long at all, that the day became horribly disordered.

A man walked out of the ocean, his head darkly bright with seawater and sunlight. He wore a pilot's suit – iridescent, sleek and permeable – which would dry as swiftly as bare skin in the hot breeze, but his hair he gathered up in his hands as he approached, wringing water from the great length of it and wrapping it high on the crown of his head with a band from his wrist.

Recognition came to Dllenahkh gradually. At first, when the figure appeared, it was a pilot; then, as it began to walk, it was a familiar pilot; and finally, with that added movement of hands in hair, it was Naraldi – a man well known to him, but not so well known as to excuse the early breaking of a retreat. He opened his mouth to chide him. *Six more days, Naraldi! Could anything be so important that you could not wait six more days?* That was what he intended to say, but another thought came to him. Even for a small planet with no docking station in orbit, it was highly uncommon for a mindship to splash down so close to land that a pilot could swim to shore. Although he knew Naraldi, they were not so close as to warrant a visit at this time and in this place.

The pilot slowed his step and looked uncertainly at him with eyes that streamed from the irritation of salt water.

'Something terrible has happened,' Dllenahkh said simply.

Naraldi wiped at his wet face and gave no reply.

'My mother?' Dllenahkh prompted to break the silence, dread growing cold and heavy in his stomach.

'Yes, your mother,' Naraldi confirmed abruptly. 'Your mother, and my mother, and . . . everyone. Our home is no more. Our world is—'

'No.' Dllenahkh shook his head, incredulous rather than upset at the bitterness and haste of Naraldi's words. 'What are you saying?'

He remembered that he was still thirsty and tried to raise the bowl again, but in the meantime his hands had grown chilled and numb. The bowl slipped. He snatched at it, but only deflected it so that it struck hard on the side of the water jug and broke just in time to entangle his chasing fingers.

'Oh,' was all he said. The cut was so clean, he felt nothing. 'I'm sorry. Let me . . .' He crouched and tried to collect the larger fragments but found himself toppling sideways to rest on one knee.

Naraldi rushed forward. He grasped Dllenahkh's bleeding right hand, yanked the band from his hair and folded Dllenahkh's fist around the wad of fabric. 'Hold tight,' he ordered, guiding Dllenahkh's left hand to clamp on to his wrist. 'Don't let go. I'll get help.'

He ran off down the beach towards the temple. Dllenahkh sat down carefully, away from the broken bits of glass, and obediently held tight. His head was spinning, but there was one small consolation. For at least the length of time it took Naraldi to return, he would remember the words of the guestmaster: he would not be curious, he would not seek to know, and he would not worry about how to right the tumbled world.

THE BEST OF ALL POSSIBLE WORLDS

I remember when the Sadiri came. We gathered at the port to cheer their arrival and, frankly, to gawk a bit. The Sadiri consider themselves to be the pinnacle of human civilisation. Imagine them settling on Cygnus Beta, a galactic hinterland for pioneers and refugees! Well, these ones, apparently, were willing to break the mould – but then again, a lot of things had been broken past repair and sometimes it makes more sense to create something new.

They looked almost Cygnian – eyes, hair and skin all somewhere on the spectrum of brown – except for the bright iridescence of the hair and a subtler sheen to the skin that was only noticeable in full sunlight. As it was dry season, there was plenty of that. They looked up into the sun and appeared relieved at the heat. Don't tell me they weren't; that 'impassive Sadiri' stereotype is a load of crap. They have body language. They have expressions. Just because it's not their way to yell their emotions out like most people doesn't mean they don't have them.

Parliamentary representatives welcomed them, formally but briefly, and they were taken to their homesteadings in fine diplomatic style. Everyone felt sorry for the Sadiri in those early days, and maybe we were all a little bit over-proud of ourselves for hosting them. Cygnus Beta isn't a rich colony by any means, but we understand fleeing disaster and war and disease, and struggling to find a place where you're wanted. A lot of people act like misfortune is contagious. They don't want to be exposed to it for too long. They'll take you in and make all the right gestures and noises, but when the months wear on and you're still in their house or their town or their world, the welcome starts to wear a bit thin.

So we understood, and maybe we were making a point, too. There isn't a group on Cygnus Beta who can't trace their family back to some world-shattering event. Landless, kinless, unwanted – theoretically, the Sadiri would fit right in.

Those were the thoughts that were foremost in my mind the day the Sadiri came. I barely even noticed when my friend Gilda said to me, 'But where are the women?'

I should have paid attention.

It's not that all-male homesteader groups don't come to Cygnus Beta. Many times people send the strongest and most intrepid to establish a level of comfort on the homesteads before sending for the rest of the family, and for some cultures that translates as men only. The reality of Cygnian society is that those men often end up settling down with someone who's already here, because, let me tell you, there's no long-distance relationship like an interstellar one, especially when you're all but marooned on a rock where communication with the rest of the galaxy means week-delayed real-space transmissions from the nearest long-range sat. But . . . *Sadiri* men? The epitome of morality and tradition, savants too absorbed in their mental exercises to succumb to base urges? It was hard to imagine them going native like most frontier boys.

Fortunately for my curiosity, I was in a position to find out about them. I'm second assistant to the Chief Biotechnician of Tlaxce Province, which means that I get to travel a lot because it's the biggest province, and it's also the province with the largest number of new homesteads. Sadiri homesteads galore, in other words. Plus – and keep this one quiet, please – I'm kind of a language nut. Old languages, new languages, made-up languages – whatever, that's my hobby. I already had a smattering of Sadiri, so it was inevitable that I would get stuck with the duty of liaison for the Public Health and Agriculture departments.

My opposite number was a joy to work with. No chitchat, no wasted time. I'd turn up at his office, he'd go over the schedule briefly with me and off we'd go in a groundcar to do our inspections. His Standard was better than my Sadiri, needless to say, so many times I just did a lot of listening while he talked with the homesteaders, and then afterwards he'd summarise for me so I wouldn't miss anything. I didn't expect them to speak Standard to me. When you've been almost exterminated, language is the first thing you cling to, one of the main roots of identity.

One day, while we were driving back to his office, a very interesting conversation took place. 'Dllenahkh,' I said to him (learning to pronounce his name had been a fine challenge, but once I substituted a Zulu 'dl' and a Scots 'ch', I got it), 'tell me how we can help you in the long term. What kind of settlement do you plan to establish? We understand if your aim is to keep as much of Sadira alive as possible. Do you require Sadiri plants? Hardy variants crossed with the indigenous flora, or hothouse specials in biodomes? We can requisition anything we like from the galactic seed bank, or even check with New Sadira to see what strains they're developing.'

'Thank you, Second Assistant Delarua, but at present it is enough for us to adjust to the environment and achieve basic self-sufficiency with what is readily available. Closer consideration of our long-term goals will follow after the completion of the initial phase.'

I must confess, I liked listening to Dllenahkh. He had a very soothing voice – deep, somewhat slow and very precise. It was a voice that matched his thoroughness and professionalism. I wish I had a voice that matched what I do. I've been told I sound like an overexcited rooster when I start rambling about my work.

'There is one matter in which you can assist us, however,' Dllenahkh continued. 'Our community is relatively isolated, and it has been suggested that it would be appropriate for us to take the opportunity to experience other cultures on Cygnus Beta. To participate. To . . . mingle.' He used Standard for that last, there being no precise equivalent in Sadiri which could convey the frivolous intent behind such a word.

'Mingle?' I repeated incredulously.

'Yes. Mingle. While much remains to be done, we are beginning to suffer from a lack of mental stimulus. Cygnus Beta is reputed to have some of the most complex and vibrant cultures in the galaxy. It would be appropriate to study them.'

I gave him a slanted look. I'd been around the Sadiri long enough to learn that whenever they start claiming something is 'appropriate', either there's something they're not telling you, or something they're not admitting to themselves. Dllenahkh had said 'appropriate' twice now.

He mirrored my look, which I'd learned was his style of humour. 'So. Do you have any recommendations?'

'Do I have any recommendations for a Sadiri boys' night out?' I shrugged, smiled, and allowed myself a laugh. 'I can come up with something.'

I did, too. The Ministry of Culture has all kinds of programmes, and I got someone to put together a package that even the Sadiri might enjoy. But people, this is *Cygnus Beta*. Yes, we have a few large cities and several towns – we're not all country bumpkins, vagabonds and adventurers – but there are few professional artists and actors, few galactic-standard museums and theatres. We simply can't afford them. It's true that most of the action happens in the urban belt, but often bands of entertainers travel about and test their luck – some venues they might get paid in credits, other places it'll be in kind. I did speak to one performer who waxed poetic about the joys of the road and how he'd made a map with locations marked for the excellence of their particular product: the best wines and spirits, of course; the best baked goods; the best cured meat and smoked fish; the most fragrant smoking herbs for incense or pipe – you name it, he could tell you where to get it.

I should point out that amateur or semi-professional doesn't mean low quality. It means *variable* quality. You get serious thespians next to dilettante wannabes because theatre companies have to take people as and when they become available. Your best King Lear might be the security guard at a small branch of a city bank. He's only going to get two or three weeks off for performances, then you're back to the understudy . . . the very earnest but not really that good retired schoolmate of the director.

I offered two options: either a series of overnight trips to the urban belt,' or visits to the Sadiri homesteads by some of the touring companies.

'Both,' said Dllenahkh.

'Both?' I repeated, raising an eyebrow, my tone more flat than querying.

He raised an eyebrow back.

Both it was.

I've mentioned my friend Gilda before. I love her dearly, but I swear she's a bad influence on just about everyone. I suspect that three out of her six children aren't her husband's, and that he knows it but doesn't care. He's so under her thumb, she must have had more than one Zhinuvian ancestor. She has three main groups she hangs out with, and she tries to annoy each one. She bores her housewives group with her science research, she makes her drinking buddies miserable with her tales of domesticity, and she scandalises her co-workers (that's me) with her lurid sexcapades.

So Gilda was happy to hear that the Sadiri were venturing out, because she too wanted 'the opportunity to experience other cultures', if you know what I mean. She insisted on being the coordinator and guide. At first I was glad when she took it out of my hands so I could go back to ordinary stuff, but this was Gilda, and something told me to enquire more deeply.

'So,' I asked her at the office, when she set up the first theatre visits, 'what's the playbill for this trip?'

'*Grease: The Space Musical*, *Titus Andronicus* and that new monologue by Li Chen where he first spends ten minutes criss-crossing the stage in silence, then sits in a Bagua-inspired design in the centre and periodically plays the uilleann pipes.'

'Aie-yi-yi,' I yodelled mournfully. 'Do you *want* them to judge us?'

'They'll judge us anyway. They're Sadiri and we're Terran – well, mostly Terran. Judging other humans and finding them wanting is what the Sadiri *do*.' She was quite unperturbed about it.

At first I said nothing. Strictly speaking, it was true. The Sadiri and their fleet of mindships had been the backbone of galactic law, diplomacy and scientific discovery for centuries. Even though other humans slightly resented them, I knew I wasn't the only one who quietly hoped that the pared-down version of their government would be just as effective at running the fleet. On a personal level, I hadn't noticed a judging attitude from Dllenahkh, but when one considered that their home planet was poisoned by their own close cousins, the Ainya, well . . . they didn't have that much high ground to stand on to look down at others any more, did they? Before I could voice that thought, there was a polite cough at my door.

'Dalenak!' Gilda said in cheery greeting. How *did* Dllenahkh manage not to wince at the woman's atrocious pronunciation? 'Are you here for the inaugural trip?'

Dllenahkh thanked her courteously and said no, he had but come to consult me regarding the matter of the hydroponics on the homesteads of the southwest quarter, which had been experiencing some difficulty. She took the hint and her leave so that I could close the door and speak to Dllenahkh in privacy.

'I thought lying wasn't a Sadiri thing,' I began. Then I looked at him more closely. 'Dllenahkh? Who hit you?'

'It is an internal matter, already resolved,' he said.

I frowned, but there was nothing I could say to that. 'You seem' – *depressed* – 'distracted. What's brought you to town if it's not Gilda's entertainment tour?'

'There is a visiting emissary from the Government of New Sadira. We have a meeting scheduled for tomorrow.'

That still didn't explain why Dllenahkh was in my office. 'Would you like to come with me to the Museum of History?' I said.

'Yes,' he acquiesced, somewhat absently. 'That would be quite interesting.'

We walked there. I kept silent, waiting for Dllenahkh to talk to me.

He waited until we had passed the geological displays and entered the Hall of Names before breaking into speech. 'Do you know why we came to Cygnus Beta?' he asked.

I glanced at him. His eyes were staring straight ahead at the writing etched on the granite walls.

'We came to find the taSadiri.' He turned his head very slightly and looked at me. 'Do you know of whom I speak?'

'Sadiri who do not practise the mental disciplines,' I replied immediately. 'They left Sadira and founded Ain, and a few settled elsewhere in the galaxy. But they did not found Cygnus Beta. It was already here.'

'I have heard of the beings you call the Caretakers.' He said it neutrally, and I was glad of the small courtesy. Some people think the idea of the Caretakers is just another one of those saviour-guardian myths that primitive societies dream up to deal with the uncertainty of the universe.

'Yes,' I said firmly, 'they are the true founders of Cygnus Beta, but we acknowledge other early settlers – mostly Terrans, it's true, but also Ntshune, Zhinuvians and taSadiri.'

'There are strong psionic and proto-psionic strains in your ancestry,' he noted. 'That was another of the reasons why we chose to come here.'

I wondered where this was going. 'So what's wrong, Dllenahkh?'

He struggled. Clearly these were very private matters. 'There is a lack of consensus concerning our path. Securing the future of our people is, of course, the primary concern, but the way this can best be achieved is in dispute. Some feel that preserving genetic and cultural integrity would be the most effective course of action. With so few of us surviving, every person would be needed for this endeavour to succeed. Others believe that negotiation with the Ainya with a view to eventual integration of our tribes is the best option.'

'But perhaps that was their reason for . . . doing what they did,' I said awkwardly. 'They've never had your level of galactic influence. Wouldn't integration be kind of like giving them what they want?'

He paused. 'Yes,' he said at last. 'Many of us hold the same view. However, from the Ainya perspective, *we* drove out their forefathers and denied them their birthright; hence their pride in claiming responsibility for our downfall. Perhaps they wish to see us not merely humiliated but destroyed completely.'

He sighed and continued, 'A third way has been proposed: colonies of hybrids selected for Sadiri physical traits and mental abilities and raised according to Sadiri values and traditions.'

A wry smile twitched my lips. Terrans: the chicken stock of every human genetic soup in the galaxy. Terra was the newest of the crafted worlds and Terrans the youngest breed of humans in the galaxy, but what they lacked in technology and mental development, they made up for in sheer evolutionary potential. Other humans patronised them and overlooked them, but just mention *hybrid vigour* and suddenly Terrans became very popular. Of course, since Terra itself was still under embargo, that meant Cygnus Beta got all the attention.

'So,' I asked him, 'which Sadiri are you? The second way, or the third?'

15

His face went still in that manner I had come to interpret as profound uncertainty. 'No decision has yet been made. We are a reserve.'

I tilted my head and frowned at him, confused.

His eyes glanced briefly at mine, then he blinked and looked aside again as if acutely embarrassed. 'As many of our off-planet occupations are filled by men, more Sadiri males survived the disaster than females. This has created some . . . disruption to our usual bonding customs. For this reason, the excess of males was sent to this colony. The Science Council of New Sadira will as a priority select for a greater number of females to be born as soon as possible. Given our lifespan, it is possible that they may be our future wives.'

I pondered this, realising the truth of what he said. Most of the Sadiri on Cygnus Beta were, by their standards, very young. But how distressing and strange, to spend decades on some kind of genetic backroom shelf waiting one's turn to clinically contribute to the expansion of the species!

I said something of the sort to Dllenahkh. He let me know my views were inappropriate. I shut up.

The Hall of Names is a very complicated place. The obvious part of it is the walls with the names of the thousand dying nations who came here or were brought here, but there is also a low susurration of a thousand extinct languages; the occasional whiff of smoke, incense or perfume from various half-forgotten rituals; the distant moan and skirl of ancient instruments that no one knows how to make any more. It's a very apt place to ponder the future of an entire world, but it's a little depressing as well.

'What do you think the emissary is going to say?' I asked.

Dllenahkh said nothing. Perhaps he did not know. Perhaps he knew, but would never tell me.

'Let's go have lunch,' I said.

We fell back into our usual routine after that, which is to say we were all business. I knew that the Sadiri homesteaders continued their cultural outreach, visiting the towns and other provinces and permitting visiting groups in return. They did indeed seem to be taking note of how various cultures had adapted to social conditions on Cygnus Beta, so even what appeared to be recreational also had some element of anthropological study to it. I did not delve deeper, and although the Sadiri emissary returned for another visit some months later, I did not quiz Dllenahkh about it.

Gilda, on the other hand, was a fount of information. She called me at my desk one day, too excited and impatient to walk the few metres to my office. 'Have you heard the news? Ain has been quarantined. Nothing goes in, nothing comes out.'

That got my attention. I dropped everything and drew close to my monitor. 'What? Has the tribunal given verdict already?'

Gilda looked very sober, which was extremely unusual for her. 'The trial isn't over, but Ain is incommunicado.'

'That's impossible,' I stated. 'The Terran embargo works because we can see everything they do and show them what we want them to see. Ain's technology is too advanced. Maybe they did it to themselves. Maybe they're hiding.'

She scoffed. 'They're not *that* advanced. People are saying it was the Caretakers. Personally, I'm glad. Sadira's going to be nothing but sterile rock for a very long time.'

My eyes widened and I felt a little thrill. *The Caretakers!* It was

17

as if angels had descended to avenge the Sadiri. 'I guess they don't like people undoing their work. How are the off-planet Ainya handling it?'

Gilda gave a wry smile. 'Here's the irony. You know only two fleets have ships that can travel as far as Ain.'

I laughed without humour. She meant the Zhinuvians, who'd charge an arm and a leg for passage, and the Sadiri who . . . well . . . I wasn't sure what they'd do, but any Ainya would have to have a lot of gall to approach a Sadiri pilot now.

The sequestering of Ain was a big change in more ways than one. Even though there's bad blood between Ain and Sadira – *seriously* bad blood – I'd had a vague hope that they might come together after a generation or two, out of necessity if nothing else. It looked as if the options had been whittled down from three to two, and where that left the Sadiri I had no idea. New Sadira was a small planet, a former science outpost that had gained an unexpected promotion. It would serve for a drastically diminished population, but as it had neither the resources nor the size to properly replace Sadira, the Sadiri would be forced to make a decision about their future sooner rather than later.

It was difficult to tell what they were planning to do. Some of the Sadiri were definitely mingling – in fact, given their youth, one might even say *experimenting*. I detected from the sternness of Dllenahkh's expression when some of the more amusing tales were related in his vicinity that the elder Sadiri of the group were barely tolerant of this behaviour – but what could they do? Kick the youngsters out? Every Sadiri capable of procreation was precious, and any of them could be brought back into the fold later, no matter how they might now be choosing to deal with their shared tragedy.

That said, about a couple of months shy of a year after their arrival I found myself in the unenviable position of being mandated by my boss to 'find out what's going on with those Sadiri'. I chose a long road trip to broach the topic with Dllenahkh, reasoning that if we were driving through the middle of nowhere, he wouldn't have any place to escape to. To give myself a level of protection, I took off the autopilot and nav and drove the groundcar myself.

'I understand there's been a bit of a Sadiri baby boom,' I said delicately, keeping my eyes on the road as I manoeuvred through freshly gouged potholes, the result of a strong start to the rainy season.

Dllenahkh's teeth clicked as we bounced through a bad patch. 'It does appear that way,' he said eventually with clenched jaw.

'Is this an indication—?' I started, then, 'Does this mean a way has been chosen?'

The silence continued for long enough that I regretfully concluded I'd pushed my luck too far. Then Dllenahkh spoke, sounding slightly injured. 'Little choice has been offered where these births are concerned. Three of the fathers have been unable to obtain anything more than visiting rights, while a fourth has been charged with sole custody. Two are in a particularly difficult situation – their children have been acknowledged by other men and are being raised with no recognition of their heritage. In only one case has there been the formation of something resembling a bond, and that man has requested to move to the homestead of his child's mother, there to live, no doubt, according to the culture of her people.'

I whistled. Added to the other stories I'd heard, those were more births and far fewer marriages than I had expected.

'So, you're telling me you're being fetishised, used and dumped. Good enough to sleep with, but not good enough to marry. Fresh blood. The new kink in town. The—'

'Your observations,' said Dllenahkh, quietly but quellingly, 'are not particularly welcome at this moment.'

I felt genuinely ashamed. 'Sorry. I got a bit carried away. The thing is . . . we've always been a matriarchal society. Cygnian fathers have little say in decisions about childrearing. I thought you realised that.'

We continued in silence while I focused on a nasty bit of road slippage. At one stage, Dllenahkh had to get out and push the car through a slurry of fine limestone before it could find purchase once more on firm ground. He got back in, placing his caked work-boots on the centre of the mat with fastidious precision. It had been a trivial but welcome diversion, easing some of the tension from the atmosphere.

My thoughts wandered as I tried to think of what to say, and then, of course, my subconscious took over. 'Dark they were, and golden-eyed,' I quoted dreamily.

'The reference escapes me.'

'It's a classic work of fiction about Terrans who go to colonise Mars. Except . . . Mars colonises them. It turns them into dark, golden-eyed Martians who exactly resemble the extinct indigenous people. I'm telling you, if you think you can colonise Cygnus Beta and turn it into Sadira, centuries later all you'll have is a slight tendency to shiny hair and pedantic speech in the common Cygnian stock. Oh, Dllenahkh, I am so sorry. I tried to warn you.'

'I do not recall—'

This was too serious for multitasking. I pulled aside, turned off the groundcar and faced him fully. 'I asked you what you wanted in the long term. Do you want to be all-Sadiri, or Sadiri-Cygnian? Because if the former's your aim, you're going about it the wrong way.'

His head dropped wearily, which is as close as a Sadiri can get to a wail of anguish. 'I do not know what we want. We wish only to survive, and we are trying all possible means to do so.'

I closed my eyes, struck by a pang of loneliness. If I can tease Gilda about having a dominant Zhinuvian gene in her make-up, then I must also admit there might be a little too much Ntshune in my own background, an occasional echo of emotions not my own. And Dllenahkh *was* lonely, no mistake. It poured off him like mist and settled into my bones with a pain as insistent as the ache of an old injury. It was most upsetting.

'All right. You need to coordinate with the Ministry of Family Planning and Maintenance. But Dllenahkh, you have to come clean, none of this juvenile – sorry, *culturally conditioned* – embarrassment over the details of Sadiri marriage and bonding customs, and no underhanded plots to seduce and indoctrinate women into the Sadiri way of life. Be upfront. I mean, you *have* chosen the right place. We've already got a mail-order-bride mentality, and we've been selecting for fecundity for centuries. How many other places could produce so many births in such a short space of time?'

'This is true,' said Dllenahkh with what sounded like a glimmer of hope.

'Plus, you could have it *both* ways: take a short-lived Cygnian wife for the first part of that long life of yours, then go home to your girl-brides and start a fresh full-blooded family. Just be . . . respectful. Honest. And stop thinking *you're* the superior ones! You're just another drop in our gene pool! We're all descended from peoples who thought they were kings and gods, and who found themselves to be almost nothing at all in the end. Don't let that be you.'

He sat in chastened silence for a while, then said humbly, 'There is merit in what you say. I will discuss the possibilities with our local council and approach the Ministry as you have suggested.'

I exhaled in relief. If only they knew how close they had come to wearing out our patience. If there is one thing a Cygnian cannot bear, it's the stench of superiority. Too often it had been a precursor to atrocity and a rationale for oppression. The Sadiri wouldn't change overnight, but at least it was a start.

'Dark you are, and golden-eyed,' Dllenahkh said quietly.

'My eyes are brown,' I replied, puzzled to hear a Sadiri say something so nonsensical.

'I understand that on Terra, gold is considered a rare and precious metal. To be golden is to be special, cherished.' He looked at me. 'To me, your eyes are golden, because they have perceived who we truly are.'

I said nothing. I opened my mouth, failed to breathe and lowered my eyes from that intense gaze. It hurt too much, like bright sun on tender skin, bright and searing with the beauty of both what had been lost and what remained. For a moment, the blood of my ancestors called out in empathy and I almost embarrassed myself by crying in front of a Sadiri.

I bit my lip, took hold of myself, and the moment passed. Then I started the car, and we travelled on to the next distant home-stead.

MATCHMAKER, MATCHMAKER

'What's this?'

The department secretary/courier glanced back at the envelope he had tossed onto my desk. 'How would I know?'

I looked him up and down. Gilroy was a gawky youngster, too tall yet still growing and plagued with a limp, the result of a bad break on a distant homestead, days out from the reach of advanced medical care. He poured all the energy that should have been spent punching cattle into gossiping – sorry – *gathering intelligence*. I picked up the envelope and twirled the ends of the ribbons on the seal, all the while staring at him meaningfully.

'Well . . . all right.' He gave his usual precursor to a juicy scoop: a quick glance around to make sure no one could overhear. 'I understand that you've made a good impression on someone, and you're going to have a slight change in duties.'

I frowned, scared now. The First Assistant Biotechnician was new to her post. Unless she was going on maternity leave or had been sacked, there was no way I was taking her place – not that I wanted to. There's only so much deskwork I can stand before I'm desperate to be out driving through the homesteadings. And there was definitely no way I could be making Chief. What other twists were possible on my career path?

I realised Gilroy was watching me and smirking at the panic I hadn't bothered to hide.

'Right, thanks, close the door behind you,' I said, dismissing him brusquely.

I shut my eyes and spun my chair around once, maybe trying to lighten my anxiety, maybe trying some weird little made-up luck ritual. Then I broke the seal and pulled out my orders.

'They want me to do *what*?'

As if on cue, my monitor chimed and flashed. I glanced irritably at the message box, then my eyes widened and I tapped the channel open. 'Delarua here.'

'Second Assistant Delarua, I believe you must have opened your correspondence by now?'

My boss tries to get away with stuff by being cute. She's short and stocky, with big round cheeks and deep dimples. She fools no one. The more she dimples, the more you know you've been screwed over.

'Chief, I can't believe you didn't discuss this with me first. Whatever happened to the Human Relations and Vocational Guidance Department? Everyone there die of the plague? Fell into a coma? Got amnesia?' Even as I spoke my frustration I reined myself in a little. As dangerous as the dimples were, it was worse if you said something to make them disappear suddenly. My boss didn't permit subordinates to take liberties.

'Sorry, dear. This came in from over my head.' She shrugged. 'It's only a year's secondment. Why not see it as an opportunity to broaden your curriculum vitae?'

'I'm a biotechnician! The longer I stay away from my field, the more my CV suffers – *you* know that!' My eyes narrowed. 'Wait a minute. Someone above you messed with the personnel structure of your department, and you're still smiling?' I felt suddenly ill, my stomach going into freefall. 'You *wanted* to get rid of me? Why didn't you say—'

'Delarua, relax! I have no problem with you or your work. And yes, I'm not shattered, but it's because of who your replacement is.'

Then she spoke the name Dr Freyda Mar, a name which will mean nothing to you or, let's be honest, to most Cygnians, but for those who know the up-to-date research in the biotech field, it was almost as if Albert Einstein had decided to take a year off from research and teach secondary-level general science.

'*Her*? What would she want with my crappy little job—? Sorry, Chief, but even you must admit that the least glamorous work of the department falls under my remit. I mean . . . hydroponics, and health inspections, and *sewage*, and driving hundreds of klicks and sometimes sleeping in barns if you're lucky and in the car if you're not. I mean yes, I like it, but everyone knows I'm strange.'

'Well, maybe she's strange, too. She wants to write a book about the practical applications of her research. More power to her, I say. I've always thought academics should get a little slurry on their boots from time to time.'

I took a deep breath. If Freyda Mar was coming to fill my place for a year, there was no way I was getting out of this. 'Fine. I see I've got two months before I go. When's Doctor Mar coming?'

'In a month's time. You'll have the joy of showing her the ropes.'

The idea of me – *me* – showing Dr Freyda Mar how to do my job for a *whole month* so thrilled me to the depths of my techie soul that I completely forgot I was supposed to be angry about leaving for an entire year to go . . . where? On a wild goose chase as part-anthropologist, part-diplomat?

The latter half of the week rolled around and I was on my way to Dllenahkh's office at the usual time to discuss the inspections schedule. I did have a moment's pause at his door, wondering how he would react to the news of my assignment, but it was only a moment. Dllenahkh's secretary was of the Gilroy stamp: young, gawky and more than a little curious at my hesitation.

'Councillor Dllenahkh *is* expecting you,' he prompted kindly.

'Thank you, Joral,' I muttered, and went through.

I tried to explain to Dllenahkh what I thought was going to happen – my secondment, my replacement and so forth. I kept my tone neutral – I don't believe in behaving either disgruntled or gleeful about work-related matters, especially around people outside my department. He leaned forwards, set his elbows on the desk and contemplated his fingers in silence for a while. During that while, I finally realised he was not in the least surprised.

'Oh. Oh no. Oh—' I began to swear. One of the advantages of having languages as a hobby is that it can take you quite a while to run out of swear words. I hadn't even exhausted my list from the dead languages I know when I paused for breath and Dllenahkh spoke up, still apparently addressing his fingers.

'Could it be that you are vexed with me, Second Assistant Delarua?'

'Could it be that you are *laughing* at me, Councillor Dllenahkh? Are *you* the reason for this complication in my life? Please, explain this madness!'

His brows drew together briefly, erasing that faint suggestion of suppressed amusement that had so irritated me, and he finally looked me in the eye. 'I fear that you have not been fully briefed as yet. No doubt your superior has informed you of all that she knows and a more detailed mission dossier is forthcoming. I assure you, this is not madness.'

He got up and walked to the archaic map board that showed Tlaxce Province and the regions bordering it. He faced it, placed his hands behind his back and unexpectedly exhaled a large sigh.

'Before I begin, I have not properly thanked you for your recommendation that we seek the assistance of the Ministry of Family Planning and Maintenance. As a result, some of the custody cases are being reviewed, and counselling is being provided for the parents and families involved. While it is unlikely that all cases will be resolved amicably, the situation is less fraught than previously. Furthermore, any future attempts at cross-cultural partnering will be channelled through the Ministry's programmes for that purpose.'

'Not bad,' I said, pleased and mollified. 'They've been establishing and maintaining unions for generations now. They're quite good at what they do – not perfect, but far better than nothing.'

He glanced back at me briefly, then raised a hand to indicate the provinces. 'Tlaxce, which is the largest province, is also one of the most genetically homogeneous provinces due to the presence of the capital and the main spaceport. We have been advised that if we are seeking Cygnians with a high percentage of taSadiri genetic heritage, we should go to the outlying regions of the neighbouring provinces.'

'Still clinging to your concept of purity?' I said quietly.

Dllenahkh turned and looked at me in a way that I fancied meant *when* you *lose your home and all but a remnant of your people, feel free to return and lecture me on the ethics of purity.*

I lowered my eyes. 'So, the mission is to find Cygnian groups that are more taSadiri than the average,' I paraphrased meekly.

'Your facility for the languages of Cygnus Beta is what led me to recommend you as Civil Service liaison. That and your insightfulness.'

First the stick and then the carrot. He had become quite talented at manipulating Cygnians with a little flattery, I thought sourly. 'And what role will you play?'

'I have been authorised to assess both the settlements and the people that we encounter in order to determine whether it would be more efficient for us to join those settlements, or to encourage potential wives to remove to our settlement here in Tlaxce.' While Dllenahkh would never stoop to smugness, there was an unwarranted certitude in his tone that suggested he had already decided what the obvious choice would be.

He took a last look at the map and returned to sit behind his desk.

'The First Assistant to the Chief Biotechnician is a year younger than you and is likely to serve in her post for at least another five years. The Chief Biotechnician will not retire for at least another twelve years. All higher positions in the department require greater managerial experience and less technical skill. I estimated there was a low probability that your career would be harmed, and . . . I have noticed that you derive a certain amount of enjoyment from our field trips. I hope I did not misinterpret the case.' There was the merest hint, the tiniest suggestion of humility and concern in his gaze.

I shrugged. 'I'm sorry I swore like that. It was a bit of a shock. I'm sure it will all work out.'

He nodded. 'Excellent. Then let us begin our rounds and I will tell you about the other personnel on the mission team.'

What he did not tell me, what would have been more useful, was the name of the higher-up who had managed to deepen the dimples in my boss's cheeks with the bribe of Freyda Mar! Because let me tell you, I want to kiss that person. We were already starstruck and willing to welcome the most eccentric, knee-sock-wearing, port-drinking, absent-minded professor type that ever came out of Tlaxce University. But Freyda Mar dressed normally, drank water, remembered everything and . . . okay, she was a *little* eccentric, but in a way that everyone could appreciate.

She bore a striking resemblance to a tall, middle-aged Wicked Witch of the West – except not, you know, actually being green. A few days before our first field trip, I looked at her long, wavy black hair and all I said was, 'Are you sure?' She took one look at my own close-cropped do and said, 'You know, you've got a point.' Whereupon I stepped out to get us some coffee for the mid-morning break and when I got back the scissors were out of the drawer and on the desk and the wastepaper basket was bristling with a metre-length's worth of hair. I'm telling you, my mouth fell open, but she just laughed at me and took the mugs from my hand before I dropped them.

In spite of all that, she seemed a little bit nervous about working with Sadiri, so I gave her a quick, casual primer while she worriedly tapped notes into her handheld. 'Trust me, they'll love you. They don't do small talk and they have a constant need for mind-fodder, so feel free to discuss your work in detail. Let them do the heavy lifting – they've got the high-grav build for it and they're happy to show off their physical strength. Don't try to shake hands with them. Don't touch anyone's head, *especially* not their hair. That's a big no-no.'

'Custom? Or something else?' she asked, stopping mid-input.

'That's canny of you,' I said approvingly. 'I don't know for certain, but I think it might have something to do with the telepathy.'

She nodded, looking thoughtful and a lot more relaxed. 'Years ago I spent some time doing research at a university in the Punartam System. I met a Sadiri mindship pilot there. He always wore gloves, always kept his head covered. I thought it was cultural at first, but maybe there's more to it than that.'

Freyda had just proven herself to be a typical techie. Ask her to remember the arbitrary rules of some foreign etiquette and she fretted. Give her a possible scientific explanation for a social behaviour and she was fine.

Road trips, now, are a real test of character, and I had no idea how she would handle the long and sometimes boring drives. I soon discovered that you could get her to sing from any musical or opera, very loudly, as the car rolled along, and sometimes I'd join in, though with less volume and skill. Poor Dllenahkh, who was accustomed to far quieter rides, would look at us sideways with an expression of mild terror. But even Dllenahkh warmed to her when she switched into technical mode. He listened to her very, very closely, their heights almost matching, constantly nodding and nodding as she rattled off some aspect of her latest theory. At one point, I could swear I saw him looking at her almost dreamily, as if he had ceased to listen to the content of her words and was thinking about something else.

I was getting ready to tease him about having a romantic crush to rival my professional crush, but then he caught me by surprise the following week. I had been expecting Kavelan to replace him as the homesteading liaison, Kavelan being a young but sober-headed subordinate in the office whom I had encountered several times over the past year or so. Instead, a completely new face turned up. It was difficult to guess how old he was, but I estimated from his aura of maturity that he was closer to Dllenahkh's age than the average Sadiri male of the homesteadings.

Dllenahkh did the introductions. 'This is my replacement, Doctor Lanuri. He will be joining us for inspections henceforth.'

Dr Lanuri inclined his head, and Freyda and I gave little bows in turn. He had creases on his face that looked suspiciously like laugh lines, but if they were they had not been used for a very long time. He still bore the slightly vacant expression of deep depression that had characterised Dllenahkh and many of the other Sadiri in the earlier days of settlement.

I wish I could say I was given the opportunity to get to know him better, but after a quick briefing on the inspections schedule, Dllenahkh led us out to not one groundcar, but two.

He said, 'Given that our vehicles must occasionally serve as temporary shelters, I considered it unwise to approach the passenger limit too closely. Therefore, each team will go in its own groundcar. The nav systems have been linked. I wish you a safe and pleasant journey, Doctor Lanuri, Doctor Mar.'

And then he positively dashed towards a car with what, for a Sadiri, smacked of unnatural and unseemly haste. I followed, bemused by the teasing lilt to his formal and unnecessary farewell to Dr Lanuri (the first leg of our rounds was only a two-hour journey, after all), and wondering if I had imagined seeing an exasperated glint in Dr Lanuri's eye – rather like the one I usually get when my mother starts hinting that a second son-in-law and more grandchildren would be nice.

'You know,' I said to him once we had started off, 'I'm thinking the Ministry of Family Planning would be more subtle than you were just now. Perhaps you should leave the matchmaking to them.'

Dllenahkh pretended to look aggrieved, but his demeanour reeked of too much satisfaction for it to be convincing. 'I do not understand what you mean by that statement. It is more convenient for Doctor Mar and Doctor Lanuri to go together in one vehicle, so they can begin the "team-building" process which is so important to Cygnians.'

'Mm-hm,' I replied with deep sarcasm.

Dr Mar, like any urbanite, was sufficiently cultured to tune her natural enthusiasm to a volume and frequency that would be appreciated by her new colleague, which is to say they seemed to have a fair rapport at the end of the first two hours. Still, I was fairly impressed the following week when we got out at one destination a little ahead of the others and we distinctly heard *singing* – loud, full-on opera singing – coming from the second groundcar. Of course, by the time the car stopped and the doors opened, there was only mild, professional chatter between the two.

I looked at Dllenahkh in shock. He merely raised his eyebrows in a way that was as good as an *I told you so*.

'How did you pull this off?' I demanded when the others were out of earshot.

'Pull what off?' he asked coolly, his tone mildly mocking the colloquialism.

'How did you know they'd click? That requires a level of intuition that seems to me unlikely to reside in the methodical Sadiri mind.'

'I extrapolated from what I knew of Doctor Lanuri's late wife. She was very similar in both manner and appearance to Doctor Mar. Lanuri has found it . . . difficult since his wife's death. I hoped that he might find solace in Doctor Mar's company, and, let me admit it, perhaps even consider the possibility of marrying again.'

On another day that might have meant more teasing about being a matchmaker, but today I was in a grumpy mood.

'So, even Sadiri men find women interchangeable,' I scoffed under my breath.

'That is not what I said,' he murmured, looking at me oddly.

I waved my hand, trying to brush away the words. 'Forgive me. I was thinking of something else, something irrelevant. So, the second spouse is often very close in temperament and appearance to the first spouse.'

'Yes. The first bond is, in a way, never completely broken and constantly seeks the absent partner. Marrying someone similar assuages some of the shock and helps with the grieving process.'

'Some people think widowed Sadiri pine away and die,' I remarked, referring to a common trope in Cygnian literature and drama.

'That would be inappropriate,' Dllenahkh said, infusing the word with a measure of distaste that was new. 'There are degrees of depth of bond. All Sadiri experience a bond with each other, and there are rituals that deepen the connection, the marriage ceremony being but one. However, one can be telepathically connected to one with whom it is difficult to live peaceably. The ability to know another's mind does not preclude the likelihood of misunderstanding it.'

'Good point,' I said. Unsaid but also understood was that no Sadiri would take the selfish luxury of choosing death as a way to escape emotional pain. All were bereaved, and now life was the priority.

The following week's inspections were routine. Dr Lanuri looked slightly less depressed and Freyda was cheerful and professional as always. It wasn't much to go on. I caught Dllenahkh frowning to himself.

'They've only just met,' I told him. 'Did you really expect a love at first sight?'

'Hmm,' he replied. 'Has Doctor Mar given any indication . . . ?' He was unable to finish the sentence, but I realised what he was asking.

I was aghast – only slightly aghast, really, but I played it up because there are so few times that Dllenahkh is anything but the consummate Sadiri savant. 'I can't believe you asked me that. That's rude even by Cygnian standards.'

He frowned some more and dropped the subject.

But I did find out. Not by asking – I'm not that inquisitive – but by alcohol, and not even *my* alcohol, so it really wasn't my fault. The last day of our inspections together, Freyda showed me a bottle of some fortified Cygnian vintage hidden in her knapsack. We snagged a groundcar for ourselves and put nav and autopilot in control.

Then we got chatty. I told her my thoughts on the mission, that it was essentially a waste of time, but at least I was getting paid to travel the world for a year, and the Sadiri would have the satisfaction of knowing they'd investigated every possibility. She told me she was tired of academia, and taking a sabbatical to write a book seemed a bit tame, so this way she'd be out for a year and *still* have the sabbatical year to write, thus staying away from the university for two years instead of just one.

34

The wine went down rather smoothly. I discovered that she did, in fact, have a fair bit of taSadiri in her background. She found out that I had just enough Ntshune in me to start people off on a giggle-loop. You've heard of someone's laughter being infectious? Well, many Cygnians of Ntshune stock have the knack of giving people the giggles in a serious way, probably some unintentional emotion-feedback thing.

We spent the next inspection choking back snickers while the Sadiri gave us puzzled looks.

The next journey was for more sober talk. She said she'd been engaged, but there'd been a mutual decision not to marry after her academic career took off, leaving her tied to the city and her fiancé still wanting the life of a homesteader. I said I'd been engaged too, and also broke it off by mutual agreement, though my career was nowhere near as illustrious as hers.

'You still have time,' she said generously.

At first I thought she was talking about my career, and I was flattered, but then I realised she meant time to have a family, and I felt a little less flattered.

'Well, what about you? Have you considered early retirement and going back to be a housewife on a homestead?'

She looked embarrassed. 'I suppose I could register my name with the Ministry of Family Planning, but I keep falling for the wrong men and getting distracted.'

The words were general, but there was something in the guilt that crossed her face that made me gasp and blurt out, 'Lanuri?'

For the first time, I heard bitterness in her laugh. 'I hope I'm not that obvious!'

'No! No, you're not. It's just . . . well, you do seem to get along

35

quite well together, and . . . hmm . . . how do the Sadiri show they care, anyway?'

She pushed back the rough bangs of her hacked-off hair and scowled. 'Well, I'm sure they don't do it by constantly mentioning how beautiful and intelligent and completely irreplaceable their late wives are!'

'Oh,' I said sadly.

'Yeah, I'm a sad, sick person, jealous of a woman who died in the greatest genocidal attack since – well, since Cygnus Beta was founded. And if you so much as breathe a *word*,' she concluded sharply . . . and it was time to change the subject.

We got back a little earlier than the other two, and rather than sit and wait outside we persuaded Joral to let us move the farewell party into Dllenahkh's office. The rest of the place was empty – inspection tours often took us past the usual work hours – so we left the door open, put our feet up on his desk in a kind of rebellion against all Sadiri sensibilities and set to finishing off the wine.

After a short half-hour had passed, we heard Joral's hushed voice through the open doorway. 'Doctor Mar and Second Assistant Delarua seem to be engaged in some kind of female bonding ritual.'

'In my office?' came Dllenahkh's bemused reply. I think both of us were picturing the expression on his face, because we went off into another giggle-loop that put paid to any lingering illusion of professionalism.

Fortunately that wasn't the final farewell. We had a nice, sober, proper seeing-off a week later at the main train station in the city. Gilda was there, and Dr Lanuri and Freyda. I hugged Gilda hard, making a mental note to send many souvenir trinkets to her kids, and got cheek smooches from Freyda, all the while thinking, *I'm drinking buddies with* Freyda Mar! *How cool is that!* We clasped arms briefly and exchanged looks. Hers said, *Don't tell anyone how pathetic I am*, and mine said, *Hang in there, you're not pathetic, you'll be fine.*

The three Sadiri men, Lanuri, Dllenahkh and Joral, stood slightly apart, making their sombre farewells, far more absorbed in the meaning of the mission and their hopes for its success than any trivial sadness over the temporary absence of a colleague. I felt a little jolt when I looked at them, a sudden awareness of the insane reality that had brought them here, a flash of insight into how death and devastation had completely reshaped their lives and destinies. Like Freyda, I suddenly felt foolish for being annoyed at them over a small matter of unrequited love.

We boarded and found our seats. I leaned my head against the window by my seat, looking at Freyda as she lingered to give us a final wave, and blinking back tears. Silly matchmaking – and now she would have a year to suffer through, pretending her feelings didn't exist. I was vexed with Dllenahkh. Dangling an emotionally unavailable Sadiri male in front of her – hah, that was a tautology if there ever was one – that was more than cruel, it was irresponsible. I thought of the messed-up attempts at courting that had left tangles even the Ministry wouldn't be able to unsnarl. Would any of them be capable of forming normal unions, unions based on more than a desperate need to keep their cultural and genetic heritage alive? Did the Sadiri *ever* admit to needing therapy?

My struggle with my emotions did not go unnoticed.

'You will miss Doctor Freyda Mar very much,' said Joral, examining my face curiously.

'Yes,' I said, my tone firm, calm and neutral. 'I wish I could have had more time to work with her.'

Joral nodded in understanding. 'Doctor Lanuri speaks of her often. I believe he finds her to be almost Sadiri in her clarity and depth of thought. Furthermore, he says that her appearance is very pleasing, and in many aspects reminiscent of his late wife—'

'Joral,' Dllenahkh chided.

'But it is true. I am only repeating what Doctor Lanuri has said on several—'

I stared at him as suddenly all the fragments that I knew came together in a gestalt that looked *nothing* like what I had at first assumed.

'Joral,' said Dllenahkh sternly, 'it is not appropriate to discuss—'

'Joral, you've got more sense than any of us!' I cried. I jumped up and ran to the door, paused with a skid, went back to grab the startled youngster around the face and plant a kiss on his forehead, then took off again. Freyda was just turning to leave the platform. I thundered towards her and she looked back at me in shock.

'He loves you, you *remind* him of his wife, he'll never admit it, it's a stupid Sadiri thing, it's up to you – go, *go*, GO!'

She gaped at me, her eyes gradually widening during my whispered babble and ending up filling with tears, the jaw-drop becoming a wide grin. I squeezed a quick hug about her shoulders and pelted back to slither through the carriage doors before they slid shut.

I returned to my seat with a small smile of bittersweet triumph. Dllenahkh looked at me with a strange expression that I couldn't quite read, but I didn't care. I was thinking about the year ahead and hoping for at least one happy ending for a friend.

Joral leaned forward and said earnestly, 'You seem to be very sad about leaving. It is all right if you wish to cry, First Officer Delarua. We will not think badly of you. We understand that this is common behaviour for many Terran females.'

'Well, I'm Cygnian,' I snapped. 'And I wasn't going to cry.' I swear, nothing irritates me more than being overemotional in front of a Sadiri. They make you feel so silly.

Dllenahkh coughed almost apologetically. 'First Officer Delarua, at one stage you suggested that I had complicated your life by asking for you to be assigned to this mission. Is it now the case that you are beginning to enjoy the complications?'

'That's an almost Cygnian streak of smug-bastardness you're displaying there, Dllenahkh,' I warned with a small, rueful grin of acknowledgement.

He straightened slightly and his eyebrows rose by a fraction at the sly insult. Then the train pulled out and we were off to start our grand adventure, around the world in one Standard year.

Zero hour plus eleven months twenty-eight days

Standard Time was invented by Sadiri pilots. Most Sadiri procedures and quantification followed straight lines and linear progressions, created for the convenience of the ten-fingered. But Time . . . Time belonged to a higher realm. It could not be carried in human hands, not while it constantly carried human minds. It was all circles, wheels within wheels, a Standard year of three hundred and sixty Standard days coiled up in twelve months, which in turn were composed of the small whirlings of twelve hours day and twelve hours night, tiny spinning minutes and seconds, ever-cycling breaths and blinks and beats.

To be described as having a pilot's mind was both curse and compliment; it could mean being unable to tell the difference between prophecy, memory and mere déjà vu.

Dllenahkh knew that it was almost one Standard year since the destruction of his home and his life. He knew it not like a memory, but like the vague dread of a possible death, a death yet to come. He left the thought and the feeling while he could still breathe and focused instead on the present. The train vibrated gently, its windows filled with the rich black of a moonless night in deep country. Delarua had already retired to the sleeping car, leaving them to continue their work. Dllenahkh looked into the soothing darkness, then made himself examine his handheld screen once again. The ambient light was too dim and the screen over bright – but perhaps, he admitted, that was not where the fault lay. The minute tension around his eyes might be caused by the fact that he was staring too intently at the reports and briefs, as if willing them to create the world he wanted to exist.

Behind closed doors, the Council had wrangled over the mission proposal with a pettiness and lack of direction to rival the callow youths they claimed to represent and govern. Then again, from what he had heard and seen, the Government of New Sadira was hardly doing any better, something that he found reassuring and dismaying in equal measure. If the Cygnian Government's response had been the least bit lukewarm, the mission would have been dropped for good, but they had been enthusiastic, offering specialists, funding and resources until the project gathered unstoppable momentum and even the most cynical Councillors softened.

Hope: that was the key. They were all clutching at straws, despairing and drowning, then clutching at a fresh set of straws. It was exhausting. It was all they had. Naraldi said it was important to keep moving forward – yes, forward, one clutched straw at a time. Highly ironic advice, considering, but useful nonetheless and something to hold on to now that Naraldi was off on his own mission, beyond the reach of any comm or courier. His last words, perhaps? No, never that. He expected Naraldi would have a safe journey and a safe return. What was one more straw to add to all the rest?

'First Officer Delarua is not what I expected,' Joral mused.

Dllenahkh kept his head bent over the mission schedule. Sometimes it was best not to engage when Joral indulged in his habit of thinking aloud.

'She kissed me.'

Dllenahkh glanced up at the young man. As a statement it was innocuous, but Joral's face held that anxiously pondering expression he used whenever women were being discussed.

'She is too old for you,' he replied firmly, though not unkindly. 'Now, let us go over the Acora, Sibon and Candirú briefs again. I would like us to be fully prepared when we meet our new colleagues.'

A MEANS TO OTHER ENDS

'We *have* a doctor on this team,' I said through gritted teeth.

Dllenahkh raised his head for a momentary glance. 'We have a Commissioner who is an anthropologist and a geneticist. Such expertise is not necessary for trivial injuries.'

The only expertise Dr Daniyel had that I wanted was the skill of understanding my need to howl shamelessly while having centimetre-long spines picked out of my palm. I hissed and twitched as Dllenahkh's tweezers probed too deeply. He gave me a tired look, firmly positioned my wrist between his knees and gripped. Then he held the tips of my fingers and applied the tweezers with a will. I twisted in my chair, turned my head into the crook of the elbow of my uninjured arm and kept it there.

'You may cry out if it makes you more comfortable,' he said kindly. 'It was only the movement that was problematic.'

'I'm good,' I whimpered.

After a few more minutes of torture, the barbaric, antique tweezers were laid aside and a modern medical scanner was passed over my hand. Having satisfied himself that the wounds were indeed clear of debris, Dllenahkh picked up another instrument and began to seal the punctures and lacerations. I emerged from hiding, sighing with the bliss of the absence of pain, and slowly flexed my hand.

'I would recommend that you stay away from that particular plant in future.'

'No disagreement here,' I said firmly.

'She only did it to get out of her turn at poling the punt,' Lian said to Joral with a laugh. They were at the back of the shuttle unloading the last set of supplies from storage.

'Mm-hm. That elegant trip and fall was all part of my cunning plan,' I said with distracted cheerfulness as I cautiously ran exploring fingers over my healed skin.

Lian and Joral went out, carrying a box between them. In a few minutes, having reassembled and put away the medkit, Dllenahkh also left. I gave my hand one final pat and was about to join them when Joral came back into the shuttle, a slightly furtive expression on his face. He slid into the chair beside me and placed his hands flat on his knees with an air of resolve.

'First Officer Delarua, is Lian male or female?'

I looked at Joral in utter shock. 'That is not a question you should ask anyone but Lian. In fact, I don't even think you should ask Lian that. Why do you even need to know?'

'Lian is highly intelligent and has features that are visually pleasing, but I do not know whether it would be appropriate to—'

'Joral, should you *really* be assessing the wife-potential of every female you meet?'

He looked slightly abashed. 'Such matters would have been arranged for me before, but now, with things as they are, it makes sense for me to review all possible options.' He began to tap his fingers on his knee, counting. 'Nasiha is already bonded, you are too old – at least, too old for me – Doctor Daniyel is *definitely* too old, and that leaves Lian by a simple process of elimination – *if*, of course, Lian is female.'

'Joral,' I said quietly, 'a word to the wise. First, it is best to steer clear of any assessment or discussion that uses the phrase "too old" to describe a woman. Second, fraternising with members of the mission team is not recommended. We will have to live as close as family while maintaining a high standard of professionalism. Complications would not be helpful.'

Joral looked at me apprehensively. He had already learned that it was not a good sign when I spoke slowly and quietly. 'I will take your advice, First Officer Delarua.'

'Good. Now, Lian is . . . Lian. Lian has chosen to live without reference to gender. This may or may not mean that Lian is asexual, though many of those who are registered as gender-neutral are indeed so. However, it doesn't matter, because this has no bearing on our mission and is thus *none of our business*. Now come on. They're waiting for us. My little tumble has put our whole schedule out of whack.'

It was a bit of an exaggeration. Things were proceeding as usual outside the shuttle. Nasiha and Tarik, the Sadiri married couple on loan from the Interplanetary Science Council, were securing equipment on the pallet that held our supplies. Dr Daniyel was talking to Lian, and Lian was making notes on a handheld computer with a stylus. Dllenahkh also had a handheld, and appeared to be recording a memo in a low murmur. Then there was Fergus tweaking some last clamp on one of the punts, and Joral and myself bringing up the rear with the last box of supplies we'd need for this trip. We were a motley crew, with two Sadiri in dark-blue Science Council uniforms, the Cygnians in Civil

Service grey and green (semi-formal yet serviceable gear courtesy of the Division of Forestry and Grasslands), and the two remaining Sadiri in beige and dark-brown civvies.

Fergus, our security and survival specialist, attracted our attention by clearing his throat and began his briefing.

'They say it's unlucky to urinate in the waters of Candirú,' he said. 'It's true. There's a parasitic fish in the river that'll swim up your urethra and get wedged in good and proper. Very painful. Don't risk it, but if you must, the Commissioner *might* be able to remove it without calling for medevac.'

The smirk that had appeared on my face at the word 'urinate' slowly transformed into a look of sheer horror and my smothered chuckle ended in a sickened gulp. 'Oh. You're not joking, are you?'

Fergus scowled down at me from his two-metre-plus height. 'I do not joke. My job is not a joking matter.'

'Okay,' I murmured meekly. Pincushion plants and perverted parasitic fish. I could tell this place was going to be *lovely*.

Fortunately, my strong right arm was not needed to bring us to our destination before the darkening of twilight. We – or rather the rest of the team – poled our three small craft to a central platform in the middle of the tree-fringed marshes and moored them carefully. Fergus boarded first and helped Dr Daniyel up. As we gathered together on the platform, we gazed about at the houses: simple structures on piles, some with steps going down to small vessels moored underneath, and other, larger residences connected to the main platform by boardwalks. The water was flat and rich with moss and weed, which tinted the crisply mirrored images of the houses with a green-glass sheen. The place was quiet, as if all were in the middle of a siesta.

'Do we call out? Ring something?' said Lian uncertainly.

'No,' said Tarik. 'We have been seen.'

His voice sounded a little strange, but when I saw the canoe and the people who were paddling it, I understood. Thus far, we had visited two settlements, both of which had indeed registered a significant amount of taSadiri heritage according to Dr Daniyel's genetic tests, but whose inhabitants had in culture and appearance so resembled the average Cygnian as to be unremarkable. These ones, now – they had the *hair*.

We set up our government-issue shelters on a spare platform (civil servants are discouraged from accepting hospitality when on-duty in case of bias or conflict of interest). It was quite comfortable. The marsh was fed mainly by outflows from the Candirú, and it did not rain during the time we were there. Screens and repellent kept the biting insects away, and filters made collecting potable water as simple as leaning over the platform's edge. Their sewerage system was excellent, its tubing tucked away behind piles and under boardwalks leading to a treatment area some distance away on dry land. I took notes. I intended to keep up to date in my own field as much as possible.

When Dr Daniyel finished taking the blood and tissue samples she needed, I went with her back to our landing site and we worked in the mini-lab that had been purpose-built into the shuttle for the mission. It wasn't really my field, but some kinds of lab skills are pretty elementary, so I ended up helping a fair bit. It was a good thing, too. I observed Dr Daniyel and realised something wasn't quite right. She leaned over her work in a way that spoke not of absorption, but exhaustion.

'You'll get your own DNA in the samples if you're not careful,' I said lightly. 'Perhaps you should take a break?'

Dr Daniyel pulled her greying locks over one shoulder with a slow weariness that was oddly graceful, then stepped back to let me help with the analysis. 'There will be time to rest after the mission's done. I've been pushing for a global genetic registry for years now. Perhaps this can be the start of it.'

'It's early in the mission. You mustn't forget to pace yourself,' I said, expressing my concern with care. I didn't want to appear to be telling my boss she looked unfit for command.

'Oh, this?' She smiled, waving a hand at herself. 'Chronic. Still within Service parameters, but I do have a condition that makes me tire quite easily. That's why I have Lian for the heavy lifting, but as for the rest of it, I'm pretty much the only person with the skill and experience for this job.'

I adjusted the meters and toggled the last few switches. 'There. That should do it.' I looked at her. 'With all due respect, ma'am, I can get the results later and save them to your files for you.'

She seemed amused and gratified at my solicitude, which was good because it could have gone either way, but then her face changed. 'Aggregated data,' she said, her voice suddenly alert and firm. 'We don't do individual scans. This is an anthropological analysis, not a medical report.'

'Yes, ma'am. I am familiar with the bioethics section of the Science Code,' I answered calmly.

She smiled once more, unoffended at being humoured. 'It's going to be a long mission. Feel free to call me Qeturah when off duty.'

'I'm Grace,' I responded. 'But everyone calls me Delarua regardless.'

The results were interesting. These Cygnians did *not* possess a greater percentage of taSadiri genes compared to those in the last two settlements, appearance notwithstanding (genetics can be a funny potluck, let me tell you), but what they did have was a surprising amount of cultural integrity. Tarik and Nasiha went off to speak to the people, recording words, stories, myths and customs in a far more detailed and directed manner than Cygnian anthropologists had yet accomplished. Of course, they had something we didn't – a knowledge of some of the more obscure and ancient Sadiri dialects, and with that they were able to make far more connections and discoveries than we could.

Once the bio tests were all finished there wasn't much for me to do, but our stay was extended so that Dr Daniyel could satisfy herself with more anthropological data and the Sadiri could explore the potential for links between their settlements. For a few days, I just relaxed and took it in. Sometimes I'd watch Joral, who was ostensibly helping the Science Council officers or taking minutes at meetings for Dllenahkh, but . . . quite honestly? Checking out the girls. It was an education in Sadiri flirting. One in particular must have been his favourite, because he all but disassembled one of the biosensors in order to spend time explaining its workings to her. Sadiri mating displays seemed to consist of flashing bright mental plumage at the object of desire in as cool and disinterested a fashion as possible.

Otherwise, I'd sit on the edge of a balcony staring at the mesmerisingly slow flow of the green water and hearing – overhearing, really – Dllenahkh debating some principle of Sadiri philosophy with the settlement's Chief Councillor, Darithiven.

'Of all the humans of the galaxy, we Sadiri have developed the greatest mental capacity,' Dllenahkh contended. 'We have realised our potential through use of the disciplines, which enable us to control our thoughts, emotions and urges, and improve our ability

49

to process data. Without the disciplines we might still be powerful, but we would be rudderless.'

Darithiven smiled the slightly condescending smile of a man who is prepared to humour his opponent, but not to yield the argument. 'Your disciplines are indeed impressive. Your pilots use them to navigate ships on interstellar routes, and because of them all Sadiri have acquired a reputation for impartiality and diligence. Even now, our systems of justice and scientific endeavour continue to be headed by Sadiri. But here we live simpler lives, with less to trouble our minds. We need only enough self-control to maintain a harmonious society.' He extended his arms, embracing the view of his settlement and his people like a proud father.

Dllenahkh actually hesitated before replying. 'Your settlement is indeed well organised and efficiently run. But there is more to the world, to the universe, than these waters. Perhaps you do not wish to explore the galaxy yourself, but what of your children and your children's children? The earlier certain things are taught—'

The Chief Councillor shook his head and interrupted gently. 'I hope you are not implying that we limit our children by what we teach, or do not teach. We have our own version of the disciplines, and they are not lacking in rigour. It is simply that our goals differ. Is that so inappropriate?'

By this time, I'd be almost slipping into the water from boredom as they went back and forth on the question of the scope and purpose of the Sadiri disciplines. I could see Darithiven's point. To tell the truth, this was one of the sleepiest settlements I'd ever encountered. People kept to themselves, not in an unfriendly fashion, but as if truly uninterested in our presence. We saw them coming and going – men up to the river to fish, women to the nearby rice paddies and the other crop fields south of the marshes, the remainder busy at home with their arts, crafts, studies or whatever else they chose to occupy themselves with. Whatever form of mental discipline they employed, it clearly worked for them. The settlement had the same atmosphere of measured efficiency I'd encountered on the Sadiri homesteadings of my own province.

'How are the talks going?' I asked Dllenahkh.

His eyes lit up. 'It has been most intriguing. They are, of course, quite attached to their simplified variant of the disciplines, but I believe in time some of them could be persuaded to return to the orthodox methods practised by most Sadiri.'

I gave him a look. 'Mmm-hm. So, will your guys come here or will they go to you?'

'They would encourage males from our homesteadings to come here, and are willing to send in exchange groups that would be mostly female.'

'Sounds reasonable. Well done,' I congratulated him.

I was a little chagrined, actually. I'd been so cynical about this mission, and here we were, already third time lucky. It wasn't storybook perfect – I could tell they'd be debating for generations to come – but at least there was a foundation.

Dr Daniyel told us at our evening meeting that it was time to wrap up and move on to explore other areas. Dllenahkh, Nasiha and Tarik reluctantly agreed. When I looked at their faces, I remembered Dllenahkh saying to me that all Sadiri shared a low-level telepathic bond. If that were indeed the case, visiting the marshes of Candirú must have felt like being immersed in a constant buzz of subtle connection. I could understand why they would be hesitant to leave.

Joral didn't want to leave at all. 'I have already identified two potential candidates for betrothal in the five days we have been here. Surely it would be worthwhile for me to remain and gather more anthropological data. This could assist our homesteaders in making an informed choice as to whether they should remove here or no.'

Dr Daniyel shot a sharp look at Dllenahkh, which he missed because he was already frowning at Joral. I smiled to myself, waiting to hear him tell the young Sadiri to be patient, to remain disciplined and to focus on the mission.

'Joral, *no*.'

'But Councillor Dllen—'

'I said no.'

Lian and I looked at each other, ludicrously wide-eyed with shock and amusement. Dr Daniyel's lips twitched, but she said nothing.

That was when the commotion started outside: shouting, the thud of running steps on the wood of the boardwalk, a woman's scream.

Fergus was first out, Lian close behind, but we all scrambled to see what the fuss was about. There was still sunlight at that hour, though the long shadows of the trees and houses darkened the waters. A small fishing boat was drawing up to one of the walkways. The smell that came from it was not the odour of gutted fish, but the strong metallic tang of blood. A hand trailed carelessly over the side into the water, and the sickly grey hue that overcast the skin was visible even from where we stood. People gathered around and the shouts grew louder.

'What's happening?' said Dr Daniyel at my ear.

'Their boat was attacked,' I said, listening and translating the fragmented, overlapping speech into a coherent explanation. 'There's another settlement off a tributary upriver, and they've quarrelled over fishing rights for some time, it seems. I . . . I think that man's dead. They're talking about going to the other settlement for . . .'

I paused. I couldn't believe the word I had just heard. I'd heard the words in Sadiri separately but never together, and so it was with a panicked glance at Dllenahkh that I said, 'Blood-price? Price for blood? Price *in* blood?'

Dllenahkh gave me a look I could not understand. Sorrow? Shame? But he did not correct me.

'There's Darithiven,' said Nasiha suddenly.

It was indeed the Chief Councillor of the settlement, and he had to pass us to reach the fishing boat. His gaze flashed across to us, he hesitated, then he appeared to make a decision and came towards us.

'May we be of assistance, Chief Councillor Darithiven?' asked Dr Daniyel immediately.

He was already shaking his head. 'A small matter, a local matter. It is nothing new. We can manage without outside interference.'

I grabbed the hard muscle of Fergus's arm. A muted glint of edged metal had appeared amid the crowd – and there again, a blade in one hand, a spear in another.

'I see it,' Fergus said gruffly. He exchanged a look with Lian, and I saw them release the catches on their holsters and adjust their pistols to a high but non-lethal setting.

Darithiven saw it too, and his expression was resigned but approving. 'You have your own security. That is wise. Now I must

53

leave you. There is much anger here, and it must be appropriately directed. We have had too many incursions into our waters and it is time to deal with the culprits sternly.'

'There are other, civilised ways of dealing with the matter,' Dllenahkh insisted.

Darithiven looked at him with pity. 'Then, by your definition, this cannot be civilisation.'

He strode off towards the gathering mob.

Nasiha inhaled sharply and began to whisper to Tarik. Their stance changed from relaxed stillness to defensive tension as they drew closer to each other.

'What is it?' I demanded. Their behaviour irritated me. Perhaps it was because they were both spouses and colleagues, but they were such an annoyingly cosy little self-contained unit. *My* Sadiri, as I had labelled Dllenahkh and Joral in my head, understood the simple courtesy of explaining themselves from time to time.

'They are making themselves angry,' Dllenahkh muttered, profoundly disturbed, as he stared at the growing crowd. 'They have lowered their mental shields to each other and are projecting and augmenting a desire to fight and kill.'

Suddenly his head snapped to Joral who stood stiffly, breathing heavily, his fists clenching spasmodically at his sides. 'Joral! Remember your disciplines!'

'It is . . . difficult, Councillor Dllenahkh,' Joral admitted.

'Stand with Commander Nasiha and Lieutenant Tarik,' Dllenahkh ordered.

Before I could ask him why he didn't follow his own advice, he started off in the direction of the crowd, saying, 'I must stop this.'

'No!' shouted Dr Daniyel.

To my shock, Dllenahkh ignored her and walked on. I wavered, eyeing her, hoping for permission, however subtly conveyed, to go after him. Instead she did the sensible thing and actually followed our mission protocols. 'Lian, Fergus, load everything essential into the punts. We must get ready to leave as soon as possible. Delarua, find Darithiven for me. I have a few things to say to him.'

I noticed that she did not issue orders to Tarik and Nasiha, but she did give them one of her sharp looks. It seemed to break them out of their cocoon because they started to help Lian and Fergus while keeping an eye on Joral. He followed them meekly, still looking shaky.

I dashed off along a path, already knowing where to go. Darithiven was not far away. He stood on the balcony of his residence and surveyed the scene below with an unsettling expression. It was not peace exactly, but . . . satisfaction? A sense of seeing something come to pass that had been planned for a long time? As I halted halfway up the steps, he looked down his nose at me, as if I were something small and unimportant come to bother him. I glared back. I would not allow him to forget that whatever rank he held in his own little patch of marsh, Dr Daniyel and I represented the government that allowed him to exercise that rank.

'The Commissioner wishes to speak to you,' I growled. 'Now.'

Dr Daniyel was waiting on the central platform. She stood meditatively with arms folded and head slightly bowed. She looked calm and resolute. I knew she was tired.

'Thank you, First Officer Delarua. Please inform Councillor Dllenahkh that we are ready to leave. Lian, go with Delarua.'

As we rushed off, I heard her begin to speak to Darithiven in

55

the slow, disappointed tones of a scolding parent. 'As it seems you can no longer guarantee the safety of my team . . .'

'Where *is* Dllenahkh?' Lian said, glancing about nervously.

I stared. I couldn't see him either, and I didn't relish going into the midst of that loud, surging mass.

'There!' I pointed to the edge of the crowd.

He had stepped up onto a low balcony and was speaking with two of the older men. Their faces were masks of bitter fury, his a study in intense determination, as if he expected to persuade them through sheer force of will. I shouted to him, my voice thin and distant in all the noise, and he did hear me, but he looked at me with a brief, dismissing glance and went back to his argument.

'Damn,' I said.

'Let me,' Lian said grimly.

Long soldier-strides took Lian to Dllenahkh's side in seconds. I followed close behind.

'Come with us, Councillor Dllenahkh. The Commissioner's orders,' Lian said simply and quietly.

'Not yet, Lian, I must—'

'Not a request, Councillor Dllenahkh,' Lian replied.

It was only when I saw Dllenahkh flinch ever so slightly that I realised Lian had nudged the pistol into his ribs. His lips pressed together, the one angry sign in a face that refused even now to lose control. 'I see,' was all he said.

'Let's go,' I squeaked, agitated by the atmosphere around us, and we walked away briskly, unchallenged and unmolested in the growing maelstrom of anger that was, thankfully, not directed at us.

It felt like a retreat. It was all done according to procedure, but it felt like a retreat. Lian sent off a preliminary bulletin to the nearest government outpost so that the situation could be monitored by the appropriate authorities. Dr Daniyel sent a more detailed report the moment we returned to the shuttle. Nasiha, Tarik and poor Joral were clearly relieved, their condition improving the further we travelled from the marshes. Fergus was pleased that the 'bug-out' drill he had insisted on had been used so early in the mission and had worked so well. Dllenahkh . . .

I didn't dare look at Dllenahkh. When I finally, furtively glanced at him, just as the shuttle was taking off, his face was impassive, his demeanour as calm and controlled as ever. I knew he felt my gaze, but he did not meet my eyes.

We flew for a little less than an hour before landing near our next destination, a bit of savannah country further south. Fergus set out perimeter alarms while we wearily put up our shelters and sought sleep. We did everything right. It still felt like a retreat.

When I woke up the next morning, emotion came before memory, so my first coherent thought was to wonder if it was a hangover that had me feeling so miserable. Then I remembered the previous day and felt thoroughly sick. I pulled myself together, freshened up and went to see if Dr Daniyel needed me for anything, but Lian said she was still sleeping, so I went away again with a vague idea of checking on Joral. He was sitting in meditation posture in the doorway of the shelter that he shared with Dllenahkh. I hesitated when I saw him, not wanting to disturb him, especially given the mental turmoil he had so recently experienced. I must have trodden too heavily, however, for he opened his eyes and stared at me.

'First Officer Delarua,' he said.

'Joral. Are you well?' I asked, formally and in Sadiri.

'I am well,' he replied in a steady voice. Before I could exhale in relief, he continued, 'But Councillor Dllenahkh will not get up.'

'Beg pardon?' I said in Standard, genuinely confused as to his meaning.

Still speaking Sadiri, Joral tried for greater precision. 'It is possible that he is awake, but his eyes are not open, he is not moving and his mind . . . His mind is closed.'

I stood still, completely at a loss. 'What do you want me to do?'

'I do not know,' he replied with simple honesty.

'Nasiha, Tarik—' I began.

'He would not wish them to see him like this.'

Something about the way he said it gave me a clue. 'This has happened before,' I accused him, a statement, not a question.

He nodded, stood up and stepped aside, leaving the way clear for me to enter. I stared at him, then went in slowly, not knowing what to expect.

Dllenahkh lay on his side in the narrow government-issue cot, not quite foetal but certainly curled into himself, the blanket pulled up to just below a bare shoulder. There were signs that he was awake. The firm grip of his left hand on his right wrist, the tension around his eyes as his eyelids pressed tightly closed and his shallow, uneven breathing all spoke of distress.

I knelt by his head, too astonished to feel awkward. 'Dllenahkh? Will you get up?'

Feeble, I know, but amazingly it got a response. 'I am tired,' he said slowly. 'Leave me alone.'

'For some reason, I don't think I should,' I replied. To my own incredulous ears, my voice sounded as ordinary as if discussing

58

an inspections checklist. 'I think you should get up and come for a walk with me.'

He remained still for a while, but his eyes opened, though they kept looking carefully past me. I glanced around for something to help restart the conversation and saw an undershirt and tunic neatly folded nearby. Trust a Sadiri to have a breakdown but still not neglect the small domestic rituals.

'Here's your shirt,' I said inanely. 'Let's put it on, shall we?'

Still looking away, he heaved a great sigh and sat up slowly. He allowed me to manoeuvre the undershirt over his head, then heavily moved his arms to finish putting it on. His hair was mussed, and I resisted the urge to pat it back into place.

'What's happened to you?' I whispered.

'Overextended myself,' he mumbled. 'So much anger, back there. So tiring to keep it out.'

I knew there was more to it than that, but I said nothing, only handed him the tunic and looked around for his boots.

'There,' I said at last with a weak attempt at cheerfulness. 'You're all ready. Let's go.'

Joral joined us as we came outside, discreetly ignoring his superior's rumpled appearance – or so I thought. Then I realised he was distracted by Lian. Already dressed, the Commissioner's aide was trotting past with biosensor in hand.

'Something's tripped a perimeter alarm,' Lian explained. 'Fergus is on it, but he wanted a sensor reading to be sure.'

I was glad for the diversion. We could pretend we were still functional when lurching from crisis to crisis; it was the time for quiet and introspection that was dangerous. We jogged along behind, following Lian up a low hill to where Fergus was already in place, half-kneeling with his pistol held point-down but ready. He gestured for us to approach cautiously.

I didn't see it at first against the blond colour of the grass, but then it moved – a short-haired animal rather like a wild dog in size and shape. The creature snuffled around briefly, tossed its head in the air as if sneezing from the dust and then turned away to lope down the other side of the hill.

Joral was the first to unfreeze. Mute, expressionless, he simply turned about and quickly went back the way we had come. I watched him go, frowning in puzzlement.

'Wild dog?' asked Lian in hushed tones.

'Savannah dog. I've never seen one before, but I hear they show up sometimes in this region,' Fergus said. 'They shouldn't be any trouble as long as we don't bother their pups.'

The two Science Council officers came rushing up the hill with Joral, biosensors at the ready. We followed them as they swept ahead for readings, followed them right to the sloping crest of the hill and crouched there, obedient to their silent, frantic hand signals. I peeked through the coarse grass that fringed the crumbling edge and saw them: a small pack of dogs comfortably at home in the den they had made, sheltered and safe in the cleft of a small valley.

'No,' said Dllenahkh.

His voice sounded so strange that I looked at him sharply, immediately afraid that he was slipping into that frozen depression again. He felt my concerned gaze and turned to me.

'No,' he repeated with the most brilliant and beautiful smile that I never expected to see on a Sadiri. 'Not a savannah dog – Sadiri. Look.'

He gazed down intently into the valley, and one by one, first adults, then pups, they went from a panting, relaxed demeanour to closed-jawed alertness. Their noses pointed enquiringly at the air – *Who? Who?* Then they looked at Dllenahkh, looked straight at him through all the brush and grass. Their jaws relaxed once more as if grinning in welcome and their short whip-like tails thumped the ground and whisked the grass in slow, cautious approval.

'Sadiri dogs, so far from home,' murmured Dllenahkh. 'The taSadiri must have brought them. So few remain now. The Science Council keeps them under protection.'

Nasiha and Tarik did not once take their eyes off the scene below them, nor did they set down their biosensors, but their free hands met and clasped together with a quiet passion that was like a promise. Joral's face was more conflicted; subtle shades of anger and grief mingled with awe and gratitude. Dllenahkh . . . the first brilliance had faded, tempered with sorrowful acceptance, but still he smiled.

I don't know how long the team stayed on the hill – the Cygnians watching the Sadiri, the Sadiri watching the dogs. I left them there and went for a short walk and a cry before going back to camp. I wanted to be the first to tell Dr Daniyel all about it when she woke up.

HAPPY FAMILIES

'So,' I said to Qeturah, 'I have this friend . . .'

She gave me a smile. It was the classic opening line for any counselling session. 'Go on,' she prompted.

'Well, they've got some fairly strict ethics about stuff like . . . telepathy and emotional control and such. They feel pretty strongly about it. Thing is, they've had to deal with a situation where someone was operating without those ethics.'

'I see,' she said. 'Did they feel vulnerable in this situation?'

'Maybe they did. Maybe they felt they were strong enough to handle any direct attack. But I think what's worse is that they felt responsible for others who might be hurt by this person.'

'The person without the ethical standards,' she queried.

'Yes. Because no one else seemed to think that there was anything wrong with how that person was behaving. Maybe they couldn't see it, or maybe they thought it was normal. I don't know. I think I'm kind of afraid to ask.'

'What do you want for your friend?' she asked quietly.

'I want them to feel . . . like they don't always have to be responsible for other people. Like it's okay to not be the strong one all the time. Maybe even okay to ask for help.'

She was silent for a while. 'Well,' she said carefully, 'you can let your friend know that if they ever want to ask for help, I'm here to listen, I won't judge and I have ways of getting things done without breaching confidentiality.'

I swallowed, feeling a thickness in my throat. 'Yes, ma'am. Thank you. I hope I can get my friend to come talk to you directly.'

Some people might think it's kind of strange having your boss also be your doctor and psychiatrist, but we were a small team and Qeturah was a very good small-team leader. She took an interest in everyone, and she knew instinctively which 'voice' to use and which hat to wear in which context. There were a lot of hats to juggle over the next few days. Central Government wanted the Sadiri and the Commissioner to come in for an inquiry over the situation in Candirú, which remained volatile. The day after the flight from Candirú we were off to Ophir, the nearest town with full facilities for teleconferencing.

Dllenahkh gave his brief testimony first. There was a Sadiri savant among the investigators, and though he spoke little, he looked at Dllenahkh as if cataloguing any and every sign of unusual behaviour. Superficially, Dllenahkh seemed fine to me, apart from an air of constant preoccupation, and yet I was aware that unexpectedly discovering a much-loved breed of hometown fauna isn't really what you might call a complete cure. That Sadiri savant must have seen something I missed, because during the tea break, Qeturah was kept in for a brief, private consultation which then turned into orders for me.

'Delarua, you know the Montserrat region pretty well?' she said as soon as she emerged from the meeting room.

'I've got some family there . . . Why?' I asked. Instinct honed by years of experience in the Civil Service made me drain my teacup and reach for an extra slice of cake to add to my napkin. It was good cake, and I didn't want a little thing like duty getting in the way of enjoying it.

'I want you to go with Councillor Dllenahkh to the Benedictine monastery at Montserrat. They've got a Sadiri priest and some monks housed there, and they'll help him realign his nodes or reverse his polarity or whatever it is he needs doing to him. Fergus will fly you in today and pick you up Sunday afternoon.'

Serendipity and guilt knocked jointly on my conscience. 'Um . . . it's a silent monastery. Do you need me to stay there with him, or just take him there?'

Qeturah frowned slightly. 'I thought he was your friend. I want to have someone nearby to check on him, and you're a familiar face. We can't spare Joral – he's got all the reports of their meetings.'

I felt even guiltier. 'No, I didn't mean . . . What I meant was, d'you mind if I take a couple of days to visit my sister? I'll make sure Dllenahkh can reach me at any time, and I'll get her to drive me back to the monastery the day before Fergus returns for us.'

I bit my tongue. I hoped she wouldn't think I was just taking advantage, though in a way I was, but it was for a good cause, an appropriate cause, even.

Her face cleared. 'Of course. All my family's in Tlaxce, and I keep forgetting what it's like when your kin are further afield. Take a couple of days. Just don't miss that shuttle.'

'No, ma'am,' I said in relief.

She glanced down at my stash of cake with a smile. 'And yes, I do want you to leave immediately.'

The half-hour trip was fairly quiet. I spent the first ten minutes of it psyching myself up, then excused myself to go to a monitor at the back of the shuttle and call my sister. Just to be sure, I called her personal communicator first, not her house comm. She answered in seconds, audio only.

'Identify,' she said, her tone offhand and slightly rushed.

Of course. I was calling from a general government comm, so my ID wouldn't show up. 'Maria, it's Grace. How are you? How're the children?'

There was a slight, shocked pause and the video flipped on. She hadn't changed too much. A little fuller around the face, maybe, but I wasn't going to tell her that. 'Grace? How are you! *Where* are you! My goodness, it's not a birthday or a special occasion – what's happening?'

I smiled. At least she seemed happy to see me. 'Work's happening. I'll be in Montserrat for a few days. Think I could pop by for a quick visit?'

'Yes!' Her response was breathless, and wholeheartedly sincere. 'The children will be so happy to see you, especially Rafi, and Ioan is always complaining that you never come by.'

My heart lightened. It was going to be just fine. 'Well, then, don't tell them; let me surprise them! Is it all right if I land in the back yard in . . . oh . . . about three hours' time?'

She began to giggle. 'Sure! Oh, this is amazing! I can't believe it. Oh!'

There was a voice in the background. She turned suddenly, one hand reaching out to swiftly kill the vid. 'Nothing, dear! Coming in a moment!' She whispered hastily, audio-only, 'Must go! See you soon! Bye!' Then the link died.

I sighed, smiling slightly. Blood is blood, you know? There's too much shared history and too many cross-connecting bonds to ever totally extract yourself from that half-smothering, half-supporting, muddled net called family.

Speaking of which . . .

'Dllenahkh,' I said, coming back to my seat at the front of the shuttle. 'I'm going to abandon you for a couple of days, but you have my comm ID and you can call me any time. You know that, right?'

He gave me a vaguely bemused look. 'I have the comm IDs of all the members of the mission team. However, given that I am going to a monastery, the chances of anything happening over the next two days that I should need to report are—'

'I know, I know,' I interrupted with a grin. 'However vanishingly small a chance it might be, you can call me, okay?'

He paused and seemed to recollect something, then graciously said, 'Thank you. And you may call me as well, should you wish to do so.'

I was warmed by his awkward little dip into small talk for the sake of courtesy.

When we landed, a part of me almost expected the Sadiri priest to come flying out, grab Dllenahkh by the head, look deeply into his eyes and exclaim, 'My God, get this man to a meditation chamber, stat! Can't you see his rudimentary telepathic integument is about to disintegrate?'

Or not. But the image almost made me giggle, which would have been unfortunate.

Of course, it was all very sedate and proper. I was intrigued that the Sadiri monks didn't seem very distinct from the Benedictines. Their garb was different, but there was no separate building, no invisible bisecting line that said 'Here be Sadiri'. The Cygnian guestmaster and his Sadiri counterpart showed us where Dllenahkh would be quartered, took us to the refectory for a little refreshment and then saw Fergus and me to the door where we bade Dllenahkh farewell.

The flight to the homestead took less than ten minutes. I asked Fergus to set me down a little way from the main house so that the noise of the engines wouldn't alert them. Fittingly enough, that meant I had the chance to run into one of my most favourite people in the world, my thirteen-year-old nephew Rafi. He was coming from the direction of the orchard, carrying a bucket of starfruit. At first he squinted at me in a very puzzled way, then recognition transformed his face into a wide-eyed, open-mouthed shout of happiness as he dropped the bucket and ran towards me. His exuberant warmth blew out uncontrolled like a hot gust of savannah wind, singeing me with a burning yet benign energy that matched his rough boy-hug.

Rafi has always been a beautiful boy, with his mother's amber-brown skin, his father's wavy brown and blond-streaked hair, and big brown eyes from both parents. He's also my godson and I adore him. He'd write me long letters filled with sketches and stories, and send them by post that took at least a week to arrive. I'd always write back immediately, usually sending a small memory disc with games and other entertainment that I knew he'd enjoy. I doubted his parents were aware how often we corresponded. He had begged me not to tell them and I indulged him, secretly glad to be the favourite aunt. I dreamt that we'd go travelling together when he was older and I was retired and properly eccentric. We'd ride elephants in the savannah, or join the crew of a sailing ship, or something.

It felt silly to say it, so I never did, but I always felt like I'd never want any children of my own as long as I had Rafi.

'You haven't come to see me in *ages*,' he complained, tugging me by the hand to the main house.

'Well, I'm here now.' I laughed. 'Boy, go get that fruit. You can't leave the bucket lying in the road so.'

He gave a grimace and went to quickly gather up the scattered fruit. I snagged one from the bucket as he came back. There were mangoes under the starfruit, and I hadn't had a proper Montserrat mango in years. It was warm and fragrant when I held it to my cheek.

'Ahh,' I sighed.

'If you came to visit me more often, you could have as many of those as you liked,' Rafi said pointedly.

I smiled at him, pleased at his clean, honest indignation, mock persuasion and adolescent sarcasm. 'I love you too, boy.'

'Maybe I should move to Tlaxce,' he hinted as we walked on to the house.

'Maybe you should,' I said, even more pleased. As if Maria would let her golden boy out of her sight, but at least he had thought about it.

Maria came onto the verandah wearing a blue cotton dress, looking very matronly and homely with little Gracie clinging to her side, still sucking a thumb. She looked older than me, older in a way that only two children and homestead living can accomplish, but happy, both happy to see me and happy in general. I hugged her hard and tousled Gracie's hair affectionately. She looked a bit too shy to hug just yet. She didn't really know me.

'Oh, Grace.' Maria sighed as she smiled at me and ushered me inside. 'Only two days?'

'I'm lucky it's even that much,' I said, letting Rafi take my small bag. The living room was full of memories, all stuff my mother had handed over when she gave up the homestead after Papa's death and retired to a condo on Tlaxce Lake.

'Look who's here, Ioan!' Maria called out.

He came into the room, dusty and sweat-streaked from working outside. He wore his hair longer, brushing his shoulders, the gilt bands in the seal brown even more fiercely bleached by the sun. He was still lean, still handsome, still golden. He had been my fiancé once. My heart stumbled as a flood of half-remembered yearning seemed to pour out from him and envelop me. His eyes glowed with an inhuman warmth and I thought I heard a whisper in his voice . . . *Shadi*. A strong memory, to echo so loudly.

'Hello, Ioan,' I said, and smiled proudly at how ordinary I sounded.

'Shadi,' he said, breaking out into a huge, radiant smile. He'd always called me by my middle name. In a few quick steps he reached me and hugged me, picking me up half a metre from the ground in his fervour. 'You came back. I knew you'd come back.'

'Well,' I said breathlessly, looking over his shoulder at Maria's beaming face, 'just for a little while.'

He stepped back suddenly, looking anxiously at my uniform. 'Man, I'm filthy. Sorry about that.' He brushed at a few reddish stains on my shirt and trousers where the clay soil had transferred and left its mark.

'Don't worry. Time I changed out of this anyway,' I said, gently pushing away his hands.

After changing clothes, I started for the kitchen, hearing the

70

familiar clatter of meal preparation. As I passed the door to the small pantry, something made me turn my head. There was Gracie, standing on a stepladder, glaring at the top shelf where a cookie jar sat just out of her reach.

'What are you doing up there? Come!' I demanded.

She tumbled from the stepladder into my outstretched arms for a hug. I squeezed her skinny four-year-old frame with a gleeful grin. She may not have been my favourite, but she was my namesake and it was early days. Maybe if she learned to write long letters . . .

'Hey, you two.'

The voice was close enough to make me jump. Ioan stood behind me and wrapped his arms around both of us, bending past my cheek to smack a kiss on his daughter's forehead. The slight stubble of his jaw grazed my skin. I took a half-step sideways, trying to keep our bodies from brushing together. He didn't seem to notice, or care, because he moved with me in a slight sway, appearing to relish the lengthy embrace.

'Two of my favourite girls,' he murmured, then finally let go.

I turned around and set Gracie in his arms. 'I'll go see if Maria needs any help with dinner.'

He put Gracie down. 'Sweetie, go see if your mother needs any help.'

She dashed off silently.

'She's so *obedient*,' I said accusingly. 'Did she even *have* the "terrible twos" stage?'

'Not really, no,' Ioan said, looking after her with a smile.

'Not like her mother, then. She drove me mad when she was two.'

'Shadi,' he said, and that was all he said, but something in the tone made me duck my head down and walk to the door which, unfortunately, meant going past him.

He seized me by the wrist. 'Shadi, look at me.'

'No, Ioan. That doesn't work on me, remember?' I tugged my hand free and kept going, trying to ignore the echo in my head . . . *Shadi* . . . *Shadi.*

At dinner, Maria kept talking about how long it had been. The first few times, it was heartwarming, but then it became almost nagging. When she started talking about how I could have stayed a homesteader rather than going to university, Rafi and I exchanged weary, eye-rolling looks. Maria missed it and made the mistake of trying to enlist Rafi's help.

'Rafi's always talking about how much he misses you, aren't you, dear? Wouldn't you like it if Auntie Grace lived with us on the homestead?'

I was startled. How did we get from 'visiting more often' to 'moving in entirely'?

'I think she should live her own life,' Rafi muttered.

Maria was furious. 'Rafi! You apologise to your aunt right now!'

'It's all right, Maria, he—'

Ioan overrode my protests. 'Your mother's right. Apologise.'

Rafi glared at him. 'You're always messing things up. I hate you!'

Now I was shocked. 'Rafi!'

He pushed away from the table and stood up, giving me a look that was both anguish and reproach. Then he shook his head in frustration and ran out of the room.

Little Gracie looked wide-eyed from parent to parent, jaws motionless, her last mouthful still bulging her cheeks.

'Teenagers,' Ioan said carelessly with a reassuring smile, smoothing his daughter's hair. 'They hate everybody at that age.'

He looked at me, still smiling. His foot gently bumped mine under the table and for a full second I didn't feel inclined to pull away. Then something buzzed on my wrist, distracting me. I slapped at it absently and it went away.

I kept up my mask of indifference pretty well, but that night Ioan haunted my dreams in a way he hadn't done in years. Memories and might-have-beens tangled in a mad jumble. I remembered how it felt when our hearts and minds came together, at a time I thought *I love you* meant for ever. I dreamt I had never left, I was in Maria's place and Rafi was truly my son. It made me angry and confused. *The ability to know another's mind does not preclude the likelihood of misunderstanding it.* That was true. I knew that all too well, and that's why I hadn't married him. So why was I dreaming about him again?

I avoided him by spending more time with Maria. It was her I'd come to see, anyway.

If anyone had asked me what I was looking for, I couldn't have answered them. Some things you know more by intuition than by reasoning. I told myself that I just wanted to be reassured that Maria was happy and Ioan was behaving himself, but to tell the truth her unwavering contentedness was beginning to aggravate me. What with that and the dreams, mostly I just felt guilty and mad at myself. Then one afternoon, after a large Sunday lunch, when we were sitting in the living room with the children sprawled on the carpet playing cards, Ioan tried a little too hard.

'You know, we could use another pair of hands on the homestead,' Maria said. 'You're helping those Sadiri with their homesteadings. Don't you think family should come first?' Her smile was oddly fixed.

I frowned a bit at that. 'Why would you say that? You know it's not like that.'

'Then explain it to me. Here you have people who love you, who want you to be part of the family, and you act like you can barely stand to see us!' Her voice cracked.

Rafi stiffened, not looking at her but listening hard. Gracie stood up and went to stare out of the window. Ioan sat straighter and made a movement as if about to rest a pacifying hand on his wife's shoulder, then seemed to decide against it.

'Maria, you're not making sense!' I said, aghast that she looked on the edge of tears. 'What's the matter with you?'

'You can have him if you want, you know. That's the only thing keeping you away. You can have Ioan,' she cried out, right in front of the children and all.

I was thunderstruck. Then, when she finally burst into tears, I knew. Ioan went to her, speaking to her quietly. She got up and left the room without looking at anyone, and after a moment, still silent and expressionless, Gracie followed her. Rafi stayed, eyes wide with something like fear as he stared at his father.

I knew how he felt as I too stared at Ioan. 'That was you. I *know* that was you.' I got up and backed away from him.

'I didn't mean for her to get that intense. She always was a little too susceptible,' Ioan replied with a sad, sweet smile.

'You bastard,' I said. 'I warned you – if you hurt her, if you hurt any of my family, I will deal with you!'

'I'm not hurting them,' he protested. 'I take good care of them. They're happy.'

'Happy little puppets,' I spat, gripping my right wrist in an effort not to slap him. 'I should report you to the authorities.'

'You won't,' he said simply. 'You love me. Never stopped.'

'It doesn't work on me, Ioan. It never did, and that's why you couldn't keep me. That and a small problem you have with honesty. You like life to be easy, don't you, with everything and everyone exactly as you like.'

'It was just a mistake, Shadi, but I do love you. I shouldn't have given up on us. I want you to stay. We all do. Can't you see that?' He was pleading now, using words and gestures alone, unpractised and desperate.

My gaze rested on the one person in the room that I trusted. He looked up at me helplessly.

'Rafi loves me so much that he's willing to let me go,' I said. 'That's what I see.'

Rafi jumped up and grabbed my hand, and we ran out of the house. I didn't know where we were supposed to be running to, or why, but it seemed like a good idea to get as far away from Ioan as possible. Unfortunately, when I glanced back, I saw that he was right behind us, moving at a leisurely pace, knowing we had nowhere to go.

But Rafi knew where to go and in a little while a growing, humming vibration that had been pressing on my ears turned into a recognisable noise. It was the shuttle, landing once more in the field near the orchard. Fergus disembarked first, looking moody and suspicious as usual. Dllenahkh followed. He wore a novice's robe with the hood up, which I thought rather suited him and gave him a very peaceful air. They came walking briskly towards us over the grass.

Dllenahkh looked almost relieved to see me. 'We have been calling you for some time. Did you forget our departure date?'

I looked at the comm on my wrist. Fourteen missed calls – when the hell did that happen? And was it really Sunday already?

'Fergus, Dllenahkh, I'm sorry! My comm must have malfunctioned, and then I forgot . . . I don't know what to say.'

Ioan came to my rescue. 'I'm sorry. The reception out here is so variable. And we've been completely monopolising her – it's no wonder she forgot.'

'No problem,' Fergus said. 'We're hours early. The Commissioner won't expect us till evening.'

I looked at him anxiously. His face was relaxed, smiling even – in fact, completely unlike him. 'I can leave now if you like,' I said, suddenly frantic.

Fergus waved a hand. 'No worries. Stay a while with your family. I can run the Councillor back to Ophir now, pick you up whenever you like. It's only a half-hour trip.'

'An hour round-trip,' I tried to remind him, a firmness to my voice that I did not feel. I felt hemmed in and scared.

'I wouldn't want to keep the Councillor waiting,' hinted Ioan helpfully.

Dllenahkh, who had been silent for all of this, quietly put back his hood and stared at Ioan. 'No. I don't think so.'

Ioan literally faltered, taking a step back. Dllenahkh continued to look sternly at him, then rested a hand on Fergus's shoulder, an uncharacteristically tactile gesture. 'Sergeant Fergus, would you be so kind as to go and start up the shuttle?'

Fergus blinked, nodded slowly and went back inside the shuttle.

Rafi looked up at Dllenahkh with an expression of immense relief and gratitude. 'I'll go get her stuff.'

'Thank you,' said Dllenahkh, inclining his head. His gaze followed the boy as he ran off, then returned to fix coldly on Ioan.

Rafi soon returned, out of breath, with my bag. I took it from him and made an impossible promise. 'It'll be all right. I'll make it right, I swear.'

He nodded, his eyes bright with tears, and ran back into the house. I gave Ioan one glance, then retreated to the shuttle with Dllenahkh at my back.

He gave Fergus the order to lift off, then faced me with a very sombre look. 'I apologise. I should have realised earlier that you needed help.'

I was breathing more easily as I looked out of the window and watched the homestead getting further away. 'It's all right. Ioan knows he can't get to me. I just wish I could do something for Maria. It's not right, the way he treats her.'

'Then you should report him,' Dllenahkh said, his tone adamant. 'I understand that there are procedures for dealing with Cygnians who have strong psi abilities and use them inappropriately.'

'He does love her,' I mumbled. 'And they might take Gracie and Rafi away from them – that would be horrible.'

'Nevertheless,' Dllenahkh said gently, 'he was prepared to force you to stay with them. Can you overlook that?'

'He knows he can't get to me,' I repeated sulkily. 'I would have got out of there – not being ungrateful for your help or anything. I just don't think it's serious enough to warrant a report.'

Out of the corner of my eye, I noticed Fergus give Dllenahkh a quick sideways glance.

'Delarua, look at me.' Dllenahkh's voice was still gentle, but there was a hint of steel in it.

I faced him angrily. 'Don't you "Delarua" me. I told you, I can handle it!'

'Then let us be sure. Let me touch your mind, a brief touch only, to be certain that he has not influenced you.'

A sick feeling shot through me. I stood up and stumbled to the back of the shuttle. 'Keep away from me,' I whispered, turning my head so they couldn't see the tears starting.

'Delarua—' Dllenahkh said again, implacable.

'Don't touch me, don't you dare come near me—'

'Delarua!' This time it was Fergus, shouting over his shoulder from the pilot's seat. 'This isn't you! Can't you see that? You have to trust the Councillor, because I am *not* setting down this shuttle until I know for a fact that you are in your right mind!' He heaved a frustrated breath and continued, 'I've been through training for this kind of thing, learning to recognise when someone's tampered with your thoughts. And let me tell you, that man back there? He's subtle. He's *good*. I've never known a Cygnian that could do what he did just now. Don't underestimate him.'

I slumped to the floor. I wanted it all locked up in my mind – the dreams, my secret longings. I thought about the shame it would bring on my family to have all this known. I pulled my knees up to my chest and pressed my fists into my eyes, struggling to be calm, to breathe deeply, to think clearly.

When I lowered my hands and opened my eyes, Dllenahkh was kneeling in front of me. His face was neutral with no trace of judgement.

I spoke softly. 'A brief touch only? You won't look at my thoughts, my memories?'

He nodded. 'A brief touch. Not an invasion, not a link. Only what you permit.'

I bowed my head. A moment later, I felt his fingertips brush my forehead and press firmly as if setting his fingerprints there. Then they withdrew. That was all.

I looked up, relieved. 'There! That's taken care of—'

Then it came flooding back. All the times I'd silenced my own comm, the forced surge of an old passion long laid to rest, dreams that were not of my mind's making, and every look of disappointment and despair that poor Rafi had given me.

'That bastard,' I choked out. 'That *bastard*!'

Dllenahkh stood up and backed away gracefully. Adrenalin pushed me to my feet and I slammed the wall behind me with a fist. 'Fergus, how much longer to Ophir?'

'Twelve minutes, ma'am,' he said. The words sounded as if they were coming through a savage grin.

I marched back to my seat. 'Make it five. I need to speak to the Commissioner as soon as possible.'

Dllenahkh returned to his seat beside me. I looked at him steadily, still feeling that slick veneer of shame over my thoughts but refusing to give in to it. 'And Dllenahkh – thank you.'

He only inclined his head in response, but I imagined I saw a hint of approval amid his neutrality. I didn't know why he was being so generous. He had gone straight into the heart of a brewing riot with nothing but his principles to arm and shield him. I was finally standing up for the truth after fifteen years wasted in equivocation.

Yes, equivocation. It was still my call, still my responsibility. If there was one thing that shook me after Ioan's influence was wiped from my mind, it was the realisation that he never manipulated an emotion that wasn't already present to some degree, no matter how small.

I remembered this as I went to Qeturah. It helped keep my anger and motivation high. I went straight to where she was sitting in the conference room, going over the last of the inquiry notes with Joral, Nasiha and Tarik.

She looked up at me.

'I'm here to talk to you directly.' My throat closed up, making my voice crack, but I gritted my teeth and pushed the words past the barrier. 'I have a problem, and I need your help.'

Zero hour plus one year one month nine days

Dllenahkh stood on the main balcony of the hotel and regarded the city streets and distant banlieues of Ophir, dreamlike in a haze of damp morning air. He breathed lightly, not merely to avoid the moisture, but to keep the last of the calming air of the Montserrat monastery deep in his lungs. It had been unusually difficult to put aside the novice robe the night before.

Footsteps approached, but he did not turn. Eventually Dr Daniyel stood beside him and rested her hands lightly on the dew-damp stone of the balustrade. Recognising the diffidence in the gesture, he merely offered a nod of greeting and waited for her to speak.

'Thank you for helping her,' she said quietly. 'We didn't know.'

He frowned slightly as he looked at her. 'We are all of us somewhat damaged, whether or not it may appear on our medical records.'

She took the gentle rebuke with a rueful smile. 'I have withdrawn my recommendation that you be removed from the mission team,' she informed him. 'I understand now that the circumstances were unusual, and I trust your ability to function in the future.'

He bowed his head and lowered his eyes. He did not want to seem rude, but neither did he wish to appear grateful. He settled for staring at the landscape again.

'First Officer Delarua is insisting that she too is able to continue in her role.' Dr Daniyel spread her hands palms upward. 'I'm not convinced, but I don't like to make the same mistake twice. There's also the question of her psi profile.'

He frowned in earnest. 'I have seen it. It does not match her demonstrated abilities.'

'In light of recent events, no. Cygnians have always been hard to assess. You'd expect something with Ntshune, Sadiri and Zhinuvian lineage, but some of the strangest things come out of Terra – a touch of second sight here, a little miracle there. Most of them charlatans, it's true, but even the simple power to persuade and be persuaded can be a psi ability. We're very good at fooling others . . . and fooling ourselves.' She shook her head, momentarily pensive, then added, 'I'd like you to keep an eye on her, not only professionally, but personally.'

He let his surprise show.

'She trusts you,' Dr Daniyel said.

He faced her fully. 'Does she trust *you*?'

She let the rhetorical question pass, her gaze flickering away as if her conscience had been touched. He would have withdrawn once more into quiet courtesy, but the small glimpse of vulnerability made him push harder.

'Tell me, Commissioner, have you had this same conversation with Delarua? Have you asked her to keep an eye on me? Have you told her that I trust her?'

She relaxed and laughed lightly. 'Of course not, Councillor. Don't be silly. I had that conversation with Joral.'

He smiled in spite of himself, conceding the point.

'Councillor,' she said, gracious in victory, and walked away, leaving him to enjoy the morning view.

BACCHANAL

'Why me?' I asked. 'I mean, I know, you've told me, but tell me again why this is supposed to be a good idea?'

Tarik gave me a look that suggested he found my nervousness absurd. 'Your updated psi profile indicates that you have developed an above-average ability to discern and suppress imposed emotions.'

'The Board of Inquiry has recommended that we add psi-profile data to our genetic and anthropological data,' Nasiha continued equably, waving a scanner of some sort over the tiny sensors stuck to my various pulse points and nerve nodes and whatchamacallits.

'We require Cygnian as well as Sadiri data to calibrate our readings,' Tarik resumed. 'You are the only Cygnian with an operable level of psionic ability on the team. Therefore, you have been assigned to us for testing purposes.'

'Thank you, Qeturah,' I muttered sarcastically. 'Now, what are these for?' I waved a hand at four injectors laid out with precision on a tray of implements.

'To inform you of their contents and effects would compromise the neutrality of the tests,' Nasiha said in a tone that was almost soothing, which only increased my worry.

'Try to relax,' added Tarik, easing the medtable from vertical to nearly horizontal with a swiftness that had me gripping the edges.

The two Sadiri watched the readouts for a while, then looked at each other and nodded. Nasiha picked up the first injector and pressed it against my arm. I gulped quietly as it hissed its contents into my bloodstream. Seconds passed.

'Well,' I said, slightly relieved, 'I'm not sure what—'

Then I screamed.

After an hour spent alternately laughing, weeping, screaming and mumbling, 'Whoa . . . cool!' I went to Qeturah to complain. She refused to be swayed. 'Psionic ability results from a combination of nature and nurture. It can't be measured using genetic data alone, and it's an intrinsic part of what it means to be Sadiri. We need this information.'

'Yes, but why *me*?' I asked plaintively. 'I never scored particularly high on psi tests before. Can't they use some average readings from the database?'

Qeturah shrugged. 'This particular method of testing has never been done before. There *is* no data.'

'Fine,' I snapped.

Only a few days had passed since Ophir and already we were back in savannah country, this time at a Forestry and Grasslands outpost that offered a little more comfort than a temporary camp. The aim was to prevent another Candirú fiasco through better preparation, and that meant taking an extra week or two to refine our mission brief before continuing to the next assignment on the schedule. Qeturah was working feverishly on documentation with Lian's assistance, Fergus was acquiring all kinds of new and exciting survival equipment and regionally appropriate advice from the rangers, Dllenahkh and Joral seemed to be spending an inordinate amount of time in meditation, and Nasiha and Tarik were torturing me.

Then Dllenahkh turned up at the next session.

'Please tell me you're not here to add to my misery,' I said with mock cheerfulness.

He shot a look at Nasiha and Tarik that didn't reassure me, then sat down beside the medtable. 'You have found the experience thus far to be intolerable?'

I struggled with myself. 'It could have been worse, but really, not having your own emotions under control is pretty miserable, yeah.'

His mouth twitched – I swear I saw it! But his face was dead calm a moment later, and he said, 'We apologise for not previously detailing the nature of the experiment to you. However, we had the approval of the Commissioner to . . .' He trailed off, constrained by the habit of truth, and amended, 'The Commissioner conveyed to us the permission of the government to carry out these tests.'

'Thanks for that,' I said quietly. 'I had an inkling Qeturah doesn't really like my involvement in this. She thinks I should be getting therapy.'

Dllenahkh held my gaze for the precise amount of time necessary to warn me that I should take his next words very, very seriously. 'And you have refused therapy.'

I matched his neutral tone. 'I'd have to leave the mission for that. Besides, fifteen years of functioning won't break down in a few months. It can wait.'

85

'I believe they had hoped to counsel and treat you, your sister and her children as a family unit.'

'It can wait,' I repeated. 'Some things might go better if I'm not there. Now, you were about to tell me what's going on here?'

He looked away, withdrawing for the moment, and picked up an injector. 'A simplified explanation will suffice. The contents of these injectors have been designed to stimulate or suppress one of the two ranges of the limbic system that contribute to emotion. One range has satisfaction at one extreme and dysphoria at the other. The other range varies from frenzy to lethargy. The first range is additionally complicated by the fact that it actually consists of two separate scales of pleasure and pain which overlap in the lower values. For example, the emotion categorised as anticipation consists of small elements of pleasure, caused by looking forward to the moment of satisfaction; pain, caused by the fact of the present absence of satisfaction; and frenzy, manifested as an urge to seek out the aforementioned satisfaction.'

I blinked. 'That's fascinating. Complicated little buggers, aren't we?'

'Indeed. Incidentally, it is not only those of Terran or Ntshune origin who experience this. It appears to be common, by one physiological mechanism or another, in all humans.'

I think I felt a mingling of mild pleasure, pain and frenzy at that point. That was the first specific bit of information he'd given me about Sadiri neurology, and I was hoping he'd say more.

He didn't. 'At present, Cygnian psi-profile tests are designed to detect levels of ability which could significantly impact a person's capacity to function in a largely non-psionic society. Strong telepaths and empaths are provided with training and a system of ethics to regulate the use of their skills. Most Cygnians are not at the level where this is required.'

'Including me,' I said with a frown. 'So why am I here on this medtable being pumped full of different kinds of crazy juice?'

'Because there are other aspects of psionic ability which the tests do not address,' Nasiha interrupted. 'For example, we have discovered from monitoring our own reactions that you are capable of quite strong empathic projection in two very specific areas.'

I grinned. 'I bet I can guess one. Pleasure, right?'

'Yes. That is the stronger one. When your pleasure range was stimulated, Nasiha and I both experienced a strong desire to laugh that was only mitigated by increasing the shielding on our telepathic receptors.' Tarik's face was so deadly serious, almost mournful, as he admitted this that I had to bite back a laugh.

'Less intense but still significant was the projection of lethargy,' Nasiha continued.

I stared at her, taken aback. 'I bore people?'

'You calm people,' Dllenahkh said diplomatically. 'But it is a much subtler effect.'

I contemplated the ceiling for a while, processing this. 'Okay. So, how does "discerning and suppressing imposed emotions" come into this? Because I was completely at the mercy of those injectors, let me tell you.'

Dllenahkh explained further. 'It is difficult, if not impossible, to stop the action of chemicals introduced directly into the body. It is, however, possible to shield from external attempts to alter brain and body chemistry. That is the aim of today's session.'

The three Sadiri around the medtable suddenly seemed to loom with menace. 'You're going to try to influence my thoughts and emotions?' I squeaked.

'With your permission,' said Dllenahkh.

I thought about it. I took a good few minutes while they remained there in silence, waiting on my word. I thought about what Ioan had and had not been able to do to me. I thought about Rafi who, I strongly suspected, possessed a similar talent to his father's, and wondered what might become of him in the future.

'Knowledge is power,' I said at last. 'Let's do it.'

First, because it was already there to work with, Dllenahkh tried to increase my sense of unease. It worked. I bolted upright, choking as if pulling myself out of quicksand, but then, with an indignant, 'Hah!' I exhaled my real tension, turning fear to simple discontent, and pushed back the false sensation with a feeling of triumph.

'My stars, you're strong.' I breathed rapidly, looking at him with wide eyes. 'Less with the elephant feet, please.'

He was examining the readouts on the monitor beside my head. 'My apologies,' he said absently. 'How do you feel? Please use the scales we discussed to describe your emotions.'

'Genuinely? I was a bit up there on the frenzy scale, and even a little up on the pleasure scale. You tried to project dysphoria and it combined with the frenzy to produce fear. So I dumped the frenzy and tossed back the dysphoria. And now I feel quite up there on the pleasure scale, thank you very much.'

'Remarkable,' said Dllenahkh.

It was better than therapy, in a way. While the Sadiri were getting their data and creating their new tests, I was finding out what my strengths were. For example, it seemed that I was even able to control my real emotions far better than you'd expect from how I usually behave. I'd just rarely had need to do so, but the proof of it was how I had been able not only to switch off Ioan's attempts to make me feel comfortable with him, but also to damp down my own inclination to feel that comfort. Telepathically, though, I had no talent whatsoever. I could be influenced into doing all manner of nonsensical, trivial things and rationalising them afterwards, like the time I randomly picked up an injector and aimed it at Nasiha who, fortunately, was agile and aware enough to leap out of the way. If she hadn't shot Dllenahkh a very nasty look for that trick, I would have sworn it was all my idea.

Which brings me to another point. I never saw Sadiri the way others do, as being in complete control of their facial expressions. It became clear to me that while I would never have the level of telepathy to fully sense them as they did each other, I did have a level of empathy to detect the emotions that they did not express, though I interpreted it as a physical expression. I once had a raging argument with Lian over the simple premise 'Joral smiles at you all the time'. Lian swore I was crazy; I swore Lian was oversensitive about being the object of a Sadiri crush. Now I understand that Lian honestly couldn't see that faint hint of a smile that I'd persuaded myself was there to account for my certainty that Joral derived pleasure from Lian's company.

Another good thing about the testing was that by the time we were ready to leave, I had acquired some respect for Nasiha and Tarik. They were wrapped up in each other – well, fair enough. Theirs was one of the few bonds not broken by the disaster, and they deserved to celebrate that. But their professionalism and skill were incontestable, and their dedication to rebuilding Sadiri culture absolute. I found that admirable.

Because the settlement we were visiting consisted of widely scattered homesteadings, much like the Sadiri one in Tlaxce, we had arranged our schedule to arrive for one of their festivals. People would be gathering at a public area called the Grand Savannah over a period of two days. Initially, we had planned to spend time at one of the major homesteadings and conclude our visit with the festival, but given the delay we were going to do it the other way around.

Our first sight of the Grand Savannah was a long, high berm with an arched entrance cut into the centre. Underneath the arch ran a road of flagstones. We came in government vehicles with a wagonload of gear, having left the shuttle at the outpost. Inside the earth-walled enclosure was a huge field with a tent city, the colours so bright and the designs so varied that it looked like a scattering of kites on the ground waiting to take flight. There were rangers there acting as marshals, and they pointed us to a space where we could set up our camp. We hadn't been there more than fifteen minutes before a visitor arrived.

'Welcome to the Grand Savannah! Do I have the honour of addressing Doctor Qeturah Daniyel, head of this government mission and renowned academic in her own right?'

The words were measured, even stately, but there was hidden laughter in the tone. When I saw the speaker, and the suppressed smile and almost-wink that passed between him and Qeturah, I instantly had the impression of some shared encounter in the past. He was a notable man of the tall and distinguished variety, but there was something irreverent in the gleam of his eye that warned of a love of fun. Qeturah, in contrast, looked unusually shy and coquettish. Must have been some encounter.

'Leoval,' she said, and her voice sounded richer and more

resonant as she held out her hand to be kissed. 'Not too old for this yet?'

Leoval gave her a droll look of mock injury. 'Qeturah! What a suggestion!'

Introductions were made. At first, when he bent over my hand as well, I feared him an incorrigible flirt, but when he proceeded to clasp arms with Fergus and Lian and bow to the Sadiri gravely with the appropriate phrase in perfectly accented Sadiri, I then realised I was in the presence of a consummate diplomat. I was right, too. He was a retired civil servant, and he had been one of the first anthropologists to revisit and update ancient research on the region. He made Qeturah promise to visit him, telling her to send word by a marshal and he would have a sedan chair come around for her. Then, with that carefully modulated sense of courtesy, he bade his farewells and departed.

'What an interesting man,' I said innocently.

Qeturah gave me a sharp look. 'Yes,' she replied firmly. 'He is. And a gentleman. He always found ways to help me without ever once mentioning the dreaded phrase "Dalthi's Syndrome". Like offering to send a chair for me – that's his kindness all over.'

I hesitated, then decided to speak my thought. 'Dalthi's Syndrome? Isn't that a treatable genetic condition?'

'Yes, it is, but I've never liked the idea of flipping the switches on my own genes,' Qeturah said in a matter-of-fact tone. 'Seems like cheating.'

I was more than surprised to hear this. It was a bit like learning your local butcher is a vegetarian.

'Besides,' Qeturah continued calmly, 'for some time I had unresolved issues about being the weak one of the family. My siblings used to tease me and say no homesteader would ever marry me because I'd be as much work to take care of as the homestead and my children would probably be weaklings, too. When you start thinking of yourself as damaged goods, you put up defences to make sure no one has the chance to reject you, so I told myself I would never get married, never have children and never do anything to change who I was. It was only after I had my own status, my own money and the contraceptive benefits of menopause that I began to allow myself to have a different view. Playing the cards I'd been dealt became my badge of honour, not a burden.'

I was silent for a while, almost shocked that she was being so blunt and open with me, but then my eyes narrowed and my jaw tightened slightly. 'I didn't realise we were in session.'

'I'm only doing what I can. Delarua, *have* you been in any serious relationships during the past fifteen years?'

Hot, sudden anger flashed through me, but I kept control of myself, merely giving her a reproachful look before I walked off to lose myself in the crowd. 'Stick to genetics,' I called back over my shoulder. 'Your counselling's a bit off today.'

'Ah, look, a breakthrough,' she said with a wry smile, but she let me go.

Gilda had always teased me, saying that I had a talent for surrounding myself with safe or unavailable men. I used to tell her that if she understood the meaning of the word 'profession-alism' she wouldn't have to speculate about my love life or lack thereof. But now Qeturah had me wondering, what were my Ioan-issues? When I first left, did he selfishly set something in my mind to make sure I'd never get attached to someone else? Or was it my own doing – was I afraid that attracting a man like Ioan once might mean I was doomed ever after to fall for that type? Perhaps I *made* men possessive and manipulative, because it seemed to me that Ioan hadn't been all that bad fifteen years ago. I hated the last one in particular, because I now had empirical evidence that I could project significantly on the pleasure scale. Was I like some bad drug, ruining good men?

I was growing disgusted with my own self-pity.

Fortunately, a distraction immediately appeared. He walked past me with a swagger, a bottle in each hand and in his eye a twinkle that wouldn't understand the concept of rejection if it was explained to him in nine languages and fourteen dialects. Then he paused and turned back. 'I'm off to hear the bands. Would you like to come, my lovely?'

I looked at him. What he didn't have in looks he made up for in self-confidence. 'Yeah. Whyever not,' I said – and yes, there was a little bit of 'I'll show them all!' in my decision.

The music was good. The stuff in the bottle was good. There was alcohol in there, but mainly it was surprisingly thirst-quenching in the heat, yet terribly more-ish at the same time. The crowd was energetic and there was much dancing. I lost my first acquaintance and found several more friends in succession, finally sticking with a rather nice young man called Tonio who looked . . . well, maybe he looked a bit like Ioan, but only a little, okay?

I forgot about the rest of the team entirely until Joral turned up where I was sprawling on the steep angle of a berm, still listening to the drums and pipes on the field below and Tonio's snoring as he napped beside me. Joral looked a little apprehensive, moving as if he hoped to preserve a small exclusionary zone around himself. I watched with a smirk as two young women breached the zone, danced up against him and moved on, leaving

93

him frozen as if unsure whether to be glad or appalled. Finally he pulled himself together and clambered up to where I was sitting.

'Enjoying yourself, Joral?' I asked blandly, handing him the bottle.

He looked at it blankly for a moment and then, in response to my hand gestures, tipped some of the contents carefully into his mouth. His eyes widened slightly and he made a considering moue.

'Piquant and refreshing,' he proclaimed, and handed it back. 'I am finding the experience very educational. The Commissioner informed me that she already has a significant amount of genetic data for this settlement, and while the phenotype is mostly Terran, there are sufficient taSadiri genes in the population that a combination of selection and switching could easily produce a child of Sadiri appearance and physiology. Moreover, the anthropological data clearly show that a number of Sadiri traditions have been retained.'

'Is this festival a Sadiri tradition?' I asked, having drunk and passed the bottle to him again.

He took a good gulp, no longer shy, and returned it. 'In fact, it is not. While it does appear to have a few features of certain ancient festivities – except with less blood and . . . um . . . other activities – its origin is Terran, specifically the festival of Carnival.'

'Farewell to the flesh,' said my linguistic self mockingly. 'It needs to be followed by a fast to be true, not preceded by one.'

'I . . . do not understand.'

I passed him the bottle once more in apology and answer. He drained it. 'This beverage is delicious. May I have another?'

I hauled another two bottles out of a nearby cooler and gave him one. He popped it open and immediately took a swig.

I looked down at the Savannah. 'If we stay here for a couple more hours, we'll get to see the fire dancing. That should be good. Oh, I forgot to ask – did you come to find me for a specific reason?'

Silence. I turned to Joral. He was contemplating the already half-empty bottle in his hand with a strange little smile. 'Oh. Yes. Councillor Dllenahkh wishes me to tell you that after the festival, we will have a meeting with some of the elders of the settlement.'

'Joral, are you feeling all right?' I asked, concerned at the look on his face.

He turned to me and smiled fully, which completely freaked me out. 'I feel fine, Delarua, just fine. I wonder if I should go down and try a bit of dancing. It doesn't look that hard.'

I hit my comm immediately. 'Nasiha! Something's wrong with Joral! He's *smiling*. I think he's drunk.'

Nasiha spoke with her usual calm. 'How much has he had to drink?'

'About four hundred mils of . . . something,' I stammered, trying and failing to find enlightenment on my bottle's label. 'There's alcohol in it. Six per cent.'

'That is far too little to affect a Sadiri,' she mused. 'Can he still walk?'

'Ye-es – I'm not sure. Joral, stand up.'

He did so obligingly, canting on the incline of the berm with a stability that hinted at least at physical sobriety. 'I feel fine! I am standing up. Tell her I am standing up!'

'Hm,' Nasiha said. 'Joral, return to the camp immediately.'

I escorted him back to camp, which is to say I herded him like an inexperienced sheepdog as he pinballed his way through the crowd, dancing from partner to partner. Nasiha and Tarik were waiting, and they immediately gripped him by the elbows and hustled him into one of the shelters. I followed them in time to see them wrestling him down onto a cot, still protesting he was fine. They quickly took a blood sample, tested his breath and looked at his eyes.

Then they looked at me accusingly. 'This is not inebriation,' said Tarik.

'Well, don't look at me,' I wailed. 'Look at this!' I waved the bottle at them.

'Yeah, that'll do it.'

I jumped. It was Tonio. I had been so preoccupied with Joral that I hadn't noticed when he woke up and followed us. He stood casually in the entrance of the shelter, completely unworried by the scene before him.

'That'll do it,' he said again. 'It's got fireberry juice in it.'

'And what,' said Nasiha severely, 'is fireberry juice?'

'It's like, another kind of alcohol, you know? Kinda takes the edge off your emotions and calms your thoughts, but doesn't take out your legs or fuzz up your head. Mothers give it to their kids to settle them down, no worries. Works great on teenage boys, especially when they start to get . . . y'know.' He shrugged and flicked an expressive eyebrow upwards while realigning the crotch of his trousers with a practised cup-and-shake of his hand.

Nasiha and Tarik looked at each other, then stared at Tonio. 'Tell us more about this fireberry juice,' said Tarik.

'Well, here, try some.' The enterprising Tonio took a small flask from his pocket and handed it to Tarik.

Tarik opened the flask cautiously, poured a tiny amount into a clean sample cup and sipped it. 'Intriguing,' he commented.

Nasiha took the cup from him and drained the remainder. 'Most interesting,' she agreed.

'But this makes no sense,' I complained. 'Why would it make Joral *more* emotional?'

'Oh, forgot about that,' said Tonio helpfully. 'Also removes inhibitions, like alcohol. Bit of a paradox. Feel less, express more.'

The two standing Sadiri were looking at him very curiously. 'This calls for further research,' said Nasiha. 'Can you take us to someone who makes this beverage?'

'Sure!' said Tonio cheerfully.

He went out, Tarik and Nasiha followed, and just as I was bringing up the rear, Nasiha turned and said pointedly to me, 'Someone should stay with Joral.'

I grimaced. 'Fine.'

Watching Joral very quickly turned into watching Joral sleep. I put him in the recovery position just in case some nasty afterreaction should occur and then curled up on a nearby cot, listening bitterly to the shouts and cheers and drumbeats of the fire dance show I was missing.

A shadow appeared at the entrance. 'Tarik?' I called out, tapping on a light.

'No,' came Dllenahkh's voice. 'Nasiha has just informed me about Joral's condition. How is he?'

I sat up and yawned and looked over at Joral. 'Still sleeping peacefully, it appears. Where are Nasiha and Tarik?'

A very strange expression came over Dllenahkh's face. It was the look of a man who had seen things he could not unsee. 'Dancing,' he said shortly.

I gaped. 'Beg pardon?'

'They decided to test the effects first-hand by sampling the various beverages that contain the active ingredient. They are now . . . blending in.' A faint, cool disapproval touched his voice.

97

'Well, good for them, I say. After all that madness they put me through, I'm glad they've got the guts to experiment on themselves. But I still don't get it. What's the big deal about this stuff?'

Dllenahkh moved to pick up a handheld and came to sit beside me on the cot. 'Perhaps a look at the data will clarify matters. Here is a summarised form of the data collected from the sensors during your experiment. And here' – he tapped and went to split-screen view – 'is the summary for Sadiri data. Nasiha was the test subject, naturally, in order to maintain sex as a constant variable when comparing your readings.'

'These are Sadiri readings,' I said, tracing the line of data.

'Those are the markers of the biochemical reactions we experience during sensory input and processing, yes.'

'And these are mine,' I said, tracing a much lower set of values. 'How do you live with that?' I asked with muted awe.

'Carefully. With meditation and strict adherence to the disciplines,' he replied. 'But without this high neural sensitivity, we could not be who we are. We would not be able to pilot the mindships, nor could we sense each other, communicate with each other, form telepathic bonds with each other.'

I gave a slow nod of admiration. 'Now that you've discovered the properties of fireberry, will you use it as an alternative to meditation?'

'It may serve for recreational use, but I do not believe it is to be depended on in the long run. One might find oneself in a situation where the ingredients are not available. The disciplines, however, can be taken anywhere that the mind goes.' He gave me a considering look. 'Would *you* recommend this sense-suppressant for regular use?'

I thought about it. I pondered Qeturah's comment about how playing the hand she'd been dealt became for her a badge of honour. 'That can only be an individual decision,' I hedged.

'Then let us consider a specific example. Would you recommend it for me, for example?'

'No,' I said finally. 'Like you said, it's who you are. I wouldn't want you to be anything less than yourself. I don't know if that makes sense, but there it is.'

There was a rustle at the entrance and Nasiha and Tarik came in. They were glowing with energy, but smiling only very slightly. I was a bit relieved. I had been afraid they might come in laughing or doing something shocking. Nasiha was carrying a small bowl in her hands.

'First Officer Delarua,' she said with a touch of breathlessness, 'we apologise for making you miss the festivities by asking you to watch Joral. Please accept this traditional regional dish as a token of our regret.'

I took it with a smile and a twinge of anxiety, but when I looked at it, it was familiar to me. A genuine grin spread over my face. 'Thank you, Nasiha! I *love* chocolate decadence cake!'

I broke off a bit and put it into my mouth. Now *this* was a drug worth taking. My taste buds positively hummed in bliss at the creamy richness. I closed my eyes and moaned.

There was an odd echo. I opened my eyes and caught Nasiha and Tarik watching me avidly, their palms pressed lightly together in a poor attempt at intimacy. There was a slightly guilty look on Nasiha's face, but it was spoiled the next instant by a suppressed giggle. The two then exchanged a smouldering look and departed hastily.

My mouthful turned to ashes. I swallowed it with difficulty

and set down the dish. 'Perverts,' I said truculently. 'Now I've lost my appetite.'

'Eat your cake,' said Dllenahkh, and there was definitely a tinge of amusement in the tone of his voice. 'They're gone now, Joral is asleep and my shields are strong.'

NEVER FORGET

I hated talking to Qeturah about certain things, but for certain things she was the only source of information.

'She's decided she hates me, hasn't she?'

Qeturah looked down at her handheld. 'I'm not privy to the counselling notes of this case.'

Liar. 'Has she told Rafi not to write to me?'

She met my eyes at last. 'I don't know. But I do know that if you write to him, we will make sure that he sees it.'

I nodded and walked off before she could start on me again. I could write to my godson. That was all I needed to know. That made things easier.

Dear Rafi . . .

I had to write. I couldn't call, because they were all under protection until the lengthy and thorough process of Ioan's assessment and trial was concluded. Fergus had been right – the authorities hadn't seen anything like Ioan on Cygnus Beta, and they weren't about to take any chances.

Dear Rafi, ~~how are you, how is therapy,~~

They'd probably read whatever I wrote. Analyse it too, for both our sakes.

How are you all doing? ~~I'm fine,~~

I grimaced at the handheld. After several efforts, the only unchanging bits of the message were *Dear Rafi* and *Love, Aunt Grace.* Perhaps I should just send that. Perhaps it was too soon. I could try again next week after I got back.

I tossed the handheld into my backpack and sealed it up. 'Ready, Lian?' I asked the aide.

Lian, who was securing our shelter to a much larger, military-issue backpack, gave me a narrow-eyed look. 'This is a date, right?'

'Why are you harassing me, Lian?' I sighed.

'Payback?' Lian replied, wrestling on the pack with the ease of years of experience.

'At least *I* can't be accused of fraternisation.'

'Neither can I. Nor cradle-snatching,' Lian said, taking it up a notch.

'Tonio is not that young!' I snapped defensively.

'He is not that old,' Lian countered, amused.

'Okay. I'm sorry if you interpreted my entirely professional attempt to warn you about being too friendly to Joral as a demonstration of inappropriate and frivolous interest in your social life. I believed I was acting in the best interests of my colleagues. Now, can we have a little détente here?'

Lian leaned forward, took hold of my face in both hands and looked at me searchingly, all the while on the edge of laughter. 'You are wearing *kohl* for a field trip. Forestry fatigues, boots and kohl. What's that for, hmm? To impress the elephants?'

Then Lian backed off, smirking, and left before I could think of a scathing rebuttal.

We had temporarily split up the team. Qeturah, Fergus, Nasiha and Tarik were going to continue along the settlements of the grasslands using the shuttle. And you remember Tonio, the guy who looked a little bit but not really like Ioan? It turns out he was a ranger, off duty for the festival, but still very much a civil servant. Qeturah seemed to think it would be a good idea to ask Leoval to pull some strings and have him assigned to us as a guide and extra security. One of those serendipitous things I've learned not to question. So, Lian, Dllenahkh, Joral and I were travelling with Tonio on a side-expedition into the forest uplands to the north. It was a place too thickly wooded for shuttles and too changeable for roads, so we were going to use a traditional, efficient and proven form of transportation – elephants.

I was excited at the prospect, but when we arrived at the mahouts' village, I was a little surprised.

'They're a bit . . . small,' I said in puzzled disappointment, resting a cautious hand on the shoulder of the elephant assigned to me. It wasn't much taller than a large-sized cart-horse. It flapped its ears at me in a friendly fashion and winked its small, long-lashed amber eye.

Lian smiled at my expression. 'These are forest elephants. The savannah elephants are the largest of the species, and the ones you see most in the holovids.'

I was still excited. Big or small, elephants are elephants after all. Just before we mounted, when I was sure no one could see me, I quickly kissed the shoulder of my beast and murmured, 'Hey, sweetie.'

'Hey, darlin'.' That was Tonio, appearing suddenly by my shoulder. He gave me a laughing look that suggested he was either

103

amused by or attracted to women who kiss elephants for no good reason. Or both.

When not under the influence of alcohol or fireberry, Tonio was witty, cheerful and sharp with a kind of suppressed electric energy. Even better, he was looking less and less like Ioan to me. He wore a short hooded cape that was non-regulation but very useful under the dripping trees, and occasionally, when he turned his head a certain way, it framed his strong profile in a way that called attention to his mouth. Well-defined, curving, with a fullness to the lower lip that cried out for a biting kiss – a very nice distraction.

And then I'd look away again to see Lian watching me and quietly laughing.

In addition to freely mocking me, Lian was generally more talkative than usual. 'This is where my mother's people come from. There are legends of remote monasteries where the monks walk on water and fly through the treetops.'

Tonio rolled his eyes, not with sarcasm but with pure mischief. 'This is where my father's people come from, and there are tales of huge stone statues which point, using one appendage or another, to the secret entrances of ancient temples. There are also reports of intricate, anatomically correct carvings on the walls of those temples which demonstrate the sixty-two approved sexual positions of the Marriage Code.'

I looked away hastily, biting my lip against laughter. Lian would tease me about always laughing at the things Tonio said.

Our first river crossing occurred within minutes. The elephants, being excellent swimmers, got across quite happily by themselves, using their long trunks to snorkel through the deep water. The two-legs passed dry-shod over a small footbridge of rope and wood, and apart from the dubious joy of riding wet elephant, it worked very well.

The second river crossing was nothing like the first.

'Where's all this water coming from?' asked Lian, looking at the cascading run in dismay.

It was too flat to be called a waterfall, but too steep to be an ordinary riverbed. There were two footbridges: a high one placed well above the churning water, strung from tree to tree upstream; and a lower one whose planks were ominously wet, resting directly on the riverbanks. The water flowed more placidly there, with greater depth and fewer rocks, but when I got closer, I gulped. The bridge was not a bridge; it was a lookout over a huge water-fall.

'We will take the high bridge,' the mahout announced.

Joral looked up at the loose sag of the swaying, fraying ropes. 'The high bridge does not appear to have been maintained for some time,' he noted.

'The low bridge is too dangerous,' the mahout insisted. 'We will swim with the elephants.'

Ordinarily, I would say listen to the man. His land, his river, his elephants, right? But that turbulent current was not at all reassuring.

Tonio shrugged. 'I prefer to stay dry,' he announced, and stepped lightly onto the low bridge. It gave a tiny sway, revealing that it was not wood but rope that connected the bridge to the bank landings, but he reached the other side easily. Joral and Lian quickly followed his example. By then, the mahout had ignored the general rebellion against his advice and was swimming over with the elephants, paddling easily near the head of his own beast. Dllenahkh looked at me, his eyebrow quirked in a 'Well, aren't you coming?' expression. Still with slight misgivings, I went before him onto the bridge.

We were hardly halfway to the other side when we heard it coming, like thunder.

Dllenahkh's quickening steps set the bridge swaying so that I stumbled. He took my arm briefly to steady me and then urged me on with a light push. White water came pouring down the slope, crashing towards us with terrifying speed. Panic kept my feet moving as the wooden planks began to heave beneath me. Still trying to move forward, I watched in helpless fascination as the water surged over and under the bridge, tipping and twisting it vertical.

I remember the fall. The weight of my pack pulled me immediately backwards and horizontal. I looked down between my feet at the white froth of breaking water and saw Dllenahkh move quickly, reaching for me, fingers sliding along my left leg and coming to rest firmly around my ankle. Not the slightest hint of anxiety or surprise showed on his face, so it took me a while to realise that he was falling too, a vast weight of water following behind his back. He hauled me towards him, grabbed my belt with his other hand and hauled again, reeling me in. Then he looked beyond me with an expression of intense concentration and pulled my head protectively against his shoulder.

We hit. Water is *hard*. I lost breath, memory and finally consciousness.

I found awareness again in a dream. I was riding my elephant through wooded marshes, dry savannah and dim green forest. He moved slowly, strongly, each step striking ground solidly yet gently. Swaying slightly with his gait, I leaned over so my mouth came close to the languidly fanning giant ear.

Dark you are, and golden-eyed, I whispered to the beast.

I lay on my stomach along his broad back and patted his huge head. He brought up his trunk and found my face without seeing, gently touching my cheeks and forehead. The skin of the trunk's tip was soft, its dexterity hand-like. His breath surrounded my face like a hot tropical breeze. I smiled. I felt so comfortable. Then the gentle brush against my skin vibrated strangely as if dragging over a patch rougher than elephant skin, like scabbing on a nasty scrape. When did that happen?

I woke up – and I mean woke up, because my eyes were already open and waiting for consciousness to return. There *was* a half-healed scab on my cheekbone. There was also a warm hand on my face. I instinctively grasped it with my left hand as I blinked and tried to focus. Not one metre away, lying like me on a thin pallet on the floor, was Dllenahkh. We had been given tunics of roughly woven linen and light blankets of some material I could not identify. Dllenahkh's eyes were shut, his face perfectly blank, but it was his hand resting on my face. As I began to draw away, there was an impression in my mind of a golden eye that winked and faded out.

'Wait.' Dllenahkh's eyes were still closed but it was his voice that spoke, the voice of someone whose vocal cords have been unused for hours. 'Stay still.'

I stopped moving, biddable in my drowsiness. Warm tendrils untangled from my nervous system, withdrawing gently but swiftly, like the leaf-brush of startled mimosa. I frowned, feeling their absence like the niggling pain of a familiar but forgotten name.

Dllenahkh cleared his throat, sat up slowly and said, 'Thank you.'

I tried to speak, choked on a dry throat and merely nodded.

He gazed at me sleepily, then looked around the room. There was a low table against a nearby wall with two covered plates, two cups and a pot. He slowly rearranged his legs to sit on his heels before the table, poured the cups full and handed me one.

'Drink. Your body needs water and energy.'

I took the cup with slightly shaking hands and drank deeply, reclining on one elbow. It was both bitter and sweet and not really something I'd usually drink, but I downed it as if it were the most delicious thing in the world.

Dllenahkh drank slowly. His eyes scanned my face and looked me up and down in a cataloguing fashion. 'How do you feel? Are you in pain?'

I set down my cup, lightly touched the scab on my cheek, felt along my arms and ribs, arched my back and pointed and flexed my toes. 'I think everything works. A little sore, which is to be expected from being battered by water and rock. How about you?'

'I am well,' he replied.

'Is it you I should be thanking for the quick-heal?' I asked.

'In part. The adepts showed me how to link to you and guide your body in the healing process.'

The adepts. Interesting. I would investigate that thoroughly – after increasing my blood-sugar level. I drained my cup and scooted to the table to pour out more, but I was soon distracted by the covered dishes. When I took a peek I found nothing familiar, but the aromas were subtly tempting. I uncovered and offered a plate to Dllenahkh, part courtesy, part bribe.

'Tell me everything,' I said.

I couldn't remember much after that first icy plunge, which was probably a mercy, because when Dllenahkh began to describe, albeit in a terse, unemotional way, how we had been sucked down by the swirling currents, I began to shiver. I have no doubt that whatever my injuries had been, I would have fared far worse had he not shielded me from the hardest impacts. As for the adepts, apparently we had washed up at one of the legendary monasteries via some underwater cave or passage or secret way that lurked behind or beneath the falls. I wanted to feel excited about such a beautiful cliché coming true, but mainly I felt hungry, worried and very unsure about the place we had stumbled into. This was not an Indiana Jones classic holovid; it was real life.

Dllenahkh had no such qualms. 'I do not understand how they have managed it, but these savants possess knowledge that goes far beyond the era when the taSadiri would have arrived at Cygnus Beta.'

'Parallel development of theories and practices, perhaps? A kind of Newton-Leibniz effect?'

He pondered. 'It is a gross oversimplification to compare the discovery of calculus to the evolution of some of the most sophisticated techniques of mind and meditation the galaxy has seen, but I understand your point. Perhaps both branches of the disciplines exemplify a natural progression in Sadiri thought.'

'How do you know so much about them already?' I asked.

Dllenahkh looked away from me, not wanting to lie, but clearly not wanting to answer. I finally got a clue. 'Telepathy! And strong enough not to need touch for conversation. That *is* something.'

Dllenahkh sipped his tea and made a noise that sounded almost like satisfaction. 'They have advanced the disciplines to a level even beyond what we attained in the monasteries on Sadira.'

'Will they go to the Sadiri settlement here, or even to New Sadira?' I asked shrewdly.

His eyelids lowered slightly, a dimming of his quiet enthusiasm. 'They do not wish to reveal themselves. Not even now.'

'Well, that doesn't help anyone.' I sighed, feeling very tired. 'Will they speak to me, or am I too brain-dumb to be worth the effort?'

Dllenahkh smiled at that. 'I believe they are being mindful of your condition. You were unconscious when we arrived, and have only recently awakened.'

'Very kind of them. Well, let them know from me that a light is more useful on a high hill than under a bushel. And after you've thanked them for their hospitality, ask them when we can go home.' I spoke as if the mission team was 'home' and I suppose that's what it had become to me by then.

I spent most of the rest of that day in bed. While I was sleeping, Dllenahkh left the room to lodge elsewhere, so I woke alone in darkness. I lay peacefully listening to the sound of rainwater – or perhaps it was a heavy night dew – dripping from the eaves outside until the sun came up and filled the room with light. Minutes later, someone arrived – a small girl-woman dressed in a light woollen robe, her hair so closely cut that it was a mere shadow on her scalp.

'Good morning,' I said in Sadiri.

She looked confused and shy. 'Good morning,' she answered hesitantly in my local dialect. 'I will bring water for you to wash, and your clothes so you can dress.'

I realised my backpack must have made the journey when I saw that the clothes she brought were those I had been carrying, not wearing. When I had finished my simple cold-water ablutions and got dressed, she brought me a number of items in baskets, laid them neatly alongside a wall and departed.

'Brilliant!' I said first, recognising the contents of my backpack, undamaged by water. Those Forestry types know how to design proper gear.

'Blast it,' I said next. There was a carefully wrapped bundle of material which, when unfolded, revealed the many fragments of my handheld. No quick-message sending. Speaking of which, where *was* my comm?

Dllenahkh came into my room, no doubt in response to my cry of dismay. 'Hey, Dllenahkh,' I said cheerfully. 'They have *women* here! You *can't* keep this treasure from the other Sadiri. But I'm surprised it's a mixed community. Don't these kinds of groups separate the sexes so they won't get distracted from philosophising or something?'

Dllenahkh folded his hands into his sleeves, an action which brought to my attention the fact that he was now wearing a robe very similar to the local style. 'As they rarely use shielding among themselves, they are already aware of each others' minds, and physical separation would not serve any purpose. Instead, they have an integrated society – celibates, singles, wedded couples and children – all in full telepathic communication.'

'What a way to live!' I exclaimed. 'I bet *some* areas stay shielded, like the couples' quarters.'

Before I could laugh at my own words, I saw Dllenahkh's lips twitch in a way that was all too familiar to me.

'I see,' I said soberly. 'I have *got* to stop laughing at things. They're turning out to be true too often for comfort. Now, have you asked them how we're going to get back?'

'Have you eaten the morning meal as yet?' he asked.

'No,' I said, frowning. 'Did you just avoid my question?'

'I would prefer to discuss it over breakfast,' he replied.

He knew where to go. As I followed him, I noticed that in spite of the near-silence of the place, the few people we encountered directly greeted us verbally, sometimes in Sadiri, sometimes in my own dialect. The men kept their heads clean-shaven, and the women allowed themselves only a shadow's length, like the girl I had seen earlier. Not all wore robes, but all garments were of solid colours and in simple styles. In contrast to this superficial uniformity, their faces and bodies were strikingly, variably expressive, a constant reminder of the thousands of ongoing conversations that I could not hear.

After passing through a kind of communal refectory and gathering a tray of fruits, grains, broth and tea, we found ourselves on a balcony that looked down a green gully with a small window of blue sky at the end. The trees dripped moisture, though the early-morning mist was quickly burning off as the day warmed up. The breeze was cool, the view breathtaking and the company . . . enigmatic. He ignored my questioning looks and urged me to eat. Only when nothing but lukewarm tea remained to be consumed did he sit back slightly on his heels and look reflective.

'I was once closely connected to a monastery on Sadira, what you would term an oblate. Although I worked as a government official and lived in secular society, my free time was devoted to the study of the mind and its potential.'

I forgot my cooling tea and listened avidly. I had never dared ask any Sadiri about their life before the disaster, and though I knew Dllenahkh better than any of them, all my knowledge of him was newly minted, scarcely over a year old.

'My time on Cygnus Beta has been spent similarly. I work in the local government of the homesteadings, and I teach the disciplines at various levels. Mainly, because I cannot be everywhere, I train others to teach.'

'It sounds to me,' I said very softly, loth to interrupt him, 'as if you are among the most advanced of the savants on Cygnus Beta.'

He seemed to ponder momentarily. 'I would say your assessment is correct, with one exception. I have not sought the highest levels – the development of the skill required to pilot a mindship.'

'May I ask why not?'

He looked at me as though it were obvious.

'Unlike the Zhinuvians, who link and delink from their technology with ease, Sadiri pilots are uniquely bonded to their ships. I do not wish to deny myself the profound bond that may be experienced in the connection between human minds.'

He paused and gazed at the distant patch of sky framed by leaf and vine. 'For me, finding this place is like finding a treasure. I *have* asked about leaving. There is no problem with us doing so. They only require that we leave behind all memory of this place, so that it may remain hidden.'

I pursed my lips. I wasn't comfortable with gaps in my memory for obvious reasons, and yet I could see that maintaining the security of this community was more important than my own personal issues. 'Very well. When can we go?'

He gave me an intent look. 'But must we go?'

I was aghast. He was serious. 'Dllenahkh, *I* can't stay. I – *we* have people depending on us to return.'

He spoke abruptly, almost an interruption. 'While I appreciate that Cygnians are capable of forming attachments within a very short time period, I believe that Tonio—'

I cut him off, stung at his obtuseness. 'I was talking about Rafi. I think even Sadiri understand family responsibility. And don't you think Joral depends on you, too?'

'Joral understands that he can rely on the guidance of any elder Sadiri of our community—'

'Yes,' I said impatiently, 'but they won't be *you*. You guys are like family, you know?'

'There are so few of us left that *all* Sadiri may be considered family,' he said stubbornly.

'Then why cause him pain by letting him think you're dead?' I said gently.

Dllenahkh said nothing, but I saw a flicker in his gaze that suggested I had scored a hit. After a short silence, he said, 'Since you insist on returning, you could tell him that I am alive.'

'After they wipe my memories?' I said sarcastically.

His look was determined, and perhaps a touch irritated. 'You will not forget this. I will see to it.'

I went back to my room and packed up my things, even the bits of broken handheld. When I came out again, Dllenahkh was there with an elderly monk who looked at my readiness and smiled slightly.

'Few choose to stay with us. This is to be expected. It is not a life that everyone can understand.'

I felt more than mere courtesy compelling me to reply, and I did so in my best ceremonial Sadiri. 'Few are truly free of obligations and responsibilities to others. Otherwise they would stay, if only for a while, because your harmonious society soothes both mind and spirit.'

He inclined his head in gracious acknowledgement at both the words and the sincerity.

'And yet I wonder,' I went on, emboldened by his gentleness, 'why your secrecy is so important – important enough to tamper with a person's mind.'

Dllenahkh began to frown, clearly considering this rudeness, but the monk bowed his head in apology, accepting the seriousness of the question. 'We tried, once, to be open to the world. The effects on the community were distressing. You see, many people believed that we were the Caretakers and began to demand of us more than we could provide.'

'And you are not—'

'We are not now, nor have we ever been, the Caretakers,' he declared solemnly.

I almost sighed in disappointment. I had no strong feelings about the matter, but I had the usual amount of curiosity.

'Their powers are far beyond us,' he continued.

'So you *have* met them?' I asked quickly.

He smiled. 'I really couldn't say.'

He led us out of the building and into an orderly garden of green grass, dark rock and low clusters of pale-gold flowers. A central gravel path led to a glass-smooth pool that appeared to have no edge but blue horizon. I felt a tiny surge of worry.

'There is no safer way?' Dllenahkh enquired sharply.

'None that outsiders may see,' was the placid response.

The monks walk on water and fly through the treetops. 'So, this *is* what I think it is,' I said in leaden tones.

'She has only recently recovered. How can you be sure she is strong enough?' Dllenahkh turned to me suddenly. 'Delarua, stay.'

'No, Dllenahkh. Rafi, remember? Joral. Qeturah. Even my sister Maria, who probably wishes me dead. And yes, even Tonio, who I've known for all of two weeks.'

'Then I'm coming with you,' he declared.

'Don't.' I shook my head. 'Don't do this, don't make me feel that I stood between you and your dream.'

His look of resolve told me he had already made up his mind. 'If I am permitted, I will return some day, after I have completed my assignment. You were right, Delarua. There are people depending on us to return, and it was a lapse on my part to persuade myself otherwise.'

I glanced at the monk. He stood looking at us, as unsurprised as if he had known Dllenahkh's mind before he had known it himself. I took in a huge breath of relief.

'Well, then, what are you waiting for?' I said with a grin. 'Get your stuff.'

I walked the gardens with the monk while Dllenahkh was away. I know we had a good, in-depth conversation, because I felt light-hearted at the end of it, and I've learned to trust my emotions. He must have taken particular care to remove all trace of his presence from my mind, because I cannot remember a single thing that we spoke about. I do remember when Dllenahkh returned, once more outfitted as a member of the mission team. My mind felt a space clearing, as if a single drop of oil had touched and spread, pushing back all other influence.

I looked at the monk, knowing, but needing to hear him say it. He smiled and gestured at the pool.

'Walk on water. Fly through the treetops. Farewell.'

Indiana Jones holovid fans, eat your heart out. We did not walk, we ran. Our feet struck the water firmly, gripped impossibly and propelled us to the horizon at the pool's far edge. We hurtled into an element that should have destroyed us: high-vaulted air with a breeze too light for the wingless to hope.

And yet we soared.

We swooped down the narrow valley, following the line of the river as if it were an arrow to our destination. I was tempted to look back to see if there was a line of robed figures just beyond the edge of the pool, wafting us gently homeward, but I knew that was just a silly cinematic image, possibly a memory from some ancient holovid. So I looked forward in wonder, seeing the kind of bird's-eye view of the landscape that even a shuttle can't give.

Some people, of course, have to prove they can't be awed by anything.

'Telekinesis is a natural consequence of intensive psionic development,' he remarked after a minute or so.

'Shut up! You're spoiling it!' I screamed. (I may also have shrieked 'wheee' at some point. I admit nothing.)

However smooth our descent, as we followed the water down I began to realise something. 'I think we're going to get wet again – aughhhhh!'

But it was only to our knees, and the current was comparatively tame. As we slogged to the nearest bank, heavy and earthbound once more, I heard the most beautiful sound, the chirp of my own missing comm, miraculously coming from Dllenahkh's pocket. He had the decency to look slightly ashamed as he fished it out of hiding and answered the automated emergency call. When he signed off, I held out my hand accusingly, thinking of my conveniently smashed handheld. He placed the comm on my palm with a small, regretful smile that made me relent.

'He was right. There was no need to worry about me. You could have stayed,' I admitted.

'I believe I acted appropriately,' he replied, both smile and regret erased from his features. 'It would not be helpful to hold dual loyalties at this stage.'

I wanted to believe him, so I dropped the subject before I could persuade myself otherwise. After that, the only thing left to do was find a shuttle-sized clearing, sit and wait.

It was a grand reunion. There was the expected hugging (by some of us, at least!) and mutual relief and general elation at being home safe and sound. Only Qeturah looked grim and almost tearful, and it struck me that she must have convinced herself that she had been responsible for sending us to our deaths. I gave her a tiny, chastising shake of the head for thinking such folly. It turned out, however, that she had other things on her mind.

'There's someone waiting to speak to you on the shuttle comm,' she said.

I perked up even more. Rafi! Excusing myself hastily, I ran to the shuttle and quickly keyed on the monitor.

'Grace.'

Maria's eyes looked shadowed, as if she had been crying and might start up again without warning.

'Hey, Maria,' I said tentatively. I really had no idea what to say.

She smiled weakly. 'Good to see you alive and well.'

I gave a small smile that wasn't entirely kind. 'Thought I was dead?'

The stricken look that flashed across her face convinced me – she *had* wished it. I exhaled and looked away, tears stinging my eyes.

'Look, I—'

'Grace, please—'

We stopped talking. 'You first,' I said eventually.

'Okay,' she said, and took a big breath, bracing herself. 'I . . .

we've got a long road ahead of us, me and Gracie. The influence went on for so long, they can't just put things back the way they should be. Rafi's all right, though. He – he's more like you. Grace, you must promise me, if I can't take care of him, if they try to take him from me, you'll look out for him? Be his guardian? I'll sign whatever I have to. I just want him to be with family.'

'Of course, Maria,' I said, tears now falling freely. 'Of course.'

We spoke for a few more minutes. I told her a message would be coming for Rafi very soon. I apologised for not having done more. She told me not to be silly, and she even sounded as if she meant it.

I left the monitor with eyes red but face wiped dry. Then I saw Tonio outside and realised I had to brace myself for another encounter.

He was perfect. He took me by the hand and led me away to a quiet place under the eaves of the forest. He sat down on a fallen log and pulled me gently into his lap. Unexpectedly, in contrast to his calm face, his emotions sang against mine in a mutual cacophony of mingled joy and sorrow. Perhaps we were both a little giddy, a little susceptible to the melodrama of the moment. Perhaps not.

'Now stop that,' I said, swallowing down my tears. 'You're so loud the Sadiri will hear you.'

He gave me a wide-eyed look of innocence. 'Perhaps you're projecting your feelings onto me.'

'If that's true, then drop the "perhaps" and tell me so directly,' I challenged him. 'Hm. I didn't think so,' I added as he looked away for a moment with a wistful smile.

'We've had too little time, you and I,' he said quietly. 'And now you go that way,' he nodded to the forest, 'and I return this way,' and he looked in the direction of the savannah. 'So it goes.'

'No jokes?' I said breathlessly. 'No light-hearted humour to make it easier?'

He gave a half-smile, touching my cheek softly with the back of his hand. 'I don't want easy. I want true.'

'Then this,' and I kissed him lightly on the lips, 'is not easy, but it is true.'

He pressed his forehead to mine, then kissed me, a kiss as brief as mine had been, but far more intense. 'Worth it,' he sighed.

I know, perhaps it wasn't a grand passion by the usual standards, but can anyone understand what it meant to me? To have had for however short a time the interest and attention of a man who was strong enough to walk away from me, and strong enough to let me walk away from him – it might be too much to say it healed something in me, but it was a start.

There's a nice little postscript to this adventure. Two weeks later, long after we had left the area, Qeturah informed Dllenahkh and Joral that a remote village in the forest uplands had made an unheard-of effort to contact Central Government authorities.

'It seems they learned about your quest to find taSadiri brides for your homesteaders, and they're impressed with your courage. They've submitted genetic samples as proof of their eligibility and wish to send a delegation of women to the Tlaxce settlement.'

'That's marvellous!' I exclaimed. 'I wouldn't be surprised if—'

Yes, I was going to say it. I was going to start talking about the place I'd been to and the people I'd seen, and the things I was supposed to keep secret. But instead my voice dwindled and choked off, my mouth closed and my teeth clenched shut so fast that I bit the tip of my tongue. Lian gave me an odd look, but otherwise no one else remarked on my strange little coughing fit. Dllenahkh, who had noted with concern and sympathy my sudden stop and watering eyes, came to me after the meeting.

'I may have neglected to mention that the injunction placed on us to say nothing to others on this matter is far too strong for me to remove,' he said softly.

'No kidding,' I said, and tried to squint down at my outstretched tongue.

'But you have guessed correctly. I am grateful that they found a way to acknowledge our need without compromising their way of life.' The words were neutral, the tone calm, but his eyes sparkled with triumph.

I smiled at him. 'I've got something for you.'

I reached into a pocket. It had been in a batch of knickknacks I'd picked up for Gilda's kids, but for some reason I hadn't sent it on with the rest. 'Never did thank you properly for saving my life and healing me and getting me back safe. So . . . here.'

He took the small brown object, bemused. Then his lips twitched. 'Highly appropriate. I thank you. It is good to have someone with whom I can remember this.'

He gravely affixed the teak elephant to the collar of his tunic and gave it a pat of satisfaction that reminded me of my own dealings with the real-life, full-sized versions.

Zero hour plus one year two months twenty-four days

Some mornings, inspired by good weather and exceptional scenery, all four of them meditated together. In the initial days after his return from the hidden monastery, the communal sessions became more frequent, perhaps out of relief and gratitude that he *had* returned. For Dllenahkh, it was more; he could now sense the latent connections that would lead them into that deeper communication shared by the people of the monastery. It took away the bittersweet nostalgia of the old familiar ritual and replaced it with the new excitement of *this is what we will become*.

One day, Commander Nasiha lingered to speak to him after meditation. 'I have been thinking,' she said. 'Delarua could benefit from some of the techniques of the basic disciplines.'

Pleased that she had spoken his innermost thoughts, Dllenahkh responded promptly, 'That is an excellent suggestion. When will you start?'

She gave a brief nod in begrudging acknowledgement of the compliment and the trick, fixed him with her usual direct look and pressed on. 'We both know that you are far better qualified to train her.'

'That might be considered a conflict of interest,' he remarked.

She kept her face expressionless, and that was as bad as an out-loud laugh. 'Oh? How so?'

Patiently, Dllenahkh explained, 'I do not wish to be seen as another Ioan.'

She blinked, shocked. 'Councillor! I did not mean—'

Neither did I. He tried to explain without compromising the safety of his bridled tongue. 'Of course, but the fact remains, she can trust me while we remain colleagues and equals. Becoming her teacher would shift the balance of power, and I would prefer not to lose her friendship.'

For I have already done too much to alter that balance. He was relieved that he could not speak of what he had done, because for all his good intentions, he felt strangely close to the edge of guilt. Healing Delarua had been unexpectedly exhilarating, partly due, no doubt, to the thrill of learning a new, near-miraculous skill, but also perhaps akin to the transcendence of bonding with a mindship and feeling the bones, tendons and nerves of another being – not as a puppet master, but like a dancer fitted to a partner, able to suggest a movement with a light press of silent, invisible communication.

'I will teach her,' Nasiha said with a firmness that was as good as an oath.

'Thank you, Commander. If I may make a suggestion, be subtle. She may appear fearless, but she is very quick to retreat if she feels pressured.'

'I will be careful, Councillor,' she promised.

THE FAERIE QUEEN

Her hair was a cloud of silver foam, growing back from her temples in tiny, soft curls, then expanding up and out in fierce glory. Few crowns of the traditional mould could encompass it, but none was necessary when diamonds of all colours, rose and white and gold, sparkled freely throughout her tresses, transforming the cloud to a starry nebula. Her eyebrows were golden and perfectly shaped, each one a gentle, delicate arc. Dark pupils stood out starkly in sea-grey irises; long light-brown eyelashes framed all with a sleepy sultriness. Her look was forgiving of the ordinariness of others, and understanding of their natural desire to adore her. Slender limbs made her sprawl elegant; the very fineness of her bones drew the eye along her lines and subtle curves. Her skin defied common sense, combining translucency with an amber tint, revealing an intricate tracery of blood vessels under the paler skin of her inner arm. She would have made an artist weep for shame that neither brush nor tint could do her justice.

A catalogue of my own flaws began to scroll through my mind. The uneven texture of my hair, whose inability to decide whether to curl or ripple meant that a crew-cut was the best out of a bunch of bad options. The mundane brown of that same hair. Flat, broad eyebrows strongly marking my face, eyes that needed the help of kohl to become remarkable. Thick bones and muscles that spoke of sturdiness rather than grace – ha, the irony! Cedar-brown skin that might have been just acceptable if it hadn't been for the faint dusting of freckles across my nose and cheeks.

Ah, there. I consoled myself. We had very much the same nose, a happy medium that was neither big nor small, broad nor pointed, just well proportioned and joined harmoniously to the forehead with a gentle dip. I held on to the image of my nose and tried to feel confident as I looked down it at her – insofar as it is possible to look down at someone seated on a throne elevated on a dais.

'The Tlaxce Visiting Mission of the Central Government of Cygnus Beta thanks Your Majesty for her kind invitation, and wishes to avail itself of the opportunity to renew to the Seelie Court the assurances of its highest consideration.'

The impressive part wasn't the high diplomatic language. It was the fact that I was able to resurrect enough of my Cymraeg to say this without pause or stammer.

The Faerie Queen inclined her head graciously. 'Be welcome,' she said.

It had been blissfully mundane for almost three weeks, exactly what I needed after the excitement of waterfall-jumping. We had flown the shuttle south and made our way across open farmland, visiting settlements with scant humanity and an overabundance of ruminants. I might have glanced once or twice at the grey edge of wooded hills to the west. I might even have wondered a little, but when Qeturah told me that we had obtained clearance to go to Faerie, my immediate reaction had been that it was a

Bad Idea with a capital B I, because I was damned if I was going to explain to the Sadiri how a community of their people had ditched their own culture wholesale to actualise an obscure Terran myth. But I was stuck with the job, so I went ahead and tried my best.

'Reports are sketchy. Faerie has been closed for more than a century because visitors tended to treat it a bit like a theme park.' *Smart visitors*, I thought cynically to myself. 'But they say that for centuries the land was populated by two taSadiri clans who were constantly at war with each other. They had endured a particularly bad run of hostilities when a strange Cygnian turned up with an intriguing solution to their problem. Since the main cause of their war was the question of which clan's rituals and dialect should take precedence, the compromise was for both clans to learn an entirely new identity.'

Tarik was utterly disbelieving. 'This makes no sense. Do you mean to tell me that two taSadiri tribes abandoned millennia of tradition for a society drawn from folk tales and fictional writings?'

'I'm afraid so,' I said, trying not to smirk at his appalled expression.

As a belief, it was rather seductive, actually. Long-lived, superior and mentally dominant over the weaker Terrans, the Elves were clearly an indication of some covert, pre-embargo Sadiri visit to Terra. If you're out of your skull, that is.

'Who was the Cygnian who told them this?' asked Dllenahkh.

'Some crackpot academic descended from the Druids of Ynys Môn who made it his business to know all ancient and modern manifestations of Celtic culture. They say his forefathers founded New Camelot. I don't know. Frankly, I find it all a bit silly, but they've heard about us and they've invited us and we can't very well say no.'

Fortunately, I had set their expectations so low that when the shuttle set down on the bald brow of a tree-ringed hill, we were relieved to be greeted by ordinary Cygnians dressed in contemporary attire and with only slightly glossy hair, drawn up in a welcoming party around the Queen's throne. They did, however, hold firmly to their own language, and until Tarik could get a translation programme up and running, that meant yours truly was the main conduit of communication on our end.

The Faerie Queen was eloquent but slightly insane, and this made translation difficult. After descending the dais to gravely greet the Commissioner, she turned her attention to the rest of the team as introductions were made. Initially, she nodded perfunctorily at each name, but then she began to walk among us, her slender height both imposing and fragile. Lian earned a lingering look, Nasiha another grave nod, but at Fergus she stopped and considered. With a sideways glance at Qeturah, she murmured, 'Probably hers,' and went to Joral. Taking the poor young man by the chin, she examined him and proclaimed, 'Young,' before moving on to Tarik. Nasiha, who was quicker on the uptake than the rest of us, seized her husband's hand and stared challengingly at the woman, who merely smiled and came to stand before Dllenahkh. Keeping her gaze on him, she beckoned me over.

'You represent the newly arrived Sadiri on Cygnus Beta?' she asked him.

I translated, and Dllenahkh nodded. 'I do, Your Majesty.'

She was perhaps three centimetres taller than him, not counting the fifteen centimetres that was hair alone, but he was three times broader, and just as self-possessed. She suddenly smiled brilliantly, as if deigning to recognise him as an equal.

'I will speak to you,' she declared. 'You,' she addressed me, still without looking at me, 'will translate. The rest of you are granted the freedom of the Seelie Court until our discussions are completed.'

I repeated this in Standard for the benefit of the team, looking anxiously at Qeturah. She smiled reassuringly, but her eyes signalled caution as she said, 'Tell her that in accordance with government practice we would be happy to set up shelter near the shuttle.'

The Queen was appalled at the idea. 'Nonsense!' she said, looking at Qeturah as if she were both mad and discourteous. 'It is far too dangerous to stay on the ground at night. We have prepared lodgings for you.'

Qeturah's gaze followed her pointing hand, looking up walkways into the heights of huge trees where wooden platforms spanned branches and surrounded trunks in a vast tree city. 'Thank her kindly for us, First Officer Delarua,' she said somewhat breathlessly.

Our platform – or t'bren, as they called it – had no barrier rails, something that seemed to worry no one but us, but they did offer us rope netting to string over and around our bedding, perhaps as a deterrent to sleepwalking. I was careful with mine that first night, hooking it securely to a branch above and tucking it under the bedding. This made waking up suddenly at midnight even more exciting as I promptly got tangled up in the mesh.

'What is it? What's happened?' I whispered frantically as I unknotted myself.

Fergus's deep murmur was slow and calming. 'Someone's trying to break into the shuttle. Lian and I are going to check it out.'

I hesitated, then flung off the netting with one final effort and felt my way to the edge. A hand rested warningly on my back, another hand muffled my start at a scream and a voice whispered in Cymraeg, 'Stay.'

It was likely someone we'd met during the day, but the night was dark and all faces dim. Probably the only person who'd stand out would be the Queen, with her bright hair.

'What is it?' I whispered. 'Do you know?'

'Unseelie,' came the whispered answer.

For a moment I was baffled, then I grimaced. 'Ah. The bad guys.'

'Yes. They rule the land at night, and go underground at dawn. They do not come up to our treetops, and we do not descend to their caves. Thus we preserve some measure of peace.'

'I thought the whole point of becoming Elves was to stop the conflict.'

The hand on my back shifted as if vibrating with laughter. 'I will tell you about it tomorrow. It makes a good tale.'

'Who are you? How will I know you in daylight?'

'I am the teller of tales and singer of songs. You will make a good song, I can feel it. Which one is yours?'

Disjointedness of thought and speech seemed to be an Elvish trait, but I understood when a shadowy hand waved to the rest of the group, who were awake and quietly talking into comms and to each other. 'Tarik and Nasiha are husband and wife. The rest – we belong only to ourselves.'

'Ah.' There was a hint of laughter in that response, and I wondered too late how strong these Elves were in telepathy and empathy. I sat up and put some distance between myself and the strange Elf with his overly friendly hand.

'Here come your guards,' said the storyteller-singer, and there indeed were Fergus and Lian returning.

'Perimeter alarms scared them off,' said Fergus. 'Someone tried a light mental tweak on us, but it didn't take.'

I quickly explained the little I had just learned.

'That's not reassuring,' said Qeturah, a frown in her voice. 'Remember the legend of faerie glamour? Let's stay together as much as possible and be on the alert for influence.'

With the immediate danger over, the Sadiri soon composed themselves to rest with their usual economy of fuss. Qeturah drew Lian aside for a quiet conference. There was little chance of my getting to sleep in a hurry, what with all the adrenalin of the past few minutes, so I shifted a little closer to Fergus. He was putting away some of his gear and politely ignoring me, as usual. I'd long ago figured out that for a man like Fergus, a man who shunned unnecessary talk, I was a walking nightmare.

'I'm a bit surprised,' I began, adjusting my voice to copy his measured cadence, hoping not to startle or vex him. 'Some of the taSadiri we've encountered . . . well, it's one thing not to have the mental disciplines, but they seem almost . . . uncivilised.'

There was a silence as he paused for a moment in his work. 'Are you joking?' he said at last, sounding wary.

I was baffled. 'No. What did I say?'

'They've got all kinds of ways to reform criminals now, but what do you think the Sadiri used to do with their delinquents in the old days?'

I was struck mute. The concept of a lawbreaking Sadiri had not even crossed my mind. The perpetual stereotype of the judging, superior Sadiri was too strong, even in me.

'They used to ship them off-planet, fast and far. A lot of their so-called science outposts and religious retreats were nothing more than places to dump undesirables, people who didn't quite fit in. Worked out for the best, ironically. Pity the demographics are so skewed.'

I exhaled very slowly. 'You're telling me that of the Sadiri who survived, there are diplomats and judges, pilots and scientists, nuns and monks . . . and jailbirds?'

'Yep. Almost makes you laugh, doesn't it?'

I felt a bit foolish. Fair enough, it was Cygnian culture and language that was my speciality, but I had begun to pride myself on becoming a bit of an expert in Sadiri matters over the past few months. 'How do *you* know all this?' I asked resentfully.

'Used to work in Galactic Patrol,' he replied. 'Been far and wide myself, even as far as Ain. *Lots* of interesting tales about how Ain got founded, but I think it's obvious.'

'You do?' I thought I knew what he was going to say. Political differences arise, conflict follows and the more adventurous faction goes off to make a new world of their choosing – or the losing side gets kicked out. That was Punartam's story, and which version you got depended on whether the person doing the telling was from Punartam or Ntshune.

'Prison colony for the worst offenders. Probably people like your—' He stopped, stiffened.

'Like Ioan,' I said, my stomach plummeting as if the tree had suddenly removed its support from under our feet.

'Something like that,' he said, wary again. Maybe he feared I was going to get all confiding, or burst into tears. 'Go to sleep,' he concluded abruptly. 'I can't keep proper watch with people nattering in my ear all night.'

*　　　*　　　*

I was now suspicious that the Queen's overwhelming presence was glamour-assisted. I tagged along behind her and Dllenahkh the following morning as they walked in the mellow light below the trees, and he told her about Sadira, New Sadira and the Sadiri settlement in Tlaxce. As I translated, I absently probed at my emotions but found nothing amiss.

After she dismissed us and swept off with her small entourage, I asked him directly. 'How does the Queen strike you?'

'Cautious,' he replied. 'She has clearly heard reports, but she assumes nothing and waits for me to confirm. A very scientific approach.'

'Well, yes, but is there anything more? How does she *feel* to you?'

He raised a faintly puzzled eyebrow. 'Bored. Lonely.'

'Do you find her beautiful?' I asked at last.

'Ah,' he said in dawning comprehension. 'You are worried about the possibility of glamour. No, she uses none.'

'Well, if any of us could tell, it would be you,' I grumbled. 'Do me a favour. When you get a chance, ask her about the Unseelie Court.'

We were invited to a formal dinner that night. I could not help smiling at the seating arrangements. Qeturah was given a couch on a smaller dais with Lian and Fergus nearby, and the Elves who attended her were mostly male and . . . well . . . damn good-looking. Nasiha had the smallest dais with Tarik at her side, Joral slightly below and again some very good-looking attendants. I had no such luck. Perhaps this matriarchal society required that I have at least one pet male of my own to qualify for special treatment, or perhaps I was still too useful as a translator. I was stuck just a little back from Dllenahkh, who was seated at the Queen's right hand. On the bright side, it seemed that the most attractive attendants had been reserved for the Queen's dais, so during lulls in conversation I amused myself by ranking them. One of them, an eight-point-five on my scale, was quietly tuning a stringed instrument resembling a cithara. He caught my eye and smiled. My eyes widened and I elbowed a startled Dllenahkh in the ribs.

'Quick! Ask her about the Unseelie Court!' I hissed.

He complied, with only a disapproving quirk of the corner of his mouth to chastise me for my behaviour, and I dutifully translated. The Queen's eyes went from lazy to furious for a moment, then she instantly regained her calm.

'It is true,' she said. 'It appears that war, when deprived of one reason, simply seeks out another. We are still a people divided, having selected different aspects of legend to embody. And yet it is better than it once was.'

'How so, Your Majesty?' asked Dllenahkh.

Clapping her hands, she caught the minstrel's attention. 'Tell them a story of the Elder Days, the one about the woman with three sons.'

The minstrel set down his instrument, stood and addressed the court in a mellifluous tenor.

'A woman had three sons, and when they were grown, the first came to her and said, "Mama, I love a girl and wish to marry her." She replied, "Son, this gladdens my heart, but of what lineage is she?" "Alas, Mama," he told her, "she is half-Terran." His mother raised her hands and shook her head and said, "A tragedy, but I will cope."

'The second son came some time after to inform her of his desire to marry and, worse yet, the bride he had selected was half-Terran, half-Ntshune, with no taSadiri in her at all. But again his mother raised her hands, shook her head and said, "A tragedy, but I will cope."

'Finally the third son came to her and said he was engaged. When she enquired about the girl's lineage, he answered smugly, "She is all taSadiri, Mama." "Wonderful news," his mother cried. "Of what family?" "She is of the Other clan," he confessed. Whereupon his mother rose up with her blade and slew him without another word.'

The bard waited for me to finish translating, then spoke low for my ears, 'I hope you have rendered it well. It is one of my best tales, handed down from my grandmother.'

'Tale, or family history?' I murmured teasingly in reply.

He merely smiled enigmatically.

'Conflicts are less intense, less bloody than before. Some blame the admixture of our blood, others credit our new traditions,' the Queen said.

'And some say there is yet a third reason,' murmured the bard as he returned to his instrument.

'Peace, child, all in good time. What my impertinent great-grandson wishes me to tell you is that some of the women of the Seelie Court are long-lived, specifically the women of my House.' The Queen looked around at her attendants. Suddenly, their devotion and her goddess-like air no longer seemed unwarranted.

'In many cultures it is considered discourteous to ask a woman her age,' Dllenahkh said. 'If I may beg your pardon in advance, would you satisfy my curiosity?'

I took care to translate the elegant framing of Dllenahkh's request. I believe I succeeded, for the Queen smiled at him and said graciously, 'I am nearly three hundred and forty-seven Standard years old.'

'Cygnian law prohibits extending the lifespan by genetic means,' Qeturah noted. 'It is a risky proposition, with uneven results.'

The Queen shrugged. 'What was done was done so long ago. Were we perhaps seeking to restore the years that the mixing of our blood had taken from us? And yes, the results are uneven, as you can witness. But it has provided a core of stability in our society.'

'You are a land of true matriarchs. Is that why there is no King in your Court?' Dllenahkh enquired.

The Queen seemed delighted at this question. 'There have been two in the past, but these days I follow the example of other women of my House and content myself with my attendants.'

There was a slight choking sound as Fergus inhaled his drink, no doubt finally realising the significance of his placement at the Commissioner's feet. Qeturah smiled and patted his shoulder. 'Hush, dear, no explanations. This is no time for me to lose face.'

'What a life,' Lian said to me afterwards. 'I've never seen a woman with a harem who so obviously deserved it. I hope she keeps a close eye on her family tree. It would be very awkward to seduce one's great-grandnephew.'

'They're a small population,' I agreed. 'I wouldn't be surprised if there was a little mutual kidnapping going on with the other Elves.'

'Yep. Anything for fresh blood,' Lian said.

I frowned to myself, not quite knowing why.

The discussions continued. What made matters particularly difficult was the fact that the Queen became enthralled by the sound of the Sadiri language and pressed Dllenahkh to speak only in that tongue. Cymraeg is very poetic, even romantic, and

Standard less so, though serviceable enough. Sadiri is absolutely perfect as a programming language, but when it comes to matters of the heart it falls a little short. This became obvious when the tenor of the conversation began to change.

'Why don't you tell me I'm beautiful?' she said randomly one day.

'It would be appropriate if you were to comment on the aesthetics of my person,' I communicated to Dllenahkh.

His eyebrows rose the merest fraction. 'The fact that you are an extremely attractive woman is sufficiently obvious that it does not require my repeating it.'

'Need I tell you what so many others have told you before?' I replied to her.

She laughed lightly. I bit my lip in frustration.

'Any progress with that translator?' I asked Tarik moodily as he worked on his handheld, comfortably seated on edge of the *t'bren* with his legs dangling over high green infinity.

He gave me a steady look. 'It will not be ready before the end of our sojourn here.'

'Blast,' I muttered. 'I'm so tired of this.'

On the last day of our stay, the Queen seemed in a reflective mood. She took Dllenahkh and me up to the highest *t'bren*, whose view extended beyond the trees, across the valley and to the grey-shadowed horizon with its high, distant mountains. A small group of attendants followed, as usual, and her minstrel played his cithara in the background, singing in some variant of Cymraeg that was unfamiliar to me. The business of the Elven-Sadiri exchange had long been concluded, with the result that the only talk remaining between them was small talk. Dllenahkh noted in grave Sadiri fashion that the music was pleasingly harmonious.

'It is a love song,' she said to him, but her eyes were on me, her smile mocking though not yet cruel. 'Shall I translate it for you?'

She signalled to the minstrel with a languid movement of her hand and he began again, singing softly to the complex melody while she translated in perfect Standard.

'The mind is a golden vein
seamed in crumbling rock (also known as rotting quartz).'

And why had it amused her to have me tagging along as an imperfect interpreter when she could easily have spoken for herself in Standard? I would never understand what passed for humour among the Elves.

'The golden mean becomes a kindness
as she learns to sip the echo of his smiles.'

That was a nice little turn of phrase there. The echo of a smile – that reminded me of the subtlety of Sadiri facial expressions.

'That Sadira died,
that her heart was shorn of innocence by a conscienceless man'

. . . the hell? She couldn't possibly mean . . .

And yet my spine stiffened as the lilt of her voice and the sly slant of her looks suffused each word with a far too personal significance.

'that she tempts him to laughter
and other ruin,

138

> *that they ache,*
> *that they find their way, slowly,*
> *delicately, respectfully –*
> *passion's slow but inexorable burn . . .'*

I was too embarrassed to look at Dllenahkh and too curious not to, so I settled for a furtive glance which only told me that he appeared to be perfectly still and controlled.

> 'It's not the sun that blinds her,*
> *nor the golden rays of impossibility*
> *in an infinitely permutable and permissive landscape.*
>
> *'Light diffuses through suspended sand.*
> *They dance, exquisitely slowly, an elegant*
> *sarabande.'*

She concluded the verses with a gentle flourish of her wrist and fingers. 'I have so much time and so many to choose from,' she said to me with a beautifully condescending smile. 'I can afford to be generous.'

Then she gracefully inclined her head, gathered up her entourage with the casual command of a glance and withdrew, leaving us alone on the lookout with the minstrel still quietly playing nearby.

My ears were burning. It was impossible to pretend that I did not understand who the song was referring to, and what she had just hinted.

Dllenahkh cleared his throat. 'I have recently received some new projections concerning the planned infrastructural improvements for the Tlaxce homesteadings. Would you care to go over them with me? I believe there are some points that may be of interest to you.'

'Yes, let's. That sounds fascinating,' I quickly agreed, and we made our way back to our *t'bren* with no further incident.

That afternoon, we said our farewells and flew on towards our next assignment, stopping to overnight at another Forestry outpost. I was curious to know what the Sadiri had thought of the Elven solution to taSadiri strife, so I approached them as they sat outdoors at twilight, talking among themselves in Sadiri.

'I know we've already had our formal debriefing,' I said with careful politeness, 'but I was wondering what you thought of the Elves of the Seelie Court, and what recommendations you might make concerning them to the Sadiri settlement.'

'It was an interesting encounter, but I do not aspire to become a member of a harem,' Dllenahkh said. As far as I could tell, he was teasing me, but I was too mortified to appreciate the effort at lightheartedness, especially since Joral, Nasiha and Tarik were wearing various expressions of suppressed amusement, which was, for them, the equivalent of a belly laugh.

'Yeah, about that,' I muttered, examining my boots. 'I'm sorry she got the wrong impression about us. I swear, I translated as best I could, but—'

'You are distressed,' he said in genuine surprise. 'But surely you cannot think that this is the first time people have speculated on the nature of our relationship?'

I was finally able to look up, my jaw slack with amazement. 'What?'

'It is true,' Joral confirmed. 'It was one of the first things Tonio asked me when he was attached to the team.'

'Tarik and I have discussed the possibility more than once,' Nasiha admitted.

They looked at Dllenahkh, who grudgingly confessed, 'Lanuri continues to exact a most un-Sadiri revenge for what he terms my "well-meaning meddling" in his personal life. He has been affixing advice to the end of every piece of official correspondence he sends to me. He is of the opinion that my apparent "slow progress" with you is an indication that I need help.'

I laughed out loud, not least because I detected more than a touch of Freyda Mar in that statement.

Then Tarik spoke up. 'As more people learn about the mission's work, there is a growing sense that it would be fitting if one or both of the single Sadiri on the team were to find wives by the end of the year as a sort of symbol of success for the broader undertaking.'

My features struggled to find the right response to this news and settled on pained incredulity. 'That's ridiculous. For what Dllenahkh and Joral are doing, those people should have Sadiri princesses lined up for them when they get back, rather than speculating about every rag, tag and bobtail they happen to work with.'

Dllenahkh's eyebrows went up, as expected. 'I am not familiar with that phrase, but if the tone is any indication, I would have to say that you are hardly in this category.'

'Most kind,' I scoffed. 'Look, you guys feel free to keep searching, but I've got some contacts at the Ministry of Family Planning, and once you're both registered we can draw up a list of candidates of a certain calibre.'

'Most kind,' Dllenahkh said blandly, but for a moment I felt a strange flash of something electric, almost as if he were angry.

'Well, it's the least I can do for unwittingly blocking your prospects,' I said lightly, hiding my bewilderment at his reaction.

'I think it is an excellent idea,' Joral said. 'You could register, too.'

'I . . .' I faltered, trying to find a good excuse. Qeturah was already convinced I needed therapy, and I wanted to keep the Sadiri on my side. 'I don't see why not. Set a good example and all that. But let's be sensible about this. You've got more choices now. Women are coming to you, and inviting you to visit them. You could even return to the Seelie Court, maybe convince a few to become fully Sadiri. It might take a little time, but . . .'

Nasiha looked amused, whether at my backpedalling or at the idea of Joral as Sadiri missionary to Elven women, I wasn't sure. 'Well, Joral, what do you think of this option?' she asked.

Joral pondered for a while, then snapped out, 'Unacceptable.'

I was not the only one startled at the sharpness of his tone. Everyone seemed to straighten slightly as he went on with increasing intensity.

'I want a wife, and children, and a family of my blood. I want sons and daughters who will look like my brothers and sisters who are gone, who will speak Sadiri and learn of Sadira and practise the mental disciplines. I want to see them married, and grow old enough to see my grandchildren and great-grandchildren. I am the last of my line, the sole survivor of my family, like so many others on the homesteadings. The Councillor is right – why should any of us seek to be a member of a harem? Why should we desire frivolous things? I want—'

'Joral—'

'Leave him be.' Shockingly, the fierce words that cut off Dllenahkh's attempt to bring Joral back to proper Sadiri behaviour came from Nasiha. She knelt before Joral and spoke passionately. 'We desire these things, too. These are good things to desire, right and appropriate things. We shall see these things come to pass for you and for others. Your line will not die out.'

I backed away, a lump in my throat. Collective grief is one thing, but the Sadiri are very scary when they get intense. I turned to see Lian watching wide-eyed from a distance, and gladly found my excuse to leave.

'Lian, you're not going to help out Joral any time soon, are you?' I murmured.

Lian answered with a head-shake, still staring past me, awed at the sight of overwrought Sadiri.

'Well, if you have a sister or a friend to recommend to Joral instead, that would be a nice gesture.'

'I'll look into it,' Lian said absently. 'I keep forgetting how important this is to them, you know?'

'I'm just as bad,' I said morosely. 'Teasing you about Joral. Treating him like a boy and not a man. Treating Dllenahkh like . . .'

Lian eyed me with great interest. 'Like?'

I frowned, trying to think. 'I dunno. As if he'll always be around to be my sidekick. Like I'll never have to share him with a wife and children and – hah, from all they're saying, grandchildren, too. Don't laugh at me, Lian, but I was jealous of that woman monopolising his time and attention. I've never felt like that before.'

'Hm,' said Lian. 'Well, I won't laugh at you.'

We walked away and gave them some privacy, but later on I caught Nasiha alone just as she was coming out of her quarters.

'So,' I began cautiously, 'is it too early to congratulate you?'

Nasiha struggled, keeping her face neutral and her chin aggressively up, but then she exhaled and glared at me with a kind of proud defeat. 'It is remarkable how you are able to be so perceptive in some areas and so obtuse in others. Yes, it is too early. It will be too early until, as Joral said, I can see my great-grandchildren. Then you may congratulate me.'

'I won't be alive then,' I said cheekily. 'I'll leave you a congratulations message that you can open whenever it seems right to you.'

Nasiha gave me a determined look. 'I believe young parents will become a new Sadiri tradition. You may yet be alive to see the fourth generation, perhaps even the fifth.'

I nodded, imagining it and finding it good. 'I'd stick around just for that. Maybe even tweak a gene to be sure.'

She completely shocked me in the next moment. She put a hand on my shoulder, not at all affectionately, but more as if she were bracing me for something. 'It would be advantageous for us to seek the assistance of suitable non-Sadiri for the education and care of our child. Tarik and I have agreed that given your experience and knowledge of the Sadiri language and culture, you would be the natural choice.'

'Ah,' I said, panicked and wide-eyed under the strong grip of her hand. 'This is an important duty. What does it entail?'

'You would function as an elder member of the family. A godparent, if you will.'

'Then . . . I would be honoured,' I replied in wonderment.

Nasiha seemed to calm down at this assurance. She released my shoulder, tilted her head and considered me. 'You were not fooling us earlier. Something about marriage frightens you.'

I opened my mouth to remonstrate, and she raised a silencing hand. 'Do not try to lie to me. Remember, I have documented your empathic and telepathic data, and I know a little about your ex-fiancé. I understand your difficulty.'

'You do?' I said. Nasiha in the role of supportive confidante was boggling my mind.

'Yes. You have concerns that you may influence your spouse without intending to, or that you may again be influenced without your knowledge. These are rational concerns, but your inability to deal with them properly is turning them into irrational fears.'

'What do you suggest I do?' I said almost meekly.

'You must learn how to shield your emotions and thoughts. You must learn how to protect yourself and others. There are aspects of the Sadiri disciplines that can help you achieve this. It is a practical solution.'

'It is,' I agreed. My sense of relief at her blunt but insightful summary was so great that I felt myself grow an extra centimetre, as if a burden had literally been lifted from my back. I wondered, not for the first time, if the Sadiri had any concept of therapy in the gentle, lengthy Cygnian sense. I doubted it. It might just have been Nasiha, but there was an attitude of going straight in with a sharp blade instead of beating around the bush.

'Excellent,' she barked out. 'We will start tomorrow.'

She walked away, leaving me stunned and not a little fearful of what the morrow might bring.

RIDI, PAGLIACCIO

'Training with Nasiha going well?' asked Qeturah absently, tapping out a report with a practised staccato rhythm.

We were working in a place called Crue, a mid-sized town which straddled a few key trade routes. The population was large but constantly changing: merchants, tourists in transit to more interesting places, and of course our fellow civil servants, keeping the wheels of government moving smoothly (or, to quote Gilda at her most cynical, keeping the speedbumps of government before the greased wheels of commerce). It had little to offer in terms of taSadiri culture, but we were there for a teleconference of a more agreeable kind. The midpoint of the mission schedule was approaching and the media wanted to give us a little attention. Qeturah and Dllenahkh had been interviewed and the rest of the team got a piece of the spotlight as well. It was also a good time to catch up on paperwork and reports in actual offices with full-sized desks, courtesy of the local branch of Central Government.

'Quite well,' I replied, not hiding my pleased surprise. 'She's almost patient with me, but not too much. Keeps me sharp, y'know?'

'Those early mornings alone would keep you sharp,' she said dryly.

Of course Nasiha would not sacrifice her own meditation time for me, so I had the dubious honour of rising even earlier than the average Sadiri for my training. 'Well, she'd better let me off just this once, because tonight'll be a late one.'

We were going out on the town. I'd discovered that both Dllenahkh and Joral had managed to duck Gilda's cultural tours, and Qeturah thought we needed a little change of pace. She, Nasiha and Fergus opted for something contemporary in the form of a holovid at the local cineplex, and the rest of us were going to risk a stage production by a touring company. It was certainly rustic, right down to the paper playbill and glossy poster tacked up outside the theatre.

'*The End of the Laughter*. I recognise this one,' said Joral. 'Is this the adaptation of *Enough*, the taSadiri tale of a man who kills his unfaithful wife and her lover?'

'No,' said Tarik, shaking his head firmly. 'You have made a common error. In *this* one, he kills the man that he mistakenly thinks is her lover while her real lover gets away. This is an adaptation of the Ainya play *Deception*, not *Enough*.'

'Okay, not meaning to muddy the waters,' I said, 'but I'm fairly certain that what we have here is a version of *Otello*, one of the old Terran standards. Kills his not-unfaithful wife on the say-so of a man who was out to get him.'

Lian approached the poster more closely and read the fine print at the bottom out loud. 'Based on the Italian opera *Pagliacci*.'

We crowded around the poster. 'Who dies?' asked Tarik with interest. 'And was the infidelity real or alleged?'

'Is there some other production we might attend which does

not illustrate that dysfunctional pair-bonding is endemic in most cultures?' asked Dllenahkh with heavy disapproval.

I sighed and rolled my eyes. 'Everyone's a critic. Come on. Let's go in.'

Lian was already making for the foyer and I began to follow when I sensed something strange in the atmosphere. Turning back, I saw that the Sadiri had paused, almost in mid-stride, and were watching a pretty girl with tumbling black curls dashing towards a side-alley, presumably on her way to the back entrance of the theatre. She held a coat and a handbag tightly in one hand and a pair of shoes in the other, as if she had grabbed them up while running out the door and hadn't had time to pull herself together. It might have been better if she had, for she was wearing one of the skimpiest dresses I have ever seen. Her legs were pretty much uncovered, and I have *no* idea how she managed to run so fast with so little support for her upper assets. All the skin on view, and there was plenty, radiated a muted shimmer. I've seen some women try to imitate that look with silicon- and mica-rich lotions, hoping to be taken for a Zhinuvian woman with flexible limbs and even more flexible morals. It never looks the same.

Heads everywhere were turning, not just the Sadiri ones. There was a small collective sigh when she disappeared from view. I stared at my colleagues in amazement.

'You – all of you – you were looking that girl up and down!' I didn't know whether to be appalled or hugely entertained.

'First Officer Delarua,' Joral said in a tone so severe that he almost sounded like Dllenahkh in chastising mode, 'while it is true that we are Sadiri and therefore not prone to mental distractions, we are more than capable of aesthetic appreciation of the feminine human form.'

I had no answer to that, so I rounded on Tarik. 'Well then, you – you're married!'

'I am allowed to look,' he said uncertainly.

'I'd confirm that with Nasiha if I were you,' I said sceptically.

Dllenahkh's voice was utterly composed. 'There is no need to be concerned, Delarua. Sadiri possess far too much mental control to be susceptible to the mesmeric influence of Zhinuvians.'

'Oh, and that makes it better, does it?' I said. I was *this* close to wagging a finger and calling them naughty boys, so I made myself back off. I went and whispered to Lian instead, and we broke down in quiet tears of laughter at the concept of horny Sadiri.

Our seats were mid-house near the central aisle – decent enough for what we were seeing and hearing. It was of a style referred to as 'neo-opera'. It combined an absence of technological enhancement with a blend of contemporary styles of music, which meant that the performers had to be both vocally powerful and versatile. I wish I had time to tell you about the whole neo-opera movement and how it relates to the *rustica* backlash against audio smoothing and augmentation in musical performance, and *realissimo* effects in holovidding. I will say that there is a simplicity in the staging – not minimalist, that's another style – but a simplicity that pretends at amateurism but most definitely isn't.

I wasn't the least surprised to find that the mysterious golden girl was the leading lady, Nedda. Only a diva could risk turning up that late and not expect to be fired. I *was* surprised at the modesty of her costume, covering her to neck and ankle and wrist. She was good, perhaps a little weak in the singing, but with a presence and expressiveness that made up for it. Her husband, Canio, was played by a tall, dark, brooding type who seemed destined to go the Othello route, because this girl was just too popular. In addition to having a lover, Silvio, she had also attracted the attentions – unwanted, alas – of Taddeo. Silvio was unexpectedly weedy and scholarly, but Taddeo was boyish and sweetly besotted, offering a kind of comic foil to the unrelenting and obsessive passion of the two older men.

The performers were not Terran method actors. Method actors call up a strange mask of remembered emotion and fit it to the situation on stage. You can feel the reality of it, but something jars a tiny bit if you know what to look for. These ones were of the Ntshune verisimilitude school, which is very similar but can only be mastered by those with a touch of empathic ability. Basically, the actors draw on each others' feelings, and sometimes one great actor is all that is needed to provoke the right emotions and reactions from the rest of the company.

I'm mentioning this to give a reason for what I was doing. I was reading the actors.

Sadiri ethics on telepathy do *not* match Ntshune ethics on empathy. To the Sadiri, thoughts may be shared but are still considered private for the most part, and emotions are definitely private and must be shielded against as much as possible. Most Ntshune are comfortable reading anyone's emotions. It's part of how we communicate. We wouldn't pry for feelings that aren't intended for us, but projected emotions are fair game. A lot of Ntshune-influenced Cygnian cultures have internalised this distinction.

So when I turned and whispered excitedly to Dllenahkh that I was picking up real jealousy from one of the actors on stage, he gave me a look that made me feel like Joral on the receiving end of a lecture on Sadiri comportment. I was confused.

During the intermission, he pulled me aside and asked sternly, 'What has Nasiha been teaching you?'

I gave him a very old-fashioned look. 'What I did in there has nothing to do with what Nasiha is teaching me. I was simply reading the actors, as I always do.'

He didn't back down. 'The training you are receiving will improve and focus your empathic abilities, making casual use particularly unethical at this stage. I thought that you of all people would appreciate this.'

'Dllenahkh! They're actors! I'm not digging for state secrets; I'm trying to enjoy the play at another level! Now lighten up, please. People are looking at us strangely. I don't think they've ever seen a Sadiri arguing before.'

He exhaled slowly. 'I am not arguing.'

I had only been teasing him, but there was a tiny bit of stress on the word 'not', and for a moment he closed his eyes a fraction longer than a blink. 'Of course you aren't,' I said quietly, suddenly repentant. 'I won't do it again if it bothers you, okay?'

During the second act, I found myself distracted by Dllenahkh's unusual moodiness. He sat beside me, his attention entirely on the stage, but there was a set to his features that spoke of endurance rather than enjoyment. I began to feel guilty, but then when I glanced at Joral and Tarik, they appeared absorbed and interested. Not just a general Sadiri thing, then.

Then I saw it. It wasn't empathy – it was clearly visible on the man's face. Canio looked across at Nedda, and his eyes spoke murder.

I grasped Dllenahkh's arm. 'Tell me you didn't see that.'

'Grace,' he remonstrated, firmly removing my hand.

I did something then that was definitely unethical. In that rare moment of skin-to-skin contact between our hands, I reached out to read Canio. An ugly wave of jealousy and hatred came from Canio, washing over us like fouled water. Dllenahkh's hand convulsed on mine, for a moment gripping so tightly that it hurt, then fell away quickly.

'How did you do that?' He sounded more stunned than disapproving this time.

'Shhh! Listen!' I whispered frantically. It wasn't the right word perhaps, but he understood, because slowly, almost unwillingly, he put his arm along the back of my seat and rested his palm discreetly against my temple.

I concentrated on the scene before me. It was a moment of high drama, when Canio is acting the part of Pagliaccio and becomes so overwhelmed with jealousy and passion that he forgets he is onstage and pressures Nedda to tell him the name of her lover. When he picked up a knife, I shivered; when he chased her off the mini-stage, caught her and stabbed her in the belly, I jumped and turned away. I wasn't the only one in the audience who did so, but I was probably the only one whose disbelief hadn't been suspended. Dllenahkh broke contact with my temple and gripped my shoulder reassuringly.

Silvio was the next to be stabbed, but there was no emotion behind that one, only the actor's façade, the leftover grimace of pain and disgust from the earlier attack. I shivered again.

'I have to get out of here,' I muttered. I stood up and left just as the last notes of the final song were ringing out.

Lian was the first to come to me as I paced up and down in the foyer. 'What was that about? You looked like you were going to be sick. Are you okay?'

'Yes. No. I don't know.' I paced some more, biting my nails. 'I don't know what happened in there.'

'Well, whatever it was, you've made Joral, Tarik and Dllenahkh go into deep discussion.'

I stopped, suddenly self-conscious. 'Really? What are they saying?'

'Sadiri's not my thing, remember?' Lian remarked. 'Here they are. Just ask them.'

They looked horribly serious, more serious than even a Sadiri had any right to look. I cowered instantly, anticipating criticism. 'I'm sorry—'

'Apologies are not necessary,' said Tarik. 'We wish to know more about your experience of what happened during the performance.'

Dllenahkh looked around the foyer, now filling with people on their way out. 'But not here. Let us return to our lodgings.'

Qeturah was already asleep when we got back, but after Tarik brought Nasiha into the sitting room of our hotel, Lian frowned, shrugged and went to get Fergus, so there was almost a full house for the meeting.

Dllenahkh spoke immediately to Nasiha, not even waiting for her to be seated. 'Your pupil did something unusual tonight.'

Instantly intrigued, Nasiha settled herself in a chair and said, 'Oh?'

'She was able to obtain strong readings of an actor's emotions during the performance,' Dllenahkh stated.

Nasiha looked disappointed. 'Oh. She is capable on occasion of almost Ntshune sensitivity in reading people's emotions, but so far she has not been consistent in displaying this ability. It is nothing to be concerned about.'

'That was not what was unusual.'

I straightened in surprise.

'During the time she was detecting his emotions, our hands touched. I found myself in that instant able to read, albeit faintly, the thoughts of the actor – not his emotions, his thoughts. I found this sufficiently intriguing that I attempted, with permission, a unidirectional link with Delarua's mind. I found myself reading not her thoughts but the actor's, and with even greater clarity.'

Nasiha frowned. 'Some Cygnians *are* capable of non-contact telepathy, however it usually requires a strong level of projection from both parties. Moreover, we have already noted that Delarua's telepathic abilities are almost nil.'

'There is more,' Tarik said, giving Dllenahkh a significant look.

Dllenahkh returned the look steadily as he spoke to Nasiha. 'I consider that the actor's thoughts clearly indicated an intent to commit murder.'

'The actor *was* playing the part of a jealous husband,' Tarik pointed out. It sounded as if he had appointed himself devil's advocate.

'What is your opinion on this, Delarua?' Nasiha asked me.

'I don't know. I didn't hear any thoughts. I didn't know that's what Dllenahkh was doing. I thought he was picking up the emotions, same as I was. It wasn't acting, I can tell you that. When he took up the knife—' I shuddered again, feeling sick.

'It might be prudent to advise the authorities,' said Dllenahkh.

'Advise them of what, precisely?' asked Tarik mildly.

This was going nowhere. 'Look, Nasiha, why don't you just come see for yourself?' I blurted out. 'Sit next to me, put me in some kind of parallel link or whatever it is you need to do.'

'I would be interested in attending if only to determine what your mind is doing,' she mused.

'Wait a minute,' Fergus objected suddenly. 'Shouldn't you clear this with the Commissioner?'

'Of course we will, Fergus,' Lian said. 'But they're not kidding about this. It could be something serious, and it can't hurt to be sure.'

I was glad Lian had been there to see our reaction and was therefore on our side, because when we informed Qeturah the following morning, she wasn't convinced. 'I can't stop you from going if you think it's really necessary,' she said, 'but it sounds like a waste of time to me.'

'You could come with us,' I suggested. 'The more objective witnesses, the better.'

'I'm not that fond of neo-opera,' she said wryly, 'and I don't see why I should have to suffer. You can call me if anything happens.'

Lian stayed with her, but she let us take Fergus. Tarik stated that he would prefer not to sit through the entire thing again, and when he admitted that, Joral was happy to volunteer to stay behind as well. I didn't mind. I was well contented with the troops I'd been given. They did at least come to see us off in the hotel lobby that evening.

'Nice dress,' said Lian, all raised eyebrows. 'And the kohl's made a reappearance too, I see.'

'Nasiha insisted that we get front-row seats. A little more effort is required,' I said, primly adjusting the knee-length hem of my sapphire-blue dress. 'Ha! See?'

The others were also dressed for the occasion. I'm not a clotheshorse, but I can appreciate when someone finds a style that works for them. Nasiha was stunning in a severe, high-waisted, long-sleeved burgundy dress that fell to her ankles. Fergus and Dllenahkh had only to blend in, and chose to do so with the traditional black: Dllenahkh very dashing in a high-collared shirt under a hip-length tunic with matching trousers; and Fergus in a similar shirt, but with a short jacket which, to be honest, showed off the close fit of his trousers rather nicely.

I had no idea what to expect when we took our seats in the theatre, Nasiha on my left, Dllenahkh on my right, Fergus next to Dllenahkh. Nasiha must have sensed my trepidation, for she said to me, 'Delarua, all that is required is for you to relax. We will do whatever else is needed.'

I inhaled deeply, nodded and began the calming exercises she had taught me, closing my eyes for better focus. I felt when she touched her palm briefly to my face and when Dllenahkh did the same. Then she murmured, 'Your mind senses us dimly. How curious. I assume Dllenahkh is the elephant, which means I am the cat.'

I chuckled to myself. 'I hadn't thought about it, but yeah, that's how I picture you.'

She was silent for a while longer. 'This is most strange. Dllenahkh, was yesterday the first time that you linked your mind to Delarua's? There are connections between your minds that suggest a deeper level of bonding than could be achieved by a single one-way link.'

'Shhh,' said Dllenahkh, sounding a bit stifled. 'The orchestra is starting.'

I was very relieved that he spoke, for my usual reaction to any mention of our time with the adepts was an uncontrollable clenching of the jaw.

The production remained free of incident till intermission time and beyond. As the ending of the second act drew near, I sat forward slightly, eager to catch a glimpse of something to prove we weren't crazy. But Canio was passionately acting, nothing more. Nedda was giving an uneven but enthusiastic performance. I began to scan the other characters: Silvio, Taddeo, random people in the chorus. Nothing felt unusual, except that Taddeo's acting was a bit flat compared to the day before. I frowned, wondering if I should feel disappointed or relieved that nothing was going to happen.

'It is the knife,' Nasiha whispered suddenly.

'It is,' Dllenahkh confirmed.

For a moment I was baffled, then understanding coalesced into a horrific image. 'The knife!' I yelled. 'Don't use it! It's real!'

I started to move. I didn't expect anyone to take my yelling seriously. This was a touring production; they were probably too accustomed to shouts of 'Look behind you!' whether they were called for or not. Canio was a professional, all right. He didn't even blink at the interruption as he came down from the tiny stage onstage to confront Nedda in his manufactured fury. He pulled back his arm, blade at the ready, and drove it at her abdomen.

But Nedda knew. Somehow, between my shout and (who knows) some telepathic or empathic sense of her own, she did not stand to take the blade full on, as she had the night before. She turned her body, but too late to avoid a slash that tore costume and skin and drenched all in blood. She stumbled and fell to her knees, then collapsed completely.

Thoroughly fooled, the real audience gasped and applauded in appreciation for the unexpected twist of high-quality special effects. The stage audience, on the other hand, reacted very badly, well aware that things were not going as rehearsed.

A mad, high scream sounded over the general uproar. 'Finish it! Finish it!' Snatching the knife from the distraught Canio's immobile hand, Taddeo lunged for Nedda where she lay gashed and bleeding, but not yet seriously harmed.

It was enough time for me to scramble up the central stage steps and throw myself at him. Don't ask me how this happened. I am no superwoman, and I would never have done that sort of nonsense in a million years, but I blame the empathic connection. My adrenalin was as high as his, and I was terrified that someone was going to die in front of me. I must have surprised Nasiha and Dllenahkh because they moved belatedly and had to contend with the bedlam of the 'audience' pouring down the stage steps and jumping into the orchestra pit.

I realised my folly when he turned the knife on me. I twisted frantically and felt the blade tug my dress as the fabric was pierced and sliced from belly to shoulder. The point of the knife went mercifully up the space between my breasts and just missed my carotid artery. Then he disappeared in a crunching thud, Dllenahkh and Fergus side-tackling him with such force that I swore one or two of his bones must have broken somewhere.

'Ow,' I said weakly, and sat down suddenly on the stage, trying to hold the top of my dress together.

'Are you injured, Delarua?' Nasiha asked, crouching down beside me.

'No. Well, yes, but not by the blade. I think I pulled a muscle ducking that knife.' Even as I spoke I was looking around her to see what Nedda's fate had been. She was sitting up and surrounded by help. Someone had already brought out a medkit to begin treating her wound.

'I shall call the Commissioner,' said Nasiha, looking around in faint distaste at all the confusion. 'It will help if a high-ranking official corroborates our . . . *unique* evidence.'

She was right. If it hadn't been for Qeturah, we might have ended up detained for questioning, but her presence plus Sadiri gravitas meant that Nasiha and I were very courteously interviewed by a constable in one of the dressing rooms while I tried to patch the bodice of my dress with strips of gaffer tape. When the constable was finished, she informed us that the rest of the team were waiting for us in the green room and we were free to go.

'Won't you tell us what really happened?' I begged her.

'Can't give out the details of the case before trial, ma'am,' she said laconically. Then she looked at my pleading eyes and relented with a shrug, 'Let's just say that a *ménage-à-trois* can get really messy when it implodes. Give me a straightforward one-on-one any day, but city folk like to get creative – no offence to you, ma'am.'

'None taken,' I said. 'I'm homestead born and bred myself. I just work in the city sometimes.'

Smiling at that, she thanked us and left, taking her handheld with the record of our interviews.

I stood up and shifted my shoulders uncertainly, looking in the brightly lit mirror at my pathetic repair attempt. 'Do you think this'll hold, Nasiha? Or am I asking for trouble?'

'Excuse me?'

The shy words were accompanied by a soft knock. The girl with the glow, Nedda, the star herself, was at the door, peering in anxiously at me and Nasiha. She had changed her clothes and was carrying a garment bag over her shoulder. Apart from a slight shadowing under her eyes, she looked very much alive.

'You're okay!' I said gleefully. 'You really are okay!'

She broke into the biggest grin. 'They tell me I have you to thank for that.' She put her hand to her mouth, seemingly horrified. 'Oh, your dress! Your pretty dress!'

Some women are like that about clothes. Skin heals, but a really good dress is irreplaceable. 'I wasn't even scratched,' I told her.

'But you can't go out like that!' She cleared the counter of cosmetics with a sweep of her arm and flung the garment bag down. I watched as she unsealed it, impressed at the drama with which she invested every move, then began to stammer and demur when I understood her intentions.

'Nonsense,' she insisted. 'Here. I had it cleaned just yesterday.'

It rivalled the head-turner of the previous night. Dark-gold, extremely short and with decorative *ventilating* slits in the bodice, it would have caused an entire colony of Sadiri to stumble.

'Oh, I can't wear this!' I exclaimed. 'You . . . you've got the legs for it. I don't.'

'Yes you do,' she chided. 'Try it on.'

I stammered some more. Her face fell. 'You're right. Maybe if I wore dresses like that more often,' and she nodded at Nasiha's austere look, 'I wouldn't have so many problems.'

'No, don't say that!' I cried in dismay. 'Why would you say that? Don't make this your fault.'

'It is certainly not your fault,' said Nasiha. 'You are not even sufficiently Zhinuvian to impose any mental influence.'

Nedda looked suddenly happy. 'You can tell? Oh, that's such a relief! One Zhinuvian great-grandparent and I get smacked with the glimmer-skin and the shiny hair and stupid attitudes from men *and* women. Funny thing, genetics. Actually, I'm mostly Ntshune, can you believe it?'

'*I* can,' I said cheerfully. 'Dark eyes, wildly curly hair, sunny disposition . . .'

We grinned at each other. I started to strip. There was no way I was going to make this nice girl feel bad by refusing her help.

'Oh, it *does* fit! Just a bit longer on me, but that's . . . ooooh, hey, you've got anti-grav boosters in here! Niiice!' I threw caution, and my bra, to the wind, the former metaphorically, the latter literally.

'It's perfect,' she proclaimed. 'Keep it. Something to remember me by.' She sealed her bag again and waved to us as she headed for the door. 'Thanks again! Bye!'

I laughed happily. 'Test her, Nasiha. I'll bet she projects significantly on the frenzy scale.'

'Hmm,' said Nasiha. 'She is indeed very beautiful, and extremely vivacious. I hope you meant what you said to her.'

'What?'

'That this is not her fault.'

There was a small silence. 'Wow, you're taking lessons from Qeturah now?' I said, but without rancour. 'Okay, I get it. Barring the unethical use of Zhinuvian-strength mesmeric influence, I am not responsible for any foolishness that a man might care to perpetrate on my behalf.'

'Good. Now let us rejoin the others. Or rather,' and here she looked at me with eyes that narrowed, ever so slightly, with amusement, 'I will go and arrange transportation while you rejoin the others and tell them to meet me outside. I think it will be kinder for Tarik if I am not present when you walk in wearing that dress.'

Self-consciousness returned in a rush, but before I could reconsider, Nasiha had already departed with the shreds of my dress and my bra. I pulled myself together and went into the green room, walking with my head down as if guilty of some immense social crime. When I finally dared to glance up briefly, I almost wished I hadn't, because it only made me want to giggle. Joral's eyes were suddenly trained on the ceiling, Tarik's were fixed unseeingly on the ground and Fergus's mouth was open as he stared at me. Dllenahkh . . . I didn't have time to notice what he was doing.

'My dress *was* ruined,' I said defensively to the floor.

'Of course,' said Qeturah smoothly, 'and how kind of them to provide you with something to wear home.'

Behind her, Lian exploded into a fit of snorts and chuckles.

'If anyone would like to lend me a coat,' I said, my tone dignified and affronted.

'The night is quite warm,' said Dllenahkh innocently. 'Are you sure that a coat will be required?'

I'd had enough. I raised my chin and walked up to him, pausing at thirty centimetres, which, for a Sadiri, is well within the personal-space boundary. Everyone fell silent; smiles faltered and faded.

'You tell me,' I challenged him through gritted teeth.

He bowed his head as if in apology, but that wasn't all. Unfastening the front of his tunic, he shrugged it off his shoulders and draped it carefully around me.

'Thank you,' I told him, teeth ungritted.

Lian heaved a huge sigh. 'I'm not fat and I can't sing, but ladies and gentlemen, can we please go now? *La commedia è finita.*'

Zero hour plus one year five months four days

He fell asleep that night smiling at the memory of Delarua, adorably horrified at discovering her capacity for seductiveness, but refusing to retreat nonetheless. Such thoughts should have led to better dreams, but the recent drama had awakened other, darker memories that would not be denied.

The nightmares were lying in wait for him.

He was sitting on a ridge looking down at a familiar place, a place where he had once lived: smooth, cool residential domes in pale clusters like bunched fruit on a vine; branching, twining roadways connecting all together; a grey-green land under blue sky. It was not where he had lived last, but it was where he had lived longest, and the events that led to his leaving had been his first experience of how suddenly and utterly an ordinary life can shatter.

'How does it feel now?' A small savannah dog sat by his knee, sending the query mind-to-mind with a clarity that only a dream could provide. It focused sad eyes on him with gentle concern, waiting for an answer.

'It's empty,' he said with reluctance. 'There's no one alive there, only ghosts knocking on my soul.'

Already a sense of dread was growing, warning him that the dream was about to go badly wrong. A corner of sky obliged by turning black – not the black of storm cloud but a true malignancy boiling out like ink to tint and taint the atmosphere.

'They are already dead,' he declared defiantly. 'There is no need for this.'

The dog scrambled up. 'I'd get out of here if I were you,' it whined, looking on in terror as the sky was eaten. It skittered back, hesitated and finally dashed away into the tall grass behind Dllenahkh.

'Wait!' Dllenahkh shouted, standing up in haste.

The ridge was crumbling under his feet, but that was ordinary fear. The real nightmare came from the cold starlight shining through the encroaching darkness, the type of starlight that shines only on lifeless moons.

'It's done, it's over,' he insisted, telling the dream, telling himself. The untenanted houses and silent roads vanished in permanent dusk. He could not stop looking as the last of them went, even as his feet slipped and his hands grasped uselessly at loose soil and dry grass, trying to stop himself from falling, falling into nothing, falling for ever.

'Wake up, Councillor.'

Tarik's hand on his shoulder was a welcome anchoring. He sat up slowly, fighting the trailing remnants of the dream. 'What is it, Tarik? What's wrong?'

Tarik gestured to Dllenahkh's handheld on the table by his bed. 'A message from New Sadira just came in. Nasiha thought you should know as soon as possible.'

He woke up at last on a rush of adrenalin and grabbed his handheld. 'Do you know what it's about?'

'The Commander observes official protocol on secrecy to the letter,' Tarik said with far too much sincerity in his voice.

Dllenahkh said no more, knowing all too well that those rules said nothing about what might be communicated wordlessly by a superior officer to her lower-ranking husband. He looked at his handheld instead. When he finished reading and rereading, he looked up, but Tarik had already left. He turned off the handheld and lay down again, but the roil of emotions within him was so strong that he had to speak.

'So,' he said triumphantly to the darkness. 'Naraldi has come back to Cygnus Beta.'

THE MASTER'S HOUSE

'Do you think Nasiha will continue with us?' I asked the Commissioner. We were standing on the quayside watching supplies being winched aboard our new shuttle, a vessel capable of air and sea travel. Publicity surrounding the mission had been very positive, with more settlements asking to be tested for genetic or cultural Sadiri traits. As a result, our budget had been increased.

'I'd be very surprised if she left now,' Qeturah said with a smile. 'She seems to have some idea that to take time off for pregnancy would set a bad example. Something about "not creating the impression that females are fragile and childbearing is unusual". She checks out as perfectly healthy, so she can do as she pleases.'

'Maria was fine for Rafi. Gracie gave her a little more trouble,' I began, then shut my mouth. Even Maria's ailments might have been due to influence and were therefore not the best of examples.

'Satisfied with the verdict?' Qeturah asked after a short pause.

I shrugged. 'About what was expected.' Ioan's highly specific abilities and his apparently genuine contrition had landed him a fairly mild sentence of a year's rehabilitation to be followed by lifelong monitoring via sub-cortical implant. And he couldn't see Maria and the children again. Ever. The prosecutor hadn't been able to prove ill intent, but there *had* been reasonable doubt (hah!) and as a result the court's ruling showed both mercy and caution.

'Homestead's rented out now, and they're spending time at my mother's place. Rafi's attending a special school. He's not that impressed with it, but he'll adjust.' I knew I sounded like I was reeling off a report, but I figured I wasn't saying anything she didn't already know, and it catered to the illusion that I was once more willing to talk to her about my private life.

It seemed to work because Qeturah simply nodded, waited a few seconds, then changed the subject. 'Nasiha asked me about medical techniques to prolong a woman's years of fertility.'

I raised my eyebrows, absently multitasking as I ticked items off the inventory on my handheld and yelled an order to the longshoremen. 'Sorry, you were saying? Prolonging fertility? She's quite young by Sadiri standards – why should she be worrying about that now?'

'Oh, it wasn't for her. It was for you.'

I nearly dropped my handheld. '*What?* Why in the name of all . . . what business . . . *me*? What did I ever do to her?'

Qeturah almost laughed out loud. 'Relax, Delarua. It's a compliment . . . I think. She was saying that you should be registered on the special list for potential Sadiri brides, and when I pointed out that there was an upper age limit for that, she suggested that extending your fertile years would take care of any objections.'

I was already dazedly shaking my head at the wrongness of it all.

'Don't worry. I told her that with the amount of Ntshune heritage you have, you'll probably be able to have children for quite a bit longer than the average Cygnian. I estimate you have another twenty-five years, maybe even thirty.'

'Qeturah!' I hissed, glancing furtively at the nearest long-shoreman. '*Must* we discuss my private business out in the open where anyone could hear? What kind of doctor are you?'

I expected it to be a more-than-routine assignment. The Kir'tahsg Islands were famed for their remoteness and inaccessibility, and as such were the genetic and cultural equivalent of a vacuum-sealed flask. We always looked forward with interest to Fergus's safety briefings about the flora and fauna and the emergency-exit strategy, but this time it was the Commissioner's talk that got our attention.

'Protocol must be strictly observed,' she said.

'Is this one of the highly formal places? Even more formal than the Seelie Court?' I asked.

She folded her arms in a way I recognised as an attempt at self-support prior to saying something difficult. 'More than that. I want you all dressed in your most ceremonial garb. Titles must be used at all times. It's a society that relies on external cues to determine a person's rank and how they should be treated.'

She looked at us individually to make her point. 'Councillor. First Officer. Commander. Lieutenant. Sergeant. Corporal Lian, I'm giving you a rather sudden and substantial temporary promotion to full aide-de-camp, which inflates both your importance and mine. Councillor, I recommend that you refer to Joral as your First Secretary.'

She scanned us again, as if seeing us with an objective eye. 'Interplanetary Science Council formal blues. Civil Service formal blacks with white robe. Military Service dress whites. Whatever is appropriate for Sadiri culture, and don't be modest. Wear all medals and special decorations. The gulf between servant and master is wide and deep in this place. I don't want any of you stranded on the wrong side.'

Our first sight of the main, eponymous island was as forbidding as the Commissioner's briefing. There was nothing resembling a beach or a landing strip. High rocks surged straight up out of violent surf, and the entire landscape appeared to consist of inclines of forty-five degrees or greater. There was evidence of civilisation, however. Inland, terraced gardens girdled the hills like green ribbons bordered by hewn grey rock. The same grey rock rose up as walled cities, which then blended into bare grey mountain, making it difficult to see where man-made wall ended and natural cliff began. They say *kir'tahsg* means 'invincible' in some long-dead Cygnian language, and it was easy to see how the island had earned its name. We had to land in open ocean, submerge and then resurface in a huge hangar-like cave.

The welcome, however, was far warmer than the first impression. Our group was taken by hovercar to the Hall of the Master of Kir'tahsg, an impressive palace in the central citadel surrounded by extensive gardens with tidily trimmed trees and manicured lawns. I was expecting the minimalist decor naturally preferred by the Sadiri mind, a mind which can be sucked into pondering fractal formulae at the mere sight of a Paisley-patterned rug. Not so here, neither outdoors nor in. The servants and officials of the Master's household were richly dressed. It was not ostentatiousness; it was a more subtle show of plain though rich fabrics, simple but skilfully made embroideries. Precious metals and gems in a classic, understated design were displayed in the furnishings and ornaments, and on the wrists and necks and ears of the nobles and higher-ranked servants. The nobles also wore their hair long, tied back with jewelled velvet bands or enamelled clasps.

Oh yes, the hair. Let me tell you about the hair. It was too obvious and a little discomfiting. The Master, the officers of his guard, the Master's Heir and all other persons of rank or standing at the Hall were Sadiri as Sadiri could be. Their hair shone brightly and their skin had a very slight Zhinuvian-like glow. The servants, on the other hand, all had dull, close-cut hair and low-luminance skin. I understood Qeturah's desire to have us Terran-types look as official as possible.

The Master was as impressive as the Faerie Queen, but his was an aged and venerable appearance. He did not rise from his seat, even though he appeared to be lean and physically fit. He had us seated according to our rank and post, and listened courteously as Dllenahkh and Qeturah made their requests. At first I thought everything would go easily, because when his eyes rested on the Sadiri it was with an air of great gladness and contentment, as if he were seeing something finally come to pass after a long wait. I was wrong.

'Regretfully we must decline to participate in this genetic testing,' the Master stated baldly.

Qeturah was taken aback at this stark refusal, given without excuse. 'We find genetic testing useful to determine compatibility. We also use it as a guide to assessing the average psionic potential of members of a community.'

The Master smiled. 'With respect to psionic abilities, I can immediately inform you that we have none. The practice of the mental disciplines has, alas, died out, and with them all the telepathic skills of our ancestors. As for compatibility with the Sadiri . . . well, look at us.' He waved languidly as if to indicate their entirely

Sadiri appearance, but I couldn't help glancing at the short-haired Terran servants.

Still bemused, Qeturah reached for a glass from a tray offered by a small boy, but her fingers failed to grip it safely and it smashed on the floor. 'I'm so sorry—' she began.

The butler of the Hall interrupted her with a terse command to the boy which sounded to me like 'See you do not fail again' or 'We will ensure that you do not fail again'. It might have been the latter, because the boy went wide-eyed with fear and fell to his knees, trying to gather up the pieces of glass.

While I was watching this closely, I heard the Master say, 'Take the boy out and bring another glass of refreshment for the Commissioner.'

The boy, naturally, looked even more terrified and cut his hand on an edged fragment.

Nasiha erupted from her seat, stepping heedlessly over the broken bits and debris with an intimidating crunching noise. She picked up the boy and held his fist firmly to staunch the trickle of blood that was now threatening to stain the marble tiles. '*I* will take him out,' she informed the Master bluntly. 'Have this cleaned up,' she told the startled butler. 'Delarua,' she continued, 'our medkit. Hurry.'

The Master only smiled faintly. I think he was accustomed to something that I was only just learning – pregnant Sadiri are not to be trifled with. I raced to Qeturah's rooms for the medkit and returned to the corridor outside the reception room where Nasiha was speaking soothingly to the boy. We got him cleaned and sealed up in a matter of minutes. He stood gazing in awe at his hand as I packed away the medkit.

'Run along, now,' said Nasiha kindly.

He did so, giving us an uncertain smile.

'Nasiha, I don't mean to be rude, but have you found yourself to be a bit . . . well . . .' I couldn't use the word *emotional*. 'A bit more vehement than usual, perhaps?'

'Of course,' she snapped. 'It is a natural consequence of the pregnancy. The maternal, protective urge must increase.'

'Oh well, as long as it's *natural*,' I mumbled dubiously.

She looked at me impassively and handed me a small sample vial filled with red fluid.

'What's this?' I said, thoroughly confused, but taking it nonetheless.

'The boy's blood. Likely some skin as well. I think you should test it.'

I frowned. 'I'm not sure I should. There's no real medical reason for it, and the Master did bar us from genetic testing.'

Nasiha nodded. 'I understand. But answer me this, Delarua. When I held the boy's hand, I detected that the concentration of telepathic receptors in his palm was far above the average amount for Terrans. How does he come to be a servant in a household that seems to have taSadiri nobility and a Terran servant class?'

I blinked at this new information. 'That does make me curious,' I admitted. 'But don't tell the Commissioner, okay? This is off the record.'

I went to her quarters early the next day. 'Terran, yes, but also a bit of Sadiri and quite a lot of Zhinuvian. How did you guess?'

Nasiha shrugged. 'When the Master speaks, there is much that he keeps back. The nobles of the Hall and the higher-ranking servants have taken similar lessons in evasion. It has been my experience that a rich and well-run household is like an iceberg.

You see the tip, but you must ask about the invisible ninety per cent that holds it up.'

Tarik, who had been quietly listening for some time, said something disconcerting. 'I have further information on that ninety per cent. I rose before sunrise as usual for my meditation and looked out through our window down at the Citadel. I saw street-sweepers and garbage-collectors. I was unsure at the time, due to the distance from which I was observing, but given this new information I believe I can say with certainty that they were Zhinuvian.'

'I think it is time we spoke to the Commissioner,' Nasiha decided.

'Please find a way to leave out my part in this,' I begged her. She gave me a look.

'Fine.' I sighed. 'Why don't I fetch Dllenahkh and Joral for you?'

Joral was nearby in the quarters he shared with Dllenahkh, so I simply directed him to report to Nasiha. I had to go outside to find Dllenahkh. Nasiha had made some concessions to her 'delicate condition' and as a result had declined an invitation from the Heir to go horse riding. Tarik had opted to stay with her and be the good and supportive husband, which left Dllenahkh to bond with the Heir. They were galloping around a small race-track girdling a paddock. It looked like a lot of fun. The Heir was winning, but not by much, in deference to his guest.

'You're a natural, Councillor!' I heard him cry merrily.

Dllenahkh carefully reined in his mount, which was still excitable after the brief run. 'We have similar beasts on the Sadiri homesteadings. I have ridden a time or two before.' Then he looked around and saw me. 'Delarua!'

I made a bow. 'By your leave, Your Grace. Councillor, your presence is requested up at the Hall.'

It was partly my fault, I know. As I bowed, I peeked up to look at the Heir. His hair was tied back with a scarlet cord, except for two long locks falling almost into his eyes. When I straightened, I even took a glance at Dllenahkh, assessing his hair in comparison. It was windswept from the gallop, pushed to one side of his forehead in an untidy dark brown wave, but even with hair cut more like a servant than a noble, he still managed to look more regal than the Heir. The Heir, however, saw only the glance directed to him, and took my caution for flirtation and my curiosity for interest.

'You're new,' he said, swinging himself down from the saddle with a grin.

He walked up to me and set the tip of his small whip under my chin. I barely had time to go wide-eyed with shock and outrage before a shadow fell over us.

He looked at Dllenahkh with a sly smile. 'Sorry, Councillor. One of yours?'

There was a moment of complete silence as Dllenahkh pointedly ignored the question.

'May I present First Officer Grace Delarua, member of this mission and second in civil rank to the Commissioner,' Dllenahkh finally said, his bland tone a warning all unto itself.

The Heir raised his eyebrows, blinked and dismissed me, turning his attention back to Dllenahkh. 'We should race again before you go. Tomorrow, perhaps? See you at dinner.'

He strode off, striking his leg idly with his whip.

'What was that?' I said, stunned at such discourtesy.

'I suspect you are not noble enough to marry nor yet common enough to bed,' Dllenahkh mused clinically, following the Heir's departure with narrowed eyes. 'I gathered from his conversation that in his world women rarely serve any other purpose.'

175

'Creep,' I said succinctly. 'Look, I'm here because Nasiha and the Commissioner want to have a chat with you. Think you can tear yourself away from your new friend?'

'With pleasure,' Dllenahkh said, matching my flat tone. 'It strikes me, Delarua, that this society is far more about appearance than substance where being Sadiri is concerned.'

'Oh, you wise, wise man,' I replied, sighing.

I escorted Dllenahkh to Qeturah's rooms, where Nasiha and Tarik were already waiting. Fergus, who was stationed at the door, seemed to be glowering a touch more than usual, but he gave me a sideways glance and something in his eyes lightened briefly.

'Like to get your hands on some genetic samples?' he said, in much the same tone that a Tlaxce City hustler would use to describe rare and reasonably priced merchandise that might or might not have fallen off the back of a freight car.

'You know I would,' I breathed just as quietly.

'Good,' he said, and turned to his colleague. 'Lian, if the Commissioner needs anything, cover for me. I'll be back soon.'

Lian looked disapproving, but merely went into position beside the door in reproachful silence.

Fergus looked me up and down, assessing my appearance. 'Take off the white robe. The blacks will pass for ordinary wear.'

'What about Joral?' I asked, removing the garment and pressing it into Lian's hands. 'Shouldn't he come, too? I might need help.'

'He can't come. He looks too much like *them*,' Fergus muttered as he started off.

'Okay,' I said, following his long stride with some difficulty. 'What's going on, exactly?'

'Lian and I discovered a few things yesterday that we thought should be brought to your attention.' He ducked down a small staircase.

I was just about to ask him why he hadn't simply spoken to Qeturah when he came to a closed door, knocked, and said something unrecognisable.

'What language is that? I don't know it,' I said.

He gave me a sombre look. 'I'd be very surprised if you did.'

The door opened, a few centimetres at first, then wider. Inside was a small group of people seated around a table, a very mixed company indeed. Fergus drew me in while I stared, reading the social language of their attire. There were higher-ranked servants and lower-order domestics. There were also menials who I had not seen before, with rough, plain garments, shaven heads and skin that gleamed in the dimly sunlit room.

Fergus broke the oppressive silence. 'Tell her, and speak quickly. We don't have much time.'

A tall man with pale eyes and shining skin stood up. 'I am Elion. These are some of the people who have been told to disappear for the duration of your visit. Let me show you why.' He indicated himself. 'Zhinuvian, you'd think, by the look of me, but my father was a noble. But with these eyes there's neither status nor work for me within the Master's household.'

He moved on to a beautiful woman with dull olive skin, brown eyes and long, shining locks that fell over her face. Surprisingly, she was wearing the clothes of a higher-ranked servant.

'My half-sister. My mother had such hopes! She was the first of our family to rise above the servant class. But none of her children has lived longer than a week. The first had no eyes, the rest had deformed hands and feet, all of them had weak hearts. Now they fear to allow her to bear more children, hence the demotion – and the warning.'

He drew aside her hair so I could see the brand that marred her face from temple to jaw, a broad, featureless scar that had neither letter nor symbol, and served no other purpose but to make her ugly. She kept her head lowered, blushing ruddy with shame.

The next woman at the table was a little darker of skin than Qeturah, but with hair so brightly black that it glowed with an iridescent green, clearly unlike the glossy browns and blue-black common to the Sadiri.

'Zhinuvian and Terran. You've met her son. You helped him when he cut himself. No matter. He's been punished since in a place where they don't mind if the blood flows.'

'What—?' I began, then faltered at my rudeness in interrupting. 'I mean, I think I understand what you're telling me, but what do you expect me to do about it? Our Sadiri colleagues are already aware that they are not being shown all of Kir'tahsg. They're not easily fooled. And if you're worried about how the boy is being treated, why not simply go to the local authorities?'

A Zhinuvian-looking woman who had not yet been introduced spoke up, worriedly addressing Fergus in that strange tongue. He replied in a reassuring tone.

'This is Karya,' said Elion. 'She is a new arrival to the household. A Zhinuvian slave – bought, not Citadel-born.'

'Slavery doesn't exist on Cygnus Beta,' I said sharply, not keen on being played for a softhearted fool. 'Aren't you paid wages? Every one of you must be registered on the Revenue and Pensions System. There's no way the Master could get around that.'

Elion's mouth curved up in a cynical smile. 'All you have to do is claim the credits appropriately. The cost of our food, our shelter, our clothing – somehow it all balances out perfectly.'

'Impossible. The government looks for that kind of dodge.'

'Oh, there is an excess of credits. But it doesn't come to us. It's paid in instalments to our former owners.'

'The Master has ties to a cartel on Zhinu,' Fergus said quietly. 'They've been buying from them for generations, and when there's infertility, or birth defects, or rebellion, some selling happens, too.'

'You don't have to believe us,' said Karya proudly, 'but take our genetic data. Someone might still be registered as missing. You'll get the genetic profile you want, and we'll get the chance to be found.'

People always think genetic analysis can do miracles. There was no global database, yet. We were not connected to any galactic database. There was no guarantee that we could find a missing-person file with matching DNA. I shook my head at the folly, even as I heard myself saying, 'Yes.'

The data that came to me was disturbingly thorough. They did not only provide samples of their own DNA. The nobility of the Citadel was well represented as their maidservants, valets and cleaning staff ransacked their rooms and personal effects for genetic traces. Lian gave me a slightly anxious frown as I accepted the first of the stolen samples, but I replied with silence and Lian acknowledged with a slow, still-worried nod. I could not leave Kir'tahsg without answers, ethics or no. I left Fergus and Lian to see to the collection of the rest of the samples so I could get started in the lab, but I was still forced to press Joral into service to get the analysis completed within three days. The results were all too clear.

Joral was puzzled. 'I do not understand. Have we not encountered three genetically distinct groups on Kir'tahsg: taSadiri, Terran and Zhinuvian?'

'Looks are deceiving, Joral,' Lian muttered dourly.

'Exactly,' I snapped. 'You could choose a mirror-skinned, pale-eyed, dull-haired servant and you'd have the same chance of getting Sadiri characteristics out of the brew as with any of those shiny-haired elitists.'

'But we have seen this before. What has made you so angry?' Joral queried.

'Besides the borderline slavery, you mean?' said Fergus, his tone caustic.

'Easy, man. He didn't see what we saw,' Lian tried to pacify him.

'We only have Elion's word for the wages set-up,' I cautioned. 'Let's not fling accusations without a proper inquiry.'

Fergus gave me a stare. 'Not you too,' he snarled.

'What do you mean?' I asked, frowning.

'The Commissioner. She told me that we're not to interfere, that it's not our job.'

'Well, like it or not, she's right!' I exclaimed. 'You planning to be a one-man army? You think you can bring down the local government?'

His face set in a determined mask. 'The army's already there. All they need is a little leadership and some key bits of intelligence.'

'Oh no,' I laughed hollowly. 'That's not going to happen, Sergeant.'

'Not feasible,' murmured Lian, though a touch regretfully.

He grinned fiercely at Lian, part gallows-humour, part warning.

'That field promotion you got is just for decoration. I still outrank you, so if I say we go—'

'You'll say nothing of the sort,' I shouted. 'If it comes to that, I outrank you, and we're not doing anything so stupid just because your head's all tied up by a pretty Zhinuvian!'

Fergus turned on me, and for a moment I honestly thought he was going to hit me. 'I was enslaved by the Zhinuvians,' he said.

'What?' I said, my fury erased in an instant by utter shock.

'They've got the best merchant fleet in the galaxy. Do you really think all their cargoes are legal? This kind of set-up? Too familiar. I know Elion spoke the truth. That's how they work. Ironic, isn't it? Terra gets more protection from the Zhinuvian cartels than the rest of us. Makes you wonder if there's any point to the Caretakers dragging us here.' His voice vibrated deep and low with pure hatred.

I suppose up to that point I had wanted to disbelieve. The idea that trafficking could take place right under the nose of the Cygnian government, that we were no more immune from oppression than any other planet – it shook me. I had been holding on to the possibility that Elion had exaggerated, misunderstood, hallucinated, lied, but now I had to consider it as truth. I saw Lian's calmly sympathetic face and realised that this was not news – at least not the bit about Fergus's past. I looked at Joral, and he was visibly appalled, considering not only who was selling the slaves, but who was buying.

'Continue to follow your orders,' I mumbled. 'I have to speak to the Commissioner.'

Fergus's anger radiated from his glare and from the tension of his stance, scalding me even at a distance. I stumbled, set my shields stronger and left the shuttle in a daze.

'Wait!' Joral called.

I slowed my pace so he could catch up, but I did not stop and I did not look at him.

'What do I say to the Councillor?' he panted.

'You tell him everything. Everything.' I stopped for a moment, hung my head and admitted, 'I'm sorry we didn't do our research more thoroughly before coming here. We've been wasting your time.'

'Delarua!'

It was the first time without chemical influence that he had ever addressed me by name and without title, so I paid attention and looked into his eyes.

'You cannot blame yourself for this. We want to search out any and every aspect of our culture that has survived. We have learned much, both optimal strategies and pitfalls, concerning the future preservation and development of our society. We are grateful. Truly.'

Joral was so endearingly earnest that, not for the first time, I had the urge to hug him. I restrained myself and settled for a half-smile and a pat on the arm. Then we hastened on our way to brief our superiors.

I suspect his conversation might have been a lot more straightforward than mine, though difficult in its own way. Qeturah listened to what I had to say, and then she got that expression on her face, the same one I had given Fergus: the one that was weighing the pros and cons of action and trying to work out not simply what was right, but what was possible. She went to the window, looked out for a moment and then began to pace the room slowly.

'You know,' she said sternly, throwing me a frown over her

shoulder, 'unauthorised acquisition and testing of genetic material is a chargeable offence.'

I knew it. I had known it when I did it. I said nothing.

'And besides one man's word, you have no actual proof.'

'The results of the analysis—' I began, my hands open and pleading.

'Only prove that they have an ugly class system based on phenotype,' she cut in, stopping for a moment to face me before resuming her slow, troubled pacing. 'Some Cygnian societies do. It may not make them desirable, but it doesn't make them criminal.'

'Qeturah,' I tried, coaxing slightly, 'I think this one crosses the line.'

'Unless we can prove human trafficking, the most we can do is submit a report and let Central Government determine in due course whether an inquiry is needed,' she said sensibly, correctly and disappointingly.

'Qeturah—'

'Grace! *Look* at this place. They don't call it invincible for nothing.' She sank back into a chair as if exhausted in both mind and body, all considered paths leading to a dead end.

My heart sank. I had been holding back one last card, something that could destroy the ruling class of Kir'tahsg. Now I had no choice but to play it.

'I have proof of something that *is* criminal,' I said softly.

She stiffened. 'Why didn't you say—? Oh. It's based on the material you obtained illegally. Well, that'll be a lot of help.'

'Such proof is admissible once the crime is sufficiently severe and the officer who obtained the proof is suitably reprimanded. After all, you weren't planning on letting my lapse in procedure slide, were you?'

Qeturah sat up. I think the look on my face was beginning to worry her. It certainly worried me, because my facial muscles had no memory of that particular expression. It was anger, contempt and grim resignation of the kind that proclaims 'Those who are about to die salute thee'.

'Analysis proves that the Master of Kir'tahsg is the genitor of over ten per cent of the domestics of his household,' I said coldly. 'The Heir, who is yet young, has only managed to contribute two offspring to the general roll of servants. I cannot give you precise numbers. Some of the kinship lines were . . . complicated.'

Qeturah blinked and turned her face away. 'You would have had to run analyses on individual, identified data to get that information,' she said quietly. 'As civil servants and scientists we are only allowed to give aggregated results on genetic data unless there is specific medical cause. This is a direct violation not only of our mission protocols, but of the General Code *and* the Science Code.'

Again I chose to say nothing. I was too angry and miserable to speak.

'Of course, any genitor who refuses to acknowledge and provide for offspring at the appropriate social and economic level is guilty of an indictable offence. And if sexual coercion is also a factor . . .' She trailed off, rubbing her temples.

'I *have* noticed that the Child Protection Division tends to move with greater speed and efficiency than the Department of Internal Affairs,' I said derisively. 'Since we can't make the accusation of slavery stick, do you think *this* charge might do?'

She regarded at me sadly, overlooking my misdirected bitterness. 'It must. You're ending your career for it.'

'Well,' I said. 'I can live with that.' I almost hiccoughed over the lie.

She continued to gaze at me steadily. I looked back without wavering. After a few seconds of this, she gave up and tossed me a handheld. 'I'll be needing a full report and confession.'

I caught it, sat down, pulled out a stylus and began.

Our courteous but cold farewells on the morrow gave no indication of what was to come. In fact, it wasn't until our mission debriefing in a quayside inn back at the mainland port that some members of the team realised the full scope of what had occurred and what was going to be done about it. Even Fergus looked a bit startled when Qeturah said that I was relieved of my appointed post forthwith. Lian, who knew everything, looked angry. Joral seemed confused and started to whisper something to Dllenahkh, who merely nodded and spoke a few words that appeared to satisfy him. The two Science Council officers looked grave, but Nasiha caught my eye and gave me a small nod. I kept my shields up and my expression blank. I must have looked more Sadiri than the Sadiri.

Of course, the moment Qeturah dismissed us I immediately left the inn's meeting room and walked out into a dim twilight of sea mist. I was too angry to cry so I started to run, my boots pounding the flagstones of the quayside. I ran past the end of the harbour, reaching a small bay with moored pleasure craft dimly visible offshore. Flinging stones from the pebbled beach into the water helped to relieve my feelings, but then I accidentally struck a boat in the growing darkness and a startled shout made me realise that this was no time to act like a delinquent adolescent. I slunk back to our lodgings at the inn, feeling more surly than ever and hoping to slip in quietly, but that was impossible. Dllenahkh was seated outside in the inclement, unwelcoming murk, a cup and a steaming pot of tea on the table beside him, a similarly steaming cup in his hand and the light from a lantern above making the scene all golden and dreamy, like a Turner painting.

I stared. He glanced at me, then set down his cup to pour tea into the other cup. I sat down before it, picked it up and sipped in silence for a while. He offered no conversation, merely sat peacefully in the lantern light and let the steam from his tea wreathe around his face as he drank leisurely.

'Ever wonder if you've done the right thing?' I asked him finally.

'Frequently,' he replied. 'Legalities notwithstanding, to *not* wonder indicates a dangerous lack of awareness of the near-infinite array of choices presented by life. More tea?'

I held out my cup in mute assent. His fingertips brushed mine as he took it from me and I felt a wave of . . . something. Approval? Affection, perhaps? I looked at him, startled, and he held my gaze for a second before focusing on pouring.

I spoke simply to have something to say. 'I've just torpedoed my career and all you can do is offer me more tea?'

'Yes,' he replied, handing me back my cup. 'It appears to be having a calming effect.'

I smiled in spite of myself. 'Thank you, Dllenahkh, but y'know, I think that's you, not the tea.'

A faint smile curved his lips as he looked at me. For a moment, I saw . . . I don't know how to explain it, but I saw just a man – not an offworlder, not a foreigner, nor even a colleague and a friend, but just a man, relaxed, smiling, glad to be in my company. I felt an odd, fragmenting sensation of suddenly perceiving something differently and having the whole world change as a result. My smile faltered, my breath caught and I lowered my eyes briefly before glancing back up again, unsure of what I had seen.

He was still gazing at me, his face now inscrutable, but his eyes were not distant. They were curious, as if he too were questioning something he had just glimpsed.

'Drink,' he said softly. 'Do not let your tea get cold.'

UNFINISHED BUSINESS

'Enter,' I said dully.

Nasiha came into my room. 'You are late for your meditation practice.'

I was sitting on my bed in my underwear, surrounded by clothes – Civil Service formal blacks, Forestry greens, various bits and pieces that were no longer relevant to my life.

'I can't find anything to wear,' I said.

She looked at the heap, then met my eyes. 'I may have something that will fit you. I too am having difficulties with my wardrobe. Today, we will go shopping.'

I came down to breakfast dressed in my own trousers and undershirt, and a Sadiri tunic borrowed from Nasiha. I assembled a plate of food and poured a mug of hot chocolate, but before I had to brace myself to face the table where Qeturah, Fergus and Lian were seated, Dllenahkh murmured at my shoulder, 'It is a warm, bright morning. We should sit outside.'

I followed him, ducking my face into my mug for a sip as we passed my former colleagues. Outside was glorious, already starting to be scorching hot, but with a fresh wind off the sea that eased the humidity. We took a table next to Nasiha and Tarik and were soon joined by Joral. I ate and drank, absently aware of the conversation in Sadiri, but not really paying attention to what was being said.

'Are you Sadiri? *Really* Sadiri?' The slightly hushed query came from a little boy, about seven years old, standing on the pavement in front of us. He had straight dark-brown hair that spiked up messily, and the tips gleamed in the morning sun. 'I've seen you on the holos.'

They all stopped talking and focused on the boy, their faces softening to near-smiles.

'Yes,' said Dllenahkh, leaning towards him slightly. 'We are really Sadiri. Are you Sadiri, too?'

The boy grinned and shook his head vigorously, clearly pleased to have been asked. He looked ready to say more, but a girl walking about ten metres further ahead shouted back at him, her expression that of an exasperated older sister. 'Hurry up or we'll be late!'

The boy dipped a quick bow, more of a nod, which the Sadiri gravely returned, then ran off to join the girl. Dllenahkh's gaze was reminiscent, perhaps even wistful, as he watched him go.

'Do you have any children, Dllenahkh?' I asked curiously. The moment the words were out I froze in open-mouthed horror, too appalled at myself to even begin an apology. While it was true that he *might* have grown children off-planet, it was still an impossible question to ask any of the Sadiri, with so many families in the past tense.

His expression was mild. 'There is no need to be distressed, Delarua. I never had any children. The opportunity did not arise.'

There was definitely a slight ruefulness in his voice. Nasiha must have caught it, too, for she said firmly, 'You are still in your prime, Councillor. You should make it a priority after the end of the mission.'

Dllenahkh gave her a look that reminded me partly of Lanuri's bemused irritation at being handled, and partly of my own response to Joral's comment that I was 'too old'. I smirked, recalling Qeturah's revelation that Nasiha had been taking an interest in my reproductive capabilities. Sadiri pregnancy hormones must be *fierce*.

'Thank you for your advice, Commander, but you must remember that I have recently been involved in helping to mitigate the consequences of over-hasty attempts to pair-bond by the young Sadiri of the settlement. To do something similar would set a very poor example. I would rather see many children in one stable Sadiri household than several ill-chosen unions producing one child apiece. To that end I congratulate you for your start,' and here he graciously inclined his head, 'and wish you many more offspring in the future.'

It was smoothly done, and all the more so for being sincere. Nasiha looked – there's no other way to describe it – *misty*. Tarik's face held the admiring expression of a man who is taking detailed mental notes for future reference. I hid a smile, wondering to myself how Dllenahkh had learned to stroke the female ego so well.

Of course, Nasiha in a good mood meant she was in fine form when it came to shopping. She immediately discovered the port's best bazaar, uploaded a map of the layout to her handheld and began to list aloud her goals for the expedition.

I rubbed my head and tried to find the right words. 'Ah, Nasiha, I can't exactly splurge. I have only one month's severance pay, and

I shouldn't touch my savings until I get another job – and an apartment, too, seeing as how mine's sublet for a few more months.'

'Do not concern yourself. I have in mind only a few simple garments, such as would be suitable for both professional and everyday wear.'

I surrendered and let Nasiha go into mother-mode. She draped me in a long off-white wrap that trailed over one shoulder, and picked out a week's worth of undershirts in basic colours. She matched two split-skirts, one long skirt and two pairs of trousers with Sadiri-style tunics, and selected two long dresses, either of which could pass at formal affairs with the right accessories.

'After all,' she said without a blink, 'the dress you were given at the opera house event may not be appropriate for all venues.'

I was changing in and out of several outfits, all the while frantically calculating credits in my head, but by the time I approached the vendor he shrugged and said, 'The lady's already put it on her bill.'

I went over to where Nasiha was frowning disdainfully at a large, shapeless dress with a lace-up front. 'Nasiha! You can't pay for all this!'

Her expression became artfully puzzled. 'It is more efficient to charge all the items to one account, especially since I have been granted a maternity allowance specifically for the purpose of obtaining new clothing. No doubt we can settle the matter between ourselves at a later date. I understand it is a Cygnian tradition to buy educational gifts for one's godchildren?'

I was stymied, and it showed in my face because her eyes got that very Sadiri look of smug satisfaction as she said, 'Now. Accessories.'

By this time I was starting to feel as if she were in truth using me as practice for any daughter she might have. She found a clasp for my wrap, which was sensible; selected two belts, which was practical; and then she was musing over decorative hair combs, which was frankly unnecessary.

'Look at me, Nasiha! My hair is *this* short!' I expostulated, showing her my finger and thumb one centimetre apart.

She looked me over. 'Yes. I think you should let it grow longer.'

She bought the combs.

I realised she couldn't be stopped, so I tried diversion instead, pointing out wraps and tunics and dresses for her own wardrobe. While she was in a changing room, I slipped away and bought something quickly, putting it aside till the right moment.

Still, I tried reason. 'You say we can settle this at a later date, but I don't know when next I will see you. Won't you be returning to New Sadira after this mission?'

She looked into the distance, her gaze reflective. 'I do not know.'

I didn't know what to say to that. She glanced at me, then returned to looking over the fabric of the dress she was considering. 'The Councillor has invited us to stay on Cygnus Beta. He believes that Tarik and I would help to promote the right image of Sadiri family life.'

'Well, you *would*,' I said sincerely. 'They really do need more women there – and I don't just mean prospective brides. Women who can be sisters, aunts, grandmothers. They're half a people as they are.'

'You and the Councillor are much of the same mind. He has asked for female elders to come to the Cygnus Beta homesteadings.'

'Good for him. *Very* good.' I smiled with deep satisfaction. It was nice to know that Dllenahkh hadn't pinned all his hopes on the bride-search mission.

She chose a dress, put it into my arms with the others I was holding for her and started to examine another garment. 'You have a particular regard for the Councillor.'

I laughed at her casual manner. 'Oh no you don't. Whatever you may have thought, whatever speculations you and Tarik may have indulged in, we don't have that kind of relationship.'

Again that quick glance. 'But you could. You are already quite attached to each other, in more ways than one.'

I felt a twitch of warning and moved my tongue away from my teeth, just in case she came too close to matters I couldn't discuss. 'You heard what he told you,' I hedged. 'He has to set a good example to the younger Sadiri. He can't marry just anybody – and certainly not a disgraced ex-civil servant.'

'I only mention it because . . . who knows when next you will see each other?'

I stood still, half-hidden by the clothing piled up in my arms and glad for it. That hurt. That actually hurt. I'd accepted my career was over and I'd have to leave the mission to find other work, but I hadn't paid attention to the fact that I'd never work with Dllenahkh again.

'Delarua?'

'I'll miss him,' I admitted, my words somewhat muffled. 'But that's no reason for a shotgun wedding. Nasiha, I'm surprised at you. Are you—?' I couldn't say *hormonal*. 'Is this because you're . . . ?' I couldn't say *pregnant* either. '*Why* exactly are you bringing this up?'

She took the pile of clothes from me and looked at me as if I were stupid. 'It is obvious that he regards you highly as well. I was under the impression that Cygnians are accustomed to arranged marriages?'

I followed her to the vendor. 'Within reason, Nasiha, within reason.'

'Is he not physically pleasing to you, perhaps?'

I pictured myself clapping my hands to my ears and humming loudly, then banished the image and tried to act like an adult. 'I don't find the Councillor objectionable in any form or fashion, Nasiha, but *really*. Now, if you were to find some other way – like maybe I could work for him on the homesteadings as an independent consultant or something . . . that would be fantastic.'

It was the perfect red herring. She dumped the clothes down for scanning and turned to me with sudden, swift energy. 'You would like that, wouldn't you?'

'Of course!' I exclaimed. 'That way, everyone benefits, no hasty decisions are made and we pretty much continue on as before.'

Her eyes narrowed slightly as she considered me. 'I believe you, not least because you have managed to discuss the subject of marriage without once resorting to a fight-or-flight defence.'

'Well, I can thank you for that,' I said heartily. 'Oh, and by the way . . .' I fumbled in my pocket and brought out what I had purchased for her on the sly – a beautifully wrought cat-clasp for her wrap. 'I thought this might be an appropriate . . .' I shook my head and tried again. 'It's practical, but it's also a reminder . . . Oh, screw it. I'm not Sadiri – I don't have to deliver a formal speech just to say I like you. Here.'

With those eloquent words, I pinned it to her wrap.

She touched it gently with her fingertips. 'Thank you,' she said quietly. 'I will treasure it.'

Getting new clothes *was* cathartic. I gathered up all the gear I had been assigned, put it into my field backpack and brought it to my meeting with Qeturah the next day. When she saw it she looked startled, then hurt. I really didn't see why. She rallied, however, and soon we were deep in discussion about how and when to transfer my mission files and reports to Lian, poor Lian, who was going to have a time and a half fitting in all the work I had been doing. I supposed Fergus would have to be the sole security resource, to ease Lian's burden. They could have hired someone new, but with the mission already more than half-over, I guessed it wasn't feasible.

'Right,' I said, cheerfully. 'So I'll be sure Lian gets everything within ten days, some partial and some completed as we've agreed on here. Thank you, Doctor Daniyel. It's been an honour to work with you.' I rose and held out my hand.

She shook it, looking confused. 'I'll be seeing you at dinner, won't I?'

'Perhaps. I planned to turn in early, given my shuttle's departure time tomorrow morning.'

'You're leaving?' She seemed stunned.

'I . . . ah . . . thought that was the whole point of the exercise?' I said, not at all sarcastically. I was getting confused, too.

'I thought you would travel with us until we reach the next major city, probably Chukai about two weeks from now, after our next scheduled stop.'

I frowned slightly. 'I assure you, I *will* get all the documents sent to Lian within the specified time.'

'That's not . . .' She trailed off, sighed and rubbed her forehead. 'Very well. I wish you all the best, Delarua.'

'And the same to you and the team, ma'am,' I replied.

News travels very fast. Lian was the first to corner me after the meeting. 'You're leaving tomorrow?' There was a definite note of accusation there.

'Lian, you guys are leaving tomorrow, too. I don't work for the government any more, remember?'

'I thought you'd be around for a while, show me some lab procedures, that kind of thing,' Lian said almost plaintively.

I sighed. Apparently I wasn't the only one for whom things were just now sinking in. 'Lian, trust me, for your protection and mine we shouldn't work in a lab together.'

'You could appeal,' Lian insisted.

'No, no. I think my confession made it a pretty airtight case. Besides, appeals take for ever and I'd rather get on with my life. I'm sorry.'

'I'm sorry, too,' Lian said and then, unexpectedly, hugged me hard.

(Yes, I know; and no, I'm not telling! If you want to know so badly, you can go ask Lian yourself!)

'Fergus is sorry,' Lian said, stepping back.

I chuckled. 'No he's not.'

Lian smiled wanly. 'Well, you're right. But he should be. You saved his ass from a useless last stand.'

'He's never liked me. I'm too frivolous for him,' I said, speaking with just enough lightness to make it clear that this did not bother me.

'He's jealous,' Lian said, blunt and unashamed of it. 'He says I've gone all girly and giggly since I started hanging out with you.'

'You don't giggle,' I said indignantly. 'You laugh mockingly. I should know – I've often borne the brunt of it.'

We laughed briefly at that. It helped.

Still smiling ruefully, I said, 'He thinks I'm a small-minded bureaucrat and Doctor Daniyel thinks I'm a loose cannon. I went too far, or I didn't go far enough. I'm beginning to think I'm just an idiot.'

'What do the Sadiri think?' Lian asked with typical shrewdness.

I puzzled for a moment, then smiled more broadly. 'I'd hazard a guess that they think my actions were completely unethical, yet highly appropriate.'

Saying goodbye to the Sadiri was hard because I had to be stoic about it. Nasiha had all my details, and I knew I would see her and Tarik again, and perhaps a godchild as well. As for Joral and Dllenahkh – were there any professional reasons for us to associate again? I wasn't sure. I spoke my farewells to them in the late afternoon. They unbent enough to shake hands, and Joral even looked a bit concerned. But Dllenahkh was quite cool and unfazed, and for some reason that upset me. I made some excuse about packing and turned to go to my room.

'Delarua, if I could have a word?'

I turned back. To be perfectly honest, it wasn't only saying goodbye that made me feel odd around Dllenahkh now. There was a little voice in my head saying breezily, *I don't find the Councillor objectionable in any form or fashion*, accompanied by the same comic image of myself tra-la-la-ing with my hands clamped to my ears.

'I have some matters to discuss with you. I would be grateful if you would consider having dinner with me this evening. I understand there is a restaurant not far from here which specialises in Ntshune cuisine.'

'Sure,' I said with a casual shrug, ignoring the little tripping sensation in my chest. Just to be certain, I put my mental shields higher.

The moment we were actually seated in the restaurant, it all clicked back to normal. He wanted my opinion on his idea of bringing female elders to Cygnus Beta, and it was such an interesting concept that I forgot to feel awkward. I talked about the importance of grandparenting for family groups, the stability that Sadiri societies seemed to find in the matriarchal model, and the need to mimic as far as possible the societal structure of New Sadira so as to encourage a parallel cultural experience for the Sadiri of Cygnus Beta. He listened closely, absently plying his utensils as he ate, and at one stage he grew so absorbed that he sat back, put his hand to his mouth and gazed at me intently. I believe I had just suggested implementing short-term apprenticeships for young Sadiri in the Interplanetary Science Council, the Galactic Foreign Service and the Galactic Judiciary, to cycle new parents out of active service for a long enough leave to spend the formative years with their offspring before opting – or not – to return to duty.

'You told me once that there are so few of you left that you must all consider each other as family,' I said almost breathlessly. 'Well, this is the proof of it. I understand if the other Sadiri can't find you wives, but surely they can spare you family?'

He nodded, long and slow, in a way that seemed an agreement to more than my last words. 'I remember some months ago, you warned me that the Sadiri must beware of a misplaced sense of superiority. I have thought long and hard about this, and I have come to the conclusion that while superiority may be our most obvious flaw, it is not the most dangerous one.'

He pushed aside his plate, leaned his elbows on the table and regarded me earnestly. 'I believe that our main flaw, and one I acknowledge in myself, is not that we consider ourselves superior, but invincible. This makes it difficult to ask for help, even from our own.'

He dropped his gaze and began to fiddle with the table linen, a departure from his usual self-control that was both touching and worrying. 'We were sent off to Cygnus Beta, told it was for the good of all Sadiri. What could we do? We went bravely, convinced of our ability to withstand any trial . . . no, *determined* to do so. Failure was unthinkable.'

He stilled his hands and exhaled deeply. 'I can only begin with myself, to set the example. I have a proposal for you' – here he raised his hand and smiled slightly – 'not, let me hasten to add, of the kind that would please Commander Nasiha, but one that I believe will not disappoint nonetheless. On several occasions you have proven your insightfulness concerning Sadiri society. Would you be willing to continue working for us on this mission?'

My heart leapt, but only for a moment. I'd had time to ponder my offhand comment to Nasiha, and I saw the difficulties. 'I'd say yes in an instant, Dllenahkh, but it's not that simple. What I've done, theft of genetic material . . . I'm barred from working in Central Government *and* local government. I might be able work on the homesteadings in a private capacity, but this is a government mission. I can't accept.'

And there it was, that little smugness. 'We are aware of this. However, the Sadiri settlement on Cygnus Beta is in a unique position. While we are, of course, subject to Central Government in terms of the administration of the homesteadings, we have been granted a unique autonomy which leaves ultimate responsibility for the homesteaders with the Government of New Sadira. We selected you for this mission. We can rehire you.'

My jaw dropped. It was too good to be true. He saw it, and

tried to inject some caution. 'I do not have the final word. You must be interviewed and assessed before a decision can be made. I thought, if you did not object, that we might take the morning shuttle to Karaganda, a town with excellent teleconferencing facilities. The interview would take place in the early afternoon, and we would have our answer by the end of the day.'

'Then . . . yes! By all means, yes!' I stammered.

Goodness knows how I slept. I was a wreck, wavering between sweet dreams and grim nightmares about the possible outcomes. Dllenahkh and I rose early and, to my great pleasure and mild surprise, we meditated together with Nasiha, Tarik and Joral before our departure for the shuttle station.

The journey to Karaganda was made shorter by a much-needed nap, and then it was time for a brief stop at a hotel to have a light lunch, freshen up and change before the interview. Dllenahkh did not fuss when he came to my door to find me still scrambling to arrange my attire just so. He gravely advised me, eased my worries about the state of my hair and even helped me arrange the wrap about my head and shoulders and clasp it into place.

'An unusual piece,' he remarked.

I realised his hand had paused on the clasp, which was in the shape of a hummingbird. 'Nasiha chose it for me.'

'Most apt.'

'Nasiha has excellent taste,' I agreed.

I took one last look at myself in the mirror, standing calm and straight as any Sadiri. Then I wrung my hands semi-theatrically and shook them out from the wrists. 'Look at me. I wasn't even this nervous for my first interview for a government post.'

Dllenahkh turned me around and took my hands. His grip was

gentle, very warm and purposely reassuring. He held me immobile with only a look, waiting until he saw my frown vanish, my shoulders relax and my lips tentatively smile. 'I have the highest regard for you, Grace. I am sure that I have not erred in my assessment of your character.'

'Thank you, Dllenahkh,' I whispered.

The teleconferencing centre was state-of-the-art – it had to be, to give such clear reception from Karaganda to Tlaxce City. It meant I had to remind myself not to jiggle my feet or pick at my nails in the mistaken belief that I was not completely in view. I stood alone at the head of the conference table and waited for the holo of my interviewer to appear. When it did, I saw that he had already seated himself, and he indicated with a nod and a gracious wave that I should do the same. I sat as gracefully as I knew how and waited patiently for him to speak first, as befitted an elder.

For he was old, aged by years and more, with a timeless sorrow in his eyes that spoke of a galaxy's worth of loss rather than a mere planet's. He reminded me of the monks of the forest uplands, for he kept his hands tucked into the long, wide sleeves of his tunic and his head was clean-shaven. He did not smile or frown, but there was an unusual relaxation to his face that made me wonder whether Sadiri dignity became tempered after long years of wear.

'Grace Delarua,' he said, speaking my name not in greeting, but musingly to himself. 'Tell me about yourself.'

'I once worked for Central Government, sir,' I said. 'I'm a biotechnician by training, but recently I've been doing a lot of liaison work with the Sadiri. That's how I ended up on the mission, helping the Sadiri as they research different Cygnian societies to see if anything of Sadira has survived. But I think you already know this, sir.'

'Yes,' he said, drawing out the single syllable slowly. 'That was the ice-breaker, if you will. Tell me, Grace Delarua, do you like working with the Sadiri?'

A Sadiri elder, talking about *ice-breakers*? I was so baffled at this effort to put me at ease that it almost had the opposite effect, but I went on bravely. 'Yes, sir. They're efficient, no-nonsense types, and easy to work with because of it.'

'So . . . you don't simply feel sorry for them?'

'Sorry for them—? Oh!' It had actually taken me a split second to realise he was referring to the disaster. 'Well, I'm sure we all want to help as much as possible, sir, but I don't think that's my main motivation. I'd work with them even if Sadira hadn't been destroyed – but then of course they'd hardly have any reason to put up with me.'

His lips twitched, but where Dllenahkh's would have quickly returned to a disciplined line, his retained a slight upward curl of humour, then leisurely came back to the default professional position.

'About your actions on Kir'tahsg, how would you assess them now?' The words were delivered with perfect neutrality, but the atmosphere grew tense. I realised that this was, in a way, *the* question I had been brought there to answer. There was no other option but honesty.

'A friend once told me that feeling invincible leads to the mistake of not asking for help. It seems to me I've made that mistake more than once, and I may have done it again. I understand the Commissioner's disappointment that I didn't have faith in her ability to take care of the matter in the usual way. I could have asked for help, or advice, at an earlier stage when things were still salvageable. I didn't. I acted as if I was the only one who could get the job done. That was, in hindsight, a mistake.'

The grave nod of acknowledgement gave nothing away; it was as perfectly neutral as the question had been.

'But,' I said slowly.

An eyebrow quirked silently, inviting me to continue.

'But I'm mostly Terran, which means sometimes I don't do what's sensible and methodical, or even appropriate. Sometimes I listen to my intuition. I'm sorry, sir, but that's who I am, and at the end of the day all I can do is take responsibility for the consequences.'

I miss a lot of cues by holovid, something about unconsciously relying on empathy when in proximity to others, but I couldn't miss the warmth in his eyes. 'Thank you, Grace Delarua. That will be all. Would you please ask Councillor Dllenahkh to join me for a moment?'

I stood and bowed, then went out in a daze to deliver the message to Dllenahkh. He was in there for much longer than I had been. When he emerged, he looked extremely pensive and not a little disquieted.

'What took you so long?' I demanded anxiously. 'Did he change his mind?'

'No, no,' Dllenahkh assured me hastily. 'We did not discuss you at all. The Consul is . . . an old friend. We were talking about other matters.'

I eyed him closely. 'Ah . . . Dllenahkh, I can't help but notice you look a bit . . . unnerved. Are you *sure* everything is all right?'

He nodded firmly, though his eyes were distant and his mind clearly elsewhere. 'Yes. Everything is perfectly fine.'

That kind of certainty sounded very familiar. I had often employed it myself. 'Do you want to talk about it?'

'I don't think . . .' he began, then trailed off and finally looked at me properly. 'I will if I can. Some day, but not now.'

'Fair enough,' I agreed. It helped that he looked more startled than upset, as if whatever news he had heard was surprising rather than distressing. 'Now,' I continued, changing the subject, 'how are we going to distract ourselves till evening?'

It turned out that Karaganda also had excellent museums and art galleries. We wasted a pleasant two hours before Dllenahkh's comm went off just as we were in search of a café. He paused on the pavement, gave me a quick glance and opened it up to answer. His responses were terse and not at all illuminating, but something in the way his spine lengthened and his head went up, something in his slow intake of breath and the expansion of his chest – it all added up to a positive result.

'I'm in?' I asked lightly as he closed the comm.

'They have consulted with Central Government and with the Commissioner, and although you are barred from conducting any scientific research whatsoever . . . yes, you're in. You have been assigned as my cultural attaché for the duration of the mission. After that . . . we shall see.'

I ducked my head down and laughed a low, long laugh of sheer relief. 'So here I am, back where I started, working with you again.'

'Would you like to tell Nasiha, or shall I?' he asked in whimsical voice, as giddy as a Sadiri could get. 'If you choose your words carefully, you might get her to start planning our wedding ceremony, or perhaps even arranging for our children's betrothals.'

'Nasiha *does* scare me sometimes,' I said wryly, then laughed out loud again, unable to help myself. It was okay. I didn't have to leave. I didn't have to tell him goodbye.

What he did next was almost, but not quite, a rolling of the eyes. It was more of a flash upwards to heaven in a 'give me strength' kind of way followed by a sigh and a rueful smile. 'She is very eager to see the new generation of Sadiri.'

I'm sure he felt the euphoria of the moment, same as I did, but out in public, on a street with people walking by, it was easier to express it with quiet laughter and gentle quips at our colleague's expense. Displacement behaviour, Qeturah would have called it, and Nasiha would have agreed, but I could hardly throw my arms around him and kiss him. That would have been even worse than hugging Joral.

And yet . . . the day was shading into twilight, we were on a tree-lined avenue below a streetlamp that had just flickered on, and for an instant I felt as if I were in a holovid at the point where the Ella Fitzgerald music starts to swell. I stepped up to him, hovered on the edge of his personal space, then came closer. He eyed me warily but did not move, held, I think, by a curiosity stronger than any decorum. I stretched up on tiptoe, careful not to touch any part of him, half-closed my eyes and deeply inhaled the scent of him at the join of his neck and jaw. Then I stepped back and smiled sweetly.

His eyes followed me, still wary but also alight with a sort of intrigued amazement. 'If I may ask . . . why did you do that?'

I felt – let me confess it – a little feminine thrill at the deepened tone of his voice. 'Just checking, Councillor,' I said smugly. 'I wanted to confirm that I was correct in telling Nasiha that I do not find you objectionable in any form or fashion.'

Zero hour plus one year seven months fifteen days

Lian rarely spoke to him, perhaps in part to avoid Joral, perhaps still conscious of that time he had needed the persuasion of a pistol to follow instructions, but Dllenahkh was not offended. Lian was perfectly professional and mostly kept to the Commissioner's side, with Delarua and Fergus being the only social exceptions.

(He did wonder once if Lian's distant attitude might stem from a mild bias against Sadiri, but he quickly rejected the unwanted thought.)

A few days after the upheaval in the team's roles and allegiances, he went into his shelter to find Joral staring in fascination at a plainly wrapped box on his small desk.

'What is it, Joral?' he enquired.

'Corporal Lian brought it for you,' Joral said, still staring at it.

Dllenahkh frowned in puzzlement, shifted Joral gently to one side and opened the box. Inside was a small card atop a quantity of springy padding. He read the card.

To Councillor Dllenahkh

with thanks

Lian

He cautiously parted the packing wool.

'Oh—' Joral began, and fell silent.

'How did Lian find this?' Dllenahkh asked in amazement. It was a bottle of Sadiri spirits, only three years old, which was young for that particular brand but still incredibly precious as the last from a now-extinct distillery.

'I . . . may have mentioned something,' Joral said.

He sounded miserable. Dllenahkh looked at him in surprise, but in an instant it was terribly clear – Lian, talking to Joral, asking questions, showing interest for the first time, and it was only to get information out of him.

He cleared his throat. 'A kind gesture, no doubt connected to our managing to retain Delarua as a colleague. We should . . .' He paused and rested a hand on Joral's shoulder, to better transmit his concern, regret and reassurance. 'We should have a little now and save the rest to drink at your wedding.'

We'll drink at your wedding. The phrase was a common Sadiri jest said to young and old, married or not, as a roundabout way to wish them well. It sounded hollow and strange.

'Or yours, Councillor,' Joral replied bravely. 'That seems more likely to happen.' There was no bitterness, none, only mild teasing.

'Yours and mine, then,' Dllenahkh said, playing along. 'After all, I must set a good example, mustn't I?'

'Yes, Councillor,' Joral agreed, sounding more like himself.

'Good. And tomorrow . . . tomorrow we will both register with the Ministry of Family Planning and Maintenance. Fetch the glasses and let's drink to that.'

FALLING

I yawned widely, raising my handheld to my face to hide my weakness from my Sadiri colleagues. The late nights were killing me.

I'd had some vague idea that since I was in effect an addition to the Sadiri team, I would have less work to do than when I was with the government. After all, Joral was there, Nasiha was still going strong, Tarik remained as quietly diligent as ever and Dllenahkh led from in front as always. Surely the work would not multiply in order to accommodate the number of persons available to do it.

Yes. I know. You'd think I'd never worked in the Civil Service.

When Dllenahkh said he had the highest regard for me, it wasn't just a consoling compliment. It was myriads of reports and manuals downloaded to my handheld for background knowledge, attending all Sadiri-led meetings, writing my own contribution to the mission report being compiled for the Sadiri government, and speaking the Sadiri language on every possible occasion to 'strengthen understanding of the nuances of the vocabulary'.

Do you know that there are about ten variants of the Sadiri

word for *the right thing to do*? There's the thing that's right to do because it's beneficial to all concerned. There's the thing that's right to do because it's been done that way for the last seven generations. There's even the thing that's right to do because it will impress your superior. And they mostly get translated as – you guessed it – *appropriate.* I think there's a particular inflection that means 'this may or may not be the right thing to do, but if I say that it is, you might shut up and get on with it'. I knew I was in deep trouble the day Dllenahkh said to me, 'It would be appropriate if you completed the Advanced Grammar module by the end of next month,' and he managed to combine two variants *and* that tricky little inflection with just three syllables, a rising tone and an encouraging little smile.

I have never worked so hard in my entire life.

Of course there was no way I was going to let them down. They'd taken a risk, bringing me back onto the team in a nose-thumbing gesture to Central Government – although, to be honest, it was less of a nose-thumbing and more of a 'we are continuing to experience the traumatic after-effects of the disaster and would welcome any concessions to maintaining stability and familiarity in our interactions'. For a people who claim that deception is inappropriate, the Sadiri know how to spin a manipulative sentence or two, let me tell you.

Failure would be an embarrassment not only to myself, but also to the people who had bailed me out. No way was I going to let that happen, but there were never enough hours in the day. Qeturah's carefully suppressed pleasure at my return transformed into mild alarm and finally, after nearly two solid months of watching me run myself into the ground, she pulled the doctor thing on me and took me aside.

'You look like hell,' she said callously.

'Well, don't spare my feelings,' I retorted. 'Instead of flattering me, why don't you do something helpful, like writing a small prescription?'

She gave me a very long look, then handed over a packet of the small adhesive patches I remembered all too well from my university days. 'I'm only giving you a week's supply of these. Use them sparingly, and do *not* come back for more. If you haven't adjusted to your new duties without chemical aid by the time they run out, you'll have to find another solution.'

'Fair enough,' I said.

It made sense. I didn't want to build up a tolerance to them, and in truth I only needed a little extra time to bring myself up to speed. I used nearly all of them, but only at most dire need. I was almost in the clear, but then . . . there was a visit coming up, and a rescheduling of another visit, and a possible insertion of a new visit on the schedule, and suddenly more work appeared to fill up the space that had been cleared on my handheld.

Which led to the present scenario: me fighting sleep during an interminable late-night meeting.

I fished the last patch discreetly out of my pocket and pressed it gently to my side, letting the warmth of my skin activate the adhesive. The kick was palpable, but muted. I'd be good for another two hours, nothing more. Better make it count.

'May I collate the pros and cons that have been laid out thus far?' I volunteered. 'We might find a decision easier to arrive at with a visual representation of the matter.'

Two hours later, the meeting was wrapping up and I crashed. I don't mean it figuratively; I literally got up, stumbled and fell over. I lay there on the ground, miraculously unhurt in any way, thought, 'How comfortable,' and closed my eyes for just a second.

I raised my head to find Joral and Dllenahkh looking at me expectantly.

'The visual representation, Delarua?' Dllenahkh enquired.

'Oh yes,' I said, coming alert at last. 'But I can't do it without accompaniment, you know.'

'That's why I'm here,' said an amused voice.

I turned my head to see the minstrel-bard of the Seelie Court tuning up his cithara, quirking an eyebrow at me in a way that managed to be both cheeky and quite sexy at the same time.

'Excellent!' I said happily. 'I was afraid you hadn't got the memo.'

'Pshhh,' he said dismissively as he slapped a mini-amplifier onto the wooden frame of his instrument. 'Miss a sweet gig like this? Not likely!'

I sang the first few notes of the report so we could calibrate our output, then prepared to begin in earnest. Suddenly I caught sight of Nasiha and Tarik walking a tightrope between a tree and our *t'bren* – walking *away* from us.

'Hey, guys, aren't you going to stay to hear the report?' I asked, feeling a bit hurt.

Nasiha giggled. 'Watch your feet, Grace!'

I had been walking towards them as I spoke, but when she said that I stopped short and looked down in a panic at my shoes. There was nothing underneath them but air, leaves, branches and more air.

'AHHHHHHHHHHHH . . . !'

Thud.

I jolted awake, thrashing wildly with the bed sheets. My hand brushed my side, snagging on the patch. I removed it and was about to throw it away when I dimly saw some strange markings on it. The light on my wrist comm illuminated it enough for me to view the words 'SEE ME' in Qeturah's best medical scrawl. I groaned, tapped off my comm light, cast the spent patch aside and walloped my pillow resentfully. A dream about a goodlooking man should *not* end in sudden death and a sanctimonious note from your doctor. Add to that the embarrassment of having passed out cold in front of Dllenahkh . . . But I was too tired to dwell on any of it. I curled up to fall asleep instantly.

'EEEEEEEE!'

You know it's bad when you're falling to certain death and all you can think for your blessed last thought is, *Damn, have I got a girly scream.*

Thud.

I collided, not with the unforgiving ground, but with a pair of strong arms and a broad chest, all connected to a form and face that I knew well.

What the hell? Dllenahkh? I thought.

'My hero!' I cooed as he swooped up into the open sky, carrying me safely.

This is bad and wrong, I tried to say. *Put me down, you idiot! I can fly for myself!*

No words came out to break the silence, but he did, in fact, slow down and land at the edge of a cliff overlooking the ocean. There was an overpoweringly Technicolor sunset going on at the horizon line, and the air was heavy with the scent of sea spray. He gently set me down, gazing into my eyes with a savant-strength intensity that suggested some heavy data analysis or problem solving was going in that complicated brain. Gently again, he tilted up my chin with the knuckle of a curled forefinger, slowly closed his eyes and brought his lips closer to mine.

213

And the light went out.

When I opened my eyes, it was to see the beautifully mundane poles of a camp shelter over my head and feel a government-issue cot under my back. I groaned. Fade to black? When did my erotic dreams ever fade to black? Come to think of it, when did my erotic dreams get so crappy and U-rated? One of the side-effects of the stimulant patches was odd, trippy dreams, but that was plain weird. I didn't want to dwell on what my subconscious was doing, so I swung myself upright and decided to start the day.

I woke myself some more by washing in cold water, dressed and dragged myself outside. Lian was nearby, sitting beside a field stove, and there were good smells in the air.

'Qeturah said I should let you sleep in, so I kept breakfast warm for you.' With a flourish, Lian uncovered a plate of pancakes.

I eyed the scene distrustfully for a moment, waiting for Lian to break into song or the pancakes to flap away, but when all remained sane, I muttered, 'Bless you,' in heartfelt relief and sat down with rumbling stomach.

'How late is it, anyway? And where is everybody?' I mumbled through mouthfuls of pancake and syrup.

'Wrapping up the visit to Piedra,' Lian replied, waving a hand vaguely southwards. 'It's about lunchtime now; the shuttle should return soon.'

'That was quick!' I said. 'I know it was just a courtesy thing, since we have so much data on them already, but I thought we were going to do an overnight, not a day trip.'

Lian gave me a puzzled look. 'We did.'

'Did what?'

'We *did* do an overnight.'

'How? When? Without *me*?'

'Take it easy. No one expects you to bounce back immediately from yesterday's ordeal.'

I frowned. 'What ordeal?'

Lian hit the wrist comm, whispered furiously into it for a few seconds, then faced me again with a smile that leaked panic at the edges. 'Would you like to go and lie down again?'

Within twenty minutes, the shuttle had returned. It wasn't the worried looks that shook me, nor the raised brows; it was the speed with which Qeturah, Dllenahkh, Nasiha and Tarik got me onto a medtable with sensors stuck all over my skull. 'Uh, guys, would you like to tell me what's wrong?'

'What is the last thing you remember?' asked Dllenahkh calmly as Qeturah circled the medtable adjusting things, Nasiha compared the readings on the monitor with the data displayed on her handheld and Tarik scanned his own handheld furiously, possibly looking up reference texts.

'We had that really late meeting about the feasibility of including the Travelling Clans in our schedule given their low genetic score but strong retention of Sadiri traditions. Uh, I've been meaning to talk to you about that. You *do* know Cygnians need more sleep than Sadiri, right? Because I think I've been running a little short, and as flattering as it is to be included in everything you discuss, perhaps I could just read the summaries afterwards and add a note expressing my views?'

'Nothing after that?' asked Qeturah, gently waving some scanning device back and forth across my field of vision.

'Well, apart from some very vivid dreams and a not-very-restful sleep, the next thing I recall is this morning's breakfast. Which, incidentally, I didn't get the chance to finish. *May* I finish my breakfast, please?' I was beginning to feel irritated.

215

They removed the sensors and guided me solicitously to a seat, which only made me angrier. Dllenahkh sat opposite me and said quietly, 'The meeting to which you are referring took place not last night but the night before.'

'I've lost a day?' I said, disbelieving.

'Amnesia is one of the possible effects of the drugs you were given,' said Nasiha.

'Given? By whom?' I asked sharply.

She glanced quickly at Qeturah, who in turn gave Dllenahkh a sombre look. His mouth tensed, then his expression became neutral once more as he spoke to me. 'We would prefer to avoid telling you what happened yesterday so that we can be certain any memory that returns is of the event rather than of our account of it.'

'It's possible the drugs are still interfering with your hippocampus,' said Qeturah quickly by way of diversion.

'What?' I asked, taking the bait.

'That's the part of the brain involved in the formation of long-term memory,' she clarified.

'Oh, yeah. Been a while since first-year neuroanatomy,' I mused.

I sat still for a moment. I checked myself over, twiddling my toes, flexing my fingers, running my tongue over my teeth. I didn't feel any pain or soreness. Whatever had happened to me, it hadn't been damaging in any way that I could sense. I relaxed just a little.

'Well, the fact that you haven't medevacked me gives me some small comfort,' I began.

'Funny you should mention that,' said Qeturah ominously, 'because I was thinking about that option right this minute.'

'We're on the edge of the desert. Where's the nearest neurologist? Look, I'm walking and talking and I feel fine.'

'That's what you said yesterday,' murmured Lian unhelpfully.

Qeturah looked at Nasiha and Dllenahkh. Nasiha seemed unusually quiet to me, and Dllenahkh had a slight frown on his face. 'One day,' Qeturah said to me, still looking at the two Sadiri as if asking for their permission. 'One more day, just in case all that's required is for the last of the drug to cycle out of your system. By then we'll be on our way to Mordecai, and they have decent medical facilities.'

That was satisfactory. I went back to my food.

I spent the afternoon brooding over what had happened. It felt funny, and not particularly nice, to have this big gap in my life that everyone else seemed to know about but me. The concerned looks were beginning to wear on me. I pulled out a small, old-fashioned paper journal that Qeturah had given me back when she was still trying to have me 'get in touch with my feelings' about the Ioan business, and wrote down what I could remember of my strange dreams. Then I confronted Nasiha in the shelter she shared with Tarik.

'I think you were very much involved in what happened,' I told her frankly. 'I've never seen you so subdued. Can you tell me anything?'

She bowed her head slightly, just enough to avoid meeting my eyes. 'Until your own memory returns, I think I should not.'

I looked at her. She had been wearing civilian clothes more often than not after our shopping trip, complaining that the Science Council maternity uniform was 'neither comfortable nor flattering'.

'Where's the cat clasp? You always wear it.'

'I no longer have it. Please, Delarua, do not ask any more questions. I am sorry.'

Tarik, who had been quietly working a few metres away, suddenly put his handheld down, stood up with a face like thunder and strode outside.

I attended the Piedra debriefing – which is to say I sat there and no one made me leave – but the conversation often seemed to weave around me as if I were merely an observer. As usual, I took notes for my own reports, but something made me take more thorough notes than usual: audio and vid recordings, several file attachments and also little personal notes for anything I found strange or significant.

For the first time ever, I had a strong desire to stay up late with the Sadiri. 'So,' I asked Joral, 'what do you guys get up to when the rest of us are asleep?'

'The Councillor and I are studying Cygnian culture,' he said. 'Literature, art, film, history – it is very interesting. Last night we began a series on pre-holo cinema.'

'Oooh, classics?'

'Remastered, for the most part,' Joral admitted.

'Remastered?' I clutched at my heart with an agony that was only half-feigned. 'Philistines. Might as well turn in, then,' I said, and yawned for the fifth time in as many minutes.

Just in case, I gave Lian the dream journal and pointed out which folders on my handheld contained my most recent notes. Then I went to bed, falling asleep far more quickly than I expected to. Of course this meant I was able to wake up early enough to see Dllenahkh off at the shuttleport, though why I should have gone out in all that damp, unhealthy fog is beyond me. To make matters worse, he was dressed oddly and talking nonsense.

'I've got a job to do, too. Where I'm going, you can't follow. What I've got to do, you can't be any part of. Grace, I'm no good at being noble, but . . .'

'But?' I prompted, genuinely curious. That wasn't how it went, was it?

He blinked and said in a more normal tone, '*Is* there a purpose to my "being noble" in this situation? I am not convinced it is the best choice to make.' The slight frown cleared from his face, he seemed to mentally shrug and then he tilted up my chin with his forefinger. 'Here's looking at you, kid.'

He bent his head towards mine and again, unsurprisingly, the scene immediately faded to black.

'What's with that?' I mumbled out loud.

'Delarua? Are you awake?'

I stretched, tangling my feet in the thin blanket over my cot. 'Yeah, more or less. Oh, shoot!' I sat upright suddenly. 'Nasiha! I'm sorry I overslept, but you saw what I was like last night at the meeting. No way was I going to make it to meditation this morning.'

She regarded me silently from her seat in a chair not far from my cot. She was already dressed for the day, of course, and there was a medical scanner in her hand which she held poised as if about to sweep it in my direction. 'Which meeting would that be, Delarua?'

'Don't you remember? The Travelling Clans issue?' I replied, puzzled.

'I see,' she said, tapping her comm.

In a very short space of time, a small group had gathered around my cot – Nasiha, Dllenahkh, Qeturah and Lian. I self-consciously wrapped up in my blanket and gaped at them.

'I've lost two days?' I said incredulously.

They did not argue. Nasiha showed me the date-stamped medical readouts. Lian accessed my report notes on my own hand-held and gave me the beginnings of a dream journal in my own handwriting. I got up, trailing the blanket behind me like a badly wrapped toga, and paced around in undershirt and shorts, staring at the items in my hands and absorbing the information.

'I've lost two days,' I said faintly. I felt my way back to my cot and sat down, dumping everything beside me and numbly passing a hand over my face. 'What's going on? What's happening to me?'

'We believe that something is disrupting your ability to form long-term memory,' said Qeturah. 'Each time you go to sleep, your consciousness resets to the last event stored in long-term memory. This is probably caused by a malfunction of—'

'The hippocampus, yes, I know,' I mused. 'But that doesn't explain why I'm remembering all my dreams.'

Qeturah and Nasiha spoke at the same time. 'How do you know that?' 'You remember your dreams from last night?'

I looked up, surprised at their intensity. 'Yes, I know about the hippocampus memory thing. Didn't you tell me about that some-time, Qeturah? And yes, I remember three dreams from last night, but two of them are described in that journal. Three dreams in one night is more than a little busy, so I think I must be remem-bering the night before.'

'Subconscious memory formation. I thought so,' said Qeturah triumphantly. 'I *did* tell you about the hippocampus yesterday,

Grace. You said you did basic neuroanatomy, but you'd forgotten about that.'

My mind was whirling. 'Give me a moment. I'll be able to think more clearly once I'm properly dressed. I promise, I'll come straight to the lab right after.'

I didn't, though. As I collected my thoughts, a strange idea came to me. I had never seen *Casablanca*. Heard of it, of course, read many a quote, even, but seen it – never. That old black-and-white stuff was for the real movie buffs, and in spite of my teasing Joral, I wasn't one.

I wandered to their shelter in search of information to test my hypothesis. 'Joral,' I said, 'tell me, what movies did you watch last night, and the night before?

He raised a puzzled eyebrow. 'Last night we saw the earliest Cygnian adaptation of *Casablanca*. The night before that, we watched the 3-D remake of *Superman*, which is famous for its interactive special effects. If you would like to join us tonight, we are thinking of viewing the original *E.T.: The Extra-Terrestrial*.'

This wasn't a huge surprise. Cygnian cinema, both pre-holo and holo, is filled with benign aliens and refugees from war and disaster.

'Thank you, Joral.' I smiled. 'I'll think about it. Dllenahkh, could I have a word with you outside?'

We walked a short distance from the camp to the edge of a small plateau and gazed down at a vast, barren landscape. I was reminded of the time we'd huddled together, watching the savannah dogs in their den. Now we were looking at a rocky desert land, with the low towers of Piedra faintly visible in the haze of fine sand and heat. I was sorry I'd missed seeing that famous city up close.

'So, you've been watching a lot of old movies.' I glanced up at

Dllenahkh. 'Tell me . . . you ever imagine me in them? Or rather . . . us?'

There was a profound silence. Dllenahkh turned to face me fully, his expression somewhere between alarm and embarrassment. 'Why do you ask?'

'Don't be coy. Superhero catches falling girl. Rick says goodbye to Ilsa. That's what I've been dreaming and that's what you and Joral have been watching!'

He actually paled. 'That would suggest that I have been influencing your dreams.'

'Worse. I'm dreaming *your* thoughts! And while we're on the subject, what *is* it with those strategic blackouts? You got something against kissing?'

Give the Sadiri credit: even in the midst of pure, unmitigated mortification, they never stop thinking.

'I have it,' he said suddenly. 'I understand what is happening to you and how to correct it. Quick, let us go to the lab.'

I could try to tell you what the detailed explanation was, but why bother when you can access for yourself the paper co-authored by Qeturah, Nasiha and Tarik? Suffice it to say that my brain chemistry had been altered by the drugs I had been given, with the result that my hippocampus was no longer storing long-term memory throughout the brain. It was all being stored exclusively in the hippocampal gyrus, which is the region of the brain responsible for telepathy. Coincidentally, this is also the region that I seem to be unable to access consciously, which is why I get a null result on telepathic ability. However, with the addition of another chemical from the stimulant patch, I had become a subconscious telepath. I was reading Dllenahkh's mind *from a distance* in my sleep. How cool is that?

'And we're going to do what?' I asked them, after the detailed explanation had been repeated to me two or three times.

'The Councillor is going to attempt repairs when you enter REM sleep tonight,' Nasiha said, her voice regaining some of its usual confident vigour. 'He will access the memories in your hippocampal gyrus and adjust your neurotransmitters to recommence storing memory in the usual way.'

I looked at Qeturah for confirmation, but she merely shook her head helplessly. 'I'm all at sea with this telepathy business, Grace. You're going to have to trust Dllenahkh.'

'Well, that's a given,' I said easily.

It was a small thing, but the moment I said it Tarik flashed a brief glare at Nasiha, then retreated once more behind a veneer of propriety.

Because there was only one medtable and limited space, they put an extra cot in the shuttle and dotted us all over with sensors to record the unusual event. Then they turned on the environment controls, turned off the lights and shut the door. For a short while, there was the glow of Dllenahkh's handheld as he sat on the cot and made some last-minute notes. Finally he turned it off, and the darkness was absolute. I heard the cot creak slightly as he lay down.

'Are you going to stay awake all night?' I said softly.

'If necessary,' he replied just as quietly.

'I may snore,' I warned after a pause.

'I shall try not to listen,' he said with mild amusement.

'Is something wrong between Nasiha and Tarik?' It might have seemed a nosy question, except that it came out in the plaintive tones of a child wondering why Mummy and Daddy are arguing.

'Tarik is struggling to find the right way to deal with a certain matter. Nasiha is concerned for him. They will be all right, Grace.'

There was a very long pause during which the silence rang loudly in my all-too-awake ears.

'You going to tell me about the kissing thing or not?'

He exhaled audibly. 'I suppose it was too much to hope that you would forget that. Kissing is not a Sadiri custom. To us it seems . . . unhygienic. And yet much of Terran romance appears to centre on the practice, to the point where potential partners may even be rejected solely on the basis of a lack of proficiency in this area.'

'Well, it *is* rather unhygienic,' I admitted, 'but there are variations, you know, ranging from a kiss on the cheek to the full-on, bite-for-blood kiss. There are plenty of Terran cultures that don't find the extreme versions attractive.'

'Where do you fall on this spectrum of preference?' he asked.

For a moment I had a kind of mental stumble that made me glad Dllenahkh hadn't linked to me yet: *He's asking me how I like my kisses!* Then I pulled myself together. 'I suppose I'm a bit tame by urban standards. I prefer a no-fluids approach myself, just minimal moisture at the most.' I was very proud of my clinical tone. 'Um . . . does your culture have an alternative to the kiss?'

I heard him sit up, felt him take my right hand. He gently uncurled my fingers and turned my palm towards him. I opened my mouth to say, 'Oh, yeah, that thing Nasiha and Tarik do.' But the words died on my tongue.

First he simply touched his fingertips to mine, which was pleasant enough. Then he lightly traced the length of my fingers, moving slowly, a low hum of sensation for the front of my hand, a warm tingle for the back. Finally, he set his palm to mine.

'Ohh!' I exclaimed, enlightened and entranced.

It felt like warm, golden light – not the muted gold of late afternoon, but something more sharply metallic, conducting its own electricity along the nerves in my hand directly to my brain and throughout my body. There was a ripple like light-hearted laughter, a more solemn surge like a deep, contented sigh, and then a comforting ebb and flow like the rocking of an ocean wave . . . very soothing . . . very relaxing . . . very . . .

'. . . good of you to put me to bed, Councillor,' I said, smothering my chagrin under a jesting tone.

Memory returned to me, bright and sharp as life, but strange as déjà vu in a hall of fractured mirrors.

'We sometimes forget that most Cygnians need at least eight hours of sleep,' Dllenahkh said apologetically as he set down the last piece of baggage in the hotel lounge. 'In future, we will try to arrange our meetings to take place at a more convenient hour and within a shorter time frame.'

'Don't make promises you can't keep, Councillor,' I said with a teasing grin. Then, much to my dismay, I saw Qeturah glancing in my direction as if considering whether or not to deal with me in public. I decided not to give her the chance. It was the work of a moment to slip out of the hotel with Nasiha on the pretext of a quick stop in town to take a look at a nearby craft market.

I hadn't considered the extent to which clothes are protection. Ordinarily, Nasiha would have been wearing her Science Council blues and I would have been wearing one of my Civil Service uniforms, but we had both taken to wearing civilian clothes bought in that region. That must have been why they thought we were fair game.

One moment we were walking down the road, and then we were gone – dragged into an alley, choking rags drenched in some sedative pressed over our faces. Nasiha was too strong and too quick for them. I saw the man who grabbed her go flying over her head. At that point, I blacked out completely.

When I came back to consciousness, it was in a paralysed body. I could feel the vibration of an aircar under me, but I could neither open my eyes nor move. I heard shouts and the sound of running feet, and then I felt the sudden crush of a quick lift-off. I struggled and finally cracked open my eyes, just as they picked me up by the wrists and ankles and swung me out of the open door of the rising car.

The aircar hadn't risen very far, perhaps no more than five metres. If I'd had the use of my limbs, I would have feared at most some contusions, a broken wrist, perhaps. But I was limp and helpless, and I waited to feel all my bones break and my skull shatter on the hard ground.

But that's not the way it went.

I collided, not with the unforgiving ground, but with a pair of strong arms and a broad chest, all connected to a form and face that I knew well.

You caught me, I murmured to the presence in my mind.

Of course, he answered, but below the calm was the fear and wonder of having arrived in the nick of time.

Nasiha?

I saw an image of her, wrap torn away and face furious, spinning around helplessly in a now-empty alley as the gang got away through the close gaps between the buildings, like rats scurrying into a maze. I saw an image of Tarik outside the hotel, face peaceful one moment, then wide-eyed with horror, sprinting away

226

instinctively to find her via the telepathic link they shared. In three minutes, Lian and Dllenahkh drew up in a groundcar and hauled him in. Tarik found Nasiha all right, but it was Dllenahkh who found me, reaching out with all his strength to sense my half-conscious awareness, as faint as the whirr of a humming-bird's wings.

I was unreasonably perky when the drugs wore off. 'Can't remember a thing!' I said cheerfully. 'Look at me – I'm walking, I'm talking, I'm fine!'

Qeturah scanned me, scowling at her instruments as they confirmed my words. 'Very well. But you're not coming with us to Piedra. You're on twenty-four-hours' rest and observation.'

I think Nasiha would have stayed with me . . . if Tarik hadn't tried to order her to do so. In the end it was Lian who volunteered to watch over me.

'Poor Tarik,' I said, thinking of his silent shows of anger and understanding at last how even a Sadiri, *especially* a Sadiri, could be almost incapacitated by fear for the well-being of his wife and unborn child. The fear felt like falling . . .

. . . *falling through darkness . . . falling for ever . . .*

. . . because there was nothing to fall *to*. Deep space had no pull, no solidity. There was only hopeless spinning in the void, and tumbling fear within.

What life begins, death must end . . .

. . . but so much death had its own gravity well, impossible to escape, an open grave that had drawn millions from existence – friends, strangers, enemies, lovers – turning everyday loss to utter loss.

He was falling, so I caught him, grasping his wrist as the arc of his orbit passed me. I tugged him down to the ground and turned him right-side-up so he could see the huge silver moon rising over the horizon. I touched the tip of my forefinger to his, kindling a golden glow, and placed my hand gently over his heart as I whispered the timeless cliché for all those who no longer had voices to tell him.

The light from the opening shuttle door woke me. They came tiptoeing in.

Shhhh, I signed one-handed, and pointed down at the cot.

His hand loosely gripping mine, chest rising and falling slightly, Dllenahkh was asleep.

REMEMBRANCE DAY

Something changed. It was bizarre. We had been side by side in the dark, hands touching, minds touching, and some of that intimacy lingered in speech and shared silence, but I still could not find a way to ask him directly about his nightmare. True, much of our time together was spent in a purely professional setting, but even so I wasn't sure I had earned that right. I read voraciously instead, my desire to impress giving way to an insatiable curiosity about old Sadira, New Sadira and the disaster in between.

The hidden motive behind my new obsession was not professional, but personal. During our close communication, I had seen myself through Dllenahkh's eyes. It had been disconcerting, even alien. I found myself wondering how the average Sadiri would view me, something I'd hardly cared about when I was visiting the settlement. The standards for courtesy and professionalism could not be the same as the standards for . . . friendship. Kissing was a minor detail. I'm no Gilda; I didn't want to experiment. I wanted to get things *right*, and I had no idea how to go about it. I stood before the mirror, paused and pondering, a stick of kohl held loosely in my fingers. Everything else was as usual. I was wearing a long black skirt and a belted white short-sleeved tunic. My wrap remained on the bed in my hotel room. I would go bare-headed tonight and see if I could get accustomed to the unruly thumb-length fuzz that my hair had become after nearly four months without a trim. A band pulled it back smoothly from my forehead in an attempt at elegance. I looked fine. The concert hall wouldn't throw me out.

A knock at the door startled me. Lian came into our shared bathroom and in two seconds took in my slightly guilty look and the stick of kohl, which I was sheepishly trying to make disap-pear behind my back.

'Don't worry,' Lian said with a gentle, understanding smile. 'Some things are too important for teasing.'

'You look sharp tonight,' I said quickly, opting for diversion.

Lian went to the mirror and ran a professional eye over each crease and fastening, each braid and ribbon, ensuring everything was in place. 'It'll do.'

My colleagues from the Cygnian Military Service and the Interplanetary Science Council had been invited to a Remembrance Ceremony commemorating those who had died in the crisis events that had brought various peoples to Cygnus Beta. The entire team had already attended a general service of remembrance earlier in the day, but this was something exclusive for the military and quasi-military bodies, perhaps a special reminder of their mandate to protect humanity.

We were in town for only a couple of days en route to another visit, so I hadn't been surprised when Qeturah declared she was happy to stay in and rest, and Joral said he had to catch up on some work. Dllenahkh, on the other hand, was interested in going to a local performance of Pakal's *Requiem* and asked me if I'd like to come along. I said yes. It wasn't an unusual invitation by any means, and yet there I was, standing in the bathroom with a stick of kohl held indecisively in my fingers.

Lian gave the shoulders of the dress uniform one final brush, looked at me and nodded. 'I'll give you some privacy.'

When the door closed, I laughed a short, quiet laugh at myself and applied the kohl.

Ganymede is a small town but it prides itself on its history and culture. As a result, the concert hall was impressive and the orchestra magnificent, rivalling even the finest in Tlaxce City. I did not regret my efforts to look my best, and I was foolishly proud of Dllenahkh, too. He could take the simplicity of a formal suit and make it as crisp and stylish as any military dress uniform. The small teak elephant I had given him rode discreetly on the collar of his shirt, adding to my satisfaction.

Pakal's *Requiem* is very moving but not particularly long, which suited my mood perfectly that night. We spent a mere thirty minutes with the orchestra and the audience, then went out with the rest of the crowd to mill about in the brightly lit town park. We were both rather silent. It was that kind of evening. Everyone, couples and families alike, seemed a bit hushed and reflective as they walked, as if it were a planet-wide holy day.

'Does Sadira have a Day of Remembrance?' I asked Dllenahkh. I meant to say New Sadira, but he overlooked the slip and answered directly.

'Different tribes have had different ways and times for honouring their ancestors and fallen heroes. There is nothing as specific as this, although in time there may be.'

I stopped walking and looked up at him with a small frown.

'There hasn't yet been a ceremony for the loss of Sadira? It's been well over a year.'

He bowed his head slightly, matching my frown, as if genuinely puzzled that such a thing had not yet taken place. 'The day was remembered, but not as a formal event. I suppose . . . I believe we have been too busy to think of such a thing.'

We walked on in silence for a while.

'Although,' he continued in a low voice, 'to do so would have meant accepting that there could be no returning to Sadira in our lifetime, nor for many generations to come. I suspect we were not ready to admit that.'

My hand brushed his tentatively. His fingers curled around mine, briefly answering the touch, then withdrew. With a look and a nod, he indicated a bench a little off the path, half-screened by high shrubbery. I followed him and we sat down to watch the people walk by.

'I promised some time ago to tell you the story behind my meeting with the Consul when we were in Karaganda,' he said.

I stared at him, my attention caught. 'You did. That was a few months back. Are you ready to tell me now?'

He nodded. 'There is much you have learned from reading our government reports. It may be easier for me to explain now.'

I racked my brain, trying to think what could have been in the several extremely dry reports I had read that would have a bearing on our conversation now. I drew a blank, so I simply smiled invitingly and waited for him to begin.

His opening sentence was unexpected. 'How did it feel, when you were recovering from your injuries and I linked to your mind to speed your body's healing?'

Dllenahkh would never ask an idle question. I paused and

pondered over the memory of it. 'It felt like your blood was in my veins. It felt like your neural electricity was in my nerves and brain and spine. I wish I could be clearer. Your awareness was tangled up in mine. Am I making any sense?'

He was looking at me and smiling very gently, somewhere between the proud smile of a master whose student has answered correctly and the fond smile of a friend who finds himself perfectly understood. 'Go on. You are doing very well.'

I continued courageously with my wild guessing. 'I suppose, from what Nasiha tries to teach me and from what I've read of the mindships, that's how the Sadiri mind works. You extend your awareness of yourself beyond the boundaries of your physical body. It's generally a benign psionic influence – case in point, when you took over the parts of my body that were not under my conscious control and helped me to heal faster. That's also how a mindship pilot operates. He or she becomes the ship – no, wait . . . not quite. The ship becomes part of the pilot.'

The smile was my barometer and it did not falter, though he gave one clarification. 'Simplified, but not inaccurate. The Sadiri mind, as you say, works in this way. Remember, however, this is due to early training and constant practice. The Sadiri brain is still a human brain, only with more of its potential realised.'

He raised his hands and regarded the palms meditatively, tilting them to catch the warm light of the park's solar lanterns. 'Zhinuvians have a higher concentration of semiconducting material in their skin, which permits them to talk to machines with greater ease than to other sentient minds. Their way of navigating their interstellar craft reflects this difference in approach. We too possess some of this ability to interface with man-made intelligence, but our skill mainly lies with the organic, independent mind.'

'I am aware,' I said carefully, because I could not say that I understood, 'that your ships, unlike the Zhinuvian ships, are alive, not crafted.'

He lowered his hands and nodded. 'I enjoyed our brief time at the mahouts' village. Their attachment to their elephants is very like how our pilots bond with their ships. It is a lifelong commitment. I have heard of only one instance of a pilot who gave up his ship willingly. That is the story I am about to share with you now.'

He relaxed and leaned back, gently putting aside a few untrimmed leafy twigs from the nearby bushes that tried to dangle about his head like a sparse laurel crown. I turned towards him, drawing my feet onto the seat and under my skirt. A talkative Dllenahkh was rare, and most welcome. I would let him speak uninterrupted and ask my questions later.

'During my years of training and study in the mental disciplines, I encountered many people who became pilots. Most of them were off-planet when the disaster struck, and yet a significant number died in futile attempts to transport people from the surface of Sadira.

'One of the survivors came to Cygnus Beta to speak at a special meeting held by an emissary from New Sadira. The entire local Council of our settlement was in attendance to discuss and decide on a matter that would affect us all – a plan to save Sadira.

'What I am about to tell you may sound as far-fetched as the tales of the Caretakers sound to some non-Cygnians, but I ask you to proceed for the moment as if both were equally true.

'A mindship can travel in space and time. For most interstellar journeys, a pilot plots a short cut through the unseen dimensions of space-time in order to travel swiftly between distant points in the visible dimensions. It is also possible to plot a course which makes use of a second dimension of time, but it is a rare and still-experimental practice which is only done far from the usual shipping routes as our scientists continue to assess and document the effects.

'In short, we had the technology to send a pilot back to a time before the disaster. What could be achieved there was a matter of debate. Some felt that averting the disaster would only create a parallel timeline in which Sadira remained alive, but we would continue in this timeline, unaware and unaffected. Others were convinced that the method by which Sadira was destroyed was so advanced that it must have come from the future, thus creating a parallel timeline in which we are now living. They further believed that parallel timelines are not sustainable, and if we were to stop the disaster from happening, this present existence would evaporate, leaving only the original reality where Sadira never died.

'Then there were the pessimists, who believed that nothing could be changed. They were, however, willing to believe that the pilot could uncover evidence of how the Ainya had triggered the disaster and bring the information back to us so we could ensure that no other planet would face devastation of this magnitude.

'Naraldi, an experienced and widely travelled pilot, was selected for the mission. I know him well. He has always been highly pragmatic in his approach. Cutting short the debate, he accepted the three different mission briefs, to be acted on according to his own analysis of the situation. He then gave up his mindship to link with a specially modified vessel. Travelling far from the populated sectors of the galaxy, he set out on the new, untried course . . . and disappeared. And we waited.

'Months later, the emissary returned to confirm in person the news we had already received. The mission had been a success, and yet not so, for our fate had not changed and no evidence had been discovered. We were to continue as if we had never attempted such a thing, and no further discussion would be entertained. In time, reports from the scientists analysing the mission would be made available to higher ranking government officials.'

He paused, coming out of storyteller mode to meet my spellbound gaze. 'You have read one of these reports, from my own handheld. Do you remember it?'

I tried. 'I think I remember the occasion, but as for the report, I mainly recall that I didn't understand very much at all. It was highly technical.'

The corner of his mouth quirked briefly upwards in wry agreement. 'The amount of complex multivariate calculus in that report *was* somewhat off-putting. However, the gist of it was that there are already stable parallel timelines in existence. Naraldi was not able to change our fate because he had no way of navigating to our past. He was able to reach many other pasts of different timelines, and see other presents and futures as well. But his own line he could not touch.'

His expression became shadowed, regretful. 'Now you can understand why no ceremonies were held. We were still hoping to make the nightmare simply vanish away.'

'What happened to Naraldi?' I asked.

He blinked away the sadness, his look growing sharp and assessing. 'He returned safely after about five months. You met him – he is now the Sadiri Consul on Cygnus Beta, an honourable and restful assignment from a grateful government.'

That aged face, those sorrowful eyes. Creeping horror stilled me as I absorbed this. 'How *long* was he out there?'

Dllenahkh shrugged. 'No one can tell. What chronometer could have made sense of his journeys? He was seventy years old when he left, barely middle-aged by our reckoning. Now he appears to be at least fifty years older than that.'

'Fifty years, in only a few months!' I was appalled.

Dllenahkh took pity on me. 'Do not be distressed on his behalf. When I spoke to him, he told me he had had some pleasant experiences, and some less so, but he had never once been bored. For a mindship pilot, that is more than enough.'

Suddenly he leaned forward, looking sideways at me in a manner that was half-secretive, half-triumphant. His voice became very quiet. 'There was one very interesting thing that he learned which is extremely relevant to our timeline. He discovered, well before the fact, how Ain was quarantined.'

I shifted closer to catch every word, every nuance of his tone and expression. 'Go on,' I urged, both amused and excited that he had indulged in a little theatrical pause.

'Anyone trying to enter the Ain system will simply find themselves on the opposite side, having passed only empty space between. The planet has been placed in an elegant pocket of folded space-time, a feat well beyond the abilities of anyone from this time – anyone we know, that is.'

'What happened to those off-planet Ainya who tried to return after the quarantine?' I wondered.

Dllenahkh's face became completely expressionless, which spoke to me of hidden anger. 'No Sadiri pilot would have taken them, and as for the Zhinuvians – I think that we have seen for ourselves how they would treat a passenger who did not have the funds for a return trip.'

I nudged his knee with the back of my hand and was rewarded when his bleak look lifted.

He spoke lightly, changing the subject. 'It may be of interest to you that in one of the timelines Naraldi visited, it was the Ntshune and not the Sadiri who became influential in galactic government.'

I laughed out loud. 'Come on!'

He shook his head in amusement at my cynicism. 'I know that at times we Sadiri give the impression that we consider our minds to be the finest in the galaxy. I assure you, I know this is not the case. A more ambitious Ntshune government could easily have surpassed us as diplomats and judges. Even the Zhinuvians, who already have the fleet to challenge us, only lack unified government to guide them into a position of power.'

'Well, thank you for telling me that. It'll be our little secret,' I joked. Humility was not a common Sadiri trait – but then again, Dllenahkh had always been unique.

He smiled. 'You can do something for me in turn. Tell me about the Caretakers.'

My eyes widened. 'What can I tell you? It's not like . . . I mean . . . we don't have reports on them; there's no branch of study dedicated to them. It's all folk tales and oral history. Not a religion, not even a superstition, but just . . . there, part of our identity as Cygnians.'

'Then tell me what you can,' he insisted, facing me fully and pointedly giving me his complete attention.

I paused. I'd never discussed anything remotely metaphysical with the Sadiri. It made me realise that for all I pretended otherwise, I *did* care what they thought about me. It *did* matter to me that even if they saw me as talkative, emotional and half-out-of-control most of the time, at least they could not fault my scientific mind. My tongue felt strangely heavy as I tried to talk of things I had secretly forbidden myself to discuss.

'To Cygnians, the Caretakers are the guardians of humanity. They're supposed to save the best of us from the worst of us, even if it's only a remnant. We're not perfect here on Cygnus Beta, but at least for those who claim to have been brought by the Caretakers, there's an additional claim that they were saved for a reason, chosen for a purpose. Not because they're better than any other group, but because there's something unique they possess, some characteristic that contributes to the fullness of humanity. It's a responsibility, not a point of pride. It's something to live up to and it helps us keep going.'

'Admirable,' said Dllenahkh, and his tone was neither cautiously neutral nor subtly judging, as I had feared it might be. It was mildly but distinctly approving. I felt encouraged enough to continue.

'If all the tales are true, no one's seen the Caretakers face to face. No flaming chariots, no wheels within wheels, no wings. It's a very boring legend, when you think about it – just some people following the music of an invisible Pied Piper, disappearing into one cave near Hamelin, Terra, and emerging from another cave near Hamelin, Cygnus Beta.'

'Do Cygnians have any theories about what exactly the Caretakers are?' Dllenahkh enquired, apparently rapt by the little I was telling him.

I shrugged. 'No one thinks they are gods. That's religion, and

239

we've got plenty of that already. Some say they are humans from the past and pour out a libation for them. Others say they are people from the future and light fragrant incense to them. Another group says they are souls tasked after death to do all the work that wasn't done in life. They don't venerate the Caretakers in any way. They just work very hard, to be sure they won't have to make up for lost time after they're dead.'

'What do you think?' he asked.

'Perhaps a little of all three,' I said. 'Remember your ancestors, dream of your descendants and work hard while you're living. It's . . . nice to think the universe has a purpose – well, more than one, probably – but at least one of them is about helping humans fulfil their potential as a species.'

'Strong anthropic principle?' Dllenahkh murmured.

'At least medium,' I conceded with a smile. 'And I know that sounds very strange and unscientific, so thank you. Thanks for listening to me.'

'Why wouldn't I listen? You listened to all I had to say about parallel timelines, and that sounded very strange, though scientific.'

'Not strange at all,' I disagreed. 'The Caretakers did some fairly interesting things when they went about collecting their endangered humans. I understand there's a community of Cygnians who say they're descended from the last survivors of a nuclear winter on Terra.'

'From a parallel timeline?' Dllenahkh queried, his eyebrows rising with surprise and interest.

'Must be, and it's not only them. All I can say is if any Cygnian tells you they're a direct descendant of Will Shakespeare, don't be too quick to call them a liar.'

I stretched out my legs, which had grown almost numb from being tucked under me while I was absorbed in conversation. Dllenahkh also moved into a more relaxed posture, leaning his elbows on his knees. I looked at the slight smile on his face and decided to take advantage.

'What about you? Are there any similar, unscientific beliefs in your culture?'

He answered easily, not in the least offended. 'With respect to ancestors, descendants and working hard, most certainly. However, there are no Caretakers in our lore. Sadira was always where we started and where we ended, no matter how many years and light years lay between. In a way, the elders of the family are our Caretakers. There is an old saying that no elder can truly die who has a hundred descendants living. Many elders do act as if the larger the pyramid of offspring below them, the better their chances of ascending to some afterlife. They have a hand in arranging every adoption and marriage, divorce and shunning. Family is blood, and more than blood.'

I said nothing. Female Sadiri elders had already answered the call and begun to settle on Cygnus Beta. Some of those elders had a few descendants, most had none. It was particularly satisfying to think of those who had never had children suddenly heading their own clans of adoptees and foreign brides, and perhaps, just perhaps, secretly and unscientifically thinking of the ladder they were building to a previously unattainable heaven.

'Gennea, Falve, Collan, Lauri.'

Startled, I struggled for a moment to understand the language Dllenahkh was speaking, and then I realised they were names. I held my breath and waited.

He continued, 'My older sister, my younger sister, my younger brother, and my mother. My father, Nahkhen, died many years ago. Also two nieces, a nephew and one brother-in-law. Among the living, I can count a sister-in-law, now remarried, and three cousins, two of my generation and one of my mother's generation, all resident on New Sadira. One second cousin of my generation is here on Cygnus Beta.' He bit his lip, looking rueful, then confessed, 'I know my kin far better now than I ever did.'

I didn't know what to say, but I had to think of something because the silence was making my throat close up. 'There's a small lake in the middle of the park. People go there to light floating candles in memory of their dead. At midnight, they turn off all the park lights so there's nothing but stars and candle-light.'

I waited fearfully as a few more seconds ticked by, then he said hoarsely, 'I think I would like to see that.'

The long silence that followed was more tolerable, breathable and peaceful.

A thought struck me. 'Dllenahkh, you told me *how* Ain was quarantined, but you didn't tell me *who* did it. Does anyone know?'

He gave me a slightly surprised look. 'I was under the impression that most Cygnians give that honour to the Caretakers.'

'*You* believe it was the Caretakers, too?' I asked. I was sceptical, not about the Caretakers but that any Sadiri would seriously consider this to be a possibility.

'As a hypothesis, it has some merit. Ability to manipulate time and space, telepathic influence strong enough to erase memory or inhibit discussion of witnessed events – we have seen the fledgling versions of those skills both here on Cygnus Beta and among mindship pilots of Naraldi's calibre. Why not speculate that humans in the future could do as much and more?'

242

'Has merit,' I repeated mockingly. 'Just admit it – we've turned you into a Cygnian.'

He got to his feet and extended a hand to help me up from the bench. I accepted the hand, careful to touch only the fingertips, and only for a second. He surprised me by taking my other hand and drawing it under his arm to rest near the crook of his elbow, so that we looked very much like the other promenading couples.

'And would that be such a terrible thing to admit?' he said in a tone of cheerful surrender. 'This is my universe, my time, my world. There is no going back to what was. There is only the future.'

We had more than two hours till midnight, plenty of time to walk the length and breadth of the park before a pause to visit the lake's small boardwalk and crouch there to light several candles. Dllenahkh looked at them as they floated away to twinkle amid a growing constellation of tiny lights in the lake's centre, then gazed up at the stars. I thought I knew what he was seeking. The newer arrivals always did it – looked for the light, actual or imagined, of their home star.

'I wonder how long it will be before starlight shines on Sadira once more,' he said quietly.

I stopped breathing for a moment, a surge of pity seizing my heart. On Cygnus Beta, mentioning a recent disaster in detail is taboo. It is referred to obliquely, delicately, in general terms like 'the great war' or 'the big wave'. The Sadiri had fallen into that habit with swift gratitude, and not once had I heard them specify how Sadira had been laid waste. Not until that moment, when Dllenahkh looked to the sky and acknowledged the world-girdling, poisonous cloud that covered Sadira in perpetual night.

We walked, rested and walked again, but just before midnight we came back to the lake and waited for the lights-off. When it came, it was as remarkable as the holos I'd seen, and more. The moonless night pressed on the eyes like thick, heavy felt, making the small flames sear the vision as they danced on the dark water. The stars added their cold fire overhead, and yet the night remained dim enough to hide my attempts to dash away tears. Of course I spoiled it by blowing my nose, but there were other sighs and rustles and coping noises in the respectful but imperfect silence, so I did not feel completely alone. Dllenahkh was perfectly silent and absolutely still, though he did clear his throat at one point.

When the lights came back on, we left the park and found transportation to the hotel. He bade me goodnight at my door and, with neither prior thought nor self-consciousness, I stretched up to kiss his cheek quickly. He gave me a searching look, then gently brushed his forefinger along my cheekbones to the corner of each eye, wiping away the slight moisture my furtive swipes had missed earlier. The tender gesture almost made me tear up again.

'Sleep well, Grace,' he said in farewell before he turned away to his own door.

I went into my room feeling a bit dreamy. It lasted all of three minutes, up until the moment the bathroom door opened to reveal Lian, yawning and dressed for bed.

'It's all yours,' Lian started to say, then got a good look at me. 'Hm.'

'What?'

Lian shrugged. 'I'm a fan of the kohl myself, but I forgot to warn you – don't wear it on Remembrance Day or at any event where you might be crying. You're a bit . . . smudged. Goodnight.'

Zero hour plus one year ten months six days

Dllenahkh walked the short distance to his own room. He felt at peace, at peace with his sorrow and fear and loneliness, and it was such a new sensation that he held it carefully, observing it curiously, wondering how long it would last and whether he could call it back the next time he had to face the things he did not wish to remember.

The moment of introspection was too brief. He found his door ajar and the light on. He entered his room with caution to see Joral, worried, and Sergeant Fergus, drunk. Resigned, he braced himself for unpleasantness.

'Sergeant Fergus insisted on waiting to speak to you,' Joral said nervously.

'It won't take long, sir,' Fergus said, his speech still clear but with an edge of belligerence that warned Dllenahkh to be careful.

'Very well, Sergeant. I am listening.' Dllenahkh did not close the door. Fergus looked at it and hesitated, but Dllenahkh merely walked further in, removed his jacket and tossed it onto the room's only chair. He then sat on the bed and began to take off his boots.

The sergeant took the hint and began to talk quickly. 'It's about Kir'tahsg. I've been following the case, and it's not going well.'

Dllenahkh straightened up and paid attention. To his chagrin, he had not given any recent thought to the Kir'tahsg situation.

Fergus continued, 'The government's been dealing with the children, but they haven't gone after the cartels. They say that's a galactic matter.' He paused uncertainly. 'They've filed a complaint with the Galactic Judiciary, but . . .'

Dllenahkh felt unexpectedly embarrassed. 'These things take time, Sergeant, even more now than previously.'

'I thought . . . if you knew someone,' Fergus muttered.

'I have sent my own report to the Galactic Judiciary via our Council,' Dllenahkh said quietly. 'I am afraid I have no further influence at that level.'

The explosion was anticipated, but it still made both Sadiri jump when Fergus began to shout, '*You* set yourselves up as the incorruptible guardians of the galaxy. You created a system where everyone had to go to you. Now you're holding on to that power with a . . . a hollow government and a skeleton fleet. It isn't right! Someone has to stop pretending!'

Instinctively, Dllenahkh mentally reached out to brace Joral – an unnecessary act given the sergeant's low psi levels and Joral's improved steadiness. He bent his mind to Fergus instead.

'Sergeant, it is late,' he suggested. 'We must not disturb the other guests. We must not disturb the Commissioner.'

Fergus looked around in sudden fear as if expecting to see Dr Daniyel standing in the doorway, but he immediately caught himself and turned back. 'You're influencing me,' he accused.

'Hardly,' said Dllenahkh with complete honesty. 'I am only appealing to your common sense. You know we can discuss this in the morning.'

Still suspicious, Fergus glanced at the open door again. 'Another time, then,' he said unwillingly.

When he left, a few tense, silent seconds passed, and Joral let go a held breath. 'Nicely done, Councillor,' he said with admiration. 'A light and skilful touch.'

'Close the door as you go, Joral,' Dllenahkh replied, too ashamed to accept the compliment.

Joral bade him a subdued goodnight and went to his own room. Dllenahkh prepared for bed, his movements automatic. They had been given so much sympathy for so long that the sergeant's rage was disorientating. Were there others who had stopped feeling sorry for the stricken Sadiri and were instead beginning to question their place and purpose? What did Fergus expect him to do for Kir'tahsg, when it took all his efforts to keep the young men of his own settlement from despair and self-destruction? And yet . . . who could help Kir'tahsg now, if the Sadiri were too busy surviving to arbitrate the lives of others?

He lay in darkness for several minutes, asking himself unanswerable questions. He knew only one thing: his brief equilibrium was a ruin and his dreams would only mirror that brokenness.

Soon he was once more outside Delarua's room, this time leaning tiredly against the doorframe as he knocked. She came to the door, looking rumpled and sleepy, and he quickly straightened, unsure what to say, but relieved that she was there. It charmed him to see that they were dressed similarly for bed, in trousers and tunic. He wondered what she would say if she could read his mind. Would it amuse or vex her to learn that although he thought she had looked very pretty all dressed up for the concert, he preferred her like this, in her usual unstudied simplicity of body and mind?

She took him in with one glance. 'Oh. Bad night?'

'It could be,' he confessed.

She stepped back. 'Come in.'

THE LAST ASSIGNMENT

It should be obvious by now that I'm not good at dealing with change. I'd settled into my new role on the mission team. I probably knew more about the Sadiri both on and off-planet than any other Cygnian. My friendship with Dllenahkh was as strong, comfortable and close as it was kiss-free (which is to say completely, but like I said, kissing isn't *everything*). I'd finally restored a level of routine to my life and I simply could not bend my mind to consider that the mission would be over in a couple of weeks. Everyone else had a job and a life to return to. I should have been making plans for my future. I wasn't. I was hiding from uncertainty by immersing myself in the excitement of our final visit.

We'd saved the strangest for last. The taSadiri had settled mainly in the equatorial and tropical belts, keeping to a warm climate whenever possible. It was what they were best adapted to, and the Sadiri are nothing if not traditional *and* practical. The last settlement on the schedule was the most distant, sited on a peninsula barely clear of the polar regions. We travelled by air and set down near a fjord under the shadow of a large, low volcano. When

I stepped out, braced for the worst in my insulated jacket and hood, I slowed in shock.

'Stinks,' said Lian, exiting close behind me.

'*Hot*,' I said in utter surprise, lowering my hood and unsealing my jacket.

And it was. The waters of the fjord steamed and the atmosphere was a curious mix of warm, heavy air and puffs of sharp, icy wind. The landscape was treeless, sloping down the narrow inlet with a cradling effect, and alternating between green lichen and black basalt. Nasiha, Tarik and Joral exited the jump-jet looking ambivalent – unimpressed by the fluctuating heat and humidity, but curious at the idea that Sadiri would have chosen to live in such a place.

Fergus, who had been piloting, stuck his head out and sniffed the air suspiciously. 'You sure you know where you're going?'

'Quite sure, Sergeant,' said Nasiha calmly, making slow, sweeping movements with her geosensor. 'All we need to do is find the entrance.'

She deserved to feel a bit complacent. It had been her hard work and brilliance, and Tarik's too, of course, that had uncovered this place from the various legends and folk tales they'd diligently collected in every settlement and town we'd visited. A little cross-checking with the records of the Ministry of Energy and Mineral Resources and the Polar Exploration Institute had borne fruit that would be worth at least one paper, maybe two. The taSadiri settlement had been *underground*, sheltered from the extreme weather, running on geothermal energy, and thus still the right temperature to remind them of home.

Of course, this was a scientific expedition, not a diplomatic one. The settlement had been unpopulated for centuries. The

Commissioner and the Councillor were back in Tlaxce, already bogged down in interviews with Cygnian and Sadiri media and meetings with representatives of global, interplanetary and galactic bodies. That left us to have the fun – and it *was* fun. Of all the places I'd been to, this was the one that I took care to record with my comm. I'd probably never be this far north again in my life.

'Over there.' Tarik pointed.

It looked like rock at first, but it was a regular, man-made structure, built low and strong against the wind into the hillside. We found a door at the side, half-sunk into the ground with steps going down, like the entrance to a bunker. When we entered and the lights came on, I felt first disorientation, then vertigo.

'Do we all go down?' asked Joral doubtfully, hitching a large, bulky bag higher up on one shoulder.

Tarik examined the small elevator-like structure hanging suspended in the centre over an unfathomably deep mineshaft. 'The carrying capacity is more than adequate. However, there are also emergency chutes at the circumference if you prefer.'

Joral turned to examine them as Tarik pointed them out. He blinked. They were narrow tubes of some transparent material, even more claustrophobia-inducing than the main lift. 'No,' he said quickly. 'No, that will not be necessary.'

Tarik turned to Nasiha. 'There is no need for you to come with us.'

'So you have already told me,' she said. 'You have my response on that matter. Further discussion at this stage is—'

'Then at least grant me this. You will return to the surface immediately if I consider it to be too dangerous.'

I was impressed. I had never heard Tarik interrupt Nasiha before.

'That sounds reasonable,' she admitted reluctantly.

I looked away from them to hide my smile.

The ride down was long, dark and filled with ominous creaking sounds, but I wasn't too worried as I knew this technology was a relatively recent addition by the Mineral Resources people. Nasiha led us out of the lift to the rim of the single pool of light around the shaft. Pale lights came up and slowly strengthened as she tapped access codes into her comm. Joral opened his bag and handed out hard hats with miners' lights – old, solid technology, but with a few modern additions like built-in nav and emergency oxygen generators. I put mine on gladly and vidded myself with my wrist comm looking all adventurer-like while Lian laughed at me.

'Where do we go?' asked Joral, and it was a good question because the mine's lights illuminated at least six different paths leading away to God knows where in the vastness.

Nasiha's reply was reassuringly prompt and confident. 'This way.'

She led us for half an hour along a path with damp, dripping rock above and around. The water was warm, and I couldn't help but feel that there must be some pools nearby worth soaking in, fed by hot springs and rich with minerals. Decadent taSadiri of this austere outpost, kicking back in their hot tubs while the weather above them went to sub-zero – I could picture it.

We turned away from the lights onto a less even path, scrambled through a few narrow places and then we were there! It was worth it! I'd missed seeing Piedra in real life so I had no comparison, but as far as cities carved out of sheer rock go, this was damned impressive. I hurt my neck swivelling around trying to get my headlight to capture the full scope of an arch two storeys high and bracketed by windows that hinted at rooms within the rock. The arch itself led into a cathedral of a passageway, with more windows high in the walls and arched doorways a little above path-level, their steps crumbling as if eroded by running water. I could imagine the subterranean street lit by cool, pale lamps during the night and warm, bright lamps in the day. Greenhouses near the surface were a possibility, Nasiha had said, close enough to take advantage of skylights but deep enough to tap into the earth's heat. Rivers and inlets were filled with fish adapted to living underground, feeding on algae swept in by the tides of the fjord. A glitter caught my eye and I went closer to see the muted sheen of crystal in the rock, not excavated but incorporated into the carvings of the door lintel. It was a rich place, an unexpected Eden. Why was it deserted?

Tarik approached one set of steps more closely and beckoned us over. 'Look,' he said. 'The path has risen. We are walking on the remnants of a lava flow.'

That put my vivid imagination to work in a less pleasant direction. I imagined the street illuminated with a hellish red, oozing past doors and trapping people in . . . Wait a minute.

'Tarik, was this place abandoned before the lava came through? Did they find any remains?' I asked.

He nodded approvingly at the question. 'None. They must have had warning of the eruption and evacuated to some other place. Then when they returned they found it uninhabitable.'

I understood what he meant when the path went sharply upwards, allowing us to walk along the level of the first-storey windows, and then past them until the ceiling of the tunnel stopped us.

'Who knows how much more lies under that rock,' Lian said wonderingly. Lian had also missed seeing Piedra. 'How do you know for certain that taSadiri lived here?'

'This is similar to the stone-carving of Piedra, and some of the symbols here can also be found in ancient Sadiri texts,' Joral explained. 'However, there may have been other—'

We froze. There was a sudden scuttling patter that made me think uncomfortably of giant spiders – my own fault for having watched pre-holo monster movies with Joral and Lian two nights previously.

'Rockfall,' said Nasiha crisply after the echoes had died away. 'Small earthquakes are common in this area. It is nothing to be concerned about.'

I would have believed her in an instant, but Tarik was frowning and checking his geosensor. 'Seismic data from the mine's sensors do indicate that caution may be advisable. How much longer do you need to record—?'

The path beneath us fell away by ten centimetres or so, then surged up higher, leaving us first stumbling, then gasping on our knees.

'We go now,' Tarik ordered, clipping his geosensor to his belt and seizing hold of his wife's arm.

Nasiha tried to collect herself. 'Wait, the—'

'Good idea,' Lian interrupted briskly.

We staggered out, disorientated by the occasional vibration of the ground and the wavering shadows as our headlights bobbed. That's how I ran into Tarik's back.

'What is it?' Joral asked sharply.

There was no answer, and for a moment I wondered hysterically if the way was blocked and he was afraid to tell us, but then one by one, we turned and squinted up through the dust, half-unsure about what we were seeing.

'Everyone, turn off your lights,' Tarik commanded.

Far from the mine's lamps, and with our own lights out, it was obvious. There was a slender beam of illuminated dust, as if someone had cracked open a window several storeys up.

'But we're so far down,' Lian murmured in awe.

'A light well,' Nasiha said. 'Another part of the city must have been opened by the earth tremor.'

Lian switched a light back on and swept it along the ground leading to the beam. The terrain was steep but passable. 'You guys stay here. We'll scout ahead, see if there's anything worth investigating.'

I dithered, trying to decide whether I wanted to be classified as a 'you guys' or a 'we', but as Joral followed Lian, curiosity got the better of me. With an apologetic glance back at Nasiha, I scrambled to catch up with them. When I arrived, out of breath, at the source of the light, they were crouched beside the gap, staring transfixed. I huddled in to take a peek and saw a huge cavern lit by massive tubes of mirror and glass. Some were dim and dark – perhaps covered over by earth where they were meant to emerge into sunlight – but there were enough tubes still functioning for us to see that the street we had just walked was a mere back alley. *This* was the heart of the city, its *forum magnum*. I vidded what I could see, and stuck my arm out to vid what I couldn't.

Lian began to pull at the rocks around the edge of the gap, trying to clear more space. 'Let's see if we can get down there.'

Stair-connected balconies ridged the walls of the cavern. Lian went through the gap and carefully climbed down a few metres of rock face to stand on one of them.

'I'm sure that's dangerous,' I said nervously. 'Joral, don't you have some rope in that kitbag?'

'A very good idea,' he said, also looking apprehensive. He took out a length of slender cord. Securing one end to a projection of rock, he lowered the other end to Lian. Lian caught it and hooked it onto a belt loop without comment.

'Tarik should see this at least,' I said. 'I'll go back and stay with Nasiha so he can come up.'

I made the switch, consoling Nasiha with some images from my comm vid while Tarik went to examine the find. Then the earth shook again, a long, powerful tremor.

I gasped. 'Let's get out of here,' I said to Nasiha.

We stumbled a short distance, and then she cried out, 'Tarik!'

'Delarua! Take Nasiha to the surface now!' he shouted back.

'You promised,' I told her, unfairly perhaps, but it had an effect. She let me pull her into a near-run as we headed for the main path, and once the way was lit she outpaced me to the shaft lift.

'Get in,' she snapped. 'They can use the emergency tubes.'

I got in. The earth had calmed again, but I felt as if I'd had my fill of adventures of this kind. Several different phobias assailed me as we ascended. We were so high up – what if the lift failed and we fell? What if it got to the top and didn't open, trapping us in a box? What if it failed, fell and left us to be buried alive in the dark? I breathed deeply, marshalling everything that I had learned in meditation practice to keep myself sane. Nasiha had only one fear, and I could read it in her eyes.

'Tarik will be right behind us,' I promised.

The lift opened. I grasped Nasiha's hand and ran out and up the stairs into the open, not giving her the chance to even think about waiting for the others inside that windowless chamber. We collapsed on the hillside, sitting facing the door. Nasiha frowned at her geosensor, then tried her comm, tapping and calling Tarik's name, then Joral's, then Lian's. There was no response.

'I am a fool,' she whispered, her face bleak.

'Come on, come on,' I muttered at the empty doorway. 'You're all okay, you've got to be.'

A long, agony-filled minute later, Tarik came out, coughing and covered in dust. Nasiha went to meet him, took his hands and seemed to sigh. I ran past them.

'Lian! Lian? Joral?' I whipped back around. 'Where are they?'

Tarik looked at me, sombre and ashamed. 'We must call for help. There has been a significant collapse of the exit tunnel.'

I slapped on my comm. 'Fergus! Call Emergency Services. We have two missing.'

By the time we got down to the jump-jet, we found that Fergus had called Emergency Services and also managed to contact Lian using the jet's comm. They were both uninjured but there was no way out. Nasiha scanned the data provided by the Ministry, but to no avail. The newly discovered cavern was unmapped.

I tried to be cheerful as I chatted to Lian and Joral. 'Look on the bright side. You're in the warm, there's sunlight all about and you're in the middle of the discovery of the century. Walk around, take some pics and vids for us. Find something Nasiha can write a paper about.'

As we talked to them, the first team from Emergency Services turned up. They were a small group from a nearby science outpost, and while they lacked excavation equipment, they did have all manner of scanning technology to determine the extent of the collapse and figure out where to start digging when the heavy equipment arrived. They also checked us over, giving Nasiha particular attention, then declared us fine and tried to ignore us as we told them everything we knew and a few things we didn't and, frankly, breathed down their necks in a very unhelpful way.

'The fact that communication is still possible suggests that transponder technology could be used to locate them,' Tarik said.

'I have no doubt that we will locate them in time,' the Emergency Services chief explained patiently. 'The challenge is factoring in the interference from magnetic fluctuations caused by the volcanic activity.'

He was a pale-skinned man, regrettably spare of fat for such a cold climate, and his short frame was made even smaller by the bulkiness of his parka. His eyebrows had a perpetually worried slant that did not reassure. His voice made up for it, though, deliberately slow and slightly soft, so you felt you had to dial down your own hysteria in order to be able to hear him clearly.

'But the fact that we can still communicate with them *is* good, isn't it?' I asked.

His expression turned wary. 'It is good in that we may be able to find out roughly where they are so we can plan how to excavate, but there's too much interference for certainty. Let's not get carried away—'

'Well, what about those light tubes?' I insisted. 'Shouldn't we try to find where they come out, maybe use—?'

'Ma'am,' he said, firmly cutting me off. 'We appreciate that you're concerned about your friends, but we do know our job. Our networks have been informed and there are people working to solve the problem.'

'Of course,' I said, defeated. 'But . . . you understand why we can't lose them? Especially not Joral. Not now. Not like this.'

He blew out a breath, looking as if he were trying to choose his next words very carefully. 'I'd like to recommend that you return home as scheduled. To be honest, we can't afford to have non-essential personnel using up our resources. You might be able to do more for your friends by being in Tlaxce than being here.'

It was a kind but definite brush-off, and it meant we had to have a final conversation with Lian and Joral.

'They're kicking us out,' I said casually. 'We have to go back, stop getting in their way and stuff.'

Lian played along. 'Well, you know what that means. Can't put your name in the acknowledgements when we make our big discoveries.'

I laughed, then sobered. 'About what I said earlier, walking around and so on? Be careful. Conserve your resources. I know Joral's got a thing or two in the bag, but—'

'Delarua, I *am* a corporal, you know,' said Lian, gently teasing. 'I didn't forget all my survival training when they made me a pencil-pusher. To replace *you*, I might add.'

My laugh was a little too close to a sob, so I cut it short. 'Yeah, man, sorry about that one. So, I'll be seeing you later, okay?'

I waited for Tarik and Nasiha to finish speaking with Joral, then I started a conversation in rapid Sadiri so that Lian would not understand. 'Joral, I know that if you remember all that Councillor Dllenahkh has taught you, your chances of survival are excellent.'

'Delarua, I have considered this. I know it will be more difficult for someone who has not been trained in psychosomatic control. I am not sufficiently advanced in the disciplines to exert this control beyond my own body, but I will at least ensure that our colleague consumes more food and water than I do.'

I smiled at his careful efforts not to attract attention by using Lian's name. 'Joral, I hope it will not be necessary for you to deny yourself what little food and drink you have, but I know that whatever you choose to do, you will choose well.' Time to treat the boy like a man. Heaven knows he deserved it by now.

When the jump-jet took off, we all gazed down at the land we were leaving. I couldn't guess what everyone was feeling at that point, but I bet Fergus was thinking that if he had been underground with us, he could have done something. As for myself, I was damping down my emotions, that thing I'm so very good at, and scrutinising the slopes for any flash of glass or metal that might suggest a protruding light tube. I saw none.

A few minutes into the flight, we called Qeturah and Dllenahkh and updated them. An hour later we arrived at our stopover point, changed, ate and switched from the jump-jet to a slower but more comfortable shuttle. At first it seemed natural to talk a bit about the old underground city and what new discoveries might be made there, but as we monitored the bulletins from Emergency Services, the journey grew quieter and quieter. The revised time to reach Lian and Joral was no longer being given in hours, but in days.

When we arrived in Tlaxce City that evening, there was still no good news. The small welcoming ceremony at Central Government Headquarters had been quietly called off, and all that remained of the end-of-mission reception were a few napkin-covered plates of assorted finger-foods. In case we were hungry, Qeturah said in an offhand fashion as we filed into her office, but I saw eight plates on her meeting-room table and a dying hope in her eyes. I couldn't blame her. I'd half-expected to step off the shuttle and find that Lian and Joral were fine and at home, flown ahead at supersonic speed just to surprise us. Dllenahkh seemed depressed, but in a healthy way, if that makes any sense. From the questions he asked us, I knew he was trying to convince himself that nothing would have happened any differently if he had been there.

'It was nobody's fault, Dllenahkh,' I said wearily. 'Nobody's or everybody's, take your pick.'

'This isn't a post-mission debriefing,' Qeturah said hastily. 'We're not in the frame of mind for that.' She glared at Dllenahkh and added pointedly, '*None* of us. This is . . . well, even if we couldn't have a proper homecoming, I wanted us to meet one last time.'

I was miserable, but strangely glad to be there because I didn't want to be miserable alone and there wasn't anyone else I wanted to be miserable with. We weren't grieving for Lian and Joral. We were worried about them, but we still had hopes of seeing them very soon. We were dealing with the fact that the mission was over, that the life we had made ours for a year was not the life we would be facing on the morrow. Not having Lian and Joral there only emphasised how much we were going to miss each other. I blinked back tears so many times that I had to excuse myself to go to the ladies' room to have a proper nose-blow and wash my face.

When I returned, Fergus was standing outside Qeturah's office door. He was speaking into his comm as I approached, but by the time I reached him he had finished the call and was staring oddly at the device in his hand. Curiosity overrode my initial intent to nod and pass by. 'What is it, Sergeant?'

At first he didn't look at me. 'That was Lian. Just wanted to make sure we'd made it back to the city okay.' Then he met my eyes and we exchanged a brief, sympathetic look of shared pain before he remembered he didn't like me and looked away again.

'I can't believe the range those comms—' I started, then froze in mid-sentence, struck by something.

He gave me his usual lowering frown. 'If you're getting any bright ideas that might help those two, you'd better share. *Do* something without thinking it to death for a change.'

I didn't get it. Qeturah toed the line and he was fine with that, and yet he'd written me off because I hadn't been enough of a maverick. I was peeved and I let him know it.

'Enough, Sergeant,' I said sharply. 'Central Government's taking care of Kir'tahsg, so stop blaming me for that. Besides, I have at least as much reason as you to care about what happens to Lian, and a hell of a lot more reason when it comes to Joral.'

I took the comm from him and examined it curiously. It was a top-of-the-line military-grade comm, far better than any wrist model or civilian handheld.

'Bullshit,' he said. 'Sadiri or Cygnian, we're all endangered when we're facing death. Got anything useful to contribute, *ma'am*?'

I looked at him and wished for a moment that I was on better terms with this man. 'I might. But I'll need to take this comm with me, just for an hour or two.' I was lying. I didn't know how much time I needed.

He swore under his breath. I stared at him impassively.

'You can choose to say no, Sergeant, but say it quickly. Time's wasting.' Big bluff. I hoped it would impress him just a little. Was that Qeturah's trick? Act as if you're in command, and suddenly they'll start following your orders?

'Take the damned comm,' he said at last in resignation.

I took it all right. I took it straight to Dllenahkh. 'You're staying at the Sadiri Consulate while you're working in the city, right?'

He raised an eyebrow at the incongruous juxtaposition of the mundane question and my conspiratorial whisper. 'Yes.'

'Any way to get an immediate private audience with your pilot friend? The man who's seen things mere mortals only dream of? The man who's been to several futures and who may or may not have the advanced technological know-how to use the fact that Fergus's comm is still picking up a clear signal from Lian's halfway across the globe and through a ton of rock?'

Dllenahkh then did something completely Sadiri and utterly adorable. He blinked at my babbled words, filled in the blanks speedily and arrived at a course of action. 'Come with me,' he said.

Our leaving broke up the meeting. Qeturah looked a little bemused, but Fergus gave me a stiff yet encouraging nod. I so badly wanted to tell Nasiha and Tarik, but I didn't dare risk the possibility that they weren't supposed to know about Naraldi's unique experiences. They hardly noticed. They were once more wrapped up in each other, and this time I didn't mind one bit.

'Thank you, Dllenahkh,' I said as I got into his aircar and belted myself in.

He frowned in puzzlement as he tapped in our destination. 'Why are you thanking me? I haven't done anything yet.'

'You listen to my crazy ideas and make sense out of them. That's worth some thanks.'

He let the autopilot take us and turned to face me, eyes flashing. 'What *you* describe as the product of a mental imbalance, *I* would classify as swift, intuitive thinking to arrive at creative solutions.'

There is no passion like the passion of a Sadiri complimenting your mind. For a moment I was speechless, completely speech-less. I gawked up at him like a lovestruck teenager. 'You . . . you really mean that.'

'You *know* I do. Why is it so difficult for you to believe that?'

I rested my hand over his, a gesture of apology and truce. 'I believe it,' I said softly.

He looked down at my hand and slowly turned his so that we fitted palm to palm. Touching him was never a simple matter, but touching him now, when his emotions were so close to the surface, was like standing on the seashore with the tide drawing out, pulling the sand from under my feet. I wanted to fall into the water.

The aircar smoothly grounded. The Sadiri Consulate is, in fact, very close to Central Government Headquarters. 'We're here,' I said, trying not to sound disappointed.

A quick comm call to the Consul ensured that he was at least a little prepared when we invaded his living room for an impromptu meeting. He was too professional to show irritation in front of me, but he still managed to give Dllenahkh a very pointed look when he said, 'I believe it was clearly stated that you were to tell *no one* about my travels.'

Dllenahkh was unperturbed. 'I'm sorry, Naraldi. I was under the impression that the restriction did not apply to Sadiri above a certain level of government.'

The Consul looked at me – in fact, he looked at my head and its fuzz of dull brown hair – in silent comment at the un-Sadiri sight of me, then surrendered with a small shrug. 'Show me the communicator.'

I handed it over and watched him excitedly as he opened it up and pondered the innards, taking occasional glances at a handheld for reference notes. Then he sat back, eyes narrowing as he contemplated his drumming fingers for further enlightenment. Eventually, he returned to the handheld and made some quick audio and written inputs, at least one of which was a message by the distinctive sound of the 'send' chime.

At last, he pulled a datachip out of his handheld, stood and gave it to Dllenahkh. 'Dllenahkh, if you will permit the indignity to your position, kindly deliver this personally to the Consulate's communications office. It is of a sensitive nature, and must go out as soon as possible.'

Dllenahkh bowed, gave me a quick, reassuring glance and left the room. I watched him go, feeling even more lost than before. 'Your Excellency,' I said plaintively, 'could you tell me what's happening?'

The Consul sat down again, his expression suddenly tired. 'Can I, or should I? I do not want to raise your hopes unduly, Ms Delarua. You assumed correctly – I *do* have technological knowledge that might result in a swifter rescue – but knowledge can only go so far. I would need a certain level of existing technology to effect a quick solution, and such technology is not yet available.'

My heart sank. He saw how my face changed and relented. 'There is a small hope. I have sent a message for help. I cannot be sure it will be answered, but I can do no more.'

'Who is it? How long will they take to get here?' For all that I tried not to sound excited, the words still came out too quickly, too eagerly.

He lowered his eyes and his jaw tensed as if he were biting back words. After a brief silence, he sighed and answered, 'I am sorry, Ms Delarua. I really couldn't say.'

I opened my mouth to plead with him, then paused, closed my mouth and frowned slightly. '*Couldn't* say,' I repeated.

His quick upward glance begged me to understand. 'Couldn't.'

My heart began to pound. I swallowed and tried to compose myself. 'I think I understand you, Your Excellency. At least . . . I hope I do.'

THE UNLIKELY ANGEL

On the first day after I spoke to the Sadiri Consul, I went to visit my mother.

This was a bit of a mistake because Maria and Gracie were still there, Rafi was only home from school every other weekend, and my mother had taken to spending long periods of time at another retiree friend whose apartment was uncluttered by offspring. Okay, perhaps it sounds a little unkind, but that was my first impression of the situation. Then, when I got there, I was entirely on my mother's side. Maria was refusing to continue therapy – wait, refusing is too strong a word. She was apathetic. Gracie was at the other extreme, suddenly acting out after years of suppression. My mother was at her wits' end and would escape for a little sanity from time to time.

'Darling, she's my daughter and I love her, but she's making me crazy,' my mother confessed to me. We were sitting on her balcony plotting strategy and carefully ignoring the yells coming from the kitchen as Maria struggled to get Gracie to finish eating lunch.

I put on my dead-calm, responsible voice. 'This family already has its full quota of crazy, Mum. Let's not go over the edge. There'll be no one left to act as anchor.'

'Well, what can I do? I mean, I was even thinking about proposing to Connie just to have an excuse to get out of the house permanently. Then I could leave this place to Maria and—'

I blinked. 'Proposing to *Connie*? What happened to the guy you kept talking about – Davi was his name?'

'Well, dear,' she said, lowering her voice to a hushed whisper, 'I didn't want to shock you, but it was Connie I meant all along. Davi's her husband, but I *think* I've almost persuaded her that she's better off without him.'

I tilted my head and pondered. 'Mum,' I said, 'you're still a homesteader at heart, so I'll say this gently. Are you sure *she's* interested in you, or is it *both* of them?'

My mother began to scoff, paused and looked suddenly startled, then confused.

'Right then, it seems to me we'd better make sure you hold on to your apartment for a little while longer. Better if Maria and Gracie come to my apartment. I'll be doing more work down on the Sadiri settlement anyway, and it'll be harder for her to avoid therapy when she's near all the best institutes.'

'But dear,' my mother protested, 'are you sure you want to do that? I mean, unless there's someone you're thinking of moving in with, I wouldn't wish Maria on you either.'

Too much Ntshune in my family. Too damn much. Her eyes lit up.

'There *is* someone,' she said, leaning forward avidly. 'Go on! What's he like? How old is he? Oh, it is a *he*, isn't it?'

He's Sadiri. Furthermore, he's a Sadiri savant who is, in fact, older than you. 'But I think we were discussing *your* love life?' I chided her with lofty dignity.

'Oh. I do seem to have made a mess of that,' she said ruefully.

I zapped a contact from my comm to hers. 'There. That's my friend Gilda. She's lovely and approachable and will give you all kinds of good advice about negotiating the currents of city polyamory. Just . . . don't date her. Please. I would find that awkward.'

I picked up my handheld. 'I'm making arrangements for Maria to move into my apartment within a couple of weeks. Please find a way to talk her around to it by then. I'll do my best to push her back to therapy, but I think even a part-time job would work wonders. The credits from the divorce and compensation are only going to last so long, anyway. Now, how's Rafi?'

'Terribly unhappy,' she admitted, looking very distressed.

I felt a pang of dismay. She'd been our rock all the time we were growing up. She shouldn't have to shoulder these burdens at her age. 'Never mind. I'll go see him tomorrow.'

Thus it was that on the second day after the Consul sent for help, I went to visit my nephew at his boarding school. Fortunately, Rafi wasn't so much terribly unhappy as quite naturally stressed by the new environment and the fact that he had come into it in the middle of the school year, when friendships are already sealed and group allegiances formed. He also viewed his being there as a kind of sentence rather than a privilege and a mark of distinction from the average Cygnian. We walked the immaculate school grounds and I tried my best to cheer him up.

'They all show off so much. Talking mind to mind. Levitating scraps of paper, even,' he said, glum and resistant to consoling.

I looked him over, noting his extra six centimetres of height and a face that was moving from cute to handsome with less adolescent awkwardness than the norm. He could be popular. He must not be trying. 'I've seen your psi profile. You're stronger than any of them. Why don't you show off a little yourself?'

He shrugged. 'I could make everyone like me, but that sort of thing is frowned upon, oddly enough. As for the telepathy – there's no one I really want to talk to, I guess.'

'Hmm,' I said. 'Who's in charge of your welfare around here?'

'My House Master, I suppose. Why?' He looked a little wary. 'Don't embarrass me.'

I gave him an incredulous look. 'When have I ever not been cool? Don't turn all teenage on me now. Just answer me one thing. Do you still like elephants?'

A quick consultation with his House Master ensured that Rafi and one other student would spend the next half-term holiday on an educational visit to the forest uplands.

'There's more than one way to be popular, my boy,' I told him as I was leaving. 'Elephants are cool. Eccentric aunts who send you and a fortunate friend to ride on elephants, they too are cool. You're lucky I've had no reason to dip into my holiday fund this year. I can't do this too often. Anyway, once should be enough to seal your reputation.'

He grinned at me. He knew I was up to something, more than was evident on the surface, but he trusted me enough to be amused and excited rather than worried.

'And by the way,' I added, 'I'd practise my telepathy while I was out there if I were you. Loudly. Vacation is no reason to slack off.'

*   *   *

Transferring the lease on my apartment and spending such a large sum on impulse meant that I had to consider my future sooner rather than later. And so on the third day after the Consul's leap of faith, I collared Nasiha in her temporary office at the Sadiri Consulate and asked bluntly, 'Want to work with me?'

She raised an eyebrow. 'You appear to have made certain assumptions about my future plans.'

'Or perhaps I'm trying to influence them.'

She smiled then, just a little. 'I *had* noticed that in spite of the fact that your breach of the Cygnian Science Code has caused you to be barred from empirical research, you have somehow managed to become the cause of academic papers by others. I would welcome the opportunity to examine the phenomenon further by continuing our association within an entrepreneurial framework.'

'Tarik?' I asked. It was interesting, this new vocal shorthand. I was finally living my life as if I had no time to waste.

Nasiha's gaze softened, and I was reminded just how much those two did love each other – although they would have found some other way to phrase it, no doubt. 'We have assessed various locations in terms of safety, stability and support networks. We have decided to spend at least one year living in the Tlaxce Sadiri Settlement so that our child can be born there. After that, Tarik will probably return to working with the Science Council while I remain as primary parent for the first seven years. At the end of those seven years . . . who knows? I may return to the Science Council while he becomes the primary parent. We may all return to New Sadira or to whatever planet we may be assigned. But that is in the future.'

I smiled. 'Tarik is a good husband and will make an excellent father.' *He loves you so much.*

Nasiha gave me an amused look. 'Of course.' *And I love him.*

For two days after that I didn't try to save the world or solve anyone's problems. I worked on my reports diligently from home, having wisely turned down the offer of office space at the Sadiri Consulate. With everything that was happening, I didn't trust my professionalism that far. At home, I could at least periodically get up from my desk, look at the calendar and scream into a pillow set aside for that purpose.

Then I got a call from Dr Freyda Mar herself.

'I heard you'd come in, but I thought I should wait a bit. I'm so sorry,' she said.

'Freyda, it's so good to hear you.' In spite of everything, I smiled when I heard her voice. 'Things have been a bit grim, but where there's life there's hope.'

'That's so,' she agreed. 'Look, I'm going down to the home-steadings this afternoon to start the week's rounds. Would you like to come with me?'

My gaze drifted to my handheld. I had been checking my messages in the minutes prior to Freyda's call. A rather large number of the messages were from Fergus – several variations on the tune of his comm and the fact that I had not returned it, no doubt. Since I had last seen it in bits and pieces in the Consul's living room, I was beginning to think that it might be a prudent move to try a change of scenery.

'Why, thank you, Freyda! That'd be perfect. We can catch up.'

Freyda was as kind as ever. She opted for nav, but no autopilot, so that I wouldn't feel pressured to make small talk for the entire journey. I dived right into the important stuff, using my new blunt-and-direct mode. 'You and Lanuri. Progress?'

Her face was calm, her tone light-hearted. 'You are aware, Ms Delarua, that government officials are not encouraged to fraternise with colleagues. It might interfere with efficiency. What they do at the end of the assignment is, of course, their own business.'

'Entirely appropriate,' I agreed.

There was a small silence and then we burst out laughing.

'I can play "Sadiri" for about ten minutes, tops,' I admitted. 'Longer if I'm really concentrating. So, you guys looking to get married soon after?'

She nodded happily. 'Yeah. It's funny, I didn't even have to make any moves. Once I started looking at things differently, it all seemed to unfold naturally somehow.'

'How do you attract a Sadiri's attention?'

'Sound intelligent,' she answered. 'Tell them something they didn't know or hadn't figured out for themselves. How do you know you've got their attention?'

'Intensity like whoa,' I said immediately. 'They drop everything and listen to you and then come up with all kinds of reasons to keep you around. How do you know they "like" you?'

'Unusually touchy. Brushing fingers when handing you a cup or a handheld. Protective, solicitous behaviour. Very quick to catch you if you stumble or lose footing, very concerned if you're unwell. Personal distance decreases significantly. Then one day, next thing you know he's holding your hand and gazing into your eyes,' she concluded dreamily.

But do you ever kiss? I wanted to ask that really badly. I just smiled instead.

273

She smiled too. 'And you?'

'Better ask when my assignment's formally over, Doctor Mar,' I said archly. Then I fell silent, remembering the number of days till then, and also the unknown number of days before the Consul's miracle would arrive. *Might* arrive.

When we reached Lanuri's office, he greeted me with unexpected warmth, clasping my hand and saying, 'It is fitting that you should be here for the memorial.'

'What memorial?' I asked, confused.

He looked slightly concerned. 'You have not received word? The rescue has been called off. Increased seismic activity in the area has made it impossible for excavation to continue safely.'

The unopened messages from Fergus, I thought. The room slid slowly to one side and I was surprised to find that Freyda was gripping me by the shoulders. I shrugged her off.

'I'm all right,' I insisted. I took a step, and swayed. 'I just need to sit down for a bit,' I amended in a small voice.

They were very attentive. They took me to Lanuri's residence and made me sit still and drink tea. It was all I could do. My brain simply shut off, refusing to accept any possibility that I would never again hear Lian's laugh and Joral's earnest voice.

The following day, I was at a Sadiri memorial service – or, as I preferred to call it, a funeral for bodies that were very likely still breathing. Two memory trees were planted before the Local Council Hall in a ceremony that was a curious mix of Cygnian and Sadiri traditions, and then the attendees retired to the Hall for a few solemn minutes of awkward interaction.

I found it indecent. 'They could have waited,' I said angrily.

Nasiha, who didn't even know about the Consul's call for help, also found it unseemly, but she tried to excuse it. 'The chances of survival are now negligible,' she stated, her morose expression suggesting that she disliked the sound of her words even more than I did. 'Furthermore, the Council was of the opinion that delaying the customary rituals would give the event more weight than is warranted.'

'It's the settlement's first funeral,' I murmured.

'Yes. And there will be more, in time. That is the point. These young men must learn to face death again.'

'But couldn't they at least have waited till we knew for sure?' I demanded.

She shrugged. 'They have no reason to believe in miracles.'

'I do,' I said fiercely.

There was, however, a limit to the sympathy Nasiha and I could share. Thank God for Freyda Mar, because we exchanged a single glance across the crowded room, made our excuses, then went together to a private corner, fell into each other's arms and wept silently for fifteen minutes or so.

'How did you know?' I asked her when we had both composed ourselves.

She smiled ruefully. 'Lanuri says that when I want a hug but I'm afraid to ask for it, I clasp my hands behind my back. You've been gripping your wrists for the past hour now.'

I had been trying to avoid even the sight of Dllenahkh, afraid to ask him if he had any news, afraid to glimpse something in his eyes that might destroy my hope, but when she said that, I had a yearning to go find him. He seemed to know I wanted him because the moment I looked in his direction, he disengaged himself from a knot of grim-faced Councillors and came towards me.

'Delarua,' he said abruptly, 'where are you staying?'

'Doctor Lanuri's residence. I'm going back to the City with Freyda tomorrow, when she's finished her rounds,' I replied.

'Come back with me now.'

'Okay,' I said immediately.

On the way there he explained to me what needed to be done. 'Naraldi does not wish to involve himself directly, nor does he wish the Consulate to be implicated in any way. I have the reassembled comm. He wants you to take it and wait at your apartment. Someone will come to you at the designated time.'

I looked at him, looked at him *properly*, and dared to allow myself to feel.

'When last did you sleep?' I asked quietly.

He glanced aside in that way he had when he was hesitating to speak the truth. 'I—'

How many times had we slept in a groundcar on autopilot? Too many times. I touched the controls, darkening the windows and adjusting the seating. 'Take a nap. We can talk when we get to the City.'

We lay down side by side. Dllenahkh started to move, hesitated and then reached out to place his hand gently on the side of my face, reminding me of the time he had helped to heal me. Instead of the expected delicate brush, a heavy warmth poured into my brain. It felt like nothing I'd experienced with him before.

'What are you doing?' I asked, holding very still.

'Making sure you won't forget *anything*,' he replied in a near-whisper.

I would have questioned him further, but before I could, I fell into a deep sleep.

*   *   *

And so, the following day, the eighth day after meeting with the Consul, I nervously waited in my apartment, holding the comm in my hand. I didn't know what to expect. Would there be a mundane buzz at my door? Would the heavens open and the earth shake? I knew neither *who* nor *how* in this adventure, and the only thing keeping me sitting expectantly in my living room was faith.

The reality was somewhere between the two extremes of my imagination.

First there was a voice, a very ordinary voice except for the fact that it seemed to be coming out of thin air. It said simply, 'Naraldi sent me.'

Then I blinked – and there it was. I jumped out of my chair. It was too bizarre to inspire awe. I had never seen a Sadiri mind-ship in real life but I knew their look, something like a manta ray, very smooth and dark and naturally designed to slip through any tear in the fabric of space-time. Not only was this like nothing I had imagined, I was sure it was like nothing anyone had imagined. It kept to the oceanic theme, at least, for it resembled the keel of a boat, all carved and sanded wood in the shape of a high, curving bow. But there was no boat, only a tall figure wearing a close-fitting metallic jumpsuit and a helmet, with one hand resting on the wood as if keeping the keel upright. *Was* there an invisible boat attached? I stared.

'Oh, good. You didn't scream, or fall down, or run away.' The voice was slightly muffled at the beginning, and then the shining helmet was removed to reveal an equally shining face and a wide, white cloud of hair.

I quickly revised my interpretation of what I was seeing. 'I should,' I said reproachfully to the gilded stranger. 'You're naked.'

He looked down nervously, then gave me a stern look. 'Don't scare me like that. I haven't lost pubic sphincter control since I was twelve.'

'Oh?' I said faintly.

A worried expression came over his face. 'That was a joke. Please don't take me seriously. Pubic sphincter. As if there could be such a thing.' He gave a short, awkward laugh, then shut up and looked at me sheepishly.

The conversation was getting away from me, getting away from any semblance of common sense in fact, so I tried to bring it back under control. 'I'm Grace Delarua. How do you do,' I said, stepping forward and holding out my hand.

The stranger eyed my hand, then looked at me doubtfully. He put his helmet back on, this time with the faceplate open, and reached out to me. 'Well, if you're sure.'

It was only in the moment that the brass-bright skin touched mine that it struck me why this would be a bad idea. Too late. The world vanished. I shut my eyes tightly and tried to scream, but it wasn't working.

The stranger's voice rang clearly in my head, sounding disconcertingly like my own tone and rhythm and idiolect. 'You can call me Sayr, by the way. I didn't think you'd want to travel with me. I just came to get the comm so I'd have a point of reference, but this way's good, too.'

'Ahhhhh!' I finally managed to make some noise. It echoed so loudly that I opened my eyes immediately. There was nothing before me but a pure, rich darkness that made me welcome the solid feel of rock under my feet, because without it I would have imagined myself floating in outer space. Suddenly a glow appeared to my left, making me jump. Sayr's entire arm had gone luminescent and he was studying a faint overlay of lines on it. For a bemused instant, I wondered why he was looking at his veins, and then I realised it was a map.

'So, this is where you were when you saw the light come through. Hm. The terrain has changed quite a bit. Would you like to try calling your friends?'

I hesitated: one second to understand that I was on the other side of the world, once more underground in the abandoned city; two seconds to wonder whether Sayr was human or machine or both; and one more second to remember and be grateful for Fergus's comm still held tightly in my left hand. I turned it on, fumbled with the lit control panel and selected Lian's ID.

'*Unavailable. Leave a message.*'

It wasn't even Lian's voice, just the generic recording. I held the comm out mutely to Sayr. His eyes widened and glittered in the dark, reflecting the glow of the comm display.

'I've found them,' he said.

The comm went dark as the connection cut out, and for a moment I was convinced I was alone in the dark. Then I told myself not to be silly. As if Sayr would leave me alone in a derelict mine with an active volcano rumbling nearby. That would be irresponsible. He was probably in deep thought or something. I tried to be quiet so as not to disturb him.

His voice rang out so close, so sudden, that I almost fell down in sheer fright. 'Sorry I didn't take you, but it's easier when there aren't any collective memories—'

'What? You *left* me here?' I squeaked. It was too much. I immediately began to hyperventilate.

Bright sunlight seared my vision and icy air pricked my skin. I gasped and screwed up my face, but at least the shock put an end to my dry sobbing. When I was finally able to squint my eyes open again, it was to see Sayr standing close to his keel, one hand in the usual rest position on his transport and the other patting me reassuringly on the shoulder.

'Look,' he urged. 'There they are. They're calling Emergency Services now. Everything will be fine.'

We were on a hill, where exactly, I wasn't sure, but it was cold enough that I knew we were still near the polar regions. There were indeed two figures, tiny in the distance, heartwarmingly familiar and blessedly alive. They sat huddled together, arms about each other. I stopped shivering with cold for a moment to shiver with pure joy.

I had no more time to be sentimental. In another twinkling of an eye, we were back in my living room.

'Thanks for the experience. Sorry I can't stay longer.' His face went from friendly to serious, and I knew what was coming next.

'Wait!' I wailed. 'Before you wipe my memory, can't I ask you some questions? A question? Just one question, please?'

Sayr paused, eyeing me warily as if suspecting me of employing delaying tactics – which might have been partly true. 'What would be the point if you can't remember the answer anyway?'

'I'd have a sense of satisfaction,' I said, guessing wildly. 'That would be enough.'

'Let me hear the question,' he said, still wary.

I took a deep breath. This was my chance to find out the meaning of life.

'Is it true that the Caretakers save people who are essential to the human race?' The words were rushed and inelegant, but I couldn't risk waiting in case he changed his mind.

Fortunately, the query appeared to interest him. 'That's a complicated question. It has a complicated answer to go with it.'

'That's fine,' I said encouragingly. I sat down in a chair and raised my hands hopefully, trying to project the image of a supplicant who would be grateful for the merest scrap.

His face relaxed, slightly amused at my eagerness. 'I'm going to tell you in such a way that you'll remember the answer, but not the question nor the asking of it.'

I suppressed a wriggle of excitement that would have been most unbecoming to my mature years. He left the keel standing by itself at the edge of the room, settled himself cross-legged on the floor and began.

'In the beginning, God created human beings, which is to say God put the ingredients together, embedded the instructions for building on the template and put it all into four separate eggs marked "Some Assembly Required".

'One egg was thrown down to Sadira. There humanity grew to revere and develop the powers of the mind. Another egg was sent to Ntshune, and the humans who arose there became adept at dealing with matters of the heart. A third egg arrived at Zhinu, and there the focus was on the body, both natural and man-made. The last egg came to Terra, and these humans were unmatched in spirit. Strong in belief, they developed minds to speculate and debate, hearts to deplore and adore, and bodies to craft and adapt. Such were their minds, hearts and bodies that they soon began to rival their elder siblings.

'When the children of God saw the Terrans and their many ways of being human, they were both impressed and appalled. Some declared, "See how they combine the four aspects of humanness! Through Terra, all will be transformed – Sadira,

Ntshune and Zhinu – into one harmonious whole." Others predicted, "How can any group survive such fragmentation? They will kill each other, and the rest of humanity will remain forever incomplete."

'After some discussion, it was decided to seal off Terra from the rest of the galaxy until Terran civilisation reached full maturity. It was also decided to periodically save them from themselves, by placing endangered Terrans where they could flourish and begin to mix with other humans.'

He smiled as he concluded, 'And that, my dear, is five creation myths for the price of one. Are you satisfied?'

'That's a child's bedtime story,' I said, but not too critically, because I'd actually enjoyed it.

Sayr shrugged. 'Doesn't make it any less true.'

'Are *you* a child of God?' I asked, keeping my tone light and conversational.

He didn't buy it. 'Aren't we all? One question only, my dear. Now, if you'll forgive me, this won't take a second.'

There was a silence. Sayr began to frown. I looked at him anxiously, baffled at his growing irritation.

'I see you've been memory-protected.' Sayr sniffed. 'This is such a difficult time period to work in. You people know too much already and you always want to know more. You'll have to come with me.'

'No!' I insisted, beginning to panic again. 'I'm home and safe, and I'm not going anywhere else with you and that . . . thing!'

Frustration edged his voice. 'Stop hyperventilating. You know I won't force you to come with me. But you leave me with no choice. I'm sorry, but I'll have to do it the old-fashioned way.'

He stood up, glaring at me, but the glare transformed once

more into that sheepish expression. 'You . . . you wouldn't happen to have any alcohol handy, would you?'

I had two bottles. One was a lovely, light, triple-distilled spirit made with honey, spices and herbs that I'd picked up on my travels and was saving for a special occasion. The other was an utterly miserable sherry that someone had given me in one of those office gift-exchange things about two years previously. I punished Sayr by making him drink one glass of sherry for every two glasses of spirits he had me guzzle. Unfortunately for my thirst for vengeance, I was only able to force him to endure two glasses. After that, I was hugging the bottle with one arm and holding him with the other, and I was far too cheerful to care when he danced us closer to the keel and got his hand onto it.

The room vanished, to be replaced by another, unfamiliar room, dimly lit and exuding the stillness of a workplace in after-hours mode. I stumbled forward, unsupported, my gentle abductor having absconded for parts unknown. To my great relief, there was another body nearby to lean on. Dllenahkh was there to meet me. He greeted me warmly – yes, warmly! I know what the word means! He hugged me! Or helped me stand upright. Maybe. But he was happy! He was practically burning with it. You can't mistake something like that. Then I looked around and was moved to comment.

'This isn't my apartment,' I said indignantly.

'No, indeed. We are in the Consulate,' Dllenahkh replied.

'Now, why did he—?' I frowned, trying to think. 'What happened? I thought this was supposed to end in alcoholic amnesia.' The last two words came out a little garbled. I pressed my fingers to my face, trying to wake up the numb patches.

'We grew concerned when we did not hear from you, so Naraldi contacted Sayr. After Sayr briefed us on the situation, Naraldi advised him that alcohol poisoning was not the best way to approach the problem. I recommended that he bring you here instead as soon as possible. Just put your arm about my waist. There. Now this way . . . no . . . the other direction . . .'

This explained the times when Sayr had been muttering grimly to himself. I thought he'd merely been cursing the sherry under his breath.

'But where are we going?' I asked after a while.

'To Central Government Headquarters. The rest of the team will meet us there.'

'What about the Consul?' I whispered to him as we navigated the corridors. 'I'd like to see him before we go. Thank him.'

'He is occupied in his office, but I believe he would not mind seeing you,' Dllenahkh replied. 'Try to focus. It will dispel some of the alcohol's effects and you will be able to speak more clearly.'

I breathed deeply, brought myself under some control just as Nasiha had taught me and steadied my steps. By the time we reached the corridor to the Consul's office, I was faking sobriety pretty well. 'I'm ready,' I declared.

Dllenahkh smiled slightly. 'Take your time. Wait here.'

He went to a door a few metres away and pressed for admittance. The door opened and stayed open, which is how I got to hear everything.

'Ah, Dllenahkh. We were just talking about you. All is well?'

'Yes, Naraldi. I contacted Emergency Services and they were able to confirm that Lian and Joral are both expected to make a full recovery. I am about to depart for Central Government Headquarters to meet with the other members of the mission team, but Ms Delarua expressed a wish to thank you personally before we go. She is waiting outside.'

Naraldi immediately came to the door, looking out rather than inviting me in. I stood straight and tried to look professional, discreetly putting my hands, and the bottle, behind my back.

'Your Excellency,' I said with a very small, very careful bow. 'Thank you so much for all your help.'

He walked towards me, Dllenahkh following close behind. 'Ms Delarua. I am glad to see that you have proved yourself more than competent in your post. Thank *you* for seeking me out and inspiring me to ask something I would not have thought to ask. Fortune favours the audacious, apparently.'

Dllenahkh came to stand next to me, radiating such an aura of satisfaction that you'd have thought the Consul's words had been intended for him. 'Ms Delarua has long been an asset to our settlement. Providing insightful solutions to unforeseen problems is a talent of hers.'

The Consul looked at us steadily, such a look as made me surreptitiously step a little further away from Dllenahkh, out of his personal space.

'I see. And this would be why you protect her from mental tampering? To maintain her talents at their peak?' He slowly shook his head in mock sorrow, and I realised with a jolt that this was Dllenahkh's Lian, the one person who would always notice when the kohl had been applied, and be happy to point it out, too.

'I wish you well,' he continued with a smile and nod to each of us, making the pronoun plural.

We gave him our good wishes in turn and then, still emboldened by alcohol, I raised my voice for the silent visitor in the Consul's office. 'Thank you, Sayr!'

There was a pause, and then a voice cautiously sang out, 'You're welcome!'

The Consul regarded me with a mixture of amusement and mild reproach.

'And thank you too, Naraldi,' I repeated softly and far more soberly. 'I'm sorry about what happened to Sadira. You helped save two dear friends today. That means a lot to me.'

He bowed his head, perhaps in farewell, perhaps to hide the fact that his eyes were suddenly shining with tears. Then he went back into the office and closed the door.

It was a poignant moment which I spoiled by suddenly smacking my forehead.

'What is it?' asked Dllenahkh in concern.

'I left Fergus's comm underground,' I exclaimed. I looked down regretfully at the bottle in my hand. 'I hope he'll accept some honey-spirit instead.'

Zero hour plus two years twenty days

The Regular Meeting of the Sadiri Council on Cygnus Beta had recently concluded. Councillors gathered in the anteroom of the Council Hall, taking refreshment and talking among themselves. They seemed far more relaxed than usual, and Dllenahkh wondered if the gravitas and endless debate of the early days of their founding had been mere posturing to hide a fear of inadequacy. But then again, he thought, relenting, perhaps that was an uncharitable view. After all, there had been a lot of good news

286

of late: Joral's safe return to the settlement, new ties with what were now called 'the heritage communities' and an increasing number of betrothals and marriages between Sadiri and taSadiri. There was much to celebrate.

'Congratulations,' Naraldi said, appearing at his side with cup in hand. 'I'm glad to see that the Council knows how to reward success.'

Dllenahkh sipped at his own drink and grimaced, a reaction only partly due to the strength of the tart, sweet cordial. 'Then why does this reward feel like another task?'

'Perhaps it is, and if so, you have only to succeed again. Look at you – you could be an elder in truth. Now it's only a small homestead on a spare bit of Council land; in the future, it becomes an odd name on a map, the ancient town of Dllenahkh, founded by some obscure civil servant a year or two after the Scattering.'

Dllenahkh opened his mouth to ask if Naraldi had seen such a thing, realised very quickly that he had absolutely no desire to find out, and changed his question. 'Will you come and visit? You can stay as long as you wish.'

He held Naraldi's gaze slightly longer than would be required for an innocent query. Naraldi narrowed his eyes, understanding. 'So, you have heard.'

'More than that. I can see the evidence with my own eyes. If it continues, if the Sadiri Government doesn't remove you as Consul, there are going to be some awkward questions asked.'

'We must keep it quiet for now. Perhaps I will simply . . . bounce back to my age before my travels, but the doctors cannot tell me what caused it to begin or how long it will continue. They want me to go to New Sadira to be monitored.' Naraldi sighed deeply. 'It is hard enough being tied to one planet. The debriefing period after my travels was long and arduous, but I had *some* freedoms. This time I suspect they plan to permanently confine me to a room filled with sensors and scanners.'

'Don't let them,' Dllenahkh said abruptly. 'You're still a pilot, aren't you? Ask for a ship.'

It was beautiful, to see the hope brightening Naraldi's face. 'You think . . . ? And yet, if old age was their only excuse for retiring me, why not?' He touched his bare scalp with a smile that was almost shy. 'I shall have to let my hair grow again.'

'But discreetly,' Dllenahkh warned teasingly. 'Remember there will be less grey than before.'

Naraldi looked around, still with that sheepish smile, like a boy expecting to be caught in a prank. 'I will visit,' he proclaimed in a whisper. 'When they give me a ship I will come to see you in your new domain.'

It was clear from his demeanour that he did not mean a common docking in orbit and a mundane transit to the surface. 'You wouldn't,' Dllenahkh whispered back, but it came out sounding more like a dare than an admonishment. Was this age regression contagious?

'I would, and I will! I have mastered the art of safe, clandestine planetfall. How else do you think I managed during my travels?'

Dllenahkh was about to answer when a strange sight distracted him. Councillor Haan, one of the more sedate and self-important members of the Council, stood nearby, shoulders bent and shaking with silent laughter, tears pouring from the corners of his eyes. Two other Councillors beside him were grinning happily, completely unsurprised at this unusual behaviour from their colleague. Dllenahkh stared at them, then glared at the liquid in his cup. 'Fireberry cordial,' he guessed. 'Don't drink any more, Naraldi, it's—'

'Dllenahkh, you've been away from home for too long. Of course it's fireberry. It's almost a tradition after Council meetings these days. They're better for it, if you ask me. Oh, don't look like that. I forget you're a purist. Here.' Naraldi kindly and gently removed the cup from Dllenahkh's hand. 'Let me take care of that for you.'

AN IDEAL HUSBAND

'Okay, now that all the unpleasantness is over, I can talk to you about something important,' Gilda said with hushed excitement.

I narrowed my eyes at her with suspicion, took a sip of my cocktail and waited.

'So? You. Him. What's it like?'

She halted me as I began to open my mouth. 'And don't you dare say "who", or "what's what like" or anything so silly.'

The last reports had been submitted and the end-of-mission ceremony and reception were finally taking place with all team members present and accounted for. There had been a bit of silly media, like those who wanted to turn Lian and Joral's story into a romantic holo, but once Lian firmly re-declared as gender-neutral and Joral stated that they were *merely colleagues*, it died down again, leaving the two free to hang out together and assess potential brides for Joral. There *had* been a bonding experience during that underground adventure, but not the sort the media was hoping for.

The other bit of media, which I should have anticipated, depicted me as Dllenahkh's consort in all but name. Faithful companion, close colleague, partner-in-crime – you name it. Not lovers, surprisingly. I suppose, since we weren't as young and pretty as Joral and Lian, the media wasn't interested in what we got up to in bed. Gilda, on the other hand, was a lot less picky than the media.

'It's fine,' I said with dignity, and meditatively licked a portion of salt from the rim of my glass.

'But what do you *do*? He's so . . . *proper*.'

I gave her an exasperated look. It was no good trying to tell Gilda that *some* people didn't divulge such intimate details, because *she* always did whether you wanted to hear it or not, and expected the same of her friends. Up till now, I'd been mercifully exempt by virtue of a boring lifestyle. Eventually I shrugged.

'We hold hands,' I confessed, lowering my voice.

'That's all?' she said in enormous disappointment.

'Well, it's more complicated than that. A sort of telepathy thing. Oh, and sometimes we sleep together.'

I should indulge my vengeful streak more often. I timed it perfectly so that she actually inhaled her beverage in shock.

'You do *what*?' she hissed as soon as she got her airway clear.

I relented. 'Oh, come on, Gilda. Clothes on, adjacent cots, same shelter. That's all. He told me I help him sleep.'

It was true. The way the team had been paired up and the fact that Qeturah had her own shelter meant that I'd usually had a smaller shelter to myself. My dreams had never completely untangled from Dllenahkh's thoughts, both waking and dreaming, after the memory-reset thing, and he found that I was at least as good as an hour's prior meditation for stopping the falling nightmare before it got out of hand. He explained to me that proximity would facilitate the effect, and quite calmly asked if he could come discreetly to my shelter for a few hours' sleep from time to time. I casually said yes, and it was literally an hour later that I experienced a jawdrop moment, suddenly realising what I had agreed to.

It didn't take Gilda that long. She slowly shook her head and looked at me as if seeing me for the first time. 'Man. Still waters.'

Her gaze flickered, focusing behind me, the slightly guilty expression betraying that it was Dllenahkh approaching. I turned and smiled at him. 'Councillor?'

'Ms Delarua,' he replied, pausing to nod courteously to Gilda. 'A moment of your time, if I may?'

I followed Dllenahkh a few steps away to a clear space, which, as the reception was well attended, meant stepping onto one of the balcony niches of the reception hall. Some journalist snagged a holo of us in conversation, standing framed in the niche with the twilight-coloured sky filling the French window behind us. I never even noticed when she took it, but there's a copy of that holo on my desk now.

'I have a suggestion for you,' he began. 'Your residence in Tlaxce City is no longer appropriately sited for the work you will be doing. My own career changes have rendered the location of my previous lodgings less than optimal. I have, however, been recommended for ownership of a homestead close to transport links to both Tlaxce City and the Local Council Hall. Of course, it is too much for me to handle by myself, but I have in mind an arrangement which may serve as a model for other homesteads in the future. Doctor Mar and Lanuri plan to marry next month. I believe you already know that Nasiha and Tarik will stay on Cygnus Beta for a period of time. Two of my colleagues from the Council offices, Istevel and Kamir, have asked to transfer from government work to homesteading until they are assigned partners by the Ministry, and Joral has requested the same. Would you care to join us?'

'Pardon?' I had been so busy cataloguing the names and the news that the invitation, tacked on like an afterthought, at first made no sense.

'Would you like to live with us on the homestead? This would greatly facilitate your consultancy work with Commander Nasiha.'

I spurred my whirling mind to stop for a moment and think clearly. 'This homestead, it sounds pretty sizeable, to be able to support so many people.'

'It is.'

I pondered. Nasiha, Joral, Tarik, Freyda – quite a lot of my favourite people in one place. It sounded pretty cool, especially if the homestead were big enough for a balance of independence and interdependence. I shook my head, laughing inwardly at myself. Working with Sadiri, living with Sadiri, speaking Sadiri more often than not – it seemed that in my own life, the Sadiri had won the culture wars quite handily. And then, of course, there was Dllenahkh himself. I freely confessed to myself in that moment that he was someone I didn't want to say goodbye to, not ever.

'It seems to be an efficient arrangement,' I decided, looking up at him with a smile. 'Yes. Thank you, Dllenahkh.'

Even after I said yes to Dllenahkh's offer to live on his homestead, I had plenty of opportunity to ponder the decision anew. Some days later, as Gilda helped me pack up the last bits of my City life, she filled me in on what people were saying. Some felt Dllenahkh was besotted with me even though I was quite clearly *not* taSadiri and therefore completely unsuitable as a spouse; others believed I was besotted with him and therefore so desperate to stay near him that I was willing to moulder away on a homestead. Some thought he was using me to project the image of a proper Sadiri family man, homesteader and government representative; others were convinced I was using him to further my own private-sector career and gradually rehabilitate myself in the government and the scientific community. Finally, one rumour all but accused us of conducting an elaborate xenofetish experiment that would only end in tears.

To the general concerns, I could have added several more. Was he attached to me because of the mission experience? Did that mental connection which I couldn't speak about and my helping him with his nightmares constitute some kind of undue influence? If so, would the influence fade as soon as he was once more in a full Sadiri community with all the telepathic support that entailed?

'Oh, shut up, Gilda,' I said irritably. 'You'd think I was going to marry the man, with all that talk.'

She looked hurt, but before she could complain there was a chime at the front door, and I gladly went to answer it.

'Excuse me? Ms Grace Delarua?'

It was a government courier with one of those buff envelopes that had so often been the bane of my life. They tended to represent upheaval at the best, and misery at the worst. I felt a pang of fear.

'What's this?' I said, taking it unwillingly.

'Ministry of Family Planning and Maintenance. Sign here, please.'

I signed for it and closed the door, relieved but confused.

'Family Planning?' said Gilda with an arched brow.

'I registered. It was a whim,' I said. I had indeed registered, about three months back when we were in a fairly well-connected town. Nasiha had complimented my meditation progress that day, and Dllenahkh had also made some very favourable remarks concerning a report I'd produced in both Sadiri and Standard. For some reason, the resulting heady rush of pride had led me to do all manner of things to prove to myself that I was definitely one hundred per cent fine in all areas of my life.

'Then why don't they just contact you via comm or handheld? Open it!' she demanded.

Curiosity overcame prudence and I opened it in her presence, laying the official document flat on the dining table. We stared at it. She swore softly, then laughed out loud. I said nothing.

'Well?' she pressed.

I put it back in the envelope. 'Come on, let's finish packing. I need to get down to the homestead as soon as possible.'

Even with nav and autopilot, the groundcar made it down to the homestead within about two hours, which was not long enough for my blood to cool. After the car passed the main gates, but well before it reached the residences, I saw something in a field that made me put on the brakes.

It was the first time I'd seen them, but it was easy to guess what they were – Sadiri dogs. There were three of them, slightly bigger and thicker-bodied than the wild savannah dog, still adapted for a heavier gravity than ours. It was evident in the way they leapt and raced, testing their new strength and speed. Three men were with them, at times running alongside them, at times standing still and observing closely. I thought they were playing with them, and then I realised they were *training* them – without leash, whip or biscuit. There was also a small group of horses, fenced off in a paddock at one end of the field.

As I watched them, one of the men put his dog to 'stay' and walked towards the paddock. The horses moved skittishly away, but one of them paused and sidled to the fence, quite possibly coaxed by some silent encouragement. The man gently put a hand to the horse's shoulder and began stroking its nose reassuringly. The horse was calm and content, but suddenly the dog came trotting forward, making the horse startle, throw up its head and scamper off. Unfortunately, the would-be horse whisperer was too close and got a faceful of hard horse-skull that rocked him off his feet and onto his backside. The dog nuzzled him solicitously while his two colleagues unhelpfully burst out in loud laughter.

'Good day. You are Ms Grace Delarua?' A young man peered into the passenger window of the car, leaning forward with a diffident curiosity that reminded me of Joral. He was dressed for rough, dusty work in trousers and shirt made of thick cotton twill. A canvas bag rode over his shoulder, clinking occasionally as he moved.

I turned off the humming engine of the groundcar, surprised that I had not heard anyone approaching. 'Yes, I am. Good day.'

He bowed politely in greeting. 'I am Kamir. I see you have noticed the animal trainers at work. Those are our new dogs, a small stock that we will eventually cross-breed with the local savannah dogs.' There was both pride and excitement in his voice.

'I thought they were restricted to New Sadira,' I said.

'Policies have changed. Hybridisation is popular now.' His words sounded slightly teasing to my sensitive ears.

I narrowed my eyes at him. 'Where is Dllenahkh?'

He straightened and pointed down the road. 'Approximately

five hundred metres further along the road, working at the smithy with Istevel.'

'Thank you,' I said, making an effort at courtesy as I restarted the car. 'Enjoy the rest of your day.'

The smithy was easy to find – a long, low building with the distinctive dish-shaped structure of a solar forge looming over it. Broad double-doors stood half-open to the breeze, showing two figures within. One man was holding something in a pair of tongs, moving it slowly back and forth under a beam of concentrated sunlight. Another man stood nearby, seemingly content to merely examine his colleague's technique. Their reflective face shields reminded me of Sayr's helmet, but everything else was low-impact, easy-maintenance technology that emphasised self-sufficiency.

I hesitated. There's something very poetic and pastoral about men working at a forge – albeit a solar forge – and on another day I would have appreciated the scene, but I reminded myself that there were more important matters to be dealt with. I turned off the car, grabbed the envelope and made for the two smiths. I nodded to the working smith first, then focused my attention on the other.

'You are the most indirect man I have ever met,' I snapped.

Dllenahkh pushed up the visor of his face shield and squinted at me. 'I do not understand.'

I impatiently waved the official document at him.

'Ah.' He nodded to Istevel, stripped off his fireproof gloves, took off his face shield, and approached me cautiously. 'Perhaps we should go elsewhere to discuss this?'

We walked about a hundred metres away to where the ground sloped under the shade of a few small trees. I sat down, carefully looking straight ahead. There was a faint rustle of leaf and dried grass as Dllenahkh seated himself beside me.

'May I?' he asked, and took the document from my hand.

I sneaked a look at him. Taking off the face shield had ruffled his hair into a slightly untidy tumble of sun-lightened brown locks. His skin had darkened after the year's break from office work. With a start, I realised that he now looked far more Cygnian than Sadiri.

He examined the document. 'The Ministry is informing you that my application to be registered as your life-partner has been approved. Our signatures, and the signature of a witness, are all that is needed to complete the process.'

'I know that.' I sounded a little frantic, so I made myself repeat the words calmly. 'I know that. But how is this possible? The only way I could get this kind of document is if you registered before me and put me down as your sole preference. And at the very least I should have received some prior notification . . .'

My voice faded. I remembered a time when any government correspondence appearing on my handheld had been rapidly consigned to the bin after a cursory look. I'd received a lot of irrelevant notices in the days when the left hand of Central Government was still processing my resignation and hadn't bothered to inform the right hand.

Dllenahkh merely blinked once as he watched my face change, but the amount of amusement he managed to convey was astonishing. 'I am only surprised that they took so long. I understand that the testing is highly intensive, consisting of genetic profiling, psychiatric assessments and financial auditing. However, due to the nature of our work, all of that data was readily available.'

'You . . . booked me in advance?' I was stunned.

He looked at my expression, parted his lips to speak, and paused.

'Go on,' I said resignedly. 'You can tell me anything, you know that.'

'I have certain . . . responsibilities,' he began tentatively, a man feeling his way on unexpectedly treacherous ground. 'Not only as a Councillor of the settlement, but also as a Sadiri, one of few remaining.'

I turned towards him slightly, listening.

'Thus it is extremely important that my actions are beneficial not only to myself, but to the Sadiri people as a whole.'

'Understood,' I replied.

He looked at me closely. 'I have tried to set an example. Careful and deliberate choice of a spouse, with objective assessment by a qualified, neutral third party, is precisely what the young Sadiri of this community need to see.'

'Well . . . congratulations,' I said awkwardly. It was difficult to be angry at him, yet impossible to be pleased about the situation.

He sighed. 'I do not know how to do this. I know I have displeased you in some way, but I am unable to ascertain how.'

I spoke honestly, if impulsively. 'I suppose it's no secret that I'm fond of you, Dllenahkh, but whether that matters to you at all I just— *ngh!*'

In a swift move that shocked me speechless, he set his hand behind my head and put his face into the side of my neck. He left the imprint of his teeth there, then soothed the skin with the tip of his tongue. It was a fraction more than a kiss, and a little short of a marking. His hair brushed the lashes at the corner of my eye; there was the slight abrasion of his shadowed jaw against my cheek. He was tender and brutal and I had no defence against him.

'Mmm,' I said, completely incoherent.

'I am relieved to hear,' he whispered under my ear, 'that you are fond of me. It matters to me a great deal.'

'Don't tell me you didn't know it,' I said shakily.

He rested his forehead against mine and spoke temptingly near my mouth. 'It would not have been right to tell you before you told yourself.'

'I *might* have listened,' I protested weakly, focusing with difficulty on his lips and wondering if he could be slowly trained to find mouth-to-mouth kissing acceptable – enjoyable, even.

He drew back and gazed at me. 'You know I will not give you emotional protestations,' he said, and his eyes looked troubled.

'Then tell me what you will give me,' I asked.

'Trust. Companionship.' His eyelids lowered, his voice grew husky. 'Children, if you wish. *Will* you consent to be my wife? I cannot imagine being better suited to any other person.'

'Me?' I laughed softly. 'Undisciplined, emotional me? I'd rather not do without you, but I won't be a burden to you, and I can't change my nature.'

'Nor I,' he replied, 'but if the past two years are any indication, we have had some success at meeting each other halfway.'

'Then . . . yes.'

His gaze grew tender. 'I believe the arrangement will be mutually—'

'Satisfactory,' I interrupted. 'Beneficial, infuriating, passionate – I'm sorry, did I hit a sensitive spot there?' I had grown courageous enough to touch him, and my hand's light passage over his side appeared to be causing him some problems if the hitch in his breathing was any indication.

'There is something you must know before we proceed,' he

said, capturing my hand. 'I am aware that many Ntshune societies and a few Cygnian ones practise short-term monogamy. This is not the Sadiri way.'

'Don't worry, it's not the Cygnian homesteader way, either,' I said. 'And they wouldn't have matched us if we didn't agree on that.'

'I know. But Grace, what I am asking is this: do you want a Cygnian marriage, or a Sadiri marriage?'

I silently questioned him with a puzzled frown. He let go of my hand and looked into the distance as he tried to explain.

'We have a need to form a meaningful telepathic bond with something or someone. There is a Sadiri saying: a man with a mindship is half-immortal, but a man without a wife is half-alive. Some men can overcome this need using meditation techniques, but never before have so many men faced a future without hope of marriage. They had no choice but to send us away from New Sadira. There were terrible incidents – men fighting over women, assaulting women, harming themselves, even threatening mass suicide. Our society was breaking down. I saw such things – things I still cannot speak of.' He gripped his wrist, a sign of distress I knew too well.

'Then don't speak of them,' I hushed him. 'Not yet. Not till you're ready. Never, if it comes to that.'

He spoke very quietly, still not looking at me. 'I have relied on meditation for many years, and I can continue to do so for many more, but I ask you now: will you bond with me?'

I leaned against him, feeling the tension in his body subside. 'I said yes, and I'll say it again. You know I trust you.'

He took up my hand and pressed it to his cheek. I closed my eyes and felt a surge of energy pushing from him to me and

THE BEST OF ALL POSSIBLE WORLDS

back again, very like the warmth and reassurance of a rocking hug. At last, calmed and consoled, we moved away from each other. He returned the document to its envelope and handed it to me.

'We will speak more on this later, after you have rested and settled in.'

He left to return to the smithy. I lay back on the grass for a few minutes, mind blown. *La, sir, this is so very sudden!* And yet . . . it wasn't, was it? We'd already moved beyond the baseline Sadiri courting rituals identified by Freyda. I knew we had been heading towards a declaration of sorts. I suppose I thought that the declaration would be multistage, perhaps an 'I love you' followed by a 'do you love me' rather than a 'here, sign this document that'll say we're married'. But dithering wasn't a Sadiri habit, and neither were 'I love yous'.

I heaved a huge sigh and sat up straight. I needed a drink.

By happy chance, so did Freyda. First I bullied her into helping me get my stuff into my rooms, then we took a well-deserved break in her sitting room. She had already completed her own move-in, and as I complimented her taste she looked around at the decor and furniture with contentment.

'I'm so glad Lanuri went along with my plan to move early and get things organised before our wedding,' she said. 'I made it sound as if it was the obvious thing for me to do, now that there's a new biotechnician in place and I'm free to start my book, but I think he knows my real motive.'

'And what's that?' I asked, making myself comfortable against the cushions as she poured the wine.

'I'm hiding,' she confessed in a semi-whisper. 'From Zhera.'

I rolled the name through my brain a few times. 'Isn't she one of the female elders who arrived recently?'

'She's seems to be the head of them, and she's *terrifying*. I thought they were supposed to be cuddly grandma and auntie surrogates for the settlement's young men. *She* seems to think it's her job to whip all the new wives and fiancées into shape. I saw her systematically interviewing a group of them at the Council Hall offices. Some came out in tears.'

'Well, as long as she doesn't second-guess the Ministry,' I said. 'I suppose she wants to stamp her authority on the community from the start. Oh, and speaking of fiancées . . .'

Freyda was overjoyed at my news, but not in the least surprised. 'Finally! Did you sign it?'

I grinned, feeling a bit bashful but very pleased at her reaction. 'Well, not there on the spot, naturally, but I will. After you guys. Don't want to steal your thunder and all.'

She waved a hand dismissively. 'You and Dllenahkh were inevitable. Lanuri's considered you all but bonded for ages.'

'Hm. So has Nasiha,' I said wryly, taking a sip of wine. 'Are Sadiri suitors too subtle for us, do you think?'

'I think it's the lack of drama. Once they've got things figured out, they simply go forward without making a fuss.'

I sat still for a while, heedlessly letting the chilled wine glass warm in my hands and drip condensation onto my lap. I remembered when I first read Dllenahkh's thoughts in my dreams. He had been trying, I think, to figure out how to signal his desire to move from friends to something more. I wondered if that had been when he'd booked me. Cheeky of him, to assume I'd say yes – and yet he knew my mind so well that he'd probably been right to think in terms of 'when' rather than 'if'.

'Well then,' said Freyda, eyes gleaming wickedly over the rim of her glass, 'now that we're in the same boat, let's talk about how much of our privacy we're willing to give up.'

'What?' I asked, confused.

She gave me a worried look. 'Hasn't Dllenahkh spoken to you about that? My God, Delarua, don't you *know*?'

'You mean the telepathic bond thing?' I said, clueing in at last.

'Yes, I mean "the telepathic bond thing",' Freyda said in amazement at my unfazed attitude.

'Yes, of course I know about it. Why are you looking so worried?'

Freyda set down her glass and leaned forward. 'Are you sure he told you everything about it?'

'Yes,' I said, beginning to grow irritated. 'He said Sadiri men have a need to form meaningful telepathic bonds. He certainly didn't give me the impression that meant having no private thoughts whatsoever.' I realised even as I spoke that he *had* said 'we will speak more on this later', but I was too embarrassed to admit to that now.

'Well, there *is* some choice about how deep the bond goes, but considering what Dllenahkh's wife did to him—'

I spewed a mouthful of wine, half through my nose and half through my mouth. I'm sure it was as unpleasant to observe as it was to experience. 'His *wife*?' I wheezed.

'Oh shit,' said Freyda. She grabbed a double handful of napkins from the table and pressed them on me. I cleaned myself up, glaring at her, but she avoided my eyes as she babbled, 'I'm so sorry. I . . . I think I'll let Dllenahkh tell you about that.'

'No, *you're* going to tell me. Now,' I said grimly.

She hesitated, but then she folded her hands together and looked at me with an earnest expression of sympathy and concern.

'You know most of them have marriages arranged for them when they're fairly young, right?'

I grew impatient. 'Yes, of course. But he never mentioned a *wife*.'

'She died in the disaster, like so many others. But even before that, they were separated.'

'Separated? What does that mean for Sadiri?' I demanded. 'He said they didn't do temporary monogamy.'

'They don't,' Freyda confirmed. 'That's why it was such a big deal when the marriage and the bond were dissolved.'

I breathed out, slowly. 'Oh. Oh, poor Dllenahkh. So, he was divorced is what you're telling me.'

Freyda looked uncomfortable. 'There was a bit more to it than that. You see, bonded Sadiri men can be possessive – *very* possessive. Dllenahkh found out his wife was unfaithful to him. He beat the other man senseless.'

'What?' I gaped at her in disbelief. She *had* to be making it up. It sounded like a bad, sordid holovid.

'Broke his jaw,' Freyda said bluntly. 'He was never charged for it. The Sadiri have different rules for a crime of passion. It's treated like a kind of temporary insanity. When he came to his senses, he told her he was releasing her from their bond.'

'Oh,' I said, unable to find words.

'I'm sorry I'm telling you this. Obviously he doesn't like to talk about it, and ordinarily I wouldn't have found out except that Lanuri told me. I think he was trying to be completely honest with me so I could objectively assess the pros and cons of a close bond.' She hung her head and glared at her wine glass. 'It didn't work. I'm even less objective about it now.'

'It's going to be lots of fun trying to look him in the eye now that I know this,' I muttered. 'Why didn't he tell me?'

'It's not an easy thing to tell,' she reasoned. 'Please, *please* don't let on that I told you. I feel terrible about this.'

'I'll pretend I never heard a thing,' I said miserably.

Pretence *did* work for a little while. There was so much to do in those early days on the homestead that there was no time to revisit the bonding issue with Dllenahkh. That was my excuse, a good excuse and an honest one, but eventually, fate took matters out of my hands. Dllenahkh continued to train others in the mental disciplines, and there was a meditation hall on the homestead for that purpose. I didn't use it myself. I could meditate just fine in my own room, and there was also a meditation room in the main house. But I did pass by it on occasion, and once I was walking with Freyda when we heard the sound of a voice raised in anger. We exchanged puzzled looks, then naturally drifted closer to listen to what was going on.

'—withhold more than you teach! You are only concerned about your own status and power in this community.'

'I withhold nothing,' Dllenahkh's voice returned calmly. 'I can only say that reliance on meditation alone is inadvisable.'

'And yet you managed for decades. You succeeded. Why not another?'

'It was never intended as a permanent solution to solitude, as you are attempting to make it. The Ministry can help you select an appropriate spouse, and there are also chemical suppressants available to ease the pain of your loss. I recommend that you choose some remedy, and quickly.'

There was a crash, and Freyda and I instinctively grabbed each other and cowered. It was a very good thing we hadn't been standing right in front of the window or we would have been hit by the heavy wooden bench that came through it. We *did* get covered in slivers of glass. Then we heard people scuffling inside the hall. Peeking through the broken shutters, we saw the beginnings of a fight. Dllenahkh was trying to restrain rather than injure, but his student seemed quite serious about doing some harm. The other students hovered uncertainly, mainly getting themselves and the furniture out of the way, but otherwise looking on anxiously, waiting to be told what to do.

I instinctively surged forward, but Freyda caught hold of me. 'Are you mad?' she demanded. 'You can't go in there!'

She was right. Dllenahkh ducked a blow and his antagonist's fist left a sizeable crack in the panelling of the wall. With a firm hold and a quick pivot, Dllenahkh brought him down to the wooden floor with a booming crash. Two students quickly piled on, keeping him pinned with their weight, while Dllenahkh put one hand to his forehead and the other around his neck, squeezing with careful timing until he slumped into unconsciousness.

'Take him to the main house,' he ordered, not even out of breath. 'Class is dismissed for today.'

Then he looked at the ruined window and saw us. His eyes went wide. 'Are you hurt?'

'No,' I said, brushing a tiny smear of blood from my wrist. He saw it and frowned.

'Honestly, we're fine,' Freyda insisted. 'Go deal with . . . whatever it is you have to deal with. We'll get this cleaned up.'

He looked like he wanted to say more, but instead he nodded, still frowning, and followed his students out of the hall. Freyda turned to me and her face changed. 'Are you *sure* you're all right?'

I didn't know what to answer. I'd accepted Sadiri strength in a 'be a dear and shift the groundcar out of this trench for me' kind of way, but it was the first time I had seen a Sadiri in full, uncontrolled rage. Freyda's story came back to my mind with a new vividness, as did Dllenahkh's sombre reminiscences about how the men had behaved after the disaster. Worse yet, I had been willing to view Dllenahkh's account of events within the context of the severe trauma that all Sadiri had experienced, knowing too well how their telepathy made them susceptible to collective anger and pain. But what of Dllenahkh's own loss of control, years and years before, in a sane and stable society where women were not a scarce commodity? It was appalling to contemplate.

Freyda guessed at the train of my thoughts and began to babble apologies again.

'I'll be okay,' I said. 'Really. Let's go inside and get this glass out of our hair.'

That night, I dreamt of elephants stampeding.

I woke up suddenly in the dark, disorientated at first, then feeling, *knowing* that something wasn't right. I put on a robe and went barefoot up the stairs to the roof terrace. It was a clear, starry night, but cool enough that the wooden flooring was already drenched with dew. A shadowy figure was lying atop the broad wall – Dllenahkh, not yet dressed for bed, wide awake and staring up at the sky with no regard for the four-metre drop below. I walked right up to him and looked down, frowning.

'Why are you still up?' I asked him.

His eyes softened; he blinked and some of the tension left his face. Still he did not look at me but kept his gaze on the stars. 'I did not want to disturb you,' he answered.

I knew he had some inkling of my nightmare. I knew he had

sensed fear and tension and all manner of things that I had never associated with him before. But this was Dllenahkh. He would never push me for explanations, only wait with patience and openness until I was ready to come to him.

I decided to be blunt. 'What I saw today scared me. You see, someone told me – quite by accident – about your first marriage.'

There was silence for a while. Then he began to speak slowly, choosing his words with care. 'I believe I was at fault. I took our mental bond for granted and was often not physically present. In addition to my career, I was very much focused on my studies of the mind, an interest that my wife did not share. One day, during a meditation session, I attained – no – *glimpsed* the state that our mindship pilots regularly experience. Before that day, I had viewed their vocation as a lofty but lonely endeavour. Afterwards, I understood why they are called half-immortal. It . . . I cannot describe it, what it felt like, how it changed me. I was a man struck by lightning – a benign, sentient lightning. I wrote poetry. I laughed. I told every pilot I met, and they smiled indulgently and said what a pity it was that I was not free to be bonded to my own mindship.

'I could not change my life. Becoming a pilot would have meant making a different decision when I came of age, and there had been no mindship pilots in my line to inspire me to choose that path. I had to content myself with what I had, and yet I could not let go of what I had seen. I studied further and became advanced in meditation theory and practice. I considered this an admirable endeavour. *She* took it as evidence that I was arranging my life to exclude her.

'She could have told me that she wished to marry another. I

would not have welcomed it, but I would never have stood in her way. Instead, she purposely hid it from me, arranged for me to discover them together, and stepped back to view the result.'

'Oh,' I breathed. 'Oh, *cruel*.'

'Yes, as cruel as she believed I had been to her. In the years after our separation, I immersed myself in even deeper study of the disciplines, looking for ways to ensure that such a thing could never happen to me again. In spite of all that had occurred, I still yearned for a bond with another human mind, but if it had not been for the destruction of Sadira I might easily have persuaded myself to become a pilot.'

'Why didn't you tell me all this, Dllenahkh?' I said faintly.

His mouth tensed. 'I should have. I would have, in time.' There was a small pause, then he admitted, 'I feared losing you.'

'Well, I'm here now,' I pointed out.

He turned his head to look at me then. 'You are. I do not understand why.'

'Think, Dllenahkh,' I chided him. 'Clearly something about you convinces me that you are the best possible choice.'

'And what is that?' he asked very softly.

I sighed. 'So many things, but the first on my list right now is that I do believe you love me. I know you are capable of living without that emotion, but you choose not to.'

'I would not classify love as an emotion, Grace.'

That startled me. 'Really?'

'Certainly it comes attended by various physical reactions which manifest as emotions, but it is one of the drives.'

'Oh,' I said. 'Like hunger, or wanting to procreate, or the desire to protect one's offspring.'

'Yes. I have identified you as the most appropriate mate, probably through an unconscious assessment of pheromones, mental capacity and, of course, social compatibility.'

'So, you're saying you like how I smell, you like how I think and you like to hang out with me?' I was amused, but genuinely warmed at such a unique declaration of love.

He sat up suddenly and turned to face me, swinging his feet down to the floor so quickly that I was half-afraid he'd go over the edge. 'What is love to you, Grace?'

There was an intensity to his gaze that made the blood rush to my face. I began to stammer something, then fell silent. Breathing quickly, I took hold of his hand, bringing it to my cheek. 'You tell me,' I whispered.

He drew me into his arms and into his mind. He saw how I valued his selflessness and trusted his integrity, even when he exasperated me by being inflexible. I showed him my admiration for his physical strength, intelligence and psionic abilities, and the gentleness that complemented all those qualities. I even allowed him to see that I had found him physically attractive from the moment we first met.

'So,' he said lightly, and I knew he was teasing me because he was somewhat shaken. 'You believe that I possess certain characteristics which you would like to be passed on, via genetic transfer and mentoring, to your children.'

I began to laugh.

'I am surprised at the strength of your appreciation for my shoulders,' he continued, still teasing, still holding me close, fitting me neatly between his knees.

'They're nice and broad,' I said, running my hands over them to emphasise my point.

'Nor was I previously aware that you had any special regard for my eyes.'

'Deep, dark and intense. They make you look almost Ntshune,' I murmured, cuddling closer as his hands stroked my back.

'I apologise for not being honest with you earlier,' he said, his voice low and soft so I could feel it rumbling in his chest.

'And I'm sorry for even dreaming that you'd ever hurt me. I won't abandon you, Dllenahkh. Invincible or vulnerable, whatever state you're in, you're stuck with me.'

He tightened his arms around me. 'A fact which gives me great satisfaction.' He sighed as he slowly brushed his nose up the side of my neck and breathed heat under my ear.

'There's just . . . one thing,' I said hoarsely, trying not to become completely distracted. 'You mentioned pheromones. There's another way to assess chemistry. Taste and smell are, as you know, closely linked.'

He pulled back slightly and gave me a wary look. 'I believe you are trying to entice me to attempt kissing.'

'Maybe,' I said casually. 'Just one? Please?'

He gave a gentle, tolerant smile and closed his eyes. 'I am in your hands.'

I didn't want to shock him or put him off, so I started with small, chaste kisses pressed firmly to his jaw. Then I quickly, lightly touched my lips to his mouth, very much a drive-by kiss, and paused to assess his reaction. His hands twitched on my back, but he did not pull away.

'Again,' he said softly. 'I am beginning to see the value of the practice.'

I obeyed, this time allowing a tiny bit of tingling gold to breathe from my lips to his, just as he had taught me to do from palm to palm. He leaned in to capture it with an appreciative murmur, added a little more of his own and kissed it back to me. The physical mechanics were still inexpert, but his energy curled in boldly and unravelled right down to my toes, making me gasp at the sensation.

'I am not averse to including this option in our repertoire,' he mused. 'But I clearly require more practice. Again, please.'

Reader, I married him. About . . . oh . . . three times, I think. First there was the signing of the Ministry document, which we did on our homestead with Qeturah as witness and a few close friends around. Then my semi-lapsed Bahá'í mother insisted on a Bahá'í wedding ceremony. I warned her that I was well past the age laid down by the Ministry for mandatory parental permission, but to my surprise and secret pleasure, Dllenahkh was quite taken with the idea. We held it on the banks of Tlaxce Lake, with more of our City friends in attendance, and even a few from the other provinces. Dllenahkh presented my mother with the non-obligatory bride price of a quantity of pure gold, which he'd had fashioned into the shape of a hummingbird.

She loved it. She told me, 'Of course, I'm leaving it to you in my will, but it's such a nice gesture. It shows he really *treasures* you.'

The third time was a secret. We went to the forest uplands, to a certain temple, and there we were bonded by law, by religion and by mind in a silent ceremony with a few physically attending and hundreds more mentally present. I . . . don't want to say too much about that, sorry. Not secret, but far too close to my heart, I think. I get a bit teary just remembering it. Deep breath! Moving on!

We did have one dramatic event, something rather akin to a 'speak now or forever hold your peace' moment. I should have guessed that in time, what with all the bride interviews, the infamous Zhera would have come across a woman from the temple and extracted her secrets using nothing but the sheer force of her presence. Or, to speak more charitably, they had likely recognised her worth and extended an invitation to her. Whatever the reason, she showed up at the end of our wedding ceremony, richly robed and closely attended by two young nuns as if she already owned the place. Her glare called to mind the evil fairy who gets vexed at being left out of the royal christening and decides to lay down a curse that will afflict not only the poor innocent babe, but the entire kingdom as well.

'So, Dllenahkh, thou hast bonded again.'

She spoke a very old and stylised form of Sadiri that hinted at too many hours spent reciting rituals with subordinates and too few minutes engaged in normal conversation with peers.

'I have, Zhera,' he replied courteously but briefly.

'Thy choice of spouse seems . . . unwise.'

I seethed quietly, but said nothing. She might think herself qualified to sit in judgement over the young ones of the settlement, but as a grown woman I wasn't going to put up with any nonsense.

While I struggled to keep my cool, Dllenahkh calmly defended himself. 'I would not call it unwise to marry a woman who is capable of strong euphoric projection.'

Still striving for control, but now for an entirely different reason, I wondered how he managed to sound so bland and yet so *insinuating*. Zhera, to my continuing astonishment, did not frown or show any kind of disapproval. Her stern look gentled to one of mild amusement, and the straight line of her mouth relaxed.

'Irreverent youth! I did not think to live to see thee considered an elder of our people, but thou hast done well. Child!'

That last was addressed to me. I tried not to flinch. 'Ma'am?'

'It is a good man, a dependable man, but when he tends to frivolity,' and she glared at Dllenahkh, 'as he has in the past, thou must not encourage him.'

'Yes, ma'am. I mean, no, ma'am. Whatever you say, ma'am,' I gasped, not so much overwhelmed by her command as utterly flabbergasted at the sudden realisation that *he* had baited *her*, and *she* was teasing *him*.

When she swept out again, I turned to him, eyebrows raised in amazement. 'Friend of yours?'

He smiled slightly. 'It is difficult to ascertain what that word means to Zhera. To me, she is a teacher of note from whom I learned much about the philosophy and science of the mind. To her, I am still the young acolyte who was sufficiently foolhardy to answer back once. She has never allowed me to forget it.'

'Why did you tell her about the euphoric projection?' I complained. 'That was embarrassing.'

He raised an eyebrow. 'Was the statement inaccurate?'

'Well, strictly speaking, no, but you certainly gave the impression that you had already experienced such a thing ... *conjugally*.'

He pondered for a while. 'I see. Perhaps not an untruth, but certainly a misleading statement. I believe there is only one remedy.'

I looked at him in trepidation, wondering if he was going to speak up and make another public announcement about my alleged abilities.

'We must investigate thoroughly the potential truth of this statement.'

'Um,' I said, because while the words were quite innocently delivered, the look he was giving me was making my knees weak. 'Yes. That would be entirely appropriate.'

'Might I recommend that we retire to our assigned chamber? The shielding built into the walls will ensure that no acoustic or mental noise will get in . . . or out.'

I was quite sure at this point that my bosom was heaving in maidenly confusion. 'Um, that sounds lovely.'

He looked at me curiously and rested a finger lightly against the throbbing pulse in my throat. 'You are agitated,' he said with grave interest.

'You are *amused* at my agitation,' I countered.

He inclined his head, acknowledging the *touché*. 'I *am* experiencing a measure of excitement combined with increasing pleasure, which is perhaps manifesting as an expression of amusement.'

It was the first time he had ever used the scales to describe his emotions. 'I love it when you talk dirty,' I whispered, and sealed the moment with a kiss.

Now

It was well before dawn, and Delarua was scrambling around in semi-darkness, wrestling with her clothes and tripping over her own boots. Already dressed, Dllenahkh observed her from his seat at the one clear corner of the bed.

Hurry. We'll be late.

As usual, she caught the meaning rather than the syntax. 'In a minute!'

As usual, he listened to the undertone of apology rather than the tone of frustration. He glanced away to signal his patience and saw her handheld in the middle of the bed. He did not intend to read it, but his attention was caught by the title: *The Homestead Years. Being the second volume of the draft memoirs of Grace Delarua (not famous yet though not through lack of trying but hey there's still time).*

'Don't look!' She yanked it out of his line of sight and stuffed it in her satchel.

'My apologies,' he said. He doubted it contained anything that would surprise him, but with Delarua, close bonding meant games of fake-privacy and pretended ignorance. He found it oddly endearing.

'Ready,' she said breathlessly at last. 'But I still don't see why we can't go in the car.'

'The car has nav installed,' he hinted with a raised eyebrow. 'We neither need nor want nav where we're going.'

She raised an eyebrow in turn, intrigued. 'Lead the way, then.'

By the time they got the horses saddled up, a faint dawn light was beginning to glow. A few minutes' easy walk was sufficient to take them out from under the trees at the heart of the homestead, through the outer pastures and onto the main road. They journeyed for a while along their own boundary line in a silence that was companionable and more.

Delarua spoke only once. 'We're going down to the sea.'

'Yes,' he answered aloud.

She laughed. It was an adventure to her, an adventure and a mystery all wrapped up in anticipation. She radiated a warm, pleasant buzz, and several vivid pictures suddenly flickered through her mind. He thought for a moment, understood and smiled at the compliment. She had imagined her mind would be bare before his, naked under a scorching desert sun, with neither shelter nor refuge. Instead, it was like playing hide-and-seek in the light and shadow of a forest, discovering and inventing a new language of double meaning, subtlety, poetry and image. As a linguist, she was captivated; as a lover, she was enraptured. Nothing could be said the same way twice.

Their destination, a small bay earmarked for future Council development, was all sand and dry, unpopulated scrubland, yet perfectly suited to the purpose. Pale, shallow water stretched for hundreds of metres up to the line where it met abruptly with depths of dark-blue ocean. Dllenahkh scanned the darker colours carefully and sighed with relief. They were too late to witness the splashdown, but in time for everything else. He dismounted, held the reins securely and watched the horizon. After briefly eyeing him with curiosity, Delarua did the same.

Dllenahkh's horse sidestepped nervously. He reassured it with a brief mental touch.

'What – what is *that*?' Delarua gasped.

A hectare of distant ocean was shifting. Solid greyness gradually emerged, surging up like a wave, but slowly, so slowly that barely a ripple chased over the water's surface to the beach. Its centre was stiff, ridged and ponderous, but the edges curled and fanned delicately with exquisite control.

'Is it . . . ?' she whispered softly, her mind a racket of thoughts and emotions.

'Yes,' he confirmed. Small, unharnessed, unladen, but unmistakable.

An aperture like a blowhole appeared on the back of the leviathan. Only then did its size become clear as a tiny human creature was ejected in a gentle rush of water to tumble over the side and into the ocean. Eyeless, yet aware, the beast carefully washed its living cargo to shore with a lazy flap of its foremost fringe. Delarua kept her eyes fixed in fascination on the small dot travelling inland. Dllenahkh also watched until he sensed some other movement, another shifting patch of grey amid the blue that made him startle and stare . . . but the sea calmed and kept its secret.

No longer old, but not yet young, Naraldi stepped out of the gentle surf, shaking salt water from his hair. It was just long enough to trouble his eyes, drenched-dark in hue with a few white streaks gleaming bright. His pilot's suit flashed in the sun, bringing an image of Sayr to Delarua's thoughts. She laughed out loud in sheer happiness, remembering, knowing.

'Dllenahkh! Grace!' Naraldi hailed them gladly. 'Have you any space in your realm for a rootless wanderer?'

Dllenahkh felt a sensation of overwhelming, devastating déjà vu – another time, another beach, Naraldi rising up out of the ocean to destroy the universe with a few words. His mind had been punctured in that instant, leaving behind a fragmented, perilous memory that could spin him into endless orbit around nothingness. For his own sake, he had learned to forget that day. Now his mind fractured again to take in the reality that he was standing by the sea and hearing Naraldi's voice, not merely without desolation, but with actual gladness. Memory and moment combined violently, and he struggled to shield Delarua from the sudden maelstrom.

She did not look at him. She did not have to. She took firm hold of his hand and silently gave him her storm of joy to navigate instead.

'Welcome, Naraldi!' she cried. 'Welcome home!'

ACKNOWLEDGEMENTS AND REFERENCES

'Golden', the poem quoted in the chapter 'The Faerie Queen', is an unpublished work by Dvorah Simon and is used with the author's permission.

The Indian Ocean tsunami of 26 December 2004 will long be remembered for the devastation it wrought on many coastal communities. Months later, the BBC reported on a distressing side effect of the disaster: more women than men were killed by the tsunami, up to eighty per cent in some of the hardest hit areas. These were women at home with their children on a Sunday while their husbands were fishing far out at sea or running errands inland; women waiting on the beach for the fishermen to return; and women who were not physically strong enough to hold on as the wave swept by. Representatives of aid organisations commented on the social impact of this gender imbalance, including psychiatric trauma in several newly bereaved men, and 'reports of rapes, harassment and forced marriages coming from emergency camps around the region'. Professor Sivathambi of

Colombo University in Sri Lanka noted, 'Men are only the bread earners. Women are the backbone of the family. Take them out and it leads to instability.'

The Caribbean is to me the new cradle of humanity. It was easy for me to imagine an entire planet just like it, with people from every corner of the world. I was also influenced by stories of the real-life Pestalozzi Villages and International Children's Villages founded after WWII for war orphans of all nationalities. A third source of inspiration came from Ray Bradbury, not only his story 'Dark They Were, and Golden-Eyed', which is referenced in the first chapter, but also 'Way in the Middle of the Air' and 'The Other Foot', which depicted African Americans of the 1950s fleeing segregation and founding a colony on Mars.

REFERENCES

Bradbury, Ray. 1950. 'Way in the Middle of the Air', in *The Martian Chronicles.* Garden City: Doubleday.

Bradbury, Ray. 1951. 'The Other Foot', in *The Illustrated Man.* Garden City: Doubleday.

Bradbury, Ray. 1959. 'Dark They Were, and Golden-Eyed', in *A Medicine for Melancholy*. Garden City: Doubleday.

Simon, Dvorah. 2008. *Mercy.* Santa Cruz, CA: Hanford Mead Publishers, Inc.

'Loss of women haunts fishermen', published 21 March 2005, 10:29:39 GMT, at http://news.bbc.co.uk/go/pr/fr/-/2/hi/south_asia/4360345.stm, accessed 31 August 2009.

'Most tsunami dead female – Oxfam', published 26 March 2005, 00:27:23 GMT, at http://news.bbc.co.uk/go/pr/fr/-/2/hi/asia-pacific/4383573.stm, accessed 31 August 2009.

REDEMPTION IN INDIGO
KAREN LORD

Paama's husband is a fool and a glutton. Bad enough that he followed her to her parents' home in the village of Makendha, now he's disgraced himself by murdering livestock and stealing corn. When Paama leaves him for good, she attracts the attention of the undying ones – the djombi – who present her with a gift: the Chaos Stick, which allows her to manipulate the subtle forces of the world. Unfortunately, not all the djombi are happy about this gift: the Indigo Lord believes this power should be his and his alone, and he sets about trying to persuade Paama to return the Chaos Stick.

Chaos is about to reign supreme . . .

Jo Fletcher
BOOKS

www.jofletcherbooks.co.uk

COMING SOON

THE GALAXY GAME
Karen Lord

Rafi Delarua, Grace Delarua's nephew, has psionic talent.
Born and raised on a secluded homestead on Cygnus Beta,
he marks his coming of age by leaving for life on Punartam,
where psionic talent is considered normal. There he can train
his mind and lead a comfortable life.

But the galaxy is changing: The Sadiri colony Sadira-on-
Cygnus is threatening to secede from new Sadira; galactic
commerce has slowed, prices have spiked and there are
rumours that the Terran embargo no longer holds.

And the Ntshune, the last stop for help, are held at bay by New
Sadira, which holds stubbornly to the crumbling remnants
of galactic rule. Only the Acadames of Punartam, quietly
researching the possiblities, may have found a solution.

PUBLISHED JUNE 2014

Jo Fletcher
BOOKS

www.jofletcherbooks.co.uk